LET *it be* ME

Annette
I hope you love
it

(signature)

BARBARA SPEAK

Chapter 1

Looking out the window as all of the trees along the roadside turned into one long blur, I tried to focus on breaking free.

I hated him. I hated him more than anything in the world for what he stood for, what he took from me, and for what he continued to do: control me.

The tree line only broke when we would pass a driveway and then it was back. I stared at it for so long that I became lightheaded, just so I wouldn't lose my focus. If I had, the only thing that would come to mind was what we were running away from. My life as I knew it was over because of the shame I brought on my family.

"Arianna, do you think I will like my new school? Will they play with me?"

Shelby, my little sister, broke my concentration by whispering her questions at a volume HE couldn't hear. She was only eight and didn't deserve any of this. It was all my fault as my step-dick, John, loved to point out.

"You are the disgrace of this family and yet we all have to endure this because of your actions!"

I heard it so many times that I could recite it word for word.

"They will love you, Shelby. Only a fool would choose not to. It's just a natural thing to adore you, don't worry your pretty little head about that."

She smiled at me and then turned to look back out her car window.

We had been driving for days. Coming from Baltimore, Maryland where my step-dick was the lead attorney at one of the most prestigious firms in the city, we had it all. The elite private school upbringing, the high-rise apartment in the middle of the city, hell, we even had a chef prepare our meals. And somehow he agreed that moving us to Montana, in the middle of nowhere, would make it all disappear. Nothing was going to make me forget. I couldn't.

Three more hours went by without a word from anyone in the car. My mother sat in the front with him, reading a book on her iPad, not even acknowledging her own children in the back seat, but that wasn't something foreign to us. She was a zombie of a person. A walking shell. I didn't expect HIM to say anything to me, I wasn't his. But for him to ignore Shelby was downright ridiculous.

Yes, I was my step-dick's burden. The one thing that reminded him that my mother had a love that could never be smothered and it wasn't his to own.

I was four when my father died in a car accident. A drunk driver with a blood alcohol level two times the legal limit hit him head on after running through a red light.

She never really did get over it. I believe the day my step-dad came into her life she gladly handed over the control. That way she wouldn't have to think. She could remain numb forever. I have faint memories of a loving woman from my childhood, and Shelby never will. That woman no longer exists.

Two more hours came and went before we started to slow down and turned onto a gravel road. Dust was circling us as HE drove so fast you could hear the rocks hitting the car.

"Did the movers deliver everything?"

It was the first time I heard my mother speak in what felt like forever.

"Yes. I have it under control, Camille. Don't question me."

She didn't respond, only making me want to slap some sense into her. I will never understand how she could choose the life she has. Why would anyone want to live with someone like him?

I wanted to ask what the house looked like, if I could see the pictures too, but I knew better. He wanted me to suffer and those questions would never have been answered regardless so I chose to use my imagination instead.

"Is that it, Daddy?"

We slowed down approaching a magnificent Victorian style farm house. The wrap around porch had my jaw hanging open. The shutters were green, offsetting the cream exterior paint covering the rest. I think the turret is what excited me most. I had never seen one in real life before. It looked like it belonged on a castle instead of a farm house out in the middle of nowhere.

"No, Shelby. That is the house next door."

I turned around in my seat, looking out the back window until it faded away from the cloud of dust being kicked up by the tires.

"This is your new home thanks to Arianna."

He never referred to me as her sister. The fact that the two of us even shared blood infuriated him.

I turned back in my seat as we pulled into the driveway of a ranch style shack. That isn't really true. It wasn't a shack, but compared to what I had just seen, nothing would have been good enough. It was blue with white shutters on each window. The front door was painted red, clashing with the color of the house itself. The shingles on the roof were green leading me to believe the previous owners had to have been color blind and my mother and step-dick were fools for picking it.

The car pulled up to what looked like a garage and was turned off. It only took a second for Shelby to jump out, slam the door shut, and then she was running as fast as she could into the house. If she thought I even cared about what room I got she was wrong. I didn't care about anything other than what I lost. My friends were my support, my escape, my happiness, and now he stripped me of that too.

Of course he would tell me this was all my fault and in a way he was right.

I heard their doors close and laughed a little to myself. I was left in the car without a word from either of them. I was invisible once again. Surprise, surprise.

I sat there looking out of the window at the fields around us. When he said he was taking us out of the city he wasn't lying. My life was officially over at the age of seventeen. He wanted me to suffer and he got his wish.

Eventually, I got bored enough that I had to get out of the car. As soon as I closed the door though I practically passed out. The distinct smell of crap hit me like a brick wall. I don't know from what animal but it was awful! I covered my nose, ran as fast as I could to the front door and threw it open rushing through it. Just as I was thinking, "No wonder Shelby ran so fast", I heard, "Damn it, Arianna! Watch the fucking door!" come from the left which was obviously the kitchen.

Internally I flipped him off, shaking my finger right in his smug face but of course I just shrugged my shoulders and said, "Sorry."

Looking around I couldn't help but hate it already. Seeing all of our furniture placed within this house didn't help it feel like home. It was just another misplaced thing in my life.

The walls were painted yellow with trim that was stained oak to match the hardwood floors. There was nothing open about the floor plan. Each room was divided by a wall cutting the house up into a maze.

"ARIANNA! COME SEE MY ROOM!"

I heard Shelby's excitement and couldn't help but let my feet carry me in the direction of her voice.

Through the family room was a hallway that held several doorways. The last thing I wanted was to have us all on the same wing but there was no guess work that this house didn't have wings at all. Sure enough, looking into the first door I passed showed my bed and dresser already put together.

One turn of the head and I was looking into my mom and step-dick's room.

"Wonderful."

Ten more steps got me to the end of the hall where I found my sweet Shelby jumping on her new bed. Looking around her room I noticed she had all new furnishings. It was pink and purple with flying unicorns painted on the walls, perfect for her. She didn't ask for any of this. The least they could do was buy her something to be excited about.

"Don't you love it? It's so pretty. What did they get you?"

I walked over to her bed and threw myself backwards, landing on the lush fabric I was now positive our mother had special ordered.

"I'm sure there is something in my room somewhere."

Lying to her became easy over the years. I didn't want her to see what was obvious to anyone else. Our family was as dysfunctional as they come and there wasn't any fun surprise waiting anywhere for me.

"Let's go see! Arianna, this is going to be so much fun. We get to make new friends. Start a new school. Daddy says I can even get a pony if I want and glue a horn on its head to make a real unicorn!"

I couldn't help but smile at her. Shelby's hair was bright red and the natural curl made her look like Annie. Her green eyes were the most beautiful thing on the planet and the spray of freckles across her nose just completed the package. We look nothing alike. My hair is board straight and black as night. My father was American Indian and I took completely after him. My eyes could be considered almost black as well. My skin always has some form of tan and there are no freckles to speak of. I actually looked adopted next to my family and sometimes I felt that way as well.

"Come on, Arianna! Let's go see outside."

Shelby grabbed my hand and pulled me from the bed, leading me through the family room and out the back door.

The smell hit me again but there was something about the space that allowed me to ignore it; it seemed endless. Mountains were off in the distance and flat land filled with trees appeared to stretch for miles. It was a sight that could steal your breath away. Shelby was talking but I didn't focus on anything but the scenery as I walked farther away from the house.

Before I knew it I had gone far enough that when I looked back, I saw nothing. The house had disappeared and I let the idea of it leave my thoughts as well. Surreal, that's the best word I can come up with to describe the view that was now mine to keep. In the madness of change, this place had come to be a sanctuary for me in just seconds.

My head snapped to the left when the sound of an engine caught my attention. I didn't expect to hear anything like it out there. "This was a place for silence," I thought, aggravated that someone would ruin this too.

Looking closer, I noticed what appeared to be a truck and the black color of it stood out in the sea of green from nature. I took a few more steps when I saw a man without his shirt on throwing bales of hay into the back of it. Quickly, I searched for the closest tree to hide behind and ran to it. Peeking around the side I went back to staring at him. Every muscle pulled and tightened as he worked. I couldn't get over how far away I was, yet how easily I could make out the fine details of his body. It may seem crazy but he was huge.

He didn't seem to notice me which I thanked the Heavens for. The last thing I needed was to be called out for being childish and hiding. Something about him kept me locked in place, though. I couldn't move. When he turned his back to me, I found myself holding my breath. I had never seen muscles look like that. His jeans rode low on his hips and...

"What are you doing? Why are you hiding?"

I whipped my head around to see Shelby a split second before I was lunging for her and throwing my hand over her mouth.

"SHHH!"

Her eyes grew huge as she looked up at me even more confused. I kept my hand over her mouth while I walked us both far enough away that he wouldn't notice us before I answered her.

Keeping hold over those lips, I whispered, "There is a man over there and I didn't want him to see me."

Her hand came up to grab mine and pulled it from her mouth. "Why not? If he is our neighbor why can't we say hi?"

Leave it to a child to simplify things.

"I just don't want to is all. Sometimes I don't feel the need to know everyone."

"You sure wanted to know what he looked like."

"Shelby!"

"Well, why else would you be hiding behind a tree staring at him?"

"Let's just go back inside."

"Fine with me. You're the one freaking out."

I gave her the dirtiest look I could muster and went back toward the place that would now be my living hell without her.

Stomping through the house, into my room and slamming the door behind me, I plopped down on the end of my bed and wanted to scream. A boy got me in that mess to begin with and nothing about that man out there was going to bring any good to my life. Even if he was pretty to look at.

"Arianna! What did I say about slamming the damn doors around here?"

This time, behind the security of my closed door I wasn't scared to flip the asshole off.

I must have fallen asleep because the next thing I knew I was sitting up on my bed in complete darkness listening to my stomach growl. Looking over at my phone I saw it was three o'clock in the morning. So much for dinner with the family.

I tossed and turned with no luck of falling back asleep. Grabbing my phone again I saw it was now four-thirty and I was no closer to sleep than the hour before.

I got up and walked quietly to the one room in the house I had yet to visit. My stomach practically screamed as I opened the refrigerator door. Reaching in, I wrapped my hands around two yogurt cups and immediately started pulling the foil tops off. I don't think I can remember a time that yogurt sounded so good. Four drawers later I finally found a spoon. Dipping it into the creamy goodness before letting it hit my tongue was quite possibly my favorite part of the day. And that brought our new neighbor straight to the front of my mind. What was it about this guy?

I finished the yogurt and was on my way back to bed when I glanced at the front door. I could either go lay there for the next three to four hours or I could go for a walk. To tell you the truth, anything would be better than laying in the dark with nothing to do other than think about how if you had only done this or that you wouldn't be where you are now.

Before I could think about it anymore, my feet were taking me from the house and down the rock covered path most would call a driveway. I knew where I wanted to go but I didn't let myself believe it was anything more than wanting to see that house again. The man I saw earlier was nothing but another person to complicate my life. Something I didn't need or want. Sure he was nice to look at, but I wanted to keep it from afar, if you know what I mean.

Twenty minutes or so later I passed the group of trees lining the road that I remembered seeing as we drove past them. My pace quickened with the thought of seeing it again. This time I would be able to focus, concentrate on all the detail put into making it.

When the house finally came into view, it stole my breath just as it had the first time I saw it. Only this time it seemed twice as big. Maybe it was because I was standing on the ground next to it but I was literally dwarfed by its magnitude. Following the turret all the way up into the night's sky, I was marveled by how many stars I could see. There had to be thousands if not millions up there. I sat in the grass bordering the road, placed my hands behind me and allowed my body weight to rest on them as I wondered what it would be like to live in a castle. To be doted on by parents that loved you, hell, loved each other. To wake up every morning being showered with kisses until you were old enough to refuse them thinking they were gross. Something I wanted so badly to give to my child.

Faintly, I heard a guitar begin to play coming from behind the house. Whoever was making that sound had talent and I had no problem sitting back and enjoying it. When the voice that belonged to those hands started to sing, chills ran across my skin. I had never heard the song before but my gosh did I want to know what it was called. He sang about a smile that lets you know you're needed, a simple touch bringing on faith that you would be caught if you fall. The next words were hard to hear. He let his voice drop low which maybe was why it got to me like it did but I know I heard something about saying nothing but it still saying everything.

I wanted to be closer. The feelings resonating within me from this music worked like a beacon calling me home.

I walked through the front lawn to the side of the house, letting my hand drag along the wood that wrapped it until it came to an end. The back corner of the house met with the view of a well-lit garden. A pergola stood over a sea of colorful flowers blowing in the breeze. The smell came straight toward the house. Someone was a freaking genius when they came up with that idea. The smell of crap completely disappeared.

I peeked my head around to find a covered, screened in porch and sitting within it was the musician that lured me here. I still didn't want to be seen so I made sure to stay in the shadows as he continued to play.

The next song I knew as soon as he began plucking the strings. I saw Matchbox 20 in concert in the sixth grade and that CD was my favorite of theirs. Why he would pick "Unwell" shocked me, but then again, I knew absolutely nothing about this guy. The longer I listened to him sing the more I knew I needed to keep my distance.

I turned and starting walking back to my prison reminding myself he was going to be nothing to me. Just like this town and everyone else in it.

Chapter 2

Monday morning came whether I wanted it to or not bringing with it Shelby and the first day at our new schools. There wasn't much debate over who was more excited.

"Arianna, wake UP! It's school day! Get up!"

"Get out of my room!"

"Fine. Go ahead and sleep. I'm going to have the best day ever meeting all my new friends and you can just sit here and mope like you have been since we got here."

"Get out!"

I waited until I heard the door close before I opened my eyes and got out of bed.

With no desire to impress anyone, I put on some old skinny jeans, a red sweater and some black ballet flats. Oh, and I brushed my hair and teeth but that was the extent of it.

Walking into the kitchen, I couldn't believe my eyes when I saw Shelby sitting at the table with a bacon and scrambled eggs breakfast. The part that baffled me wasn't her choice but who must have cooked it. Our mother hadn't lifted a finger to cook in over ten years.

"Did you want some, Arianna? Mommy can make breakfast now! Isn't that cool?"

I glanced over at my mother but she never raised her eyes to meet mine which came by no surprise.

Grabbing a banana, I turned from the room looking back over my shoulder at my little sister. "No, thanks. A banana will do. Make sure you give them your best, Shelby. They'll love you just like I do."

Once I was out of the house the first thing I noticed was the very old, extremely ugly, red pickup truck in the driveway.

"What the hell?"

I turned and walked straight back into the kitchen with my rage gunning right for my mother.

"Where is MY car?"

Of course she didn't look at me when she said, "There's a truck for you to drive outside."

So she was going to make me ask again. Well, I was happy to play that game.

"I saw the piece of crap. I asked where my car is. He promised it would be here today!"

"Your father sold it."

"He did WHAT? He can't do that! That was mine! How could you let him? You know what, never mind. You let him do whatever he wants. You have never defended me when it counts why would I think you would say something about a damn car that my REAL father paid for?"

I didn't give her a chance to respond, but she wouldn't have anyway. She knew I was right. She knew what he forced me to do and she said nothing while I begged and pleaded for another option. She would never do anything to stop him or help me, her own daughter.

Walking back out of the house, I stomped over to the hunk of shit, opened the door, hearing the creaking sound like it wanted to break off, and climbed in. The ripped seats didn't surprise me at all. Or the smell of cigarette smoke for that matter. One more of step-dick's continued attempts to make me suffer. Mission accomplished.

Turning the key, the whole thing started to shake. Honestly it felt like it was going to blow up when the engine finally turned over.

"This is my life."

Placing my foot on the brake I had to use all the strength I had just to pull the gear shift out of park.

To say the ride to school was interesting would be a flat out lie. The drive was nothing but ten minutes of farm fields on either side of the road filled with rows of wheat. All I could think about was how much these people and I didn't have in common. I had no idea what to expect from any of students but at the same time, I knew it didn't matter. They would never welcome a new kid, especially one like me.

My truck fit in with the rest of the crap parked in the school parking lot so I guess that's one positive thing that I had going for me. My Lexus would have stuck out like a sore thumb, bringing on attention I didn't want. Maybe he was actually doing something nice for a change? Ha! That is something worth laughing about.

I gripped the steering wheel with both hands looking at the tiny school in front of me. "You can do this. It's only two more months."

Grabbing my backpack and throwing it over my shoulder, I killed the ignition and slid out of the truck.

I only made it fifteen steps before it started.

"Hey, new girl, wait up! What's your name?"

I heard someone shout it out but I didn't bother to turn around to see who was asking or to answer. I just walked a little quicker until I finally came in contact with the door that I had been focused on getting to. I pulled the handle back but a hand landed flat on the glass preventing me from being able to do anything more.

"I asked you a question."

Looking down at my feet, I wanted to stay quiet until he gave up but I knew it wouldn't work. If he took the initiative to catch up to me he wasn't going to stop.

Spinning around, I placed both of my hands on his chest and pushed as hard as I could. "If I wanted to answer you I would have. Now get out of my way!"

People seemed to come from out of nowhere and each and every one of them stopped to watch the drama unfold which was the last thing I wanted. I wished I had just kept my mouth shut.

"Look, I'm sorry. I'm not trying to be..."

"A bitch."

"I was going for rude but you can call me whatever it is you want. I really would just like to go to class if you don't mind."

"Well the thing is, I do mind. Don't show up here and think you're better than..."

"Stop it now!"

I was so grateful someone interrupted him. The jerk standing in front of me was no shorter than six feet. His hair was shaved to his head and I would have actually considered him handsome had he not opened his mouth.

Off to the left a staff member was charging toward us and the crowd seemed to take notice. She was on a mission and her size didn't seem to matter; they were scared of her regardless. One-by-one people started

11

walking in different directions. When jerk boy decided to let go of the door, I saw my out and took it.

Walking as fast as I could, I made it more than halfway down the hall before, "Miss, stop!" was heard.

I kept walking until she caught up to me. Grabbing my shoulders, she forced me to give in to her will.

"Honey, are you okay?"

I turned to face her and the anger she was wearing outside was nowhere to be seen. Her whole demeanor was approachable— relaxed— and her eyes showed nothing but concern.

"What's your name?"

"Arianna."

"Well, Arianna, it's very nice to meet you. We don't get many new kids at the school. It's a breath of fresh air to see a new face."

"Thank you but I really need to get to the office for my schedule."

"Do you happen to know where the office is, Arianna?"

I looked down at my feet embarrassed to admit the answer was no.

"I didn't think so. You are going in the wrong direction, sweetheart. Let me show you. I was going there anyway."

I lifted my head to look in her eyes and sure enough she was sincere. The first person I had encountered in a long time to be so.

"That would be great."

We walked a few steps before I started to say something and realized I had no idea how to address her.

"My name is Audrey Hemswith but you can just call me Mrs. Hemswith."

"How did you know what I was thinking?"

"It was kind of obvious that you didn't know my name. I hadn't given it to you yet."

"Well that's true."

I continued following her through the halls packed with students glaring at me like I sported two heads.

"We're here."

She led me through the double doors toward the first desk you came to in the room. Behind it sat a little old lady with a smile that could melt your heart.

"Delilah, this is our new student Arianna Dubray. She needs her schedule."

My head snapped in her direction with shock written all over it.

"How did you know my last name?"

With a simple smile she replied, "Like I said earlier, we don't get many new faces around here. We have been expecting you."

She tapped the desk twice with both hands and then pushed herself off of it, taking a step back.

"It was very nice meeting you, Arianna. I hope you enjoy your time with us."

Then she walked away, disappearing through a door to the far right of the room.

"So, here you go. Your first class will be Chemistry with Mr. Hull. It's right down the same hallway that brought you here on the right. Room 814."

I took the piece of paper she was holding and glanced down at it. All of my classes were ones I had taken previously.

"Ma'am, I have already studied these courses."

"Yes, we know. But our curriculum doesn't have anything higher, dear. You are in all of our top flight classes. It was the best that we could do."

Looking down at the paper again I smiled for the first time in what seemed like forever. At least the rest of the school year would be a breeze academically.

"Thank you very much."

"You're welcome. Now get on to class. You don't want to be late."

"No, ma'am, I don't."

I turned and walked back through the doors ready for the day to be over before it even really began.

My first three classes were filled with gawking students. Not one introduced themselves to me or even tried to make me feel welcome. The guys bore hungry eyes while the girls seemed to hate me before I was even given a chance. I wasn't surprised. My friends always reacted the same way to anyone new. I always thought they felt threatened so this didn't shock or disturb me. At least they were leaving me alone.

Lunch was a different story. As soon as I entered the cafeteria I wished I had brought my food and ate it in my truck. The entire room went quiet as I neared the food line. All I could think about was Shelby as I prayed her day was going better than mine.

"How has your day been going, Arianna? Classes seem okay?"

The only one who seemed to care enough to even ask that question was Mrs. Hemswith so there was no need to look surprised when she came into view.

13

"The teachers all seem to break down the subjects well for students to grasp the information."

"And you? How has it been going for you?"

"I am hanging in there."

She took a step closer to me and dropped her voice low as to not be heard by the two students nearest me in line.

"They are a tough bunch to infiltrate but I think you can handle them."

"That's the thing, I have no desire to handle anyone. There is only two more months between me and eighteen and I can assure you I will leave this town as soon as that day comes."

She took a step back this time before saying, "I sure hope something changes your mind. I would hate to see you go before you get a real chance to see that you belong."

The line had moved forward so I took the few steps to advance with it but when I looked back, Mrs. Hemswith was no longer standing next to me, she was walking out of the room.

"So, you seemed to buddy up with the principal pretty fast. Don't think that will help you though."

I turned behind me and found what was apparently the most popular girl in school. How do I know this? Because you can always spot the leaders from the followers. Her golden blond hair hung almost to her waist with her blue eyes sparkling from the light spilling in through the windows. Cut-off jean shorts, a plaid button-up shirt and cowboy boots made this girl something that I am sure all the men in town wanted to have a slice of and the girls all wanted to not only like her but be her. Her three sidekicks were standing on each side of her proving my point.

"I'm not looking for help. I just want to graduate and leave. Do you think you could call off the dogs and let me be?"

"What makes you think I could call off anyone?"

"Because you obviously hold the power. I'm not stupid, I used to be you at my old school."

"Honey, you were never me."

Her friends laughed as I waited for her to answer me.

"Fine. You want to be left alone, you will get exactly that. But if you even think about going after one of our guys, deal's off."

If she only knew that was the furthest thing on my mind. If I could think about anyone other than Kale and what he did, it would be a Godsend. Men are all assholes that can't be trusted to do anything but break your heart and then stomp on it for good measure.

"I can assure you, all of your guys are safe for you to keep."

"We'll see, won't we?"

I had nothing left to say to her so I turned around and grabbed a tray. The silence was bliss for as long as it lasted, which wasn't near long enough.

"So, what made you move here anyways? I mean really, who moves at the end of their senior year?"

I didn't answer. Who would want to? I knew nothing about this girl yet she wanted access to my deepest secrets. Placing the most disgusting slice of pizza on my tray, I skipped over what they considered seasoned carrots and went straight for the fruit bar.

"You go asking me for favors and don't think you at least owe me answers? If I ask you something you damn well better answer me!"

I let my head fall back while I looked up to the ceiling praying this day could just end already. But I wasn't getting that prayer answered, that was for sure.

When I turned to find a table to sit down at, I was met by a wall made up of the leader and said followers.

"Are you kidding me? What part of leave me alone didn't make sense to you?"

All four of their mouths dropped open and mine followed when the reality of what I just did sank in.

"You listen to me, don't fuck with me or I swear I will make your life a living hell."

No thought went into what I was saying before I snapped, "Good luck! I'm already there!" and began sprinting from the room after dropping my tray at their feet.

I found a bathroom down the hall and sprang for it. The sooner I could lock myself in a stall the better. As soon as I made it through the door, I sat down on the toilet seat and started to cry. I hated myself for being weak. Those girls didn't deserve my tears, neither did Kale or my step-dick for that matter. That didn't stop them from coming, though.

I heard the door to the hall open and quickly started wiping my eyes. No sniffles or even blowing my nose was going to be heard. I had already given them enough ammo to take me down. I didn't need to hand them the shovel to dig my grave as well.

"You can breathe you know."

I raised my feet so I couldn't be seen and pretended like I was invisible. It's what I truly wanted anyway.

"I saw you come in here so it's not working."

I didn't move.

"Look, I'm not going to tell you not to worry about them because you should. How you managed to not only piss off Kyle McDermott but Ashlynn Stanton is beyond me. You have been here what? Three hours?"

Well, at least I had the names of my enemies.

"All right, if you don't want to come out I get it, but listen. Those two have run things since kindergarten. They aren't going away. You either play by their rules or however long you plan to be here will be hell. No one likes them but we have to respect them to survive. Understand?"

No, I didn't understand. Why would a group of people not stand up to two? The odds were in their favor and yet they bowed down to these two like royalty.

The door closed letting me know whoever was on the other side of the stall door was gone. I chose to stay on that toilet seat a good five more minutes before I got the courage to flip the latch and walk out of the bathroom with my head held high. I wasn't going to let anyone force me to do anything. I already had my step-dick, I wasn't doing it again for some strangers with hay stuck up their ass.

"So, you're finally willing to come out?"

That damn voice.

Sure enough, standing across the hall was a girl who couldn't be taller that five feet. Her short brown hair and glasses made her look almost childish in a way. Nothing about her clothes showed she had a sense of style either. Her black t-shirt was oversized and the jeans she wore had holes in the knees. Not the pre-made kind either but ones that had worn through. This was the definition of blend in and not be noticed.

"Excuse me?"

"Don't act like you didn't hear me in there."

I ignored her and started walking down the hall when she followed me still talking.

"What are you going to do? Please tell me you're not going to try to stand up to them again. There is no hope left if you do that."

"Listen, I am here to graduate, that's it. I don't care about your cliques and hierarchy. You all can conform to whatever they want you to. But me? I am not one of you."

She'd been keeping up with me stride-for-stride until I said that. Little Bit stopped walking and said, "It's your own grave you're digging."

That almost had me. The very words I had said to myself were coming back at me.

"Well then let me dig it."

I wasn't going to let anyone know how miserable I was. My life was mine. Not one person in this stupid po-dunk town was going to make a difference. No one could.

Chapter 3

The rest of the school day went about as good as the beginning. Everyone stared at me, talked about me, but not to me. At least it wasn't behind my back I guess.

I felt protected in a way while I was in class. No one would be stupid enough to start something in front of a teacher. The halls didn't go so well but I just kept my head down and got to where I needed to be. When school was over, I expected the worst to happen but all of the students rushed out of the classroom as soon as the final bell rang proving me wrong. It's not as if I thought they would lynch mob me but something about it seemed too easy. I waited a few minutes just to be safe before I stood up from my desk just as the teacher Mrs. Hawkins called out my name. I looked up to find her standing at the front of the room with her briefcase in hand.

"You made it."

"Excuse me, ma'am? I made it?"

"Through your first day. You made it. Now every day can get a little easier. By the way, it's nice to have a student who cares about what I am trying to teach. You were a joy to have today."

"Thank you, ma'am."

"You're more than welcome, dear. Now go on and enjoy the rest of your day."

I grabbed my backpack and slung it around my arms when Mrs. Hawkins who had just left the room peeked back in.

"It's all clear."

"Ma'am?"

"The halls are empty. You don't have to stall anymore."

And then she was gone again.

I smiled knowing that at the very least the staff at Highgrove High were a pleasant distraction.

She was right, all the halls were empty and so was the parking lot I noticed once I walked out the doors. I let the cool spring air hit me and thanked the Heavens there were no pastures around. It may have not been an easy first day but I made it through it only crying once and once was more than there should have been.

The truck was just as ugly the second time I had seen it as it was the first. Nothing was endearing or cute about it. He must have bought it off an elderly farmer who couldn't drive anymore because no one would be selling this beast in a car lot that's for sure. Opening the door, the same wave of stale cigarette smoke hit me. This time I slid myself over to the passenger side and rolled down the window doing the same on my side after I was done. The cracking noise could still be heard when I pulled the door closed too.

"I can't say I expected you to change while I was in class but it sure would have been nice."

I put the key in the ignition and turned it over only to hear a click and then nothing.

"NO, NO, NO! Please don't do this to me!"

Four more attempts with the same result. Nothing.

"SHIT!"

I pulled out my phone to call for someone to get me but that someone didn't exist. He would rather me never come back. My mother wouldn't dare go against his wishes and Shelby obviously can't drive.

Grabbing my purse and backpack, I started doing the only thing I could: I walked. I tried to find positive in a negative situation but there really wasn't one. My feet hurt, I was thirsty and if one more person drove by staring at me without even offering me a ride I was going to flip out. I thought country people were supposed to be nice. Isn't that what everyone says? Well, they're wrong or there aren't any in Highgrove, Montana.

My cell phone died sometime around four-thirty. Well, that was the last time I checked it and around ten minutes later it was dead. I had been walking for over an hour and a half and saw a total of two cars.

"WHAT THE HELL HAVE I DONE TO DESERVE THIS?" I screamed it at the top of my lungs hoping God would just finish the job and take me out of my misery.

All of a sudden, I heard the engine of a car coming from behind me. This was it. My final hope for humanity to restore itself. It got closer. I could feel the wind change and the vibration within it.

"Please, please be someone nice enough to give me a ride or someone crazy enough to off me 'cause I can't take this anymore."

I turned around just as the truck approached me praying for a miracle but sure enough the prick kept his foot on the pedal.

"That's fucking it!"

I grabbed a handful of rocks from the side of the road and threw them right at that pretty truck he was driving.

"Have that, asshole!"

The brake lights came on just as the clang from the rocks started hitting the tailgate. The tires screamed against the blacktop while the back end kicked to the side from stopping so fast. My eyes practically bulged out of my head when the driver side door flew open.

"OH, SHIT."

And oh shit was mild compared to what I would have said if I had known who the fury coming at me was before I decided to throw rocks at his truck. How could I not have thought it was him? I had seen that truck before.

"WHAT THE HELL IS WRONG WITH YOU?"

"ME? YOU'RE THE ASSHOLE THAT WOULDN'T EVEN STOP FOR A POOR GIRL WALKING DOWN A FREAKING ENDLESS ROAD!"

"WHY WOULD I?"

"UGH!"

I can't believe I did it. Never in a million years would I have ever even thought to do something like this but I reached down in my rage, grabbed a handful of rocks again and threw them right at his chest. Wall of muscle or not he could take that and suck on it.

A look of complete shock registered on his face but I didn't stick around to see what came next. Hell no, I walked as fast as I could away from him. I didn't get very far before he grabbed me and threw me up against the side of his truck.

"ARE YOU FUCKING CRAZY?"

His fingers were digging into my arms and they hurt. I wanted to tell him that I was sorry but the pain prevented me from being able to talk.

"Oh, shit! I'm sorry."

His hands immediately let me go and were then in the air, palms facing me as he walked backwards.

"If I hurt you...fuck. I didn't mean to..."

"It's okay. I think after what I did I kind of deserved—"

"No, you didn't. I never should have put my hands on you."

Nothing was making sense to me at all. How could he be feeling bad when I probably just dented the crap out of his truck and then, come on, I threw rocks at him! Who says sorry to someone who does something like that?

"I really think I should go."

I didn't give him a chance to respond. I simply started walking away.

"Hey, wait!"

I stopped like he asked as he came toward me wondering the whole time what on Earth he wanted me to do. Probably pay for the damage to his truck. That was going to go over great when he told my step-dick. I was completely screwed.

"Did you need a ride?"

"Wait, what?"

He looked confused at my question but I'm sure so did I because that was the last thing I ever expected him to say.

"A ride. Wasn't that the whole point of all this?"

"Well, yeah, but..."

"Just get in the truck."

He walked toward the driver side while I stood there in awe, but then clarity came and of course he was going to take me home. He needed to know who to bill for damages.

Feeling like I had no choice in the matter, I did as he said and followed him. I opened the passenger door and watched as he rushed to clear off the seat so there was a place for me to sit. From the outside his truck looked good but this guy was a slob. Food wrappers and just plain trash was everywhere. That wasn't what I was most in awe about though. His damn muscles. I mean who has muscles like that? The guy had to work out five to six hours a day to get that big.

"You can get in now."

"Huh?"

I was still staring at him. Not at all paying attention to what he was saying.

"Are you checking me out?"

"Huh? Wait, WHAT? NO! NO. I was just admiring your trash collection."

I couldn't help but smile as I said it. I wasn't flirting. I was truly laughing at how stupid that sounded even to me. Your trash collection? Who says that?

He laughed openly and then said, "Come on, get in."

I swung my backpack onto the floorboard and then pulled myself up into the cab closing the door behind me.

"Where to?"

I'm your neighbor almost came blurting out but thank God I caught myself beforehand.

"I don't know the address. It's just down this road and then you turn left on another road and then it's down around a corner on..."

"You have no idea where you are do you?"

"Yes I do! I drove to school just this morning."

"You drove? Where's your car?"

"You mean my piece of crap? Oh, that would be back at the school parking lot not working."

"You don't have a phone to call someone? You just decide to walk ten miles?"

He shifted into gear but nothing about it was making sense. He put it in reverse instead of drive and started turning us around. I mean, I knew where I lived and we were going the wrong way.

"What are you doing?"

"I'm going to fix your car."

"Why?"

"Well that's a dumb question. Didn't you just tell me that it's broke and without answering me you also told me you have no one to help you?"

"You don't even know me."

"Can't say I have had the pleasure yet. I'm Canyon."

Canyon, what a weird name. I guess it's not weird but it sure is different. It's kind of pretty actually.

"Are you going to tell me yours or just sit there saying my name over and over until it sounds normal to you?"

"I wasn't doing that."

"Yes you were. Now tell me what I can call you."

"Arianna."

"Arianna? Seriously? What kind of foo-foo name is that?"

"Shut up! You're named after a hole in the earth."

"So you were thinking about it!"

"Just shut up."

I turned to face my window, not wanting to continue being teased when his hand landed on my thigh and started rubbing back and forth as I heard, "Listen, Ari, I was just teasin' ya. Don't be mad."

I grabbed his hand and removed it from my leg while I turned back toward him and said, "My name is Arianna not Ari. You didn't hear me call you Can, did you?"

His hands shot up in the air again. "Whoa, slow down, pissy pants. It's just a nickname. Haven't you ever had one? Besides, Arianna is stuck up and I think Ari fits you quite nice."

He smiled again and the conversation seemed lost at that point. We had pulled back into the school parking lot when I heard, "That's your car?" and the smile disappeared.

"Well yeah. There isn't any other possibility is there?"

The parking lot was empty otherwise. Canyon stopped his truck and just stared straight ahead at mine.

"Are you going to pull up to it?" I was answered with silence. "Hello? What are we doing?"

His voice was low when he finally spoke. "That's my dad's truck."

"Oh, so your dad sold that piece of crap to my step-dick? Well let me tell you something, it's disgusting! Like majorly gross. Could he have at least rolled the windows down while he puffed sixty packs of cigarettes...?"

"That was my uncle."

"What? What was your uncle?"

He took his foot off the brake and pulled up next to my truck and then got out. I had no idea what just happened but Canyon obviously made his mind up about something and decided to still fix it for me. I didn't know if he needed help or if I should just stay put. His demeanor had certainly changed and after all the mood swings we both had had in the matter of minutes since we met, I wasn't confident that any decision was the right one. Curiosity won over as I opened the door and climbed out. I had watched him mess with the inside and pop the hood but then it blocked my view, leaving me with no idea as to what he was doing.

Walking around his truck, I saw him leaning over the engine with, again, no shirt on. My feet stopped moving. When did he take it off? I couldn't believe what I was seeing. Distance sure makes a difference when you are looking at someone. This man didn't have an ounce of fat on him. It didn't seem possible to be that lean.

"Oh, hey, can you do me a favor? Go grab my tool box out of the bed for me."

He had stood up to look at me and I shook my head to be able to think clearly.

"The what?"

"The bed of the truck. You know. The back end."

"Of course I knew that."

I walked away thinking, that was good enough, right? I at least didn't give myself away. How embarrassing would it have been if...

"Oh, Ari?" I turned back to see what he needed when he said, "You like what you see, huh?"

Blood red. My face couldn't be described as any other color. How could he just call me out like that?

"No, sport, you got it backwards. I was just thinking about how wrong it is to have less than five percent body fat. You need to enjoy life a little more."

Triumphantly, I continued my walk to the back of his truck wearing a smile. I grabbed the tool box and returned with almost a skip in my step.

"So do you think you can fix it?"

"Darling, I can fix it but you really should get another vehicle. This is not something you can rely on."

"Thanks for the advice."

It's not like I had any choice in the matter anyway. All of my money was in HIS control until I turned eighteen.

I waited and watched for a while as he unscrewed this and banged on that before I got bored and started to walk around. The sun was going down and the skyline was absolutely breath taking. The mountains really were unbelievable. Flat land for miles with a background that reached the clouds.

I heard the slamming of the hood but I wouldn't let myself look away from the view just yet.

"Lived here my whole life and it never gets old."

His voice caused me to jump. Not because he said something but the proximity from where it came from. Canyon was standing right behind me and his mouth was inches from my ear.

"I didn't mean to scare you."

I took a step forward, putting space between us before I turned around to face him. "It's okay. You didn't scare me. Startled is all."

"The truck is back to running and it's getting late. You need to be getting home. Your parents must be worried sick."

I laughed but then shut it down. The last thing I wanted to do was explain to him why he was wrong.

"You're probably right. Thank you so much for fixing it for me. It was the last thing I expected you to do after I dented yours."

"About that..."

Shit. Why did I have to remind him?

"I will pay for the damages. It will have to be in two months or so but I promise I will."

"I don't need your money, sweets, it was my fault to begin with. Although I should explain myself so you don't think I did it on purpose."

"What are you talking about?"

"You had every right to be angry that I didn't stop to offer you help. The part I want to explain is, I didn't even see you."

"How could you have missed me? I was the only girl in red walking down a street lined with wheat. I stick out like a sore thumb. Besides, you said, 'Why would I?'. Like you wouldn't have even if you did see me."

I couldn't believe he was giving me a pass on this.

"I wasn't even looking at the road, Ari. I was changing the song on my mp3 player. The next thing I knew I was hearing what sounded like shotgun shells hitting my car. Besides, I was pissed off."

"So you really didn't see me? That's what you're saying? I dented your truck for no reason."

"No, you dented it because you were sick of walking. Can't say I blame you there."

"I still should fix it."

"We can worry about that later. Let's get you home."

Canyon smiled as he held out the keys for me to take. I couldn't help but smile back as I reached for them either. He was nice. I wasn't convinced that existed anymore but sure enough, he was.

"Let me follow you just to make sure you don't have any more problems with it."

"That would be awful nice of you. Thanks."

"My pleasure."

After I got in and closed the door I realized where we were going. He was going to see I was his neighbor. What if he wanted to meet my family? His horn went off pulling me out of my thoughts and when I looked up he was parked right next to me with his window down.

"I put my shirt back on so you can stop dreaming about me."

I shook my head smiling and laughed as I turned the truck on and it worked.

"Woohoo!" My arms went into the air as I bounced up and down.

"Would you just drive already? I told you I fixed it."

Leaning out my window as far as I could, I said, "Like I had any faith in your mechanics. Nice job, by the way."

"Go, woman!"

I pulled on the gear shift until it landed in D, took my foot off the brake and let myself feel for the first time in weeks as I pulled out onto the road.

Life doesn't have to be all bad.

Chapter 4

The sun had set by the time I pulled into the driveway. The headlights in my rearview mirror followed me home and I can't tell you how good it felt to have someone care enough to watch over me. Even if it was only for a few miles.

Canyon's lights turned off followed by the sound of his door closing. I had ahold of my door handle but couldn't bring myself to push it open. I'm not sure what I was expecting but when the front door of the house opened with my step-dick barreling out from it, my choice in the matter was gone.

In the short time it took to get around the front of my truck, Canyon was already approaching him with his hand extended.

"What the fuck took you so long?"

He had completely ignored Canyon's gesture and was aiming his rage right at me. Quickly, Canyon pulled his offer back and walked the few steps needed to stand between my step-dick and me.

"Excuse me, sir, but I came to introduce myself. My name is Can—"

"I didn't ask and I don't care. Arianna, get your ass inside that house now!"

The biggest mistake my step-dick could have made happened in a matter of seconds. His hand landed on Canyon's shoulder to push him out of the way and in a blink he was on his back on the ground.

"Oh my god!" came out of somewhere within me.

Canyon's head snapped in my direction and regret took over his demeanor. I didn't know how to feel about what was happening in front of me.

Once again his hand extended. "I'm sorry about that. Can I give you a hand up?"

John started scrambling from the ground avoiding the help. "No, you stupid son-of-a-bitch! GET OFF MY PROPERTY NOW!"

"Sir, I think you need to calm down. Ari's truck broke down. She had no way of contacting—"

"Don't tell me to calm down, boy. And let me guess, she played the helpless card on you? Our little Arianna has a cellphone probably hiding in her purse right now..."

"The battery died! I didn't have any way of calling anyone, John. I was walking!"

"Enough! I don't want to hear another word. Get into the house NOW!"

I was humiliated. Feeling completely stripped of any ounce of humility I had left, I began my walk of shame toward the house.

"Wait!"

I didn't know what he was going to say to fix it or why he was even trying for that matter. My step-dick didn't change his mind, ever. It was a lost cause.

"There is the matter of paying me for the damages on my truck that your daughter caused."

"WHAT!" John started shaking his head back and forth and then began to chuckle. "Why am I not surprised?"

"What the hell! Why would Canyon do that?" was all that was going through my mind as I watched what was happening in front of me. I had no idea what he could have been thinking telling a raging lunatic something that was only going to add fuel to the fire. If looks could kill, Canyon would have been dead on the spot with the distaste I was showing him. Yet, he wore a smile. His eyes confused me. There was a light in them as if things were going just the way he had hoped.

"John, is it? Well, John, let me try this again. My name is Canyon Michaels. My house is the last one you pass before you get here from town. Your daughter seemed to be desperate for someone's attention and decided her only option at the time was to throw rocks at my truck. Now, I could make you pay for it, but I think a better lesson for Ari here is to work it off."

John openly laughed. Loud. "You want her to work? Seriously? She doesn't have a clue how to do anything for herself other than screw up."

Canyon's hands began to flex into fists and the light in his eyes left. "Well, it can go my way or yours. She can work every day after school on my ranch or you can go inside and get your wallet to pay me in cash. It's up to you."

My jaw fell to the ground. As much of an ass as my step-dick was, he was also right. I didn't have a clue what to do on a farm and there was absolutely no way in hell I was shoveling crap.

"You got yourself a deal."

I didn't know which way John was going with this but regardless I was going to suffer from my actions once again.

"What will it be? Work or cash?"

"Oh, she can work. I'm not paying a damn dime for this one. She's already cost us everything." He looked over at me with disdain. "Have you told your new friend here about that yet? I bet not. Well there, I gave you something to talk about while you shovel shit. Ha! This is priceless!"

My step-dick had proved what a dick he actually was as he walked back into the house laughing, leaving me to face Canyon. I couldn't. I stared at the ground while I heard the crunch of gravel under his shoes as he approached me. The tips of his red Nike shocks were now all I could see before his finger came to rest under my chin and forced me to look up at him. The long journey up his body brought me to his black workout pants first, then the red t-shirt that clung to his body perfectly until his sharp jaw, amazing lips and finally those eyes were all I could see.

"Don't, Arianna," was all I kept repeating in my head. He's nothing but another man that can hurt you.

"Are you okay?"

Damn, why did he have to ask that? Letting my eyes fall, I thought to myself, "No, I am not okay. Did you not just hear what I deal with every day?" How could I even answer that question?

"Hey, look at me. Please?" My eyes came back to his but I was done. Spent. I didn't want to do anything but go inside and cry myself to sleep. "Don't let him do this to you. Don't let it break you."

"You don't understand."

"I do. More than you could ever know." I went to speak again but Canyon cut me off. "I did this for you, you know. I saw what you have here and was trying to get you out, not make things harder. That man would never want to pay and I knew it. Now you can spend every day away from this."

"But it will never end..." A tear slid down my face at the same time his thumb wiped it away.

"It will. Someday it will."

"Arianna! You're here!"

Shelby came rushing out the door, screaming, "I had such a fun day today! All my friends at school were so nice just like you said." She came crashing into my leg. She was so excited that she obviously hadn't taken notice of Canyon until...

"Oh my goodness, it's you."

"Yes, it's me. And how would you know me, pretty girl?"

Shelby blushed at the compliment and then began to answer. "Arianna and I saw you the first day we got here. She didn't want to come say hi but I did. We were in the back when you..."

She was talking so fast I didn't get the chance to stop her before but I was hell-bent to keep her from telling anymore of that story.

"Shelby, this is Canyon. Canyon, this is my little sister Shelby."

Canyon's face lit up. "It's very nice to meet you Shelby. I sure wish your sister wouldn't have been so stubborn. You could have come over and met my horses."

If I thought Canyon's face was cute, Shelby's was priceless.

"You have horses? Like real horses? My daddy says I can get a pony and make a real unicorn out of it! Isn't that so cool?"

Canyon smiled so big his cheeks must have hurt. "That is the best thing I have heard in a long time. I can't wait to meet it. Are you going to get a boy or a girl?"

"Oh definitely a girl. They're so much prettier. When I braid her mane and tail she will be the prettiest unicorn ever."

"I bet you're right about that. Well you let me know when you're ready for her and I can help you pick her out. You want to ride her of course?"

"Well, yeah! Why would I want a pony I can't ride?"

The laugh that came out of him was adorable. "Sounds like a plan then."

Shelby was lit up like a Christmas tree. Beaming.

"Hey, Shelby, can I have just a few more minutes here with Canyon and then I'll come inside. I can't wait to hear about your first day."

"Okay. Bye, Canyon! It was nice to meet you."

"Right back at ya, Shelby."

We both watched her skip back into the house before we turned and faced each other again. All of a sudden I saw it for what it was. I was letting him in and it was a mistake.

"She's a lot of fun I bet."

"She's my happiness."

"So you wouldn't come say hi?"

"That was a quick change of conversation."

"Answer the question."

"No, I wouldn't."

"Why?"

"Because you're a man."

"Yes, you could say that. What does that even mean?"

"It means you don't need to understand me to do your chores. That's all this is. I will work for you until the debt is paid off. Then we go our separate ways."

"Huh, you're different, girl, that's for sure."

"More than you will ever know."

There was an awkward pause that I had to break. "What time do you expect me tomorrow?"

Canyon looked like he wanted to say something else but gratefully he changed his mind. "Four o'clock works for me."

I turned and started walking for the house before I said, "Then I will see you at four."

I heard, "Don't be late" just as I walked through the door and straight to my bedroom.

Shelby came running in after me wearing a huge grin on her face.

"So how was your day? Did you get to meet new friends like me? Wasn't it cool?"

"Mine was good but I want to hear more about yours. So you met some nice kids, huh? How is your new teacher?"

Nothing like deflecting.

"It's a boy! His name is Mr. Schneider and he is so nice. He even let me introduce myself to the class. I got to tell them all about me and..."

"ARIANNA, GET IN HERE!"

"Uh oh, what did you do?"

"Nothing you need to worry about. I will be back to hear more about what happened, okay? In the meantime why don't you listen to my new Maroon 5 CD?"

"You'll let me?"

"Sure thing. It's a special day, right?"

She smiled that hundred watt grin at me and I melted. Normally I don't let her go near my iPod but I needed something to drown out the screaming that I knew was coming.

Walking out of my room into the hallway, I was met with John and my mother standing in the family room.

"Who do you think you are? Throwing rocks at people's car? You are nothing but a huge fuck up." My mother stood behind him with her eyes on the floor. "I asked you a question!"

"What would you like me to say?"

"Are you kidding? You just think you can do whatever it is you want with no repercussions? Well, let me tell you something. I am done bailing you out!"

I broke. Never before had I spoken up for myself, but something in me couldn't do it anymore.

Looking him straight in the eye I conjured up as much courage as I owned. "You have done nothing for me." My voice was low but I came across clearly. "You didn't bail me out. You didn't defend me when I needed it more than anything. You are a lawyer, John. We could have fought the charges. We could have done so much more than take the money and run."

When he stomped toward me, I expected him to scream, but instead, his hand came crashing into my cheek buckling my knees as I dropped to the ground. I immediately cupped my face and felt the heat resonating but it was nothing compared to the ringing in my left ear.

"You little bitch! She died because of you! YOU! Not me. Not your mother or Shelby. YOU! I had to do what was best for my family and you dare to blame me? This"— he threw his hands in the air— "is all because of you!"

There was no point in arguing over something I couldn't change. He was right. I was responsible for everything that had happened and nothing was going to make that pain go away. Slowly, I pressed myself against the wall behind me and pushed with my legs to climb up it. Once upright I looked to my non-existent mother hoping for a miracle but was met with the same reaction as always.

I turned and walked out of the room ready to climb into bed and let this day come to an end. Rounding the corner into my bedroom, I found Shelby lying on my bed with her eyes closed. I have never prayed harder that the music was enough to keep her unaware but soon I found out that she was fast asleep.

"Some prayers get answered after all."

Chapter 5

School was no better than the day before with one exception: I got to eat this time. No, I didn't brave the cafeteria again. I made sure to pack my lunch and ate it on the tailgate of my truck.

I was tripped in the hall and locked in the bathroom while someone held the door closed from the outside for ten minutes within the first two hours of school but nothing that could be described as tragic happened. At least Shelby wasn't dealing with this. I overheard some girls talking in fifth period about how I hit on Kyle and that's what started the hatred spreading like wildfire through the school. These people had no idea what I was about or they would know I had no desire to hit on anyone.

The last bell rang and I wasn't going to do a repeat performance and wait it out. The quicker I could part from the sea of idiots the better.

I grabbed my things from my locker and joined the masses pouring from the building. Once I was out the door and in the open air, a sense of calm washed over me. I really didn't want to go work at Canyon's but it seemed like a way better option than going home to face step-dick.

All day I contemplated skipping out on the whole deal and just hiding in a field somewhere, but what good would that do? I did owe him something for the damages and I knew he only came up with this idea to try to help. Still, with all of that, I was mortified to face him. He had to have gone home and thought about what John had said. Fifty

34

million questions must be brewing and ready for answers I wasn't willing to give. Before I knew it, I was turning to the left and pulling up into his driveway. My hands started to shake as I reached for the key to turn the engine off. Dropping my head to let it rest on the steering wheel, I told myself that it was going to be okay. Whatever it was he wanted me to do I could do it. All I needed was to get out of the truck.

Bam!

My head shot up only to find Canyon laughing, standing in front of the hood he had slapped, scaring me half to death in the process.

"Come on, girl, get out. We have things to do and I don't have all day."

I shook my head back and forth, rolled my eyes, smiled and reached for the door handle.

Canyon walked over to my side and pulled the door open for me still wearing that shit-eating grin of his. "What took you so long?"

I slid out of the cab landing right in front of him. "What are you talking about? School just got out."

"Well, let's get to doing. There's no sunlight to burn. We have maybe three hours before we lose light and a lot to get done."

"I'm not looking forward to this."

"Oh, but you will love every minute."

"If you say so."

I reached into my truck to grab a rubber band to tie my hair back with. I may not have cared to do anything with myself to impress anyone but I loved my hair and getting crap in it wasn't something I was keen on doing.

"Come on, woman."

He was already five steps away when I lifted my hair up on my head and started wrapping it up into a messy bun.

"Hold your horses. I'm almost ready."

Canyon turned around laughing. "Speaking of horses...WHAT THE FUCK IS THAT?"

I had been smiling because, let's just face it, his demeanor was contagious but something happened and I didn't know what. "What's wrong?"

I spun around to see what was behind me that got him so upset but nothing was there. Turning back I found Canyon two inches from my face.

"What happened to you?"

"Me? Nothing. What is your problem?"

I took a step back but he grabbed my arm loosely and pulled me back to him. His right hand came up to the left side of my face. The calluses on his palm felt like sandpaper being dragged across my skin but the tenderness that he was using didn't allow it to hurt. His eyes went dark as his shoulders dropped almost in defeat. Only then did I remember what had him so upset.

"He did this to you after I left, didn't he?"

The simple answer would be yes but that wasn't fair. So much happened before John struck me that I didn't want to explain.

"It's a long story and not something I want to get into. Can we just get started on whatever you're going to make me do out here?"

"Okay."

One word and that was it. I expected him to argue but he let it go just as I asked of him and began to walk away.

"Hey, wait up!"

I followed Canyon down the driveway until we started approaching the house. My adoration only grew being this close in the daylight.

"Are you coming?"

I hadn't realized I had stopped walking.

"Yes. I'm sorry, I just love this house."

Canyon walked back to me and looked up to the balcony I couldn't take my eyes off.

"I wish I could see what you see."

"Does that lead to your parents' room?" His body locked up. I felt the jerk even without touch. "Did I say something wrong?"

"No. We better get to work or nothing is going to get done."

He turned from the house and began to walk away again.

"Could you get anymore moody?"

"I heard that!"

"You were supposed to."

Canyon continued to walk ahead of me until I lost him around the back side of the house. I hurried to catch up until I rounded the corner and sent dirt flying from stopping so fast.

"Holy crap!"

Those words were nothing compared to the magnitude of what I was seeing. The barn was huge. Bigger than the house. Wrapped in cedar shake siding, stained perfectly with stone pillars holding up the gable, I was speechless. There was even a cast iron M in the center of it. It was something I could only imagine seeing in magazines. How I missed this the other night when I was back here seemed impossible but then again the night sky was above me.

I let my eyes fall back on Canyon standing in the doorway wearing that smile again.

"Didn't expect this, did you?"

I continued to move closer with my jaw hanging open. When I finally could wrap my head around it, I answered, "No, I can't say I ever would have expected this. Shelby would be in Heaven."

"Come on in. There's something I want to show you."

I followed him through the gigantic barn doors and couldn't believe there was more to be surprised about. I expected a barn. What I found was a place cleaner than most people's houses. A concrete floor stretched through the center aisle all the way to the back doors. There had to be thirty or more stalls on either side made also from cedar with black iron fencing that topped the wood another four feet. The best part of all was that over half of them were filled with a magnificent horse.

"Are all of these yours?"

Canyon stood back and watched me as I walked around in amazement. I had never seen anything so utterly perfect.

"Yeah. We lost our stock a few years ago but after it was all over I began to build it back up."

"You did this? That's incredible."

"It's all I have left."

His mood became almost somber. I wanted to pry and ask what he meant by that but I knew all about secrets that needed to be kept as such. Feeling the only option I had was to change the subject, I said, "So, where do we start?"

I pictured myself shoveling crap and gagged with the thought.

"Have you ever ridden before?"

"Um, no."

"No? Seriously?"

"You asked. You had to know the possibility was there."

"Well, I had hope."

"Sorry to disappoint you."

Canyon looked deep in thought and then he said, "Okay, we don't have time for lessons today so I guess you'll just have to ride with me."

"With you?"

"Yes, with me."

He started walking toward an open area in the back filled with equipment. I followed behind him looking at all the stuff.

"What is all this for?"

He didn't look at me but continued grabbing this and that.

"This is a tack room. This"—he held up something that looked like a bunch of straps tied together— "is a harness and this is a lead rope."

"What do you want me to do?" I felt awkward just standing there while he was busy grabbing all kinds of things.

"Here, hold this."

He walked over to me and dumped fifty pounds of crap into my arms practically causing me to fall forward while he turned back to grab blankets and the saddle.

"That's a different kind of saddle."

"You know what it is?"

"Well, I'm not an idiot."

"I didn't mean.... anyway, this is an English saddle. It's easier to ride double than a western which is probably what you are used to seeing."

He didn't wait for a response but instead walked past me and out the back of the barn placing the saddle on a piece of wood supported by two legs. I thought I had almost caught up to him carrying my pile when he passed me going the other direction back into the barn.

I turned to face him and shouted, "So much for helping a girl out!"

He continued to walk away when his response came. "You're here to work, remember?"

"Ugh!"

I finished carrying everything outside, threw it on the ground and then stared at it having no idea what all of it was used for. I heard the slamming of a gate and when I looked back, Canyon was walking toward me leading a beautiful pure black stallion. I knew it only from watching the movie but I wasn't owning up to that one. Every step the horse took closer to me it seemed to grow in size. By the time Canyon was standing next to me, I was scared.

"This is Magnus. He's one of my prized stock." I raised my arm to pet him but apparently moved too fast because the horse's head flew up, jerking Canyon's arm along with it while scaring me half to death. "You have to move slower around horses. They spook easily."

"Now you tell me."

He pulled the rope back down and Magnus's head came down with it.

"Try again, but this time just hold your hand out and let him come to you." I didn't move. "Come on. He won't bite."

I sneered at Canyon but did as he said.

This time I put my arm straight out, palm facing down and waited. When Magnus didn't raise his head again I moved my hand a little closer, inch-by-inch until I could feel his breath across my knuckles.

"It's safe to touch him, just go slow."

I flipped my hand over and lifted my arm to pet him behind his ear first. I laughed when it twitched from side to side.

"See, he likes you."

"That's to be determined."

"Horses are pretty easy to read. If their ears go back, look out. Other than that it's all good. Just always remember, they are animals and think like one. Don't talk to them like they can understand you. Use simple commands and you will be good to go. Oh, and don't walk behind them unless you are at a safe distance if they kick."

"You make it sound so easy," I said sarcastically.

Canyon responded as if my sarcasm went unnoticed. "It really is. They are my pride and joy."

"Why do you have so many?"

He didn't want to answer this either and I didn't understand. Why was this a secret? Instead of letting him off the hook and giving him an out, I chose to continue petting Magnuses' head and wait.

Several deep breaths later came, "I am trying to build the best damn quarter horse this world has ever seen."

"WHAT?" I didn't think before I let that blurt out of my mouth. It was the last thing I expected him to say so it caught me off-guard.

Canyon looked down to the ground and kicked the dirt out from under his shoe before he lifted his head again to look at me. One glance was all I got before he started grabbing things and putting them on Magnus.

He took the strappy thing off of his head and replaced it with a metal bar that he shoved in his mouth.

"Ouch."

"Not ouch," he snapped. "This is a bit and it's the part of the bridle that allows the rider to steer."

He had to be bipolar. I couldn't think of anything else that would explain his mood swings. He lifted what I now knew was called a bridle up and tucked Magnuses' ears under the leather strap. Next he snapped two buckles to the metal rings on either side of the horse's mouth which I also learned were reins. Once he tied them to the piece of wood he walked over to the pile I had dropped on the ground and started picking up blankets and placing them on his back before finally putting the saddle on top of them.

I thought when he was done with that he might say something but instead he reached under Magnuses' belly and came back with a belt that he attached under the foot holder. He tugged on it so hard I thought the poor horse might not be able to breathe. I figured that might be the icebreaker I needed.

"Can he breathe with his belt so tight?"

"It's a girth strap and yes."

No, he didn't look at me but his tone was at least better.

Canyon tugged on the saddle confirming it was good and tight before he untied the reins and put his foot in the thing hanging down to pull himself up on top of Magnus. I looked up at him wondering what I was supposed to do when he said, "Let's go."

Of course I had no idea what that meant for me so I stood there and stared at him waiting for more direction.

"That means come here so I can pull you up."

"No."

The look of shock was priceless but I was too mad to enjoy it. If he thought I wanted to subject myself to any more of his pissy mood he was crazier than I thought.

"What do you mean no?"

"It's a simple word to understand, crab ass."

With one blink his leg was swinging back over the horse and Canyon was standing in front of me.

"Look, I don't know you. There are things I'm not comfortable talking about and after last night I thought you of all people could respect that."

"I can and I do but you don't have to be rude about it."

"Being quiet isn't the same thing as rude."

"You're right about that, there's a definite difference."

"Let's just go. I have to check on everything before it gets dark."

"You still want me to come with you?"

"Would you rather go home?"

"No."

"Then come on."

Canyon was up on top of Magnus again and holding his hand out for me to take seconds later.

"Put your foot in the stirrup and let me pull you up, okay?" he barked, pointing to the foot holder.

I walked over and then took one look at the stirrup.

"Will you hold him still?"

"Of course I will."

I didn't know if I could believe him or not but true to his word, Magnus stayed put while I lifted my leg to get my foot inside of it while Canyon pulled me up. The problem was I had no idea where I was supposed to go from there.

"What are you waiting for?"

"Front or back?"

"Back. I can't trust you in front yet."

I wasn't in the mood to argue standing on the side of a gigantic horse. I flung my right leg around and landed myself on Magnus's butt, right behind the saddle.

"You comfortable?"

"At least there's blankets back here."

"Good. Okay, now put your arms around my waist and hold on. We don't have as much time as I thought we were going to have."

As soon as my hands found each other in front of Canyon, I gripped them together with all of my might.

"Now, let's go have some fun."

Nothing at that point seemed like something I would ever call fun. I was scared out of my mind.

Chapter 6

I have never been more wrong. When Canyon kicked and the horse took off, I wanted to piss my pants, but Magnus was amazing. It took about ten seconds for me to settle down, let my hair loose, and enjoy it blowing in the wind as we raced through the open land. As far as my eyes could see there were mountains of various sizes. Some were still capped with snow from the hard winter I learned they had as Canyon explained it to me. His mood had changed into something I could enjoy.

"Over there is the creek I grew up swimming in. This is where I got my first kiss from Maggie Greenwood. Right there was where I got thrown for the first time."

He pointed in so many directions, teaching me all about what it was like growing up out here. It was everything I could ever want for Shelby and for the first time, I found something positive about our move. But the last bit of information didn't sit right.

"Thrown?"

"Yeah, if you piss off the wrong horse you'll go flying."

"Did you get hurt?"

"Hell yeah I did, but it started my love for bull riding."

We had slowed down to a walk with Magnus and what Canyon said had me wanting to jump off just so I could see his face and determine if he was joking or telling me the truth.

"You got awful quiet back there."

He turned in the saddle to look at me and it was then I got my answer. He was smiling.

"That's not funny. I thought you were serious."

"What makes you think I'm not?"

That smile only got bigger.

"Your shit-eating grin."

"Well, I can assure you, darlin', that I wouldn't be grinning if I was eating shit."

"You know what I mean."

"If you think I'm lying come with me Friday night."

"To where?"

"Billings. I have a few friends that will be there I want to see."

"I'm not sure."

"Scared?"

"No. I just don't know you and where ever Billings is probably far away."

"What? You think I would try to do something? Don't flatter yourself, doll, I'm good on my own. I don't need to force anyone."

He had kicked Magnus to speed up and soon we were running again, not giving me a chance to explain what I meant. Hell, he had no idea how much I appreciated what he said. The last thing I wanted was for him to get the wrong idea from me.

A few minutes later we were entering a wooded tree line. Canyon bent forward and said, "Keep your head down."

Branches were just over us and I had no idea why were even going through this in the first place.

"Damn it!"

A branch had caught on to my hair and pulled it so hard it broke off and was stuck. I let go of my other hand to yank it out but Canyon quickly grabbed ahold of it and put it back where it was.

"Hold on to me, we're going to go down a ravine. When the trees break lean back fast."

No sooner did he say it, it happened.

"Holy shit!"

Canyon was practically laying on me as we went straight down. I was petrified.

"It will be okay, just stay back."

Too freaked to respond, I did the only thing I could. I closed my eyes and prayed for forgiveness.

"It's over. You can sit up."

"Are you sure?"

I hadn't moved yet but I could feel that we were on flat ground again. When I opened my eyes we were in a whole new world. If I thought it was scary going down that hill I didn't know what fear of falling truly meant.

"Isn't it amazing?"

His voice sounded so proud in that moment. Like he was sharing a piece of heaven with me and by all rights I had to agree.

We were on a bluff overlooking the flat lands far below us and the mountains above. As if the view wasn't amazing enough, Canyon pointed down to the left and when I followed his arm, I saw hundreds of horses grazing.

"Oh my God! They're beautiful!"

"Aren't they?"

We both sat there and stared while time became nothing.

"Are those yours too?"

"No, those right there are mustangs."

"What does that mean?"

"It means they belong to no one. They're wild."

Something spooked them bringing all of their heads up to listen.

I dropped my voice to a whisper. "Did we do that?"

"No. They can hear better than we can. Something else has got their attention."

All of a sudden a huge brown horse with black hair stood up on its back legs and let out a sound that could be heard off the rocks around us, before it took off followed by the rest of them. If I thought watching them eat was beautiful I can't come up with a word to describe the entire group running at full speed.

Magnus raised his head and yelled back something, making me laugh.

"Is he talking to them?"

"He was one of them."

"What? How?"

"When I started the business up again I had nothing. There was no way I could afford to buy breeding stock. I had no choice. The bank was coming after the ranch unless I could show that I could manage to still turn a profit."

He had finally opened up a little and the last thing I wanted to do was load him down with questions. Even if I barely understood anything he was saying to me.

"So you caught one?"

"No, darlin', I caught six."

My mouth fell open. I guess my hands falling to my sides was a dead giveaway because Canyon whipped around to look at me.

"By yourself?"

"My buddy Tanner helped, but yeah."

"How did you do it? They're wild. Wait, Magnus was one? That's not possible. He's the sweetest horse ever."

"Slow down. To answer your question, he was my first. I have been breaking in horses my whole life." He started to laugh. "Can't say I ever broke a mustang before him but I was desperate at the time."

"You don't have to answer this if you don't want to but how old are you?"

"Finally! I have been waiting for this conversation."

"Really? Why?"

"I'm twenty-two."

"And why were you waiting for me to ask?"

"'Cause I have been dying to know how old you are but the last thing I needed was you thinking I wanted to know cause I was interested."

"Well then why do you care?"

"I don't know. I guess there's just something about you that makes you seem older."

"I'm seventeen. My birthday is in June."

"I knew you had to be around that if you're still in school. What I don't get is what could have gone so wrong that life gave you that shit head for a dad?"

I didn't answer at first and then felt slightly guilty for being the only one not willing to open up a little.

"My dad died when I was four and my mom married John not long after. He hates me, that's all there is to it. Shelby came along and gave him his happy little family and I am what stands in the way."

Canyon didn't have much to say. In fact nothing came out. He opened his mouth several times but then closed it again.

"Don't worry about me. I only have two more months and then I'm out of here."

"Well, that's a shame. What happens in—oh, you turn eighteen. That makes sense. Where would you go, though? Back where you came from?"

It was a valid question and deserved an answer. Unfortunately, I hadn't thought one through yet.

"I don't really know."

"Well then maybe you just might change your mind about Friday. Living a little is never a bad thing and if you're only going to be here for the next eight weeks we have to get on it."

"What's got you so hell-bent on me going with you?"

Canyon turned Magnus around and started to head for the hill. I wrapped my arms back around him preparing myself when I finally heard him answer me just before we hit the trees.

"Because, Ari, having you around just makes things seem better."

I wanted to smile but there was no way having your life flash before your closed eyes was making that a possibility. I was sure to tuck my head but going up was almost worse than coming down. It felt like at any moment I was going to slip off the back. I felt Canyon's hand cover the clasp of my own, securing my safety and once again, it happened. He was protecting me.

When we finally came to the top and were clear of the tree line, I spoke. "I'll go Friday if you really want me to."

All his teeth became visible as he grinned from ear to ear turning around to face me. "If that's the case we need to work our asses off today and tomorrow."

"Why? What difference does that make?"

"Well, judging by your choice of clothing my guess is you don't have boots or a hat."

"Oh, no you don't. I am not a Barbie doll you can dress up."

"If you plan to go to one of the country's biggest PBR events with me, woman, you will adorn a respectable hat. The boots I will have a little give on."

With that, he kicked Magnus again and we were off. Running as fast as I think a horse can go, I felt free. Like nothing mattered in that moment but where I was.

A couple of fields over Canyon pointed out a chunk of wire fence that wasn't standing up like it was supposed to be. He turned Magnus and headed us over to look at it. Clearly tools were necessary and we had none which raised the question, "Don't you need..."

"Hop down."

"How do you expect me to do that?"

"Hold onto me, lean forward, swing your leg over and slide down."

"I'll fall!"

"No, you won't. Now quit being a baby and just do it."

I did and of course he was right again. Once my feet were on flat ground a whole new feeling took over. I realized just how sore I was going to be. Squatting down to stretch my muscles felt good until Canyon started laughing.

"You got to be kidding me? You're sore already?"

I gave him a dirty look but that was all I had. He was right. I was completely out of shape.

"Why are we here? Don't we need to get tools?"

Canyon started putting on gloves without answering me but that was okay because I had another question that I wanted answered more.

"Where the hell did you get gloves?"

"They were in my pocket."

"Bull. Your pants don't have room for gloves."

"So you've been checking me out again?"

"No! I just mean I think I would have noticed gloves."

He walked away from me toward the fence still laughing. "You were checking me out. You were checking me out."

"If you sing that one more time…"

"You'll what?"

"I'll...I'll... I don't know, but just stop, okay?"

He laughed at me, giving off that amazing smile before he said, "I'll stop teasing ya. But, Ari, you need to smile more and pull the serious stick out of your ass."

He had me ready to kill him.

"Just because I don't walk around smiling all the time doesn't mean anything. And hell, if you want to know the truth, I smile when it's something worth smiling about."

Canyon put his foot on the bottom line of wire holding it to the ground and then pulled the top up over the post and wrapped it making the three rows flow like they had never been damaged.

Gloves were needed due to the fact there were pointy things all over it.

"That fence seriously holds in horses? You would think they could just jump over it."

"Glad to see you dropped the attitude. These barbs intimidate them. They don't think to jump unless they are trained too."

I didn't want to argue anymore so I stuck to the answering him nicely. "Hmm, that seems like simple logic."

"Not everything in the world is complicated."

If he only knew.

"So it's fixed?"

"For now this will do but I need to come back and secure the wire better." He walked back toward me smiling again. "Now, are you ready for the best part?"

"I don't know. Are you being serious or am I going to be shoveling crap?"

"Well, you will be doing a little of that too but you can't get into the stalls unless the horses are out of them, right?"

Imagining all of the horses getting to run free had me excited to get back.

"So can we go do that now?"

"There's that smile I was talking about."

"Like I told you, when it's worth it."

Canyon laughed and then walked back to Magnus and climbed back up.

"Let's go do this."

I wasn't nervous. I knew what to do. I grabbed onto Canyon's hand, put my foot in the stirrup and pulled. Just as I was going to swing my leg over, Canyon let the tension go of our grip and my balance shifted. I screamed at the top of my lungs as I started to fall backwards toward the ground. Just as I was emptying my lungs of air, Canyon's grip tightened again and I was pulled back toward him. My heart was racing out of my chest when I looked at Canyon and saw him smiling.

Rage. One single word that says so much.

"You son-of-a-bitch! You did that on purpose!"

His smile turned into a full out belly laugh. "Your face! Ha! That was priceless!"

I pulled myself onto the back of Magnus and then sat there while he practically wet himself from laughing so hard. I wanted to leave but I had no idea where I was to be able to get back. Fate dealt me a pretty crappy hand when they put this lunatic in my path.

"Are you done?"

He didn't say anything but I could hear him try to settle himself down. When a few large exhales happened I knew he was finally over his fit.

"That sure felt good."

He picked up the reins and kicked Magnus. I had no choice but to put my hands around him again. Even if it was the last place in the world I wanted them to be.

Running through the fields almost had me forgetting about his stupid prank until I heard him say, "You were so funny."

"It wasn't funny at all."

"Yes it was. Maybe not to you but it sure was."

About ten minutes later, we were riding up to a place I hadn't seen yet. There was a fenced in area with a gate and then off to the left the fencing ran in a complete circle.

"What's this for?"

Canyon pointed to the first area I saw and said, "That's a corral and that over there is a round pin. Both are used to contain and work with them."

"So is this where they go when we let them out? I thought they would get to run."

"Oh no, you were right. Today's not a day for training. We have actual work to do."

He steered Magnus around the fencing and across the back of the barn before we came to stop at the very place we got on. I slid down first and then walked into the barn to check out the other horses. Some were smaller than others and the color range was surprising.

"Hey, Canyon, didn't you say you caught only six? Why do they all look so different if they came from the same parents?"

He was taking all the equipment off of Magnus but still answered, "Four mares and two stallions. Breeding them became like mixing paint."

I looked at the stall across from me that was empty and asked, "Is this where you put Magnus? I can't remember."

Canyon looked up to see where I was talking about and then smiled, "No, Ari, that stall's not empty. Go look."

He didn't go back to working but chose to stand and watch me instead, making me nervous. Slowly I crept over to the bars and peered over the wall.

"OH MY GOD!"

It was hands down the cutest thing I had ever seen. Standing at its full height, the baby wasn't yet tall enough to see out. Its ears were above the railing but not the head. It was covered in white with black spots all over, like someone splashed paint on it. Its hair was black and when it looked up at me my heart melted.

"Canyon! Is it a boy or a girl?"

I jumped when he answered from right behind me. "He's a boy."

"Did you name him yet? How old is he? Can I go in? Or can he come out?"

"Calm down, woman. Give me a chance to talk." He put his hands on my shoulders and said, "His name is Triton and he's four months old." I could feel his breath on my neck. "Now, foals can be finicky, so when you handle them you have to be careful. I just started him with a halter last week so if you want to pet him always make sure I'm around, okay?"

He pushed me forward and turned me slightly so I would look at him. "That goes for the other three too."

I swear that grin was something that deserved its own definition at times but this one I had matched.

"There's three more? Where?"

I tore off from his grasp, searching through every stall until I found all three of them. Each one was still with their mother and smaller than Triton by half the size. Their legs made up the bulk of their height making them look awkwardly cute.

"Canyon, they're so cute!"

I was on my tippy toes, gripping the cold bars that separated me from the cutest one yet. It had a strawberry blond fur with white blond hair just like its mom.

"You're kinda fond of that one, huh?"

"How can you tell?" I didn't take my eyes off the foal as I spoke.

"A Palomino is striking to say the least."

"What does that mean?"

"It's what a horse is known by if its coat and mane are this color."

"Is this one a boy too?"

"No, darlin'. She's a beautiful lady just like her momma."

"I just want to wrap her up. I have never seen a more adorable creature before."

"I got something to show you that might change your mind."

He grabbed my hand and pulled me away taking from me any choice in the matter.

"Wait, what's her name?"

"Haven't given her one yet."

"Why? That's just mean."

"No, it's not. I haven't found anything pretty enough to suit her."

"Nyah."

"What did you just say?"

"Nyah. I like the name Nyah."

"Where did you hear that?"

"I haven't before. It just came to me."

50

"That sure is pretty. Nyah. Yeah, I think that could work for her."

"Yeah! I got to choose a name. Any more unnamed creatures running around that need my services?"

I wagged my butt from side to side doing a happy dance causing Canyon to laugh at me.

"You sure have some silliness to ya, girl."

I shut down pretty fast realizing I got caught up in the moment.

"Hey, don't stop on my account. I kind of need that around here."

I looked into his eyes and realized he was telling me something that ran deeper than the surface of his words. In that moment I realized I was helping him somehow just as much as he was helping me.

"So, what was it you wanted to show me?"

Chapter 7

"Oh my gosh! How does this keep getting better?"

"I knew this was the icing on the cake."

"How many are there? I can't count. They're moving too fast."

"Nine if you can believe it. Poor Dolly is dropping weight like crazy having to feed the hungry little suckers. They're going to literally suck her dry."

In a pen protected by a chain link fence was the cutest litter of puffy white and black puppies.

"What kind are they?"

"Shetland sheep dogs."

"They're so freakin' cute. Where's the dad?"

"He's here somewhere. I have never been able to catch the son-of-a-bitch. I got him five years ago and he never sticks around."

"Well he sticks something somewhere obviously."

"Was that a joke? You actually can joke? I never would have guessed." He was laughing so at least I had that.

"I'm not a stuck up person. I just like to keep to myself sometimes."

His laughter died off and was followed by, "I can respect that."

It started to feel awkward and I needed to break the silence.

"So, is this the work you were talking about? I mean, I can sit here all day and play with puppies, if that's okay with you."

"No, that's not okay with me. We need to let all the horses out and muck the stalls."

"Damn, I knew there was cleaning crap somewhere in my future."

"You got that right. But it's not all bad. I will take the piles while you handle the sawdust."

"Sawdust?"

"Just follow me. I will explain it all as we go."

Back in the barn I stood and watched as Canyon let each latch go and then led the horses out of the barn. The mere strength of them blew me away. You could visibly see every muscle grind as they moved. The babies were my favorite part though. Each one stuck right beside their mom all the way out into the pasture.

When every stall was empty, Canyon came walking back toward me with a shovel. He made a turn to the left and opened a door telling me to follow him. Once I made it around the corner I saw what he was getting at. The largest pile of sawdust you could imagine was inside of it.

"This is what you need to scoop up and spread over the urine spots in every stall."

"So I'm supposed to just cover the piss not clean it?"

"The straw absorbs it."

"Oh, okay."

That didn't seem too hard. "I can handle this," I thought, as Canyon handed me the shovel and walked away.

Taking the shovel and plunging it into the pile was one thing. Lifting it and carrying was another. Holy crap that stuff isn't light. My arms felt like they were going to give out before I made it into the first stall. Canyon was coming out of the gate with a shovel full of what looked like exactly what I was carrying.

"The wet stuff?"

"Yep, you gotta clean it out or where would it go?"

He passed me and headed out the back door. "Well, if he just took the wet stuff, where am I supposed to put this?" crossed my mind.

"CANYON."

He didn't come back so I immediately called for him again.

"CANY—"

"Damn, woman, you sure have some pipes on you. What's wrong?"

"My arms are about to fall off standing here and I have no idea where to put it if you took all the wet stuff."

"You can see where the floor is still damp in spots. Just spread it there."

Well that seemed easy enough. I walked into the stall and searched the dirt floor for damp spots and spread it out like he said. There was straw along the back wall leading me to believe that's where they sleep.

"Do we need to replace the straw too?"

"Only if there are piles in it."

"They crap where they sleep?"

"They'll drop a load where ever it comes out. Horses aren't finicky."

"Gross."

"It is what it is."

Two hours later we were finished with the stalls and I was worn out. I knew it would be hard work but damn. Country lifestyle isn't easy.

"Canyon, do you think I could use your bathroom?"

He had been closing the back door to the barn when I asked and stopped what he was doing but didn't answer me right away. It wasn't a hard question that required deep thought. I had to pee. What was the big deal?

Finally, after he finished closing the door he turned and said, "Sure thing, follow me." Like it didn't take him any time to decide. The closer we got to the house the more I wondered what he didn't want me to see and it started to creep me out.

"You know what, never mind. I can just go home if we're done for the day. It's getting late anyway."

He almost looked relieved when he said, "Okay, if you're sure" which confirmed my suspicions.

"All right then, have a good night."

I turned and walked away toward my truck without him saying a word and heard the back door to the house close behind him.

It was a short drive home but I did it with a smile on my face. Yes, I still needed to go to the bathroom and yes, he weirded me out, but all in all it was a great day. I couldn't remember having so many experiences in such a short time. By the end of cleaning the stalls I had even got used to doing that.

It was almost dark when I pulled into the driveway of the house. After I turned the truck off I sat for a second just staring at the last place I wanted to be. I missed my friends and most of all Kale which was the stupidest feeling to have. Anyone that could hurt me the way he did didn't deserve to be missed. He deserved to be hated but somethings can't be turned off just because you want them to.

Walking in through the front door had me excited for only one reason: I couldn't wait to share my day with Shelby. I knew she was going to be so happy when I offered to take her with me the next day. I hadn't asked Canyon but what harm could it do?

"Shelby," I called for her as soon as I closed the door behind me and went in search for the little monster. When I didn't find her in her room I called for her again.

"Shelby!"

"Stop fucking screaming in my house!"

The step-dick was sitting his fat butt on the couch in the family room as I entered it.

"Sorry. Have you seen Shelby?"

"Do I look like her keeper?"

I wanted to say anything but what I let come out of my mouth.

"No, sir."

"Then why are you still standing there like a dumb ass deer in headlights, go away."

I walked into the kitchen where I found Shelby at the table playing her iPad with ear buds in. The kicker was my mother was sitting next to her and clearly heard the whole thing. How hard would it have been to just say, "She's in here"?

I walked over to my little sister and tapped her shoulder. Her face lit up but then turned quickly into a scowl.

As she pulled the ear buds out she said, "You smell terrible."

I laughed realizing I probably did.

"You just laughed! Arianna, I haven't seen you do that in a long time."

I was just about to respond when I heard, "Yes, Arianna, please tell us what's funny about you smelling my house up like shit? Speaking of shit, how was it cleaning it up?" He laughed but it was as fake as his good side.

I looked back at Shelby. "I'm going to go take a shower but then I want to talk to you, okay?"

"Okay."

I walked out of the room telling myself, "Just two more months."

Once the warm water hit me it was as if it activated the smell. I half coughed, half gagged at it myself. A new bar of soap practically disappeared after I stood there scrubbing for an hour to make sure it was gone. When I was done, I got dressed and went to Shelby's room only to find her sitting on the edge of her bed waiting.

"That took a long time."

"Well, I was pretty stinky."

"What did you want to talk about?"

"Did anyone tell you where I was today?"

"Daddy said you had to work and then something about poop in the kitchen."

"Well, I went to Canyon's after school to help him. You will never guess what he has, Shelby! I can't wait to take you with me tomorrow to see."

"What is it?"

"I want it to be a surprise."

"That's just mean."

"I was going to tell you all about it but I just realized how much better it will be if you don't know. I didn't and I was amazed."

"Is it going to be cool?"

"Cooler than you can imagine."

"Then I can't wait."

"Shelby! Dinner's ready."

"Come on, Arianna. Let's go eat. Daddy made steaks."

I was starving but knew I had nothing to look forward to. His steaks were always rare and the blood grossed me out.

"Sounds great, squirt. Let's go."

The conversation over dinner consisted of me listening while Shelby and John talk. My mother and I, as usual, kept our heads down and just focused on eating.

I cleaned the kitchen after everyone was done and went to Shelby's room afterwards to hang out with her. We played a couple games on her iPad and laughed at a few YouTube videos before she shocked me with something I didn't see coming.

"Daddy shouldn't have said that at dinner."

She knew whether I told her or not how awful her father was to me. I just found it more important to make sure she appreciated what he was to her rather than let her focus on me.

"It's okay, Shelby. It's my fault I don't like steak. I should really try to eat what food he provides for us and not be ungrateful like he said."

"It just doesn't seem fair. I don't like Brussels sprouts and he doesn't yell at me to eat them."

She was figuring it out whether I wanted her to or not.

"Well, let's not worry about that. It's time for your shower any way. You stink and need to start getting ready for bed."

"Why do I have to go to bed so much earlier than you?"

"Because I am twice your age. When you get bigger you can stay up later too."

"Okay."

She drug the word out letting me know she wasn't happy but regardless, she grabbed a towel and pajamas on her way out of the room before she turned and said, "Arianna, I like seeing you happy. If what I'm going to see tomorrow did this then I can't wait."

Long after I tucked Shelby in for the night and the house was quiet I still laid wide awake in bed. I checked Facebook to see what all of my friends were up to and even saw Kale in a few pictures. Life had carried on for them without a hitch, as if what happened didn't have any effect. Envy coursed through my veins. I longed to be back there, in those pictures, laughing without a care in the world again. Knowing that it wasn't a possibility crushed me. It wasn't my fault. Well, it wouldn't have been if I had never gone to the party that night.

An hour later I had enough of self-pity to last a lifetime and decided to go for a walk. I grabbed my coat, this time knowing the temperature had dropped and I wasn't planning on coming back anytime soon.

The gravel crunched under my feet making a sound I had never heard a week before but now was becoming used to. Even the smell didn't hit me like the first day we got there. Somehow I was conforming and that bothered me.

The moon was almost full and lit up the night sky. As much as I wanted to hate this place I had to admit how pretty it was. The stars were my favorite part. In the city they never seemed to exist. In the county it almost felt like you could reach out and touch one they were so close.

Before I knew it, I was passing Canyon's house. This time when I looked there were no lights on to bring it to life. I thought about all the work we had left unfinished and how exhausted he must have been after doing it all by himself. His life was so vastly different from anything I had ever experienced. To bear so much responsibility. I didn't know where his parents were but it seemed very wrong that a man his age would have to carry that kind of burden. What was it about that house anyway? I fell in love with the outside the moment I saw it but the way he made me feel that afternoon brought on a completely different emotion. What demons were lurking inside? What formed the mood swings that came on when parts of his past were brought into question? The more I thought about it the less I wanted the answers. Some secrets are best buried, for when they surface they can suffocate you.

A mile down the road I decided to turn around and head back. School was coming in the morning whether I wanted it or not and I had to be on my toes. No sleep wouldn't give me any advantage when it came to the people in this town.

Coming up to Canyon's house again I noticed everything was different. The lights casting through the windows were shining on to the front lawn illuminating the house itself. It amazes me how much I still could love something that held so many secrets. I stopped for a moment and stared with every intention of continuing my journey home until I heard his voice again. I couldn't understand how I could listen to him sing and it seemed so far removed from the man I'd spent the afternoon with. Canyon kept everything to himself. The little bit of information he gave me still was nothing compared to his backstory. Yet, through the songs he sang I could feel his pain. I recognized it as soon as I heard his voice. "Tonight I Want to Cry" by Keith Urban was one of those songs you don't forget after you've heard it. Why he had picked such a sad song piqued my curiosity. Was he really all alone? His parents wouldn't have just left him here. Or was it about a girl? My curiosity almost won out. I snapped out of my thoughts and found myself at the back edge of the house again wanting this time to expose myself but reality slapped me in the face. Whatever happened to him was not my business. I was leaving and nothing good could come from getting closer to Canyon. He served as a good distraction but that was all I ever could let him be.

Finally I was thinking clearly enough to backtrack out to the road where I belonged. His voice carried so well that I could still hear him halfway to my house. My heart hurt with the emotion he was pushing out with the lyrics. Somebody did some major damage to that man and I wasn't the one to fix it.

As I climbed back in bed and closed my eyes I thought to myself, "I guess everyone has a skeleton in their closet."

Chapter 8

The next morning I got out of bed and almost screamed after my feet touched the floor as I attempted to stand. Every muscle in my body burned.

Showering had me almost in tears, making me angry at myself for being so completely out of shape. I was almost eighteen and had no reason to hurt this bad other than blaming my upbringing and that would be just an excuse. I pushed through the pain while drying my hair and getting dressed. Even turning the steering wheel on the way to school brought on an ache I never wanted to feel again. To say I was in a bad mood walking into school would be an understatement. I was crabby as hell.

No one spoke to me in the parking lot. I even got through my first two classes unscathed. It wasn't until third period when Kyle McDermott passed me a note in the hall that everything changed.

I was walking with my head down through the mass of people all scurrying to get where they needed to be before the bell rang. I hadn't really realized what had happened. One second I was minding my own business, praying no one would bump into me, and the next a wad of paper was shoved in my hand. I stopped walking and turned around to see who had given it to me, only to find one face looking back in my direction wearing a smile and it was Kyle's.

Immediately, I let it fall to the floor and watched as it got kicked around by the shuffling feet of students. For a brief second I wondered what it could have said but then decided it didn't matter and continued on to my class.

That decision came back to bite me in fifth period when Ashlynn came storming into the classroom, slamming her hands down onto my desk and then she leaned down so far that I could feel her breath on my face.

"I told you to stay away from them." I had no idea what she was talking about. I hadn't gone anywhere near anyone. "Don't play stupid, Arianna."

I pushed my chair back slightly to create some distance and questioned what the best move would be. The last thing I needed was more drama and if I gave her what she wanted that's exactly what I would get. On the other hand, though, my toleration level was about to implode. The only thing I could think to do was keep myself in check and reason with her.

Looking up, I calmly spoke. "I've stuck to our agreement. Now, could you please just leave me alone like I asked and stop making a scene?"

BAM

Her hands came back down on the desk so hard it jumped off the floor.

"Don't you dare lie to me, you stupid bitch. I saw what he wrote you and if you think for a second I'm going to let that happen you are dumber than I thought."

It was all over that piece of paper I never bothered to read from Kyle.

"Just go away, Ashlynn."

"Fuck you. I'm not going anywhere."

"Watch your language, Miss Stanton, and move along. Class is about to start."

Mr. Brock had walked in the room giving me the out I needed.

Once more for good measure she bent down even further until we were practically nose to nose. "This. Isn't. Over."

Of course it wasn't. I had just managed to piss off the Queen Bee without lifting a finger. No, this was the beginning of the longest eight weeks of my life.

The final class of the day was awful. Every student by then was talking about what Ashlynn was going to do in the parking lot after school. I almost laughed out loud when one girl said Ashlynn was going to beat me up. Did no one have an ounce of maturity in this town? That girl would never resort to violence if it meant she could lose. She was nothing but a prima donna looking to bully those that let her. It was quite sad. Although, at that moment, I was slightly worried they were right. I couldn't fight back if my life depended on it. It still hurt like hell to carry my backpack from class to class.

The final bell went off ending the day and it seemed like every student turned to look at me before running out of the room to get outside as fast as possible.

I stood up from my chair and grabbed my backpack from the floor, slinging it over my right shoulder. Just as I was entering the hall, Mrs. Hemswith called my name. I looked around until I spotted her walking toward me from the other end of the hall.

"Please wait one moment." I walked toward her wondering what I did wrong when she spoke again. "Would you like me to escort you to your car?"

I shook my head in disbelief. The damn principal knew about this too.

"No, thank you, ma'am, I think I can handle this."

"Are you sure, honey?"

"Yeah, I will be fine."

Her right hand landed on my left shoulder and then she squeezed, almost causing my knees to buckle. I tried keeping a straight face. The last thing I wanted her to do was feel sorry for me and take my choice away.

"Okay, I will respect your decision but just know I will be watching to make sure nothing happens."

"There's no need. I don't care to interact with the people of this town any longer than I have to."

She looked sad when she replied, "I sure hope that changes." Then she let me go so I could leave.

"Thank you for caring, Mrs. Hemswith. It really does mean something to me."

"It's not a hard thing to do, Arianna. You're a good kid."

I smiled and then went on to face the drama that was about to unfold in front of me.

BARBARA SPEAK

Entering the parking lot, I saw what seemed to be half of the students from the school waiting by their cars. No one did anything but watch me as I walked toward my truck with my keys in hand. "Just let this go smoothly," is all I kept saying to myself hoping mind over matter would happen.

I was just about to grab my door handle, thinking I was in the clear, when Ashlynn and her three minions approached me.

"Not so fast."

I didn't even want to turn around. What would be the point?

"Look at me, bitch!"

I guess that was the point after all. I turned and found I was circled in with no option otherwise.

"What do you want?" It came out as snotty as I meant it to. I was getting sick and tired of this hierarchy and I was only on day three.

"Who do you think you are? Don't answer because I'm here to tell you. You are nothing. Do you hear me? Don't think for a second you will ever be anything other than nothing. You can walk around all you want..."

"Leave her alone, Ashlynn."

I never saw it coming. In fact, I didn't understand a bit of what was happening in front of me.

Ashlynn turned as soon as Kyle said it and with flaming fury written all over her perfect face, she screamed, "Stay out of this, Kyle!"

Kyle walked closer until he came to stand within the circle I was confined in facing Ashlynn.

"No! This is all about me anyway. So what, I said I was sorry for being mean to her. What's the big deal? She's new. She hasn't done anything to any of us and you've set out to make her your biggest target."

"You asshole! You're just trying to make me jealous. Well I don't care! Take her to the bonfire Saturday night, see if I give two shits."

So that's what was in the note. Yeah right, I thought. Like I would want to go to a party filled with these people.

"Oh, you care. Look at you making a fool of yourself right now!"

I couldn't take any more.

"Both of you shut up." I looked at Kyle first. "Thank you for apologizing but if it was to get this reaction from Ashlynn then you can keep it." Then I turned to her. "You need to just stop. I don't want your man or any man for that matter. I told you to just leave me the hell alone and I meant it." And finally to both of them. "I have some place to be.

62

So, if you don't mind, move the hell away from my truck and then you can continue this dramafest without me."

I turned my back to them and grabbed for my door handle again, this time uninterrupted. I swung the door open almost knocking down one of the trifecta and climbed inside, slamming it behind me. My adrenaline was racing as I turned the engine over and practically stalled it as I fed it more gas than it needed.

My tires squealed when I punched the pedal even harder pulling out of the parking lot.

"How dare them!" I thought as the memories came flooding back to me of being cornered. By the time I pulled into Canyon's, I was hot.

Getting out, I slammed the door behind me and watched the face of the man ready to greet me fall.

"Rough day?"

"I don't want to talk about it."

I kept walking until I entered the barn and realized I had completely forgotten about Shelby.

"Damn it!"

I began walking back toward my truck, passing Canyon on the way when he grabbed my arm lightly and spun me to a halt.

"What has got you so riled up and where do you think you're going?"

His eyes showed concern and his bottom lip was between his teeth while he waited for me to answer.

"I forgot Shelby."

"Were you supposed to pick her up from school?"

"No, our mother does that. I promised her I would bring her with me today and I completely got sidetracked."

I threw my hands in the air, frustrated to say the least when Canyon said, "She can wait a few minutes; it won't kill her. Besides, you need to cool down a little before she sees you like this. What happened?"

He had placed his other arm on my shoulder and now had me pinned with no way to avoid the question.

"I just had to deal with some stupid people from school is all. It's not a big deal."

"Well I would beg to differ. I have never seen you so mad."

"Canyon, I really don't want to talk about this..."

"I'm not letting you shut down on this one. What were their names?"

"What good would that do?"

"Just tell me."

"Why?"

"Ari, I swear, I will have you cleaning every pile I can find if you don't start talking."

"You suck!"

"Yeah, I've been told that before. Now spill it."

Canyon took me up the stairs to the screened in porch I knew he sat in every night and offered me a drink before I went over everything that had happened since the first time I stepped foot on school grounds. Canyon balled his hands into fists a couple of times and chewed the hell out of his bottom lip but he remained quiet until I was done with my rant.

"Are you kidding me?" was the first thing out of his mouth. The second was, "I am taking you to school tomorrow to show those little shits—"

"No, you aren't. I'm doing fine on my own and you'll only make things worse."

"You don't know anything about this town, little woman. These people..."

"What? These people are nothing to me. I am out of here in eight weeks, Canyon."

"That doesn't give them the right to act like that. I could kick Kyle McDermott's hind end for treating you like that and Ashlynn Stanton? Well, she's been a little brat since the day she was born. When I dated her sister Brooke she would..."

"You dated her sister?"

"Yeah, three out of the four years of high school."

"Holy crap."

"She was nothing like Ashlynn, I can tell you that."

"Well neither of them are worth you getting involved in this. Besides, my poor little sister is probably crying wondering why I haven't showed up yet."

"Why don't you go get her and I can see about rounding up some of the foals for her while you're gone."

"I was wondering where they all were when I went into the barn earlier."

"It was nice out today. Besides, I needed to work Apollo for the race coming up."

"Work him?"

"I'm raising quarter horses, remember? They need to be worked to build their speed."

"How do you do that? Never mind. Tell me later. I need to go get Shelby."

I walked out the door and ran to my truck feeling like a fifty pound weight had been lifted off of me. I never thought I would want to talk about anything personal. What would happen if I slipped? I could lose everything. What I needed to remember most of all was to keep my mouth shut or I was going nowhere but hell and I didn't need to bring Canyon down with me. Having someone I could consider a friend was one thing, but a true friendship works both ways and I needed to remember that.

Chapter 9

Watching Shelby's face when Canyon brought her over to the corral was one of those priceless moments you want to hold onto forever. Her red curls gleamed in the light of the sun but were no comparison to the beam of her smile. She bounced up and down holding on to the top wood rail while standing on the bottom one. Inside contained all four babies and their mommas.

Outside the fenced in area were several other horses watching curiously from their different spots in the pasture.

I walked over to stand by Shelby's side asking her, "So, was it worth the wait?"

She began to bounce again not able to contain her excitement when she screamed, "Please bring one over here" ignoring me completely. I didn't need her to tell me, she was in her own heaven.

Canyon was pointing to each one taunting her while I openly laughed. "This one? Or do you want this one?"

"Any of them! PLEASE, CANYON."

She looked like she was either going to explode from eagerness or she needed to use the bathroom, I couldn't tell with the way she was shifting her weight from one foot to the other.

Finally, Canyon brought Triton, the oldest of the foals, close enough to Shelby that should could reach out and touch him. Unfortunately, we forgot to explain to her the smell test. Just like her bigger sister she threw her hand out toward the young horse causing him to jerk back and take Canyon's arm with him.

"Whoa. It's okay, boy. She just wants to pet you. It's okay." Canyon worked to calm the frightened horse as Shelby's face fell.

"I'm sorry."

Canyon beat me to the punch. "Don't you worry about a thing, Shelby. Triton here just needs to learn how to be around more people is all. You didn't do anything wrong. The only thing I would like you to remember is that horses are magnificent creatures with stellar strength and capability. You always have to respect that. When meeting a horse whether it's a big one or a little one like him, you always want to hold your hand out for them to smell you. I know that sounds weird but that's how they decide if they can trust you or not. Are you ready to try it again?"

I looked down at Shelby and could feel her uncertainty like waves crashing off of her. Without wanting to push her, I stuck my arm out and watched Triton size me up before his ears turned toward me and he lowered his head. I stayed put until I felt his hot breath flow over my knuckles. Slowly, I turned my hand over and raised it enough that I came in contact with his neck. Sliding my hand over his hair I looked back at Shelby and said, "You wouldn't believe how their fur feels. It's..."

"A coat." I looked at Canyon wondering what in the heck he was talking about. "It's their coat, not fur. I was just trying to help you out. If you want to call it fur go for it."

I guess my facial expression read something other than what I was thinking because he looked almost scared.

"Why would you say that? Of course I don't want to sound stupid and call it fur if that's not what it is. Thanks for straightening that out for me."

The two of us were going back and forth not paying any attention to Shelby. When we looked back she had her arm completely extended and Triton was licking the palm of her hand.

My eyes practically bulged out of my sockets while Canyon smiled at them.

"He likes you."

"I had no idea horses licked people like a dog."

"They don't. They like the salt on your skin and apparently Shelby here has plenty of it."

Shelby started to giggle once she learned he wasn't going to bite her hand off next. Well, we actually didn't learn that part until Canyon said,

"Just keep your fingers together. Don't spread them apart or he might mistake one for a carrot."

I laughed thinking he was kidding but Shelby took his advice and her little fingers went stiff as a board, like they were glued together.

"That's not funny. You scared her."

"It wasn't meant to be. I've seen it happen."

"No way!"

"Yes way."

"Wow."

We didn't get much done that day as far as chores but Shelby had the time of her life. I can't say it was a bad day for me either, actually. Canyon somehow made everything about life seem as if it needed to be cherished instead of loathed which had seemed to be my way of looking at things. He taught us about what the horses did all day and how he had to run certain ones for so many minutes and then put them on a wheel in the center of the round pin for cool down time where they just walk in circles. If they didn't do that their muscles could lock up and swelling could occur. He even explained to us what he used certain farm equipment for and if you can believe it, farmers use the crap from the horses over their fields and gardens for fertilizer. If you said yuck so did I but apparently it's good for it.

Shelby followed every word Canyon spoke as if it were gospel. I always chose to walk ten steps behind to watch the two of them in action and realized that in that moment, I had never seen my little sister so happy. With everything that happened that brought us here, for the first time, I saw something positive.

We were headed back toward the house when Shelby looked back at me with an expression I knew all too well. She had to poop. I picked up my speed with each step until I caught up and gave a look back that said, "Let's go" so Canyon wouldn't catch on. I didn't want to embarrass her and nothing is worse than having to go number two.

She mouthed the words, "I can't hold it" taking anything secretive off the table.

"Canyon, Shelby hates feeling dirty and would like to know if she could use your bathroom to wash her hands."

He looked down at Shelby and grabbed both of her shoulders, shaking her lightly, "You have to get used to a little dirt if you want to take care of your own horse someday."

"Canyon, I think she really needs to wash her hands."

68

He looked over to me questionably before the light bulb went on.

"Oh! Well, those hands do look pretty dirty. Let's get you inside."

Shelby all but ran up the stairs. We found her waiting inside the screened in porch, standing next to the door to the house. Canyon walked her in while I chose to sit down in one of the wicker chairs that faced the property.

"Hey, you coming in?"

Canyon was leaning out the door, gripping the frame above him.

"Um, I'm okay out here."

"Don't be like that. You have to be thirsty, come pick out what you want to drink." And then he disappeared.

Placing my hands on the arm rests I pushed my weak and tired body to stand, all but forcing myself to walk through the door.

I don't know what I was expecting, to tell you the truth. It's not like I thought something was going to jump out and scare me. It was just the way he acted the day before that made me think there wasn't anything good about walking through the threshold. What I found was a normal country kitchen. The cabinets were all oak, the countertops were made of butcher block, and hardwood covered the floors.

Canyon was standing in front of the refrigerator with the door open when he looked over his shoulder at me and smiled before asking, "Do you like sweet tea?"

"I can't say. I have never tried it before."

"COME ON! You seriously have never had sweet tea? Where did you come from?"

"A place where they don't drink sweet tea, obviously."

He walked over to the cabinet above the sink and grabbed three glasses. "Get ready to have heaven hit your taste buds for the first time."

"You're pretty confident..."

"Of course I am. You just wait until Shelby gets out here...."

I didn't hear the rest of what he was saying. I realized the time that had passed and wondered what was taking her so long.

"Canyon, sorry to cut you off but where is the bathroom you took her to?"

"It's through the hall and on the left. Why?"

"It's just been awhile and I want to check on her."

"Okay. I'll just make some snacks."

I walked out of the room and down the hall only to find the door on the left was open. A few steps farther led me into the family room where I found Shelby staring at a wall of pictures.

"What are you doing? It's rude to go through someone's house, you know."

She didn't look away from the wall when she spoke. "He looks so different."

My curiosity won over my manners and led me to see what she was so enamored with.

In solid wood frames were pictures of Canyon growing up. Some were from when he was born up to six or seven riding horses. Then the football pictures came. They weren't the posed kind either. Action plays on the field during games or newspaper articles stating his team won the state championship. Then the bull riding must have started. The arenas were packed around him as he held on to gigantic bulls. Only one picture caught my attention and held onto to it, though. It was Canyon with his mother. He was probably around my age and she was kissing his cheek. The look on her face was unmistakable. She was proud of her son. Canyon smiled like only he can with his arm around the woman who couldn't have been taller than five foot five, standing on her tippy toes. They looked happy.

"Hey, ladies, what's..."

I spun around like I had been caught with my hand in the cookie jar. Guilt flooded me for not taking my own advice and pulling Shelby from the room.

"You look silly in this picture."

Shelby broke the silence by pointing out a picture with Canyon swinging from a rope into water. He couldn't have been older than five. His mouth was wide open with his eyes practically bulging out of his head, making it clear as day he was scared to death.

Canyon came to stand behind Shelby and started laughing easing the tension I was sure to feel.

"That was a crazy day to say the least. My mom convinced me it was okay to jump in. After that, it took me ten years before I did it again."

"You were cute."

"Was? You don't think I'm cute anymore?"

I blushed. Being put in the spot left me with only one option, the truth.

"I wouldn't say any man your size could be described as cute."

"Yeah, Canyon, you're not cute. You're a monster."

"A monster? A monster? You want to see a monster?"

His hands went in the air with his fingers spread out causing Shelby to scream and run with him chasing right after her. I heard her scream again and then go into an all-out laughing frenzy giving away that he not only caught her but was tickling her to death. I took one last look at the wall of pictures and noticed the lack of a father. Maybe we had more in common than I thought.

Chapter 10

Shelby talked the whole way home about how much fun she had and more so about her love for Canyon. He was the best thing I had seen happen to her. He balanced the fact that she was young but didn't treat her like a child. I couldn't help but respect him for that.

The night sky fell and Shelby never stopped. Tucking her into bed, she still couldn't help herself. "Can I come with you tomorrow too?"

"No, hun, tomorrow we have to do some running around. Canyon is making me go with him to a rodeo Friday night and I need clothes for it."

"A real live rodeo? Can I come with you? Please, pretty please."

"I wish you could but it's for older people. Maybe the next one that comes into town we can go together."

"But, Arianna…"

"You need to go to sleep. I can't change my mind on this one. It's not fair for you to keep asking me."

"I'm sorry. I just want to go so bad."

I kissed her goodnight and then turned the light off as I closed the door and said, "Goodnight, sweet Shelby. I will see you in the morning."

The next day when I got to school the atmosphere was completely different. Students were smiling at me and a few even said, "Hi."

I don't know what happened to change their mind but I really didn't care. These weren't people I needed to gain approval from. By lunch I found the answer whether I was looking for it or not.

I had brought my lunch again, still finding it easier to eat in my truck and not deal with the drama. I was just about to take a bite of my sandwich when I saw Kyle come out of the door to the parking lot. Call me immature but I dove down onto the floor board trying to do anything I could to disappear. The knock on my driver's side window had me practically digging through the floor board. Even the dumbest person could figure out I didn't want to be seen. The door opened making me curse out loud for not remembering to lock it in the first place.

"Arianna, will you please sit up so I can talk to you." Reluctantly, I pushed off the floor and slid myself back on to the seat. "You've got something on your face right...."

He reached his hand out to wipe whatever off but never got to before I was sliding back toward the passenger door wiping my own mouth.

"What do you want, Kyle?"

"Why are you hiding out here?"

"I wasn't hiding. I came out here to eat in peace."

"You're trying to tell me that you wanted to eat on the floor of your truck?"

"Will you get to the point?"

He let his head fall. My guess was he was watching his shoes as his feet shuffled back and forth before he said, "Did you think about what I asked you?"

"You didn't ask me anything yet."

"You didn't read the piece of paper I gave you, did you?"

"No, I'm sorry, I didn't. But if this about what Ashlynn was freaking out about the answer is no, thank you."

"Just because Ashlynn is a bitch doesn't mean the rest of us are like her. Come to the party with me. I'll show you how we do things around here."

"Kyle, I really am grateful that you're not the jerk I thought you were. But I don't want a boyfriend or to cause any more drama than I already have with the girls at this school."

"Don't worry about them and as far as the boyfriend thing goes, I didn't ask."

Talk about being embarrassed.

"Thank you again for the offer but I still don't think it's a good idea."

He took a few steps back shuffling his square-toed cowboy boots.

"I guess all I can say to that is, don't be a stranger. There are good people here and you would be lucky to get to know them."

"Thanks for the heads up."

He walked away throwing his right arm up as a way to wave goodbye and headed back into the school. I slumped down in the seat of the truck wondering why crap like this kept happening to me.

Hours later, I was pulling up to Canyon's house dreading this part of the day much more than school itself. I was far from the country girl he was going to try to paint me to be. I may not have liked anything about myself but I was all I knew how to be.

It was the first time I had gotten there and wasn't greeted by a smiling man waiting for me. Instead, there were two other trucks in the driveway and no one to speak of. I turned the engine off and waited a few seconds before I got out deciding to go in search of him.

After walking along the gravel path that lead to the back of the house I expected I would find him on the porch. I was wrong. Next, I went out back to the barn but found all of the stalls filled with horses and no Canyon. Just when I was about to give up, something caught my attention. I turned and followed the sound around the side of the barn until I was looking at four men sitting on top of the fence of the corral talking and none of them were Canyon.

"You got it ready? Here he comes!"

"I got it. Damn that horse can move."

"Imagine when you take a hundred pounds off his back what he'll do."

Dirt was flying in the air behind Magnus as Canyon pushed him to run as fast as he could. In a matter of seconds he came into view and the next he was gone.

"Twenty three point one!" Screamed the stout man in the middle holding the stopwatch. The other three took their cowboy hats off simultaneously. One fanned his face, one circled it above his head while the last threw his on the ground.

"He's mine."

"The hell he is."

The man with the stopwatch was turning red and looked like he was going to throw down with the taller one who had lost his hat to the dirt. Whatever they were arguing about made no difference to me. It was clear they wanted Magnus and it broke my heart. Why would Canyon want to sell him?

"Fuck you, Bingdom! I told you coming here if he was under twenty-four with Canyon on his back he was mine."

"I didn't fly all the way out here to let you tell me what's going to happen."

"Both of you stop! We have a lady present," shouted the only man wearing a smile.

All four men shifted their bodies to turn in my direction. The man who hadn't spoken previously was now walking toward me with a look that made me nervous.

"Well hello there, pretty lady. How can I help you?"

"Hello, gentlemen."

He picked up my right hand and brought it to his lips, making me want to gag when I felt them make contact. I allowed the kiss but pulled my arm back quickly after and rubbed the back of my hand over my jeans in an attempt to wipe it off.

"As I said, what can I do for you?"

A cold fear took over me and the look in his eye said more than I wanted to know. Just as I was about to leave and go home, he grabbed ahold of my shoulder locking me in place. I didn't know what I should do. Canyon came from out of nowhere, jumped off Magnus and yelled, "Hey, Stucky, how about you step away before I break that arm of yours off."

The man I now knew to be called Stucky dropped his arm but didn't move away from me. The other three stood in place while Canyon launched himself over the fence and was standing before me fuming moments later. The veins in his neck were bulging while his hands were in fists.

"What makes you think you can put your hands on her?"

"Listen hear, boy..."

"Boy? Get the hell off my property!"

The veins were now about to burst. I didn't know what I should do. Leaving seemed to be the best option. I looked at Canyon one last time before I spun on my feet and began walking away.

"You heard me. Get the fuck out of here now!"

I was almost to my truck when another hand grabbed my arm but this touch I knew to be tender as I heard, "Don't go. Let me just finish up here okay. Please don't leave."

I heard how much his tone had changed from Stucky to me. His voice was almost coated with desperation. I didn't understand why me sticking around meant so much but in that moment I didn't want to deny him.

"How about I wait in my truck?"

"Do you really want to show them your weak side? Stand strong, Ari, you're better than that."

"I have nothing to prove to them."

"No, you don't, you need to prove it to yourself. No man should make you feel like you should back down."

"Canyon, he's..."

He dropped his hold on me but then I felt his fingers intertwine with my own. "Just come with me. I need you to do this."

I wanted to ask what the big deal was with me waiting in my truck but in that moment he was proving something whether I understood it or not. "Okay."

His mouth spread to show all his teeth before he led me back over to the three men still standing at the fence. Stucky didn't budge until we passed by him without giving him a look.

Kicking the gravel, creating a fog from the dust, he yelled, "Fuck you, Michaels!" before he stormed to his truck, slammed the door and peeled out backwards, taking out the mailbox before he drove off.

"That was a temper tantrum if I've ever seen one," came from the man with the stopwatch.

Canyon squeezed my hand before letting go and said, "Guys, this is Ari. She's a good friend of mine and I expect you to show her some respect or you can leave now."

All three men came toward me with their hands extended. I shook each one while Canyon introduced me to Richard, Bruce and Steve. None of them showed any signs of disrespect but instead did what they needed to to get on Canyon's good side before negotiations began.

I stood back as numbers were being thrown around. Nothing about selling him made any sense to me. Don't get me wrong, they were tossing out almost thirty thousand dollar promises but I kept thinking, wouldn't Magnus be worth so much more if he won? Ten minutes or so went by and it seemed to be coming to a close. Bruce, the hat in the dirt guy, had won Canyon over with promises of ten percent on stud fees in the future. I wasn't sure what that even meant but it all still gave me an uneasy feeling.

"Excuse me, gentlemen, but could I have a word with Canyon for a minute please?"

Canyon looked as puzzled as I felt when he said, "I'll be right back with you, Bruce." We walked over to the side of the house and as soon as we rounded the corner Canyon whispered, "What's wrong?"

He showed concern which only made it more awkward to stick my nose where it didn't belong.

"I think this is a mistake. I know nothing about any of this but my gut keeps screaming don't let him do this."

His hands went up to his head, knocking the ball cap he always wore backward off as he pulled on his hair. I regretted letting my opinion loose and began spilling apologies.

"I'm sorry. It's not my place. I shouldn't have even said anything..."

"Why?"

"Like I'm saying, I shouldn't have. I'm just going to go. Call me when you're done."

"I meant why don't you think it's a good idea?"

"Canyon, I don't know what I'm talking about. It just seems Magnus would be worth so much more if he wins."

"If he doesn't he's worth nothing, Ari."

"See! Don't listen to me. I'm going to just go."

"Do you really think he could win?"

"I don't know anything about this stuff. Don't let me sway your decision."

"Too late."

He grabbed my hand, lacing his fingers with mine again and pulled me back out into the open and over to the group of men losing their patience.

"Sorry to waste your time, fellas, but I'm not ready to let him go just yet."

"WHAT? I flew all the way out here you son-of-a-bitch!"

"And I'm sorry about that. I am willing to show you several more that I think could work out perfect for you."

Bruce was pissed. You could see it easily from the color his face was turning. Richard and Steve, on the other hand, were happy to say the least.

"Get 'em out here and let's get this done."

Two hours later Canyon had sold not one but two horses. Forty seven thousand dollars was handed to him making everyone wear a smile. After we stood side by side and watched the three men pull out of the driveway, Canyon turned, grabbed me under my arms and spun me in circles forcing me to wrap my legs around him for security.

"You are amazing!"

I didn't know what I had done for him to be giving me any credit.

"That was good, right?"

"That was unbelievably good. Ari, what just happened will put me back on the map."

I began to laugh to keep me from getting sick.

"You have to stop! Canyon!"

When he did, the look he gave me was something I wasn't prepared for. "Thank you."

"I didn't do anything."

"You gave me something I haven't had in a long time."

"What's that?"

"Hope."

He let me slide down until the weight of my feet crunched the gravel underneath them.

"You give me far too much credit, Canyon Michaels."

"Speaking of giving. Are you ready to go get you your first shit kickers?"

"My what? Or do I even want to know?"

"Just get in my truck. This is going to be fun."

We laughed about Stucky's reaction, talked about how you ship a horse and went through a few tell-me-more-about-yourself games before pulling up to the little country store in town. Walking through the door, Canyon was teasing me about the sweet tea thing again when I attempted to push him to make him stop. I didn't even make contact before he grabbed both of my hands in one of his and taunted me, "Come on, Ari, whatcha gonna do now, huh?"

I was laughing so hard I didn't have the energy to do anything when, "Are you kidding me?" was heard from the back of the store.

I looked around, trying to follow the voice just as Canyon let one of my hands go, taking the other one and intertwining his fingers with it before he said, "Have fun with this."

I had no idea what he was up to when he led me to the back of the store until I heard, "There is no way. No way!"

"How are you, Ashlynn? It's been awhile."

I was speechless. Had I known she would be here I never would have agreed to come. Her face looked like someone shoved five lemons in her mouth at once letting me know just how happy she was to see me too. I let go of Canyon's hand and put both of mine in my pockets, uncomfortable to say the least.

"I've been apparently better than you."

There was something in her tone that showed more than her usual hatred toward me.

"Your mama didn't raise you to be rude."

"Well yours didn't raise you to keep trash for company. I guess neither of us care too much for what our mamas wanted."

The grin Canyon had been wearing dropped instantly. I don't know what it was that she said but he locked up.

"Look. I'm not here for you to like me. I don't really care if you do or don't. We came here to shop and if you're the only one working I think it's best if you start. What was it that we came for… shit kickers?"

Canyon burst out laughing, at what I didn't know. Ashlynn just huffed and walked away throwing her hands in the air as she called me a stupid bitch and then walked into the back room.

Turning back to Canyon I said, "What's so funny?"

He grabbed my face with both of his hands while looking into my eyes before he spoke. "You. You're the best thing that has happened to me in a long time. I sure am glad you're here."

Two pair of the tightest jeans I had ever put on my body, a pink pair of boots (aka shit kickers), a flannel shirt, a rather-cute-if-I-do-say-so-myself cowboy hat and we were ready to go. Ashlynn did everything she could to make the experience a dreadful one but Canyon wouldn't allow it. He had her bring out every pair of boots in my size only to tell her to take them back to the stock room before I ever tried them on. The jeans were my favorite part.

"What size pants do you wear?" he asked as he was looking through the rack.

"These look small so I guess a ten."

Ashlynn pretended to cough as she said, "Fat ass."

"I don't think that's right, do you, Ashlynn?"

She pretended she wasn't paying attention when she asked, "Do I think what's right?"

"Canyon, I know my size. Why are you asking her?"

He gave me a look like he was up to no good when he questioned her again. "What size do you wear, Ashlynn?"

She had no problem looking me up and down when she spouted back, "Six."

Canyon looked back at me and then her again before he said, "Can you grab a size four in these? I think it's the Tuff copper bling fit." He looked down at the tag of the jeans in front of him. "Yep, that's the one I want."

I was just about to correct him when Ashlynn laughed before saying as she walked to the back room, "Yeah, I'd like to see that happen."

I gave Canyon the look of death before the chastising began. "What are you doing? Why would you want to humiliate me in front of queen—"

"They'll fit."

"No they won't and I—"

"Will look fantastic in them."

"Quit cutting me off!"

"Here you go. Just the size he wanted for you," she practically sang as she came back holding the pants that an Ethiopian would probably have a hard time getting on.

"Do you have a dressing room I could use to try them on?"

"Hell yes we do. I can't wait to see this one." I gave Canyon one last look before I followed her to the back of the room. "Here you go. Don't forget to come out and show us."

After she closed the door I flipped her my middle finger before slipping off my shoes and the jeans I had on. I held up the size four and laughed at myself for even attempting to put the damn things on. One leg went in smoothly so I prayed harder than I ever had in my life before I slid in the other.

"Holy shit they fit!"

I tried to keep my excitement down to a whisper but I seriously wanted to do the happy dance when the zipper came up to meet the fastened button at the top. I twisted from side to side, making sure all angles looked good in the mirror before I opened the door and stepped out. I noticed the two of them arguing as I crossed the room hoping they would take notice without me having to clear my throat or do something just as equally ridiculous. Ashlynn saw me first and the mouth open, hands on hips, lack for words reaction she had was absolutely priceless.

Canyon looked me up and down before he asked, "Turn around for me."

Normally I would have refused, feeling put on display, but I had never wanted to shove something in someone's face so much, not like I did for Ashlynn.

I slowly lifted my shirt until I exposed the waist line of the pants and turned in a complete circle.

Ashlynn stayed quiet while Canyon whistled and then laughed before he said, "Smokin' hot, just like I thought. We will take two pair and you can go ahead and ring up the rest while you're at it."

I held in the smile that wanted to take over my face until I was back in the changing room putting my clothes back on. Holding a size four in my hands felt like Heaven and when I carried them to the counter Canyon was standing at with his wallet open. Something about him paying for all of it felt wrong but I knew it wasn't something I could argue when Ashlynn announced the total. Seven hundred sixty-three dollars and thirty-five cents. Don't get me wrong, I had a single pair of shoes worth more but I didn't think much about how much things cost until I was looking at what life would be like on my own when I left.

"You're really paying for her? You don't have the money to be doing this, Canyon. It's not like when she—"

His hand slammed down on the counter halting her spew and making me jump. "What I have or don't is none of your business! Now ring it up and keep your mouth shut."

He was seething. I'd never seen him talk through his teeth and I can honestly admit I was scared myself. Ashlynn took his bank card and ran it looking just as pissed off as Canyon was.

"I'll just go wait in the truck."

He grabbed onto me before I could move. "Why don't you stay and carry some of this with me?"

My guess is that he was trying to still make Ashlynn uncomfortable. What he obviously didn't see was that I was just as much. She tore the paper off the print out machine and handed it to Canyon without making eye contact. I was sure she wouldn't say a word as we walked back through the store with our hands full but she did. "We will miss you tomorrow night," came out just as bitchy as only she could be right before we walked out the door to the street.

Canyon held the door open for me but leaned his head back in the store to say, "Don't worry. Ari and I will be there just to make you more uncomfortable. See ya soon." Then he let the door close behind him.

I walked to the truck and opened the back door to put the bags in without saying a word. Canyon walked around to the other side and did the same thing before we both were sitting inside the truck in silence.

He turned the key looking down at the ignition refusing to make eye contact with me. I didn't know what to say when he said, "Listen, Ari, there are things you don't know..."

I put my hand on his right shoulder to stop him from continuing. "It's not my business."

He let out a breath of air I didn't know he had been holding. "Thank you."

"There's no reason to thank me for being your friend, Canyon. That's what having them is for."

Chapter 11

Canyon picked me up the next night at my house after practically pulling a tearful Shelby off his leg. "Darlin', I would have bought another ticket if I had known you wanted to go so bad. Please don't be upset. How's this? I will buy you the best cowgirl hat I can find and you can wear it when I take you next time."

"But I want to go with you guys."

"Shelby, stop this. I have never been to one of these to even deem it appropriate. Let me judge it tonight and we can talk about it later. Now, we have to get going. I love you and—"

"There's nothing there she can't see."

I shot Canyon a look that could kill. "You're not helping."

He bent down and picked her off his leg, bringing her up into his arms. "Next time, I promise."

She looked at him, wiping the tears from her face. "Okay. But don't forget you promised."

"I couldn't forget you." He set her down and then scratched her head, messing her curls up, making her look like she had an afro.

"Now we really need to get going. I'll see ya tomorrow."

I had already opened my door to get in when I heard Shelby ask, "Tomorrow?"

Canyon climbed in his side, shut the door and rolled down his window. "Yep, you can watch me teach Ari to ride."

Shelby jumped up and down, back to being the happy girl I was used to seeing before she screamed, "See you tomorrow!" as we backed out of the driveway and headed on for our hour drive to my very first PBR.

The parking lots filled with trucks and trailers amazed me so you can imagine how I felt walking in to the arena packed full of people dressed just like me. I had felt ridiculous putting on the outfit Canyon had bought me only hours before. Now I realized how much I would have stood out in my normal garb.

"What's going through that head of yours?"

I looked around once more at the dirt floor, the gates where they kept the animals, and the cowboys who lined the walls waiting for their turn on one.

"You used to do this?"

Canyon turned and looked up at the seats above the tunnel we had just walked through. "I lived and breathed for it."

I was just about to say something when I noticed a man grinning from ear to ear approaching us. He yanked the hat off his head and threw it in the air before he hollered, "Holy shit, if it isn't Canyon-fucking-Michaels! Damn, it's been too long."

Glancing up at Canyon, I saw a gleam in his eye that melted my heart before he was wrapping his arms around the man, pounding him on the back as only men do. They broke apart but Canyon didn't let go of his shoulders.

"Look at you all cowboyed up. I've been watching your numbers, kid. I can't wait to see you ride again."

"I can't believe you're here. It's been years, man. I never got to tell you how sorry I am about your mom. What your dad did made all of us want—"

"You don't have to worry about apologies, Chett, it's all in the past. So, who did you draw for tonight?"

"Dark Storm, if you can believe it. It's so crazy how that worked out with you being here."

"No kidding! How in the hell did that happen?"

Canyon turned back smiling and called me over to them. "Chett, this is my friend Ari. Ari, this is Chett Morgan one of the best bull riders in the country."

"THE best! What do you mean one of the?"

84

They both laughed as I stood back and watched Canyon be someone I had yet to see. He was truly happy and it came through so vividly as he joked with his longtime friend. "You still have a record to beat before you go claiming that prize."

"Ari, is it?"

Chett stepped back from Canyon to walk over and shake my hand. "Are you ready to watch magic happen tonight?"

"Sure, I guess."

"Do you know anything about bull riding, beautiful?"

"I can't say that I do."

"Well, get ready. Tonight I am going to not only beat this guy's record but I am going to shatter it on the very bull that put him at number one."

I couldn't have heard him right. I was still trying to process the loss of Canyon's mom, something he hadn't wanted me to know. Now his friend was informing me that Canyon held the record in bull riding. There was so much I didn't know about him.

"Is that right? Well, we'll just have to see about that."

I winked at Canyon letting him know I would always have his back, getting one hell of a grin in return. "For a girl who knows nothing she sure doesn't have much confidence in me."

"That's not what—"

"No, she just has too much for me is all. Anyways, where is everybody? I want to say hi."

"Follow me. Damn they're gonna shit their pants when they take one look at you."

Chett started to walk back the way he came while Canyon took my hand and squeezed it before leaning down to me and saying, "If I forget to tell you later, thank you for coming with me tonight. I had a good time." Followed by the best smile I had seen from him yet.

"Thanks for bringing me. I had a lot of fun too. Especially when Chett didn't break your record."

"You are too much, woman."

He pulled me along as we met up with the world's roughest and toughest cowboys. Remington Airs, also known as Remy, Dalton Haywood and Trenton Moore. Each one of them were as shocked as Chett to see Canyon. Standing back and watching five grown men act like little kids, putting each other in head locks and chasing each other around was quickly setting itself up to be the highlight of my night.

Canyon introduced me and every one of them was a true gentleman. They went on and on about Canyon and his ability to predict every bull he rode like no one else could. It bothered me that we were reminiscing about someone who was perfectly capable of continuing his passion. Why he quit would be something I would love to ask about but I knew my place.

The time eventually came to say our goodbyes and take our seats. "Something's just wrong about you sitting up there, man. You belong down here with us!" Remy all but shouted as we were almost out of sight.

Canyon turned and with a somber face replied, "Some things change."

With my hand in his we climbed the stairs up into the middle area of the arena and sat down. "You were right, Shelby would love this."

"Told ya. That there is Mitchel Braxton. He's been announcing for the PBR ever since I can remember."

"So you know everybody here?"

"Not everybody but for most of us this is like family. We made this our life years back competing in rodeo."

"You still include yourself even though you haven't seen these people in years?"

"That's what family should be like. You don't have to see them every day to appreciate how important they are to you."

"I guess that's something I can't wrap my head around."

His hand fell to my thigh and squeezed. "You got me now and I don't plan to let go anytime soon."

"Thank you for that."

Our conversation was cut short when the announcer spoke over the loud speaker asking everyone to please rise to their feet for the playing of the national anthem. Every hat in the place came off and were placed over hearts. When the song ended, I wanted to scream, "Play ball!" but figured no one would find it funny other than me.

"It's showtime," Canyon all but whispered.

He looked adorable as he balled his fists up and pounded them against his thighs, almost appearing nervous.

"Ladies and Gents out there, before we begin, I would like to inform you of something that was just brought to my attention. It seems we have a legend in our mix. I would love for all of you to rise again and give applause to one of the best bull riders this world has ever seen.

Canyon Michaels, you have been missed and it's our honor to have you in the house tonight."

The stadium went wild. Everyone stood and clapped but most were looking around for him.

Canyon lowered his hat as he sunk down in his seat saying, "I'm gonna kill the guys when I get ahold of them."

I grabbed his arm trying to force him to stand up and be proud but he wanted no part in the attention. "All right since nobody can obviously see Canyon out there with everyone standing, how about we do this another way. Would everyone take a seat so Mr. Michaels can take a stand?"

My jaw dropped. The entire place sat, immediately murmuring back and forth about getting the chance to see him. I had no idea Canyon was anything like what the people that filled the arena thought of him. He was a God to them. All I could see was my only friend in the world.

"They're not really giving you a choice here, are they?"

"No they're not but I love them for it."

He stood up making him seem five times as big as he normally looked, dwarfing me. He raised his hand, waving to the roaring crowd all around and then took off his hat as a gesture of thanks. All the while pride filled me to the hilt. This man was loved by strangers and friends alike. Many could only wish to reach this kind of pinnacle in life and Canyon had done it in twenty-two short years.

He calmed the crowd and then sat back down grinning from molar to molar while saying, "That was freaking cool!"

"Heck yeah it was. I never had any idea you were this."

"I was this?"

"A rodeo God."

"Hahaha, I am no God, Ari. Not even close."

"It seems you're alone in that thought."

"So are you saying you think I'm a God?" He raised his eyebrows, wiggling them up and down.

"You're creeping me out, Mr. Michaels."

"Don't start with that crap."

"Oh, don't get bossy with me, super star."

"You are so walking home if you keep that up."

"I wouldn't want to damper your persona."

"That's it."

"What are you going to do to me?"

"You will never see it coming so stay scared 'cause it's a-comin'."

"Oh, you're going to play it that way?"

"No, doll, that was all you. Now shush and watch. It's all about to go down."

I had never seen anything so crazy, wild, and downright insane as what was before me. Men were getting tossed around like rag dolls and the bulls were huge! I didn't expect them to be small, but in person, they were two-thousand-pound beasts. The point was to stay on for eight seconds, which is something I found out is next to impossible.

Men wearing clown makeup were giving their best to try to distract the bull while the rider was running for their life back to the fence to get out of harm's way once they were either thrown or made it to the eight second mark.

Canyon tapped me on the side of my leg to pull my attention away from the chaos. "Are you getting hungry?"

"Not really but I could snack on something."

"I'm starving. Do you want to stay here or come with me to grab a bite to eat?"

"I'll come with you."

He stood and then offered me his hand to help me not only stand but maneuver through the crowd of people.

"Had enough of this yet?"

"To tell you the truth I never expected to like anything about this but I can see where you would get attached."

"You do?"

"Don't look so surprised. I mean, I would never want to get on one but to beat the odds, overpower the bull's mind and come out on top. That has to be one hell of a feeling."

He stopped walking and looked at me in a way that made me feel like this wasn't all about friendship anymore and then he looked away.

"Canyon?"

"Yeah? Oh, uh, yeah, there isn't anything like being on one."

"Are you okay?"

He let his eyes focus on something behind me again before returning to look at me.

"Canyon?"

This time it wasn't me that called his name. I turned around to see one of the most beautiful women in the world walking toward us with the bitch from hell beside her. Nothing in me wanted to continue to stare at her but watching Canyon's reaction or even putting him in an uncomfortable spot was further down on my list of wants. All my instincts were telling me to pretend I had to go to the bathroom to get away but I knew Ashlynn would see right through it. The resemblance between the two of them was uncanny, making it impossible to ignore the fact that Brooke Stanton, aka Canyon's ex, was on her way over.

I was so focused on what was coming that when Canyon whispered, "I'm sorry", it didn't click.

"I can't believe you're here!"

Brooke all but ran the last few steps until she was wrapped in Canyon's arms, being spun around in circles. "I'm so proud of you."

I watched as she placed both of her hands on either side of his face before she brought her lips down to meet his. I couldn't help but look away. I don't know what happened in that moment but the line of our friendship had gone blurry. I knew it shouldn't hurt to see him with a girl. It shouldn't have bothered me at all.

"Don't you just love seeing two people that happy together?"

Throwing daggers at Ashlynn's head sounded like a good idea at the moment but instead I just smiled and agreed.

"If only you and Kyle could have been so lucky."

Yep, score one for me. It wasn't often I welcomed confrontation but in that situation I needed to vent some frustration and oh was it worth it.

The expression she had been wearing fell off, revealing the evil beast within. "You stupid little fuc—"

"Don't you finish that word, Ashlynn Rae Stanton, or I will tell mama what kind of language you've been throwing around lately."

I hadn't realized Brooke had come up for air to even notice what her sister had said but I was thankful all the same.

"Don't act like you're perfect!"

"I never said I was. All I'm doing is pointing out that a lady finds better words to use."

I wanted to stick my finger down my throat and gag myself. How could the opposite of Ashlynn annoy me just as much? It shouldn't be possible. I had yet to look at Canyon. What was going on with me was nothing he needed to see. I was his friend. That meant being happy for him and not reacting the way I was.

"Canyon, aren't you going to introduce me to your little friend?"

Little? I didn't care for the way she said friend but little was over the top. It seemed we had a wolf in sheep's clothing. Brooke was exactly like her sister. Without paying him attention I walked toward Brooke with my right hand extended while he remained silent.

"My name is Arianna. I'm sorry, I didn't catch yours."

She played nice and shook my hand but I could see it in her eyes. She didn't like me. The feeling was mutual. "Brooke Stanton."

There were no nice to meet yous. Simple introductions seemed to be enough. I pulled my hand back and rubbed it on my pants, ready to make up whatever excuse was necessary to get away when Canyon spoke up for the first time.

"It was good to see you, Brooke, but Ari and I need to get going."

"Ari? What a cute pet name. Maybe I'll use that on the next gilt we get. You wouldn't mind would you, Arianna?"

"I would be flattered. The fact that you'd want to remember me every time you see it means the world."

"Like I said before, it was good seeing you guys but I'm starving. Are you ready?" I noticed Canyon's outstretched hand and followed it up to his waiting eyes. I may have not been able to read the situation but I knew that look. He wanted to get away from them. I walked over, gave him my hand and felt his fingers lace through mine before he led us in the opposite direction of the girls.

"See you soon, Canyon," practically echoed off of the concrete cinder block walls around us. Canyon didn't respond. In fact he didn't say anything to me either until we were standing in front of the vendor minutes later.

"What sounds good to you?"

"What's a gilt?"

His body went stiff and he refused to look at me.

"Canyon Michaels, tell me right now, what is a gilt?"

He continued to look at the menu in front of us when I felt a light tap on the small of my back. I turned around and saw a boy about Shelby's age looking up at me.

"It's what we call a girl pig before she has babies."

I turned to Canyon and busted out laughing. "Ashlynn Stanton is a pig farmer? Haha!"

His shoulders relaxed as a smile crept up his face. "You're not mad?"

"Why would I be? That's some of the funniest crap I have heard in a long time."

The little boy tapped me again. "I have pigs. Why is it funny?"

Have you ever had a moment when you wanted to crawl under a rock and hide? "It isn't funny. It's a tough job I'm sure."

It was enough to put a smile on his face which was enough for me. I twisted my body back around just in time to see Canyon trying to contain his laughter.

"You think that's funny?"

"I think that was hilarious."

We made it back to our seats with more food in hand than would be required to feed a small village. "How can you eat so much?"

"How can you not? Okay, shhh, Chett is coming up next."

I didn't care for being shushed but if Chett was riding I wanted to focus too.

Watching him climb onto the bull mesmerized me. The rope he used to secure himself looked painful at best. A few tugs to make sure it would hold up came before he raised his right arm in the air signaling he was ready and then grabbed on to the gate. I hadn't paid such close attention to the other riders but this one felt more personal. I knew this one. The gate opened and out came Dark Storm with Chett holding on for dear life. The bull was relentlessly bucking and thrashing right out of the pen. My fingernails were digging into my palms as I watched him lose his balance and fall to the left side. I thought he was done but he came back up.

"He's gonna get it! He's gonna get it!" And then all hope fell. "FUCK!"

Chett didn't predict the last turn from Dark Storm and fell to the ground under him. Canyon went to his feet as the clowns went to work, determined to get the raging bull away before he stepped on him.

Two more men ran out to pick Chett up and get him to safety. When they finally got him over the fence, Canyon sat back down next to me.

"Are you okay?"

"It's all part of the ride. I just wanted him to nail this is all."

"For you, I wished it too."

Chapter 12

When you walk into a stadium full of people, it still doesn't register just how many there are until you're stuck inside a car, waiting in line to exit the parking lot. Canyon couldn't lose his smile as he talked about how great it was to be back. I didn't want to break his mood but some things can't be helped when curiosity wins out.

"Why did you leave?" Nothing but the radio playing Luke Bryan's "That's My Kind of Night" was heard. Canyon closed his eyes making me regret asking the question in the first place. "You don't have to tell me. That was kind of our agreement from the beginning. I shouldn't have asked."

"You have every right to ask but it doesn't make it any easier to answer."

"Well, then let's talk about something else. I really liked your friends. They all seemed to be really good people and they care about you a lot."

That brought the teeth out again. "Yeah, they are pretty awesome. I wish one of them could have had a good ride so you could see how amazing it is to beat out the clock. It just wasn't their night."

"It was still cool though. I have never seen anything like that before. People don't do any of this where I'm from. We have parties on the weekends, there is no rodeo."

"We have parties."

"I know. Kyle wanted me to go to one tomorrow night with him but that's not what I was trying to say. I just meant that you guys have something we never did."

"Are you going?"

"Am I going where?"

"To the party."

"Hell no."

"Why not?"

"I have no desire."

"What if I took you?"

"How would that make it any better?"

He slapped my leg in play before he asked, "What's that supposed to mean?"

"I didn't mean it like that. I just don't do parties anymore. It's just not my thing."

"How can having fun not be your thing?"

"They aren't always fun."

My mood had changed and he picked up on it right away. The teasing had stopped and the quiet returned. The only thing positive was we finally had broken through the traffic and made it to the highway. Only an hour and a half to go.

Several minutes later, out of nowhere, Canyon blurted, "My mom died three years ago."

I had already known this but it didn't sink in truly until the information came along with the emotion behind it. His voice cracked as he let it out. What words are comforting at a time like this other than sorry? Enough people had spoken that single word to make it lose its meaning.

I felt uncomfortable and nervous wondering what to say when I suddenly said, "My dad was killed when I was four."

Canyon went completely stiff proving that was the worst thing I could have done. I sunk down in my seat wishing I could blink and the night would be over.

"How did he die?"

"A drunk driver hit his car. He was dead on impact."

Silence.

Even more silence.

"My dad did it."

That sentence destroyed me. I sat back up in my seat and turned to face him. I knew the last thing he wanted was pity but something way more than pity was filling me. Rage, sadness, confusion, I wanted to scream at the top of my lungs for him and yet hold him at the same time. How could you get past that? Your own father.

"Can you pull over?"

"Are you okay? Are you going to get sick?"

I felt like I could puke but that wasn't what I needed to do. "No. I just need you to stop the truck."

The blinker went on as Canyon slowed down, pulling on to the shoulder of the highway before coming to a stop. He put the gear shift in park and then sat back expecting anything other than what happened next. I don't know why or how I thought it could make things better. I guess I didn't think at all about the consequences. One second I was looking out the passenger side window and the next I was unbuckling my seat belt, crawling slowly over the bench seat of his truck until I was inches from his face. I could hear his breath getting labored as well as feel his chest rising and falling from where my hands landed. It was pitch black inside the cab. There were no street lights to help us see. It was as if we were blind, forced to rely on all of our other senses. I hovered over him, refusing to take the leap. Our lips were practically touching and I couldn't do it. Once that connection happened it would be real and I wasn't ready to accept that.

"Ari." I felt the air that was required to release my name from his lips land on my own and it was enough to break me. "You don't have to do this. It was a long time ago."

"It doesn't make it hurt any less. I want to take away your pain."

As soon as the last word came out Canyon's hands moved from the steering wheel he had been gripping to the back of my head as he pushed me the final few inches needed for his lips to touch mine for the very first time.

We stayed like that for a blink or maybe an hour. Time doesn't seem to be measurable in moments like those. Neither of us was trying to push what was happening. His lips parted, sucking in another breath and then came back to meet mine again one last time before his hold loosened and I could back up.

I was almost to the other side of the truck, feeling more uncomfortable than I ever wanted to be when he grabbed my arm and pulled me back to him.

"Thank you," came out so softly spoken I had to strain to hear it.

Knowing I may have eased some of his pain for the moment meant everything to me. "You're welcome."

This time he let me sit back down and get my seat belt on as he drove back out onto the road. We didn't talk for a while after that. It wasn't awkward as much as we both needed time to process where the line of friendship just went.

"Hey, Ari?"

"Yeah?"

"You know what happened with Brooke back there was nothing, right?"

"You don't have to explain yourself to me. I'm not anyone who deserves to know the whys. It's your business."

"I didn't kiss her."

I didn't feel like he owed me an explanation, even though I sure did want one, but for him to lie to me was something completely different.

"You don't have to lie or soften this up, Canyon. You and Brooke have a past that hasn't gone away. I know a lot about that. I have one of my own."

"What's that supposed to mean? I wasn't softening up anything by the way."

"All I am trying to say is feelings don't go away just because you want them to."

"What's his name?"

The way he asked let me know he was not welcoming my answer. I hadn't had any intention of bringing Kale up and quite honestly it was the last thing I wanted to discuss.

"It's not important."

"Maybe you don't see it that way but I do."

"What happened to respecting what we didn't want to talk about?"

"You're right and you have all the reason in the world to not trust me. I only hope that someday that changes and all of those walls you keep up can fall down, because I want you to see what I see when I look at you. I want you to know just how beautiful you actually are, scars and all."

"They aren't walls that can be torn down, Canyon. They are choices that I can't make, promises that weren't mine to give, and a burden I am left to bear. It's not that I don't trust you. I just can't."

"There is a way out of every screwed up situation, Ari, you just have to fight with everything you have and never give up until you're free."

"Says the man who quit the one thing he has more passion for than anything else in the world."

He didn't come back with a quick witted response. In fact, he didn't say anything for a while. He simply looked at the road as we drove for miles. I eventually gave up waiting and started watching the lines on the road illuminated by the head lights.

"I'm going back."

My head jerked to the left not expecting anything to come from him and most of all that. "Where? Did you forget something? It's getting late and—"

"No, Ari, I'm going back into the circuit. You were right. How can I expect you to face your demons if I can't go back to enjoying the thing that my mom loved most because of my guilt?"

"Please don't make this choice because you think it can help me. There is nothing that can make my situation any different than it is."

"Well, you already have plans to leave. That's something. You're getting away from John and as much as I don't want you to go that's the most important thing for you to do. If it's not overstepping boundaries again can I ask you why you didn't go with your dad's family?"

"I only met them a few times. My grandparents had my dad when they were older so by the time I was born they were already in their seventies. My dad was an unexpected only child. They didn't have the means to take care of me when I was that young. I lost both of them before I turned twelve."

"Damn."

"It is what it is."

"It shouldn't be."

An hour later we were pulling into Canyon's driveway instead of mine.

"Why are we going here first?"

"I'm not ready for the night to end and I can't imagine John welcoming me into his house."

"No definitely not. I'm surprised you're not sick of me yet. You do remember you promised Shelby you would see her tomorrow. That means me too."

"It was always going to be you. She's just a bonus."

"I have to do chores first. My step-dick doesn't let me stay there without consequences."

"I get helping around the house but what I don't understand is why you two despise each other so much. Has it always been this bad?"

He turned off the truck and got out without waiting for an answer. I climbed out after him and closed the door trying to figure out the best way to explain John and me without giving away too much.

Canyon walked around the back of the house and I followed with a question of my own. Once I made the corner he was in view so I asked, "Do you ever go through the front door like a normal person?"

He was almost at the door when he turned to look at me. "The front door is for strangers to ask if they're welcome. The back door is for those who have no need to ask."

"I sure didn't know that. I lived in a flat. We only had one door."

"Well that's just weird."

He stood holding the door open for me. "You coming in?"

As I walked through the door I asked, "Can I tell you something silly?"

"Of course."

He let the door close behind him before going straight for the refrigerator. "The first couple of days I was scared to come in here."

Stopping his pilfering he looked back at me surprised. "Why?"

"I just got this weird vibe that you didn't want me inside."

"That's probably because I didn't."

My jaw dropped and so did my butt in the chair next to me as he went back in search for food. "Don't sugar coat it or anything."

"This isn't a welcoming place. It never has been. I have never in my life invited someone here."

"That's hard to wrap my head around. I fell in love with this house the second I saw it."

"A house is not a home and this one sets the bar."

"Could we change the subject? Talking about how screwed up things are isn't fun."

He stood up with jalapenos and pepper jack cheese in each hand. "Nachos?"

"I want to tease you for eating again but nachos sound fantastic."

"What do you think about coming to the gym with me?"

"Are you saying I need it?"

"Do you always do that? Spin what people say? If I thought you needed to lose weight I would say so." My eyes went wider then wide. "Okay maybe I wouldn't but I would have come up with a more sly way to tell you. I was really asking because I go alone and it would be cool to have someone there to talk to."

"I do need it. I was so sore the day after we did all that barn work. I could use some help. So yeah, if you don't mind a girl who knows nothing about it coming with you then I'm in."

A couple of hours later I was yawning like crazy. We had watched *Blended* with Adam Sandler and Drew Barrymore, ate an entire plate of nachos, and talked about everything that was in bounds to be discussed.

Canyon drove me to my house and cut the headlights out of respect as we pulled into the driveway as to not wake up my so-called family. I reached for the door handle to get out while saying goodbye when Canyon opened his door as well. I didn't know what he was doing. I closed my door and walked around the front of the truck to meet him before he could advance toward the house.

"You didn't have to get out you know."

"I know I didn't but there is something I wanted to ask you about all night and didn't."

"What's up?"

He took a step towards me making me nervous when he asked, "Did you kiss me because you felt sorry for me or because you wanted to?" I couldn't answer him immediately because I didn't really know the answer myself. "Don't think too hard about it. Just answer me."

"I don't know."

"So it was maybe a little of both?"

I didn't want to admit that I might be blurring the lines. That I was going against everything I swore I would avoid by putting myself in this situation to begin with.

"Canyon, I...."

He didn't give me the chance to finish. That one step forward was all he needed to close the space between us. Both of his hands cupped my face as his lips met with mine again. I used all the strength I had to fight off the feelings growing inside of me for him but it wasn't working. Something about Canyon Michaels made what felt dead inside me come back to life. I felt guilty for those feelings but yet they were still there, eating at me to explore what was there right then. Just as I was letting myself relax in the situation, he pecked my lips and released me.

"Are you sure you don't know anymore?"

"You don't want to do this."

"I'm thinking maybe you're wrong."

"I'm leaving."

"I know."

"Then why?"

"Why not?"

Every reason I was trying to give him he shot down and it was frustrating as hell.

"Just trust me. You don't want to get yourself involved in my screwed up life, Canyon."

"Don't tell me what I should want. Don't tell me you're not worth it. Just let whatever happens happen, okay?"

I couldn't continue a conversation that was going nowhere. He wasn't listening to reason.

"I'm going to go in now. Thank you for bringing me along tonight. I..."

"Don't go yet."

"I have to. I don't want things to get awkward between us."

"They don't have to be."

"Then let me go for the night. I will see you tomorrow."

"Goodnight, Ari."

I walked away and into the house closing the door behind me. Only then did I smile. He wasn't giving up that easily. Maybe for once I shouldn't either.

Chapter 13

The next morning I woke up not by choice. The bouncing sister of mine couldn't contain her excitement any longer. She had no idea I was up all night thinking about Kale and looking everywhere I could on Facebook for just a glimpse of him.

Canyon scared me and I felt if I could just hold on to Kale and what we had before it was destroyed, it would be enough to clear any possibility of things moving forward with my next door neighbor.

"Arianna! You have to get up. It's nine-thirty and I have been waiting for you for hours. How long are you going to sleep?"

Without wanting to disappoint her, I swung my legs off the bed and pushed myself up to a sitting position. "I'm up."

"How was it last night? Did you see horses? What did they do? Can I go next time? Please!"

"Slow down. I can only process one question at a time right now. It was neat and I know you would like it a lot. Canyon and I talked about it and yes you can go to the next one they have in town."

She started jumping up and down verses the bouncing she had been doing before. "When? Can we go today?"

"No. Today we are supposed to be going to Canyon's to work, remember?"

"On a Saturday? Can't we do something fun?"

"I'm sure it will be fun for you no matter what."

Two hours later after a shower, chores were finished and some breakfast, Shelby and I were walking out the door when, "Where do you think you're going?" came from the step-dick from hell.

I didn't even turn to face him. My hand was on the door, ready to be opened when I answered, "Canyon needed some help today and we promised Shelby she could come along."

"What makes you think you can just take my daughter somewhere without even consulting me? Heaven knows what you two are doing over at that house. She doesn't need to be exposed—"

"Daddy, I want to see the horses. Why won't you let me?"

"I thought maybe you would like to go pick out your own, honey."

"Really? You're going to get my horse today?"

She was so excited I didn't have the heart to tell her that he just came up with that two seconds ago. John didn't have the faintest idea where to find a horse, he just wanted to keep his daughter from me.

"Well we could try if you wanted to stick around and see."

Shelby looked up at me with so much joy on her face I couldn't break her heart with the questions I knew would out him.

"Go ahead, Shelby. There will be more chances for you to go to Canyon's. If you want to stay I will just see you when I get back."

"Then you can see my horse. My own horse! Isn't this so cool?"

"It sure is."

I went to open the door but couldn't help myself from at least saying, "Where are you going to keep it?"

If looks could kill I would have been dead on the spot. He hated when I questioned anything. All the while my mother sat there staring at me with the blank expression she loved to wear. But seriously, there was no barn, fence, food— I could go on for days. Prior to meeting Canyon I didn't have the faintest idea what a horse needed and it was obvious that neither did he.

"You don't worry about what I do or how I do it. Just get out of here and go screw up your life even more than you already have."

I walked through the threshold and closed the door behind me, all the while thinking, "He doesn't even have a trailer to get it here." Idiot.

Minutes later I was pulling into Canyon's driveway. I could see him walking out of the barn toward me wearing that grin I was falling in love with. I had been battling with myself all night and one look was all it took to make my decision foggy again.

He met me at my door, opening it for me, in the best mood I had seen him in yet.

"How are you this morning, darlin'?"

I got out and let him close the door behind me before saying, "I'm good. What has you in such a good mood?"

"I get you for the day. What else do I need?"

"That's a nice thing to say."

"I can tell you nice things all day long if you want me to." That damn smile again.

"Why don't you save them for when they count most?"

"I can do that too. So, where's Shelby?"

"Listen to this crap." I put my hands on my hips and let it all out. "Step-dick decides as we are walking out the door to tell Shelby she could get her horse today."

"What?"

"Yeah, he's an idiot. What are they going to do with a horse?"

"She doesn't even know how to ride yet. Where did he say he was getting one anyway?"

"He doesn't have the faintest idea. He just didn't want her to leave with me and used the one sure fire thing that would keep her around: his money."

"Does he always try to buy her love?"

"Always."

"That is one extremely messed up dude."

"Tell me something I don't know."

We stood there for a second before Canyon grabbed my hand and started pulling me with him.

"Where are we going?"

"Well, I told Shelby yesterday I was going to teach you how to ride today and if that means dragging you I will."

"You want me to get on one by myself? Are you crazy?"

"No, I am determined. There's no reason you shouldn't be able to, especially if you're going to be helping me out around here. You're going to need to be able and today I'm going to show you how."

"I'm scared."

"Hop on."

He had stopped pulling me and not only let go of my hand but squatted down for me to get on his back.

"You're kidding, right?"

"Just do it."

I laughed as I grabbed onto his neck while I wrapped my legs around his waist. Once he had me, he stood up and started running full speed, scaring me to death that we were going to go face first into the dirt.

"Why are you doing this?"

It came out a little more like, "Why. Are. You. Doing. This," but that was due to the bouncing I was trying to endure.

All of a sudden he stopped but then he started spinning us in circles. I was so dizzy I couldn't imagine how we were staying upright. Laughter exploded out of both of us. I couldn't catch my breath I was laughing so hard. Finally we stopped going in circles and Canyon put me down on my own two feet. Both of us were trying to walk and the sight of each other was hilarious.

"Try to walk straight."

"I am trying."

We were stumbling all over the place until I finally gave up and let my body fall to the ground, still laughing my butt off. Canyon crawled over to me. I hadn't even noticed him going down also. I was too busy wiping the tears falling from my eyes.

"I love this side of you."

"What are you talking about?"

"This. You living. It's the best thing in the world to witness."

I sat up and looked at him still trying to catch my breath. "When did you get all mushy on me?"

"When you showed me it was time to live again. Life's too short to be miserable, Ari."

How he could just flip a switch and be happy made we wish it was that easy.

"I'm trying."

"Are you?"

"I keep coming here, don't I?"

"Yes you do, thanks to me. Now, let's have some fun."

"Thanks to you?"

"Would you be here if I hadn't come up with the idea of you working for me?"

"Would that have happened if I hadn't thrown rocks at your truck?"

"I'm the one who didn't stop."

"I'm the one who was walking down the road."

"You wouldn't have had a truck that broke down if my dad wouldn't have gone to prison."

The joking banter stopped there with my eyes bulging out and his head falling down. Once again I grabbed him, but this time I didn't allow the sweet kisses we'd been giving to take over the moment. I shoved his body down and climbed on to him grabbing his bottom lip with my teeth before letting it go and using my tongue to part his lips.

He didn't respond at first, I am sure due to the shock of me taking the initiative. I had never been so brash but I hated him feeling defeated by something out of his control. Words don't work as fast as actions do and the way he came back at me once it all sank in told me he welcomed the idea.

When I felt his hands come up to my waist, moving under my shirt, everything changed. My body froze up at the idea of letting things go further.

"Hey, where did you go?"

I placed my hands on either side of his head pushing up to raise myself far enough that I could look down at him. "I don't know what I was thinking. I..."

"You think too much, is the problem." He reached behind his head and with one tap my elbows gave out and I was falling back down on him. "I like you much better here."

The comfort of him was like being wrapped in a warm blanket when you're cold. I felt like I could stay there forever and be happy and once again I needed to stop myself from falling. Without warning, I pushed my fingertips into his armpits and started tickling him like crazy. Feeling him squirm under me had me laughing hysterically. I had no chance against his strength and within seconds he'd thrown me off of him. I landed flat on my back but still was laughing.

"You think that's funny, huh?" He leaped over me, landing with him straddling my waist as he raised my hands over my head and pinned them down with his knee. "How do you like the Chinese typewriter?"

He didn't give me the chance to respond before his index fingers we're pecking at my chest. It hurt so badly but I couldn't stop laughing for long enough to tell him he had to stop. He continued to punish me until I damn near peed my pants.

"STOP!"

I screamed it with the only breath I had left. He followed direction and stopped but then we were back to being just as uncomfortable as we were before I took the leap and kissed him again. I guess you can't ignore the elephant in the room and the fact that his mother died by his father was nothing a kiss or playfulness could wipe away. I didn't want to force him to talk about it. That was something that he needed to do by choice not by obligation.

"Ari, I want you to know that I understand why you do what you're doing and I appreciate the fact that you care enough that you want to help me, but I dealt with all of this the last few years. It may not be fun to talk about but I can take it. The next time you kiss me I want it to be for no other reason than you want to, okay?"

"Is it wrong for me to want to keep you from those thoughts? You may have dealt with it in your own way but it has to hurt. I don't know what your dad did to her but none of that matters, you are what's important."

"Are you sure you have to leave? I kinda like having you around."

The little tip of a smile peeked out of him and as much as I knew the last thing he wanted was pity, it still broke my heart that he was forced to live with losing both his parents in one fell swoop. He was all alone.

"Do you have any family around? I know you said John got my truck from your uncle."

"All I had was my Dad's family and when I testified against him, they disowned me."

"I am so sorry and that's not pity that's just me caring about what you had to go through. I wish I didn't have to leave but I can't stay here with him. You don't know what he has done."

"My dad beat my mom, Ari. He beat her until she was dead on the floor and he continued to hit her until I pulled him off. There isn't anything I want more than for you to get out of that house but selfishly I don't think life will be the same."

He watched his own father beat his mom. He actually was the one who had to pry him off of her dead body. This was so much worse than anything I could wrap my head around that. All I wanted to do was cry for him but I knew that would do no good. He was finally moving past all of that and I didn't need to be the reason he had to feel that pain all over again.

How could he think though, as screwed up as I was, that I could bring anything but more problems his way by staying? I knew the answer to that—he had no idea.

"I've only been here for a week. Don't give me that much credit."

"I may be dramatizing this a little but don't think for a second you haven't changed things. Only a week or not, you make me feel again and that means more than you know."

Three hours later I was screaming at the top of my lungs from the top of Magnus.

"Don't you let go, Canyon Michaels!"

"You can do this."

He was laughing and I found nothing amusing about the situation at all.

"I can't and I don't want to."

He opened the gate anyway and smacked Magnus in the butt causing him to start running into the open field. I had never in my life been as scared as I was in that moment. All of the things in my past never led me to feel like each breath I took could very well be my last.

I held both reins in my hands like he had taught me to do but without him there to guide me, the horse could choose not to listen and I would be screwed. I pulled back on the reins to try to get him to slow down when he completely stopped, throwing me forward in the saddle.

"Okay, Magnus, that was probably my fault for pulling so hard but you have to bear with me. I don't really know what I'm doing here and I'm a little freaked out."

I rubbed my hand back and forth over his neck to soothe him. I was really the one who needed the soothing but treat others as you would like to be treated is a motto that works for most.

"All right, I'm ready to go back now. I'm going to kick you but I won't do it so hard that it hurts, okay? It would be much easier if you could understand me right now. Okay, let's do this, don't hate me."

I kicked, putting the heels of my shoes into the back of his belly and pulled on the left rein to make him turn.

It worked!

"Thank you. Thank you. Thank you. You are the best horse ever!'

He trotted all the way back without going too fast or too slow. Honestly it felt great the longer I was on him. Fear disappeared and was replaced by security. He wasn't going to hurt me and being in control felt amazing.

The closer I got to the corral the more I didn't want it to end. I could see Canyon sitting on the top of the fence watching me with his perfect smile in place as we slowed down to a walk before we reached the fence.

Canyon jumped down and grabbed the reins to tie up Magnus while I swung my leg over the saddle to get down. Without seeing it coming,

Canyon grabbed me off the saddle and swung me around screaming, "You did it! I knew you could do it! I am so proud of you!"

I was proud of myself, to tell you the truth. I rode a freakin' horse by myself. That is a huge accomplishment.

He set me down but grabbed my shoulders to square me up with him.

"I'm going to kiss you right now, Ari. This is what it feels like to be kissed for no other reason than I really want to."

He came down to meet my willing lips and I melted at the taste of him. His tongue did things to me that I couldn't remember ever feeling before. I let him pull on my lips and soaked up every bit of what he wanted me to have. I was falling for him whether I wanted to or not and in that moment I let all my doubts and fears go.

When it came to an end he brought his lips up to kiss my forehead before he looked down at me and said, "How did I do?"

"I think you might have to try harder next time."

"Oh really, you're so sure there's going to be a next time."

"You're right. Let's just end this now before it gets complicated."

He picked me up off the ground squeezing me. "I have no intention of letting you go."

"You know you're going to have to, right? This can't be anything."

"Will you just stop with that? I'm tired of hearing about what we can't or shouldn't do. Just shush woman and let's have some fun while we can."

Chapter 14

Shelby was disappointed just as I predicted when I got home that night. She didn't talk at all through dinner and as soon as she could, she went straight to her room, closing the door behind her.

I wanted to kill John for it but saying something to him wasn't going to change him in any way. It would make my life harder. Some things are just better unsaid. I couldn't take any more from him. Somehow Canyon giving me time away made me feel not as intimidated but more angry instead.

I knocked on Shelby's door before I entered finding her faced down in her pillow.

"Go away," was barely heard but I got the point.

Sitting next to her on the bed, I began petting her hair and wishing I had the right thing to say to make it all better. "I'm sorry."

Her head turned toward me and the first thing I noticed were her swollen eyes from crying. "He promised and then took it all back. He isn't going to ever let me get a horse like he said. It was all a lie."

"Maybe today he couldn't but I doubt that he never will..."

"No, he said so, Arianna. He talked to a man and he told Daddy what he would need. That's all that happened and then he got off the phone and told me absolutely not."

That son-of-a-bitch. I wanted to storm into the living room and tear into him. He has the money. I know personally where it came from and it left him with no excuse to use.

"I bet we could talk to Canyon about using his stables. Let's see tomorrow what he has to say and then you can talk to your dad. How does that sound?"

She sat up wiping her face and nose. "Do you really think he would let me?"

"It's worth asking, don't you think?"

"Thank you, Arianna."

"You're welcome, hun, now go grab a shower, you need it."

"Me? You smell like horse poop."

I had gotten so used to the smell that it went unnoticed. "Then I'll go first but you have to follow my lead."

"Deal."

Later that night when everyone was sound asleep I decided to go for another walk. This time I wasn't lying to myself. I wanted to see Canyon. I picked up the sound of his voice right as I passed the trees. The closer I got to the house I started mouthing the words along with him. I loved Rascall Flatt's song "My Wish". I went to sit down in what had become my spot on his front lawn but something inside pressed me to continue forward until I was at the back corner of the house looking at him.

He was handsome, there was no doubt there but the way he could play the guitar only upped the ante. When the song came to an end I decided to be bold for once and stepped away from the house clapping my hands together for him. He jumped up from his chair holding his guitar in the air, completely shocked to see me.

"What are you doing? Are you trying to give me a heart attack or something?"

I walked forward until I reached the stairs leading up to the screened in porch and climbed them. Once I was inside the door I asked, "Was that for me?"

Canyon looked down at the ground before coming back up to look me in the eye. "How could you tell?"

"I loved it."

He looked out into the night before he said, "I've never played for anyone before. This is pretty embarrassing."

"It shouldn't be. You truly are talented."

"I wouldn't say that."

He smiled letting me know he was okay with me being there. "First tell me why you're even awake at this hour."

"Would it make things more awkward if I told you this wasn't my first time hearing you?"

"What? You've been here before? I mean this late? Why? Why didn't you say something? You were just sneaking around..."

"I wasn't sneaking at all. I went for a walk and could hear you. After that I wanted to come talk to you but it always sounded like you wanted to be alone. Tonight was the first time your song wasn't about sadness. It hit me that maybe you wouldn't mind company this time."

"I'm so used to being alone. Having you here really is changing everything." He looked out at the property again and then his face lit up. "Oh, I was going to tell you something tomorrow but you're here now."

"I'm sorry if I invaded your privacy. I seem to be here more than I'm welcome. You can wait and tell me tomorrow. Go back to whatever you were doing..."

"Ari, I got in to the rodeo coming here in two weeks."

"Wait, what? The PBR is going to be here again? I thought they...."

"No, you're right. They travel. This is a much smaller scale event but I have to start somewhere again. I can't just jump back to the PBR. I need practice."

"So in two weeks, huh? Are you nervous?"

"No, darlin', I'm excited. I couldn't sleep. I was just thinking about all the ways life is coming full circle, ya know?"

"No, I don't."

"Come here."

When I got closer, he pulled me down on his lap facing him. "I'm not going to pretend like life is easy. I am working my ass off to try to make it a better place to be though. When my mom died I really thought I wanted to go with her. Now I have you here to hold. I have to look at the bright side or I'm gonna fall into that hole again. I don't want to go there again."

The way he described himself was almost someone I wouldn't recognize.

"Will you sing me a song?"

"No way."

"Come on. Why not?"

"Because you were never supposed to hear me to begin with."

"You won't change your mind?"

"No, I won't."

"You would have if I hadn't come around the corner."

"If you would have stayed on the other side of that corner you would officially be a stalker. The creepy kind too."

"Whatever! I'm going home."

"Four o'clock doesn't ever come late enough for me. I need to get some sleep. You're welcome to join me."

I ignored the offer. "You get up at four?"

"How else do you think everything gets done around here?"

"You are a stud, Canyon Michaels."

"Why thank you, pretty lady. You're mighty fine yourself."

I leaned forward and pecked his lips. "Goodnight."

He patted my butt two times and then helped me climb off of him softly saying, "Goodnight, sweet Ari."

I walked home with a smile on my face that I couldn't wipe off. I was seriously falling for that man.

The following morning Shelby and I left without waiting for John to share his opinion. We didn't even say goodbye to him or our mother. And as soon as we pulled into Canyon's driveway she was tearing out of the truck, straight for the barn he was walking out of.

"Canyon!"

He knelt down to catch her in his arms. "Hey there, little bit. I missed ya yesterday."

I was almost to them when Shelby blurted out, "Arianna says you might let me keep my horse here. Will you please?"

Canyon stood up with her still in his arms and looked at me questionably.

"John didn't get her the horse. He said they don't have the means to hold one."

Canyon looked back down at Shelby. "So you want to get one and keep it here?"

"If you would say yes I could."

"Let me talk to Ari for a second, okay? In fact, why don't you go see the puppies? They got even bigger."

She wiggled out of his arms and was gone in a second.

"That worked well."

"You should see the puppies. I wasn't lying, they are freakin' cute."

"So what do you think about letting her keep it here?"

"Do you really think he's going to get her one if he knows she has to come here to see it?"

"Good point. Damn I hate him!"

"What if I gave her Nyah?"

My jaw practically fell off. "You would do that?"

"For Shelby? Yeah, I think I could do just about anything for that little girl."

I leapt into his arms and started smothering him with kisses all over his face.

"If this is what I get for giving away a pony I can only imagine what I'll get when—"

"Just shut up and kiss me."

He laughed but kissed me anyway. "Do you think we should run it by John first?"

"I think that is the worst idea ever. We don't need to tell him anything."

"You know full well she is going to run home screaming her head off that she got a horse."

"Well then maybe we don't tell her yet. Let her learn some responsibility first. You could tell her that she could earn money to buy her own. That way she understands what it takes to own a horse to begin with."

"I think you are a sneaky creeper with stalker tendencies but I agree."

I smacked him in the chest. "That's not funny."

"You really freaked me out last night. I had no idea people could hear me or I never would have started."

"You make it seem like a bad thing. You really are good. I'm not giving up either. One of these days I will get you to sing for me."

"Not a chance in hell."

Canyon wasn't wrong, the puppies were like little puff balls jumping all over the place. Shelby wanted nothing to do with anything but them giving Canyon insight into her reality. She wanted to call a horse hers but was in no place ready for the responsibility. He and I worked more on my riding and I am proud to say I was really getting the hang of things.

When three o'clock came, I took Shelby back home before Canyon and I were going to go out on our first ride together on individual horses.

I walked into the house with Shelby on my heels to change my clothes when John met us at the door.

"Where the fuck have you been and why weren't you answering your phone?"

I hadn't realized I left my phone in my bedroom until he mentioned it. "I left it..."

Bam! He slapped me again straight across the face causing Shelby to scream bloody murder. He must have forgotten she was standing there because this was a first for her. The blow knocked me to my knees and as I was going down he yelled for Shelby to go to her room. The look in her eye showed all the fear in the world as she didn't move.

"It's okay, Shelby. I'm fine. Don't worry, honey."

"Are you sure?"

Her voice quivered as she spoke breaking my heart with every deep breath she had to take through her tears.

"Positive."

"I said go to your ROOM!"

She ran down the hall and slammed her door shut behind her. My mother was nowhere to be seen but then I remembered her car wasn't in the driveway.

"I'm sorry I worried you..."

"You are one sorry piece of shit and there will never be a day I worry about you. You could fucking leave and never come back and it would make me the happiest man alive. What you did was take my fucking daughter again without permission. What do I have to do—" Bam! he kicked me as hard as he could in my side causing me to drop to the floor from my knees and cover my face out of instinct "—to get you to fucking understand she's mine! Mine not yours."

BAM! He kicked me again.

I hadn't realized how long all of this was going on. It felt like seconds and hours mixed together. I could hear Shelby wailing from her room. All I wanted to do was get up and beat the crap out of him but I didn't stand a chance against him. He had hate seething through his veins and I will forever be his target.

I opened my eyes just in time to see his foot coming straight for my face. I screamed, "NOOOOOOOO!" just as the impact should have happened but it never came. Instead, the front door flew open and nailed me in my side as I laid on the floor crying, too afraid to open my eyes. I heard blow after blow land, a gurgling sound and then a thud.

My head was lifted off the ground, then I heard Canyon begging me to open my eyes for him.

"Please, Ari, you're okay now. I'm here and I will never let him hurt you again."

All I kept thinking was, what did you do? I had only weeks left of enduring him until I could leave. Now those weeks would feel like years.

I opened my mouth before my eyes but only to ask, "What have you done?"

"He won't touch you again. I promise you I will protect you with everything I—"

"I'm not your mother, Canyon! You shouldn't have come here. You only made things so much worse."

His body went stiff. The soft cradle he had on my head then felt cold and unfamiliar. I forced my body into an upright position taking away his need to hold me.

"Oh MY GOD!"

I looked across the floor at an unconscious John with a face almost unrecognizable it was so swollen. Just then I heard Shelby's door open. I have never moved as fast as I did that day trying to get to her before she saw her father.

"Shelby, stop!"

"Arianna, what's happening? Why did Daddy do that? Where is he? Where's Mom?"

"Let's get you back to your room, okay? I need to talk to your dad for a few more minutes."

"Arianna..."

"This is not up for discussion, Shelby, please just go back in your room."

"Fine!" She turned back and slammed her door for the second time.

I walked back out to the family room and found the front door still wide open but no Canyon. The only thing left was John who was starting to wake up on the floor. I sat down in the chair furthest from him, grabbed ahold of my knees trying to get my legs to stop shaking. I had no idea what I was supposed to do. John grabbed his face, feeling the obvious swelling that had taken over and then he was scrambling to his feet looking in every direction for the person who caused the damage coming to land his focus on me.

"What the fuck did you do?"

His voice sounded nothing like usual. It was as if it hurt to speak. I didn't know what to say. I didn't want to mention Canyon and I had no idea what he remembered.

"I didn't. I..."

"Who did this?"

Shelby came out of her room and was down the hall before I could get to her. "Daddy? Why were you hurting Arianna?"

"I didn't mean to, baby. I was scared when I didn't know where you were. I made a mistake. Arianna and I have already talked about it and she knows to not do it again. See, everything's fine."

"What happened to you, Daddy?"

"I wish I knew, honey. I'm going to go jump in the shower and then take a nap. You can play some video games if you want."

He disappeared down the hall leaving Shelby looking at me for answers.

"I don't know either."

"You always promised you would never lie to me."

"Shelby..."

"I heard him, Arianna. I heard Canyon talking to you. If he did that to Daddy I'm not mad at him. He was hurting you."

"You don't need to worry about this. I have it under control."

"I'm not going to tell. I will never tell."

In that moment my baby sister became a young lady and I hated that what happened was the cause.

Chapter 15

I went straight to Canyon's feeling like life was no longer in the little control I felt I had left. Scared to death of what was to come, I ran straight to the one thing I felt could hold me together. As soon as I could throw it in park I was jumping from the truck and running into his house. I called for him over and over but couldn't find him. I thought about going up the stairs but that would never be my place and even in the mess my head was in I remembered that.

Outside, I ran to the barn screaming his name but I didn't find him there either. What I saw was Magnuses' stall door open and no Magnus. Realizing he must have taken him out, I sat down next to the tack room and waited, hurting like I should probably go to the hospital but I didn't know where one was and all I wanted was him. I had nowhere else to go and didn't know what to do. Time drug on longer than I could keep my eyes open. The whole situation drained me. I wished I could wake and have it all be a horrible dream.

"Arianna, wake up."

The sound of his voice had me jumping up to see him. It was dark and without the barn lights I wouldn't have been able to see a thing.

I didn't talk. I stumbled straight into his arms, only they didn't wrap around me like I expected and that is what finally broke my walls down.

I cried. Not the kind of cry you let out when someone hurts your feelings. No, this was me letting out the pain from my whole life.

"I'm so sorry I drug you into this. I am so sorry!"

The arms I needed came not only to hold me but he picked me up and carried me to the house. Every time I had to breathe it hurt but I was too afraid to admit it.

We climbed up the stairs and the next thing I knew he was setting me down on a bed. I curled in a ball wishing I could just disappear. Canyon climbed on the bed behind me until his body rested against mine and he began to brush my hair away from my face. I waited for him to say something, anything, just to let me know he understood why this was a horrible idea. Why I needed to keep distance between us. Why I needed to get as far away from John as humanly possible. Only I couldn't imagine any longer not having him. He had snuck in under my radar and become the only thing I trusted. My life was more messed up than I ever felt before.

"I'm falling in love with you, Ari. I came back here and rode for hours trying to wrap my head around all of this. I can't make it stop. You mean everything to me and that son-of-a-bitch put his hands on you. I'm sorry you didn't want me to step in but I'm not sorry for stopping him from hurting you more. I will never be sorry for protecting you." I couldn't believe he just admitted he was falling in love with me. He couldn't be. I rolled over and screamed out from the pain that went straight through my side. "Fuck I hate this! I'm taking you to the hospital."

"No. I can't."

"You can't? Ari, I think he broke one of your ribs! I am the one who can't do this again. Do you know how many times she told me I couldn't tell anyone? That it had to be our little secret. I know you said that this is different but it's not. I won't sit back and let him come after you again. I will kill him myself if he even tries."

"Am I supposed to leave Shelby? I have to go back, Canyon. She heard you in the house and told me that she's not mad at you for hurting her dad. That she won't tell. What does that say? It says she's mine not theirs. I will never leave her with them."

"Where is your mom when all this happens?"

"I haven't had one for thirteen years. She does nothing and never will."

Canyon looked down at my hands that were resting on his chest before he grabbed them up into his and brought them to his mouth before he kissed them.

"I can't protect you if you won't let me."

I had nothing to say that could make this situation better so instead I just closed my eyes and willed it all to go away knowing it wouldn't.

I slept for as long as I could hoping that if I stayed asleep it wouldn't be real. Morning came regardless and I forced myself to get up and go to school. Canyon urged me to stay in bed and let my sore body rest but I needed to feel like I had something left of a normal life. Even if it was to go to a school I disliked.

I kissed Canyon goodbye hoping that that one kiss wouldn't be our last and then got in my truck and headed home.

After I had pulled in the driveway and turned off the ignition, my body began to shake. I forced myself to get out and go into the house whether he was there or not.

The door swung open, surprisingly; I was betting on being locked out. I walked in with caution but was met with complete silence. Instinctively, I was about to shout, "Hello" but welcomed the quiet instead.

After a shower, I went to my room and got dressed, worrying that any second John would come in swinging. He never came.

I got to school and went about my day the best I could without answering the questions coming at me about why I was walking funny or how I got hurt. Even Ashlynn seemed to leave me alone. Maybe I wore an expression that read, "Not today" and for once they listened.

When the end of school came I was more worried than ever about where I should go. I knew Canyon was expecting me to come to his house but Shelby had to be a nervous wreck after waking up and finding that I never came home. The last thing I wanted was to worry her even more and then it hit me. What would she do when I finally left? I had never talked to her about it. Would she be okay? I had always convinced myself that when I was no longer there her life would be better. After the night we had just had I wasn't so sure any more about anything.

I got to my truck and started it still not sure what to do. I decided to just head toward the house and let myself decide then. Driving down the road approaching Canyon's house, my nerves started kicking in. My need to reassure Shelby won out as I passed Canyon's and pulled into my driveway moments later. His car was there; this time I checked to see. I was just about to restart the truck and leave when Shelby came barreling out the front door. I got out and met her with a hug I didn't know I needed until she was in my arms.

"Where did you go yesterday? I didn't see you this morning and got really scared."

"I went to Canyon's and fell asleep without realizing it. I'm sorry if I worried you. I will never do it again okay?"

"You are promising so no take backs!"

"No take backs."

We walked back in to the house together and flashbacks from the day before hit me.

"It's okay, Arianna, he's in the kitchen," Shelby whispered.

I didn't want to be there. I had seen Shelby and knew she was okay. That was all that mattered to me.

"I'm just here to grab a few things and then I am leaving again."

"Can I come with you?"

"I don't know. I'm not sure that's a good idea."

"Please. He hasn't talked to me at all. I don't want to be here."

The look she was giving me made up my mind. I would take another beating if it meant getting her out of there. "You let me grab what I need and we can go."

"Thank you."

She didn't thank me often which only fueled my reason to take her with me.

After I grabbed my boots and changed my dress into shorts and a t-shirt we headed out the door. I yelled, "Shelby is coming with me" but didn't wait for a response. The entire walk to the truck was terrifying. My pace quickened the closer I got to it just waiting for him to come barging out. When I reached the truck door, I flew it open and climbed inside turning it on as soon as I could. Shelby climbed up and closed her door before I put it in reverse and backed out onto the street.

"It's okay, Arianna, he won't come."

The last thing in the world I wanted to do was ask her how she knew that but I couldn't help myself.

"What makes you think that?"

"Because he knows I saw."

She was right. I hated that it was the truth but she was right. With Shelby as a witness he would never want me to go to the police. If I had the guts to do that I might out him and everyone that was involved. He would never chance it.

"I'm sorry that that is the truth."

"Me too."

There was a moment of silence before she spoke words that I would never tire of hearing.

"I love you, Arianna."

I grabbed her hand in mine so she would know how much I meant it when I told her, "I love you too."

Canyon was waiting in the driveway for the first time looking worried out of his mind. He was pacing when I first saw him as we passed the tree line and then he began walking toward the truck to meet me at my door when I came to a complete stop. He opened it, ready to yell at me, before he noticed Shelby. His entire demeanor changed.

"Hello there, little bit. What a great surprise."

"Hi, Canyon. Do you care that I came with Arianna? I didn't want to stay at home."

She was so blunt with her feelings at times I wish I had her inner strength.

"No, I don't and never will. You will always be welcome here. I never want you to feel like you have to ask again. Does that sound good to you?"

"It sure does! Can I go see the puppies again?"

"Have at it."

She opened her door and jumped out before he finished his sentence. Once she was out of range to hear him he turned back to me.

"You had me worried to death. I was two seconds from driving over there again."

"I went to see Shelby. You can't be mad at me for that."

"I can but I would never. Come here." He picked me up and lifted me out of the cab into his arms. "Are you okay? Did he say something to you? Tell me the truth, Ari."

He was more concerned than anyone had ever been for me.

"I hurt a little but other than that I'm okay. He was there but Shelby said he hadn't talked to her at all. I told him I was taking her with me but I didn't wait for a response."

"Did he go to the doctor?"

"I don't know. I didn't go into the room he was in or anything. I just changed clothes and left. Why?"

"Because I'm pretty sure I broke his jaw. He won't be able to talk comfortably for a while."

I kissed him with every ounce of my heart I could give. "Thank you for being there when I needed you. By the way, how did you know I needed you?"

He set me down gently and smirked. "I was going to pick you up and surprise you with dinner out. I thought a real date was finally in order." He noticed my expression and then screamed." Don't make fun of me!"

"You wanted to ask me on a date?"

"No, I was going to take you on one. I don't need to ask. You can't resist me."

"Oh, you think?"

"I know. Now let's get you inside so you can take it easy."

"Normally I would argue but today I think it sounds like the best plan ever."

We passed Shelby and the puppies on our way and I changed my mind instantly. "They are so cute!"

"Oh no you don't. Inside, Ari, now."

"Don't get bossy, I'm going."

"Canyon, can one of them come inside with her?"

I looked at him and smiled hoping it would pull some weight.

"How am I ever supposed to stand a chance against you two?"

I watched her pick out which one she wanted and then hurried to close the fence so the rest didn't run out before I made it to the first step. I was airborne seconds later landing in Canyon's arms.

"Stop doing work that I can do for you."

"Put me down. I'm not crippled."

"You will let me take care of you and like it. Shelby, tell your sister to play nice."

She was about to speak when I gave her a look that closed her mouth tight.

"Did you just do that?" He looked at me and pointed to Shelby. "Don't do that."

Then he went back to Shelby. "Whatever looks she gives you don't listen. You're on my side, right? I have horses and puppies."

I died laughing. "You are pathetic! Trying to lure my own sister to your side with puppies and horses, really?"

"Can I have one?"

My head snapped in Shelby's direction telling myself I couldn't have heard that right.

"You sure can. Whichever one you want it's yours." He looked at me with every one of his teeth showing. He was so proud of himself.

"Take me inside. Please."

"Your wish is my command."

He carried me into the family room and set me down on the couch while Shelby and the puppy, which she was now calling Darla, both sat down next to me. Canyon flipped on the TV and then went into the kitchen for I'm guessing a snack seeing as he is always hungry. I was busy playing with the puppy climbing all over me that I didn't pay any attention to what was on the TV until I heard his name.

"Governor Michael Thompson has won the seat as the Republican candidate going into the Presidential election."

Tears welled up in my eyes and I begged for the TV to turn off so I didn't have to see his face any longer.

"Isn't that Kale's dad?"

"Can you turn it off?" Shelby didn't move causing me to shout, "TURN IT OFF!"

She was off the couch and heading for the TV when Canyon came running into the room looking for the problem. He hit the button on the remote and the screen went black.

"What's wrong?"

"Nothing."

"Don't lie to me. You obviously are upset."

I looked at Shelby ignoring Canyon's question. "Come here." She walked over to me with her head down. "Hey, I'm sorry I snapped at you. I shouldn't have."

She hugged me. "It's okay."

"No, it's not, and I will try to never do it again."

She hugged me tighter and then said, "Why don't you want to see him?"

"He's a bad man, Shelby, and that's all you need to know."

I expected her to argue but what I said seemed to be enough for her.

Canyon looked from me to her and said, "There are cookies in the pantry if you want some."

Shelby took off with the puppy following right behind her into the kitchen. Canyon took advantage of the privacy immediately.

"What happened? I don't even know what you saw. Please don't lie to me again."

"This is the part of my life you can't be involved in. Don't take this personally, it isn't about you, it's about me and why I need to get far away from John."

"Something on the TV was about you?"

"No, it wasn't."

"I'm about to turn it back on, Ari. Tell me."

"Please listen! You can't do this. You can't make me talk about something I can't. This isn't fair."

I stood up and was ready to grab Shelby and leave when Canyon stood in front of me. "I've told you so much and yet you keep me in the dark. Why won't you let me in?"

"Because I'm not okay with bringing you into this! It's my problem not yours."

He took a step back and then walked out the door. I knew he was getting too close. I also knew I didn't want to let him go either but with Kale's father gunning for president I was never going to be able to break free from a past that wasn't mine to own. I had nowhere to go. I couldn't stay with him and let him fall deeper and I didn't want to go home. Shelby surprisingly stayed in the kitchen never coming in to see what the commotion was about. I guess she was so used to her father screaming that it wasn't an issue for her. I hated that just as much.

I decided it would be best to go talk to Canyon and try to reason with him. If I failed, at least I tried.

Chapter 16

I walked out the door and found him on the back porch looking out. He didn't turn and pay any mind to the fact I was there.

"Will you please try to understand?"

That got his attention.

"Try? That's all I have been doing. I didn't let anyone in, Ari, until you. I've done everything I can think of and you keep pushing me away."

"Because you keep coming closer. I warned you from the beginning this would never be something—"

"That's a lie and you know it. You may push me away every time I try to get close but only after you realize you want me there. I don't know what happened to you but whatever it was you can't keep running from it. It will eat you alive. Trust me I know."

"So where does this leave us? We can't be friends because I won't put you in a situation that you never belonged in the first place? Come on!"

"Friends? Yes, Ari, you are my friend. If that's how you want it."

I decided it was time to go. "We're going to get going. I will make up my work time tomorrow."

I turned and walked back in the house to collect Shelby. I found her in the cookie jar with a face covered in chocolate.

"How many have you had?"

With a mouth full I got, "Only six."

I had to laugh. "It looks more like sixteen. Come on, it's time to go."

The puppy was still at her feet feasting on every crumb she dropped.

"I don't want to leave. Where are we going to go? I don't want to go home, Arianna."

"Why don't you guys run to the grocery store for me and grab some steaks. I can barbecue when you get back. Sound good?"

Shelby's eyes lit up while my mind went in circles. What would he do this for unless he was changing his mind?

"Can we?"

She looked at me and the choice of making her go home versus being around Canyon was simple. It wasn't her I was worried about.

Canyon gave us money and we headed to the store. We were quiet for most of the ride there until Shelby asked, "Why did seeing Kale's dad make you mad at Canyon?"

"It didn't, he just needs to understand that I don't want to tell him everything. Sometimes keeping things to yourself is a good thing."

"But he likes you."

"I like him too."

When we got back from the store, Canyon had already started the grill and was making potatoes and corn in the kitchen when I walked in and set the bags down.

"Come here."

I wasn't expecting him to talk to me. I walked forward until I was close enough for him to tug on the waist band of my shorts, bringing me so close that I could smell him. All of my reservations went out the door.

"You were right. It's not my place."

"No, it's not."

He let go of my shorts, grabbed the back of my head and brought my lips to meet his. "Can I get a pass on this one?"

I knew in my gut it was a bad idea but what came out didn't apparently agree. "I think I can arrange that."

"Good to hear."

He kissed me again and we were back to where we started, or so I thought.

Dinner was delicious. I had never had steak that tasted so good. Shelby went on and on about it like she hadn't eaten in years making both of us laugh.

After helping clean up, it was time to get going whether I wanted to go home or not. Canyon walked us out to my truck keeping a distance I wasn't understanding. I expected a, "See you tomorrow." What I got was something I never saw coming.

"Tomorrow I won't be here when you get off school. I have a buddy that I used to train with. He and I are going to work on my riding so I can make sure I'm ready."

"Oh, okay."

"You're more than welcome to come here anyway. I should be back around five."

"I wouldn't feel right being here without you. I can just see you on Wednesday."

"See, that's the thing. I'm going to need to do this every day until I know I've got the hang of it."

I was shocked. Yes, I knew he needed to train, but to not see him for weeks hurt far worse than I thought it would.

"Maybe I will come by sometime."

"All right, darlin', thanks for staying for dinner."

"Thank you for having us."

No kiss goodbye or anything. I turned away from him to get in the truck as he walked away. He may have said he was okay with things but from the way it sounded to me, he was trying to be the one doing the pushing now and I hated every second of it.

Shelby and I got home around eight o'clock. It was just enough time for her to get showered and cleaned up before bed.

Step-dick and my mother were sitting in the family room watching some sort of news channel when we came in. I only knew because I heard that name again. The decision had to have just been made that day. I looked at John to gauge his reaction and found he was about as happy as I was with the news. President? They both deserved to be in a hole in the ground.

That night, laying in bed, I thought of all the people I missed. My friends had been texting, calling and privately messaging me through Facebook since the day I left but I never responded. The non-disclosure agreement kept me from being able to answer any of their questions and quite honestly I missed them so much I thought keeping in contact would hurt more than it already did. That didn't mean I didn't still read every one they sent me or each post they put on my newsfeed.

Kale is the only person who never tried to contact me. The one I wanted to hear from most didn't care enough. After everything we had, he let it go in a blink. I hated him for so many reasons but this one took the cake.

All of the posts on my newsfeed seemed to be about his dad and I couldn't look at it anymore. I threw my phone on my nightstand and forced myself to find something good in my life to focus on.

Canyon came to mind every time.

Friday came and I hadn't seen Canyon all week. I hoped on my walks to hear him but I guess letting the cat out of the bag cut that possibility off. Every time I drove by I prayed he would be somewhere I could see him but that never happened either. Four days felt like a lifetime to not see his smile.

Step-dick didn't even so much as look at me when I was there. My mother never did either, leaving Shelby and me to fend for ourselves for things to do. She talked about missing Canyon but I didn't have an answer other than the one he gave me. He was busy.

The talk of the school was the town fair that weekend. Apparently everyone goes. Rides, games, a live band and a tractor pull—which I still don't get the point of—was going to happen and Shelby wanted in on the action. The last thing I wanted to do was have anything to do with the people of this town but honestly, I was bored out of my mind.

We changed out of our school clothes and Shelby talked me into wearing the cowgirl boots Canyon bought for me with my yellow sundress. The season had gone from late spring to early summer but the nights still cooled off considerably compared to what the midday sun would bring. I grabbed a jean jacket, brushed my hair, put on lip gloss and was ready to get the night over with before it had even begun.

When we pulled onto the street where the fair was being held, we both said, "Wow" at the same time. It seemed like there wasn't a car missing from the whole town.

"They must either take this seriously or be very bored people."

"I think it looks like fun."

"I bet you do."

After we parked in a field directed by men with flags, Shelby and I walked the mile it took to get there. Music could be heard through the speakers and the lines for the rides seemed endless.

"Which one do you want to go on first?"

It didn't take her two seconds to decide. "That one!"

She had pointed out the one ride that was sure to make anyone vomit. You sit in a circular seat with a wheel in the center that you turn to spin but that wasn't all. The whole thing spun simultaneously making me nauseous just watching it let alone riding it.

"Do you want to maybe ride by yourself?"

"No. Do you not want to come with me?"

"It's not something I would want to do but I will for you."

"Oh my gosh, there's Maddison!"

I wasn't sure if I was grateful for the distraction or not. While she was running over to little girl with long brown hair I was stuck looking ridiculously alone. Maddison was with her parents and it made me sad that my mom and step-dick would never be the type of normal Shelby deserved. Seconds later, the family was walking in my direction. I plastered on a smile and welcomed them in introductions.

"Hi, I'm Arianna, Shelby's sister."

"It's nice to meet you, Arianna. Maddie talks about Shelby all of the time."

"I'm so glad to hear she's making friends here. Moves are always so hard."

"Well, no worries there. It seems your Shelby has hit it off with all of the kids at school."

I looked down to a beaming Shelby.

"Anyway, I know we just met but we wanted to offer you a break. Surely you'd like to go have some fun of your own and we have no problem taking Shelby with us."

Shelby and her friend started jumping up and down. "Please, Arianna."

"Are you sure?"

I wasn't really comfortable with leaving her with them but I caved, gave them my cell phone number and asked for them to call me if they needed anything or were tired of her. They both laughed and assured me she would be a pleasure, then off they went.

I had no desire to even be at this event and I especially didn't want to be by myself. Standing in one spot made me feel like a target so I chose to walk around and at least see what the fuss was all about.

Funnel cake, corndogs, and lemonade stands seemed to be everywhere. A barn full of livestock drew in quite the crowd as well. The music didn't sound half bad and was coming from a white tent pitched over a wooden dance floor. Country music must be all that the people in the town listened to because as I got closer, I noticed a large group line dancing to the band. It was actually kind of neat to watch. They all moved in sync with each other putting most flash mobs to shame. The way the group slapped their heels and stomped their feet mesmerized me.

One person seemed to stand out from all the rest with her long blond hair, perfect body and smile that I remembered all too well. I couldn't take my eyes off of her. The band stopped when the song ended and everyone began to clap while those on the dance floor started to walk off. I assumed that they were going on break but then the guitar began playing a slow ballad and people started their way back onto the floor in pairs.

I couldn't help but notice Brooke was walking onto the floor but this time she was with...

"Are you kidding me?"

Canyon was smiling as he led her to the center, making them the spotlight you couldn't help but focus on. I cringed as he drew her body close, swaying back and forth to the music. Brooke was looking up at him like her world was finally complete and it made me sick.

"They always made the perfect couple. Just look at them. Had it not been for his piece of shit father he would have taken his football scholarship and been with her like they always planned. You'll never stand a chance against what they have. Time to get back in his dad's truck and get the hell out of this town. You never belonged here anyway."

I hated Ashlynn but she had a point. I didn't want to be here any longer than I had to. I never knew he gave up going to college or that he and Brooke had plans that they never got to live out. I reached in my pocket for my phone so I could call Maddie's parents and collect Shelby when Kyle walked up.

"I can't believe you're here."

"Why would you think I wouldn't be?" snapped the queen bitch behind me.

"Arianna, can I have this dance?"

I had my phone out ready to dial, completely ignoring Kyle's offer when Ashlynn began to scream.

"You son-of-a-bitch! You only did that to piss me off. I don't give two shits about you anymore..."

I had turned my back to them and put the phone up to my right ear while I used my left hand to cover the other one so I could hear. The phone continued to go unanswered until it kicked over to voicemail. I was waiting for the beep to leave a message when someone grabbed my arm. I hung up knowing it was Kyle, fully prepared to lay into him when I looked over my shoulder and saw Canyon. Instinctively, I glanced out onto the dance floor where I had last seen him, only to find Brooke standing by herself glaring at me with her hands on her hips.

I turned back to Canyon and snapped, "What are you doing?"

"I didn't expect you to be here." I could smell the alcohol on his breath.

"That's obvious."

"What does that mean?"

I jerked away from him and walked back over to Kyle and Ashlynn arguing.

"I'll take that dance if the offer's still open."

The shock written all over each one of their faces was priceless.

"Absolutely it is."

Kyle took my hand and led me out on the floor right next to a fuming Brooke. I had single-handedly pissed off both of the Stanton sisters.

His hands went around my waist and mine around his neck as we began to sway to the music.

"What changed your mind?"

"Something's just aren't meant—"

"Kyle, I suggest you get your hands off my girl."

I couldn't believe him. I didn't belong to anyone and for him to stake a claim on me after he had the nerve to be here with Brooke was unbelievable!

I looked up to Kyle and said, "Just ignore him."

"I dare you."

Kyle looked at Canyon, down to me and then back to Canyon. He was visibly scared. "Dude, I didn't know."

I felt his arms press into my sides before he pushed me away and walked off. Spinning on my heels, I came face-to-face with a man who didn't intimidate me in the slightest no matter how angry he looked.

Putting my finger in his chest I began, "You're the one that put us here, not me. How dare you scare Kyle like that!"

"If I can't have you, he can't either."

"That's the most childish thing I have ever heard. What makes you think—you know what, never mind. "

I tried to walk away but he grabbed my right arm and held on taking the option away. I wondered if anyone had taken notice and sure enough, when I looked around, the dance floor was practically empty, leaving us as the focal point.

"People are staring."

"Let them stare, Ari. I don't care."

The band started playing but the people continued to stare and began whispering to each other. My mind changed in seconds. I didn't attempt to jerk away this time but instead put my left hand on his shoulder. He had no clue what I was doing. I could tell when he let go of me allowing my right hand to join my left behind his neck.

Just as I thought, the people waited a few seconds but then started walking back out and dancing like nothing ever happened.

"You confuse the hell out of me."

I wasn't positive but all signs pointed to the town plaguing him as an abusive ass just like his father. They were just waiting for him to screw up and I wasn't going to give them that.

"You aren't so easy to read yourself."

"What do you want from me?"

I had the opportunity to drill him about Brooke but I let it go. What I missed most of all was his friendship. If she was what he wanted I had to be okay with that.

"I want my best friend back."

"I never left."

"Listen, I know I'm all over the place and you never know which side of me you're going to get. That should tell you to run as fast as you can the other way and that's exactly what you did. I get it. I just missed you and wished things could be different."

"Why do you have to think so deep all of the time? Yeah I might have needed to clear my mind a little but, Ari, I seriously was training."

There was so much I felt in that moment. Ashamed was in the front of all of them. Here I was pushing him to pursue a passion of his and at the same time I was jealous of the time it took away from me. It wasn't his place to make sure I was happy. There was no place for happiness. Not until I got my money and took down the very people that destroyed me.

"Can we start over?"

"I don't want to, Ari. I kind of like the feel of your lips. In fact I miss them more than I can explain with words."

I was confused yet I understood at the same time as I met him in the middle. Once I could taste how much he still needed me it fueled me to let go of everything other than what I was feeling in that moment. I wanted to stay. For the first time I was admitting to myself that I had something I didn't want to let go of with him.

BARBARA SPEAK

Chapter 17

When the song ended, Canyon didn't want to let me go even though what the band began to play was certainly not a slow song.

"We need to go. I don't know how to line dance."

"You don't have to. Just stay here with me."

"We look ridiculous slow dancing to this."

"I don't get why you care what they think. My family has been the center of this town's drama since I can remember."

And there it was, confirmation that they were looking to label him.

"You could always leave, you know. You have nothing here to hold on to."

"That's where you're wrong. I have everything I ever wanted in the palm of my hands now to prove them all wrong."

His grip on my waist let me know I was included, causing me to smile for the first time in four days.

"What will you do when I go?"

"I will do what I was always meant to do. Raise champion quarter horses and beat out the hardest bull to ride there is."

"That sounds pretty fantastic."

He had a plan. It didn't need to include me and I think that was my favorite part. It seemed I was the only one without a plan.

The song changed again. Canyon pushed me back away from him with the first few plucks of the guitar strings only to grab my hand and pull me back to him. Keith Urban's "Somebody Like You" was a great song on its own but after that night it will always be burned in my mind as the first song Canyon sang in front of me. As he spun me around I couldn't have pulled the smile from my face if I tried. His voice melted me as he sang about how much having me in his life changed him from a place where he was going nowhere to feeling invincible. I couldn't honestly take that credit but knowing these weren't his own words helped me enjoy them.

Rocking me close while holding my hand to his chest, he sang the last few words before he dipped me and the song was over. When I came back up I surprised him by jumping into his arms, grabbing his jaw and kissing him like I never had before.

"You liked that, huh?"

"You singing to me will forever be my favorite thing, Canyon Michaels."

His face turned red showing his embarrassment making him look all the more adorable. He set me down and took ahold of both of my hands pushing me slightly so he could look me up and down.

"Have I told you how much I like those boots on you?"

"I think maybe once before."

"Well, let me tell you again. You look freakin' hot!"

"You're crazy. They're just boots."

"It's not the boots, darlin', it's who's wearing them."

I pulled on his hands to bring my body closer until I was close enough to pick up on his breath again. "That's the booze talking."

"No, that booze you speak of just lets me say things I normally wouldn't say."

"So you wouldn't have scared Kyle off without it?"

"No, I still would have done that. That punk needs to know not to come near you."

"Now you're just being stupid. I feel bad for putting him in that situation to begin with."

"Don't. He was just trying to get a rise out of Ashlynn anyway."

"Speaking of apologies, you need to find Brooke."

"For what?"

"You left her on the dance floor, Canyon!"

"So? She knows we're just friends and that's it."

"You kissing me in front of the whole town pretty much shoots that idea to crap."

"Not you, her."

"That's where you're wrong again. She loves you."

"Now that's where you are insane."

"I know when I see that look what it means and she had it out here with you before you rudely left her to come find me. You came with her, Canyon!"

"No I didn't. I came up here by myself and I'm not going to stand here and argue about my feelings for her with you. What she and I had was a long time ago. It's over. Can we please just drop it and go get some funnel cake?"

No sweeter words were ever heard. He didn't want her anymore. It still had to suck to be her because I knew what I saw and she didn't feel the same way.

"It's always about food with you."

"I'm a growing boy."

"You're big enough. You don't need to grow anymore or you're going to start looking like the Incredible Hulk."

"What are you trying to say? You don't like my body?"

"I love your body just the way it is. Me, on the other hand..."

"You are the sexiest thing God ever created."

"There you go again with the compliments. Stop already, I'm getting a big head."

"Never. You will always know how beautiful I think you are."

"That's it. No more alcohol for you tonight."

We both laughed as we walked to go get his fried, powered-sugar-covered mess of a snack.

Eventually, it was time to collect Shelby. I asked Canyon if he wouldn't mind waiting for her while I used the bathroom and of course he agreed.

Walking away from him didn't keep me from smiling. If anything it only got bigger.

I found the restroom to be a one stall facility and wondered who would ever think that would be enough with a fair this size as I waited for the person occupying it to finish. When the door opened all thoughts left me other than, "Crap"!

"So we meet again."

Brooke walked over to the sink and began to wash her hands. I could have ignored her and just entered the stall but I felt she deserved more than that.

"I'm sorry he chose to leave you standing out there like that. It wasn't nice and..."

"Just don't hurt him."

"Excuse me?"

I wasn't expecting anything less than the bitch I had built her up to be so this comment threw me. She finished washing her hands, turned the water off and grabbed a few towels to dry them before she elaborated.

"He's been through hell and back. I'm sure he told you the gist of it, seeing how close you two apparently are, but you weren't here to watch his life crumble. The trial nearly did him in. He doesn't deserve anything but to be happy so if you plan on sticking this out then do so. If not, leave well enough alone."

I got her point loud and clear but felt no need to explain myself or what was going on between Canyon and me.

"Thank you for the advice."

I knew it wasn't enough and could quite honestly be taken as harsh but I didn't owe her anything. She looked at me and then threw her towel away before walking out of the bathroom leaving me alone with my own thoughts.

Several minutes later, I was walking back to meet up with Canyon and a very happy Shelby.

"Hey there, squirt. Did you have fun?"

"It was so much fun! Maddie and I rode every ride twice. Thank you for letting me go with them."

"Aw, you're welcome. I'm just happy you got to hang out with your friend."

"Maddie comes from a great family. The Popes have been around here for generations."

"It seems most of the town has. Does anyone leave? Never mind, we covered that."

"You'd be right about that. Why would anyone ever want to leave God's county?"

Once we made it outside the designated fairground area Canyon asked, "Where did you park?"

I pointed to the field far off in the distance that went unseen due to the night sky and lack of street lights.

"Out there somewhere."

"Yeah, not gonna happen."

"What do you mean?"

"I mean first off, I've had a few beers and shouldn't be driving. Second, I wouldn't let you walk there by yourselves."

"So are you coming with us?"

"I couldn't ride in that truck again. No, you need to drive mine."

"Why not, it's just a truck," Shelby asked but it was a question neither of us wanted to answer, therefore we just ignored it.

"You want me to leave it here?"

"You think someone is going to steal it? Come on, everyone knows where that thing came from."

"Good point."

"Where did it come from?" Shelby asked again as she grabbed a hold of Canyon's hand while we walked to his truck.

"Oh, I was just teasing your sister a little bit, nothin' you need to worry about."

"You two talk about a lot of stuff I don't need to worry about. When will I get old enough to worry about it?"

Both of us burst out laughing.

Twenty minutes later we were pulling up to Canyon's driveway when he asked me to pass it up and go to ours instead.

"Why? I can drop you off and bring your truck to you in the morning."

"Please just keep going."

I passed his driveway wondering what the heck he was up to. I glanced over at him but it was too dark to see his expression. I felt his hand moments later brush the hair off the back of my neck before he began rubbing muscles I didn't even know were tense.

I pulled into the driveway, cut the lights, and turned off the engine trying to make as little noise as possible.

Shelby leaned into Canyon giving him a hug. "Thank you for making up with Arianna."

"What makes you think we were fighting?"

"I'm just glad you're back."

She climbed out of the truck and ran into the house leaving the door to the house open for me.

"So, do you want to drive home from here? I'm sure you can handle it."

"No, I can't. I've been drinking."

"Give me a break. You haven't touched a beer since I've seen you. What are you up to?"

"I need you to drive me home and make sure I get into the house okay. Hold me all night and make sure I don't get sick. I need..."

"Are you serious? You need me to babysit you?"

"No, I want you to stay with me."

My smile wasn't enough. I leaned across the seat until I could kiss his lips.

"Let me tell Shelby goodnight and I'll be right back."

"I'll be waiting."

I walked through the door expecting to see Shelby telling them about her night or to get chewed out for keeping her out so late but instead, she was already back in her room and my mother and John said nothing. I didn't want to make a big deal out of me being gone overnight again so I just leaned into her room and said, "I'm going to Canyon's, I'll see you in the morning."

"Way to go!"

"What?"

"You got him back for us."

I shook my head back and forth before I decided to walk in and kiss her forehead.

"Good night, Shelby."

"Good night, Ari."

"Did you just call me Ari?"

"Canyon does and I kind of like it."

"You do, do you?"

"Yep."

"Well okay then. I'll see you tomorrow, honey, good night."

I passed by both step-dick and my mother without a word and headed back to the truck. Canyon was waiting outside of it with his arms crossed leaning back against the hood.

"Everything go okay in there?"

"Surprisingly, yes. They haven't said two words to me all week."

"No kidding? Maybe I knocked some sense into that asshole after all."

"I doubt it. He's just stewing waiting to boil over. Shelby is his. For me to take her has to be eating him alive."

"Come on, get in. We can talk about this at my house."

I didn't think there was more to discuss but I also saw no point in arguing either. We both got in and rode the short drive to his place.

Once we walked inside we didn't get past the kitchen before Canyon went right back to the conversation we left off on at my house.

"Let's talk about Shelby and what's going to happen."

"Okay?"

"When you go do you see them staying here? I don't really understand how your family picked this town anyway. They don't fit in at all. John hasn't found a job and your mom does nothing but stare at the wall. I'm not trying to be mean I've just been thinking a lot lately about this and I want you to know I will always be here for her if she needs me. I don't ever want her to feel alone and it's important to me that you understand that."

"Thank you for caring as much as you do but I really don't know what they will do. It wasn't like they picked here, more like it was picked for us."

"What does that even mean? Let me guess, more secrets?"

"I hate that word. I'm not trying to keep secrets from you. It's just a situation where the less you know the better off you are."

"Would knowing maybe help me keep you around a little longer?"

"No, it would create the complete opposite effect. We would move again for sure if anyone found out."

"What makes you think they would find out? I'm not going to say anything."

"Can I ask you a question without you getting mad?"

"Of course."

"Can we please just enjoy our time instead of arguing over something that can't be changed?"

He didn't answer me right away. Instead he walked away into the family room. "Will you come in here with me?"

I followed his voice and found him laying on the couch. Resting my shoulder against the corner of the wall I asked, "Is there room for me?"

He patted the cushion he was laying on. "Right here with me."

I walked the few steps between us and sat in the small space left next to him. "That's not what I had in mind."

He pulled me down on top of him until our noses lined up.

"I missed the hell out of you this week. I thought maybe keeping some space was going to help me prepare for you leaving but it only made me realize I was wasting the few moments I had left with you."

I lowered my lips until they met his softly. "I never got that ride that we planned."

"What ride? Oh! No kidding. We never did do that, did we? Well, when you wake up in the morning, come out to the barn and find me. I'll make sure you get your chance then. Sound good?"

I kissed him once more before I whispered against his lips, "Being here with you right now is better than good."

"Hmmmm, kiss me again so I don't forget."

"Forget what?"

"That you admitted you like being here."

I kissed him with enough conviction he would never question what I wanted again. Even if what I wanted and what I could have were two different things.

Chapter 18

I didn't sleep in like he thought. Instead I was up pretty much the entire night wondering how I let myself fall in this situation to begin with. The way he held me in his arms as his breathing hit my shoulder was something I could see wanting to never let go of.

We both came from crap which had to be the reason we connected so well. I hadn't had friends my whole life that understood me the way Canyon did. He may have pushed a little hard at times but who wouldn't? Knowing someone is keeping something from you would never allow you to feel completely comfortable.

Something he said before we fell asleep stuck in my mind as I tossed and turned.

"I never want you to be her, Ari. My mother kept what my father did to her a secret and it killed her. Secrets never help anyone. I couldn't protect her but I would do anything to keep you safe."

I had thought he was talking about John and reassured him with, "You already are. I have never felt this safe. I mean that."

He didn't correct me but it hit me later that he was referring to my life in general. The whole thing was one big secret. One he couldn't do anything about and for that I felt terrible. He was fighting a losing battle once again.

When he woke at five I watched as his eyes fluttered to open. He noticed me staring and then buried his head into the pillows.

"What are you doing awake?"

"I told you I don't sleep well. Why do you think I could always hear you singing late at night? Good morning, by the way."

"Good morning."

He didn't move. With the pillow over his head he held still for so long I thought it was quite possible that he fell back asleep.

"Hey, don't we need to get up and get to work?"

"You're going to help me?"

"I still need to pay off my debt, don't I?"

"That doesn't include five o'clock work hours. You're more than welcome to stay in bed and try to get some sleep."

"It won't happen so I might as well help, right? Come on, sleepy head, let's get going."

He sat up long enough to throw the pillow at me and then landed hard back on the mattress.

"I didn't peg you for a morning person."

"I'm an unpeggable person all around."

I jumped out of bed and went to the bathroom to brush my teeth, even if it was just with my finger. I found some mouthwash on the counter and took advantage of that as well. By the time I made it back to Canyon's bedroom he was out of bed and stretching. He had his head back with his arms raised in the air over his head but none of that was what my eyes were focused on. The man I had once upon a time seen shirtless was now dressed only in his boxer briefs. Every muscle was flexed as he stretched and I mean EVERY one.

My hands went over my mouth without thought just as he lowered his arms and looked over to me. Instantly, he covered himself and apologized as he ran past me into the bathroom and closed the door behind him. I sat on the bed wondering why it was that I couldn't have just slept like a normal person. He obviously wasn't counting on me being awake when he got up or I'm sure he would have worn shorts.

The door to the bathroom opened with Canyon walking out with a smile on his face and straight to his dresser for some clothes.

"Sorry about that. Morning problems."

He pulled on a pair of jeans and grabbed a long-sleeved t-shirt.

"It's no big deal. I just realized something though... I forgot to grab clothes last night. All I have is my dress. I can't work in that."

"It would make my day to see you try."

"I bet it would, Woody, but I need to go to the house and get some clothes."

"Did you just call me..."

"Woody? I sure did." He tackled me on the bed and started tickling me until he had me screaming, "Stop! Pleeeeeaaaaassssssse!"

I was completely out of breath when he finally let up.

"I kept some things of hers that might fit you."

I had been laughing but went completely silent.

"That's not necessary. I can just go home and..."

"Don't be silly. You and she are practically the same size. How else do you think I would know what jeans would fit you? Just give me a second and I'll grab some stuff for you."

He walked out of the room leaving me feeling awkward at best. I wasn't sure about wearing anything of his mother's. Would seeing me in her clothes stir up memories he wasn't ready to face?

He came back with a handful of things and started laying them out on the bed as he said, "I wasn't sure what you wanted so I grabbed a sweatshirt, a short-sleeved shirt, some jeans, underwear, and some socks..."

"I think I will pass on the underwear, Canyon, but thank you."

"Oh yeah, well, I just didn't want you to not have options. They aren't used or anything. She had bought them right before... and uh...."

I stood up from the bed, walked over to him and wrapped my arms tightly around him. "Thank you."

He rested his arms around my waist while he kissed the top of my head. "It's no problem. Why don't you get dressed and meet me downstairs? I'm gonna go get breakfast started."

"You don't have to cook me breakfast. I'd be okay with a banana and a yogurt."

"You might but I'm not. I need to eat."

"Of course you do."

He slapped my butt and then walked out of the room and down the stairs.

I turned back to the clothes and told myself they were just clothes. It would be no different than trying something on from a store where ten other people had tried on the same thing.

Minutes later I was wearing all of it, aside from the underwear. The t-shirt was under the sweatshirt, the jeans fit perfectly and I had my boots from the night before. I still couldn't believe I could wear a size four but designer clothes obviously catered to the skinny girls of the world and out here they wanted a woman to feel good about her size. Something I very much appreciated.

I could smell the bacon by the time I hit the top of the staircase. The aroma only intensified the closer I got to the bottom. By the time I reached the kitchen I was practically drooling. Eggs were frying, the bacon was popping and Canyon was standing with his back to me singing softly, George Strait's "I Cross My Heart".

Listening to the radio in my truck with only country stations to choose from was teaching me some great songs that I can't say I ever would have learned otherwise.

I stood with my back pressed against the wall listening to something that couldn't be forgotten. He had the voice of an angel even at a volume you could barely make out. He turned for the fridge when he saw me standing there for the first time. The song stopped and so did he.

"Wow." I looked down at myself trying to figure out what could possibly be wow worthy when he said, "I was right. It all fits perfectly."

"Yeah, it does. Thanks again for letting me borrow it."

"You can keep it. There's no sense in it hanging around here in a drawer."

"Oh, uh, okay. So, what are you wanting to eat with that? I can slice fruit or..."

"I was just going to grab some cheese and mushrooms for the eggs. You can get whatever you want out. Feel free."

I waited until he got his things and then started rummaging through drawers for any kind of fruit I could find.

"You don't have any fruit?"

He was stirring the bacon when he looked over his shoulder and apologized. "Sorry about that. I need to go the store. I'm out of almost everything."

I closed the door and went to sit in one of the chairs at the table. "It's no big deal. I can eat whatever."

"Good because I made some killer scrambled eggs."

Thirty minutes later we had cleaned up the mess in the kitchen after we finished practically licking our plates. He wasn't lying about those eggs.

Just as my foot hit the dirt off of the last step of the porch I asked, "So, what's the plan? What do you need me to do first?"

"First things first means I need to make and spread fertilizer. I don't expect you to have anything to do with that,
so why don't you water all the stalls and troughs in the corral?"

"I can handle that."

Once that was done, it was time to feed the horses. Canyon stopped the tractor and came into the barn to show me where the grain barrels were. He even brought me up into the hay loft where he kept all of the alfalfa bales.

"Oh my gosh there is a whole other barn up here. This is huge!"

I had just climbed off the top rung of the ladder into what Canyon called a loft.

"With as many horses as we have had at once we needed a space that could hold enough to feed them all winter."

I heard a cat and then felt something brush up against my leg. Looking down I found an orange tabby staring right back at me.

"That there is Penelope. She's the head barn cat up here. You should be seeing the lot of them pretty soon."

"How many are there?"

I bent down to pet her and could feel her body vibrate from her purring.

"Seven. Well, there were three but four kittens were born six weeks ago."

"You have babies everywhere around here."

"That's what spring brings."

"Why do the cats stay up here?"

"Well, it's warm and there are plenty of mice to catch."

Canyon grabbed a bale off of the stack, opened a door on the floor and dropped it down to the ground underneath us. He grabbed another bale and lifted it up only this time I screamed causing him to almost drop it.

"WHAT?"

I had my hands covering my mouth but the scream kept coming. In my mind I envisioned seeing a cute furry kitten if I was going to be seeing anything. Not some freaky, eyes glowing, huge and I mean HUGE rat staring back at me.

Canyon threw the bale down the hole and then started kicking around the bales I was looking at.

"Ari, talk to me. What did you see?"

My hands were shaking as I tried to explain. "It was the hugest rat I have ever seen, Canyon. I mean like scientific experiment type huge."

He moved some bales around until he picked up one and the loudest hiss came with it.

"Holy shit!" Canyon dropped the bale immediately and looked over to me holding his hands straight out at me. "Okay, everything's okay, I just wasn't expecting it is all. Why don't you go back down and I will take care of the opossum."

"What the heck is an opossum? The granddaddy of all rats?"

"More like a kangaroo, really."

"What?"

"I'm going to try to get it out of here but they get mean. Do you want to stick around or go play with the puppies?"

Naturally, I wanted to be as far as possible from that thing, but I was also curious as to how Canyon planned to pull this off.

"I'll stay, just way over there."

"If you're sure."

He walked to the far wall where he got a huge fork and began heading back to the spot it was hiding while I made my way to the other side of the loft.

"You're not going to poke it, are you?"

"No. This is just to move it."

"You don't have a shovel?"

"Not up here."

He set the fork down and started moving bales around before he grabbed the fork again and pushed it down. I wasn't sure what was happening until the damn thing ran out toward him hissing and made Canyon not only scream but jump three feet in the air, causing him to throw the fork and land on the bale beside him. I have never laughed so hard in my life! Seeing Canyon scared of an opossum or whatever it was had me nearly pissing my pants.

"You find this funny?"

I couldn't stop laughing long enough to answer him. He got down and grabbed the fork again, sliding it down and under the opossum. Every time the fork touched it, it turned toward Canyon hissing. Eventually, Canyon maneuvered it to the opening where he pushed it to fall down on top of the bales below. I hurried to the hole so I could watch it land before it ran off.

"That was priceless!"

Canyon dropped the fork to the floor and then scooped me up, carrying me over to the stack of bales behind us.

"I told you they're mean."

"When you screamed like a girl..."

"Like a girl?" He dropped me on the hay and then turned and walked towards the ladder.

"Where are you going?"

"Away from you." He stepped down each rung until I could no longer see him.

"What do you want me to do about the door?"

"Close it for me, please."

At least he said please. He wasn't too mad at me.

After feeding all the horses and dogs I was exhausted. How he managed all this on his own amazed me. Canyon finished up with the crap and met me back at the barn about an hour later.

"I need to condition a few of them today but what do you say about taking that ride first?"

My face lit up. "Really? I would love that."

"Let's get the tack together first."

I remembered everything he taught me and shortly after getting the horses they were fully equipped and ready to go.

"You take Magnus, I'll grab Winston."

"Sounds good to me. Magnus and I have an understanding, don't we, boy?"

I was rubbing behind Magnuses' ears and he loved it. Every once in a while he would push his head into my side letting me know just how much.

"He likes you, that's for sure."

"The feeling is mutual."

After we were both on, Canyon made a noise and the horses took off. I wasn't the least bit scared anymore. Riding that fast through the open fields felt like home to me. The wind had my hair flying behind me as if we were flying. I looked over at Canyon and caught him staring at me wearing the hugest smile.

"Come on," he yelled. "This way."

He pulled a hard right and led us across a creek and up a hill until we reached the top and came to a stop. The sun was just coming over the mountain side and it was purely breathtaking.

"Oh my gosh. It's gorgeous."

"Isn't it? My mom would bring me out here as a kid and we would just sit here for as long as it took for it to rise."

"I bet that was amazing."

"It was."

We both sat there and stared at nature in its finest form.

"Thank you for sharing this with me."

"No, thank you for letting me."

The horses were eating the grass below us without a care in the world as we enjoyed the view. Eventually, Canyon picked up his reins again and said, "You ready to head back? I have to work on the horses especially that one if I plan to race him."

"You aren't going to ride him in the race are you?"

"Hell no! I'm twice the size of a jockey. Ever since you convinced me to keep Magnus I have been talking to a few that I know. I think I have one lined up."

"Does he come out here and work with him too?"

"No. Eventually I will send Magnus to him. That way they can bond before the race."

"Gotcha. Well, all right, let's get heading back."

Canyon and Winston led off but this time we went a different way back. New fields and trees, mountains and valleys to see. His property was a complete slice of heaven and I could understand why he never wanted to leave. I was beginning to feel the same way.

We got back and stripped Winston down but he kept Magnus ready. I climbed up on the top rail of the fence and watched as he tied Magnus up and went to grab another horse. This one was not one of the horses I was familiar with. He led him out and put all of the equipment he took off of Winston onto him.

"What's his name?"

"Bud."

"Are you kidding me?"

"I wish. I lost a bet and had to name him after a beer."

"You couldn't have thought of Guinness or something?"

"We were drinking Budweiser at the time."

"Poor horse."

"Yeah, I have to live with that bet every day."

He was on top of him and walking him to the running path when he looked back over his shoulder. "Are you gonna hang out and watch?"

"If you don't mind?"

"Not at all. See ya in a bit."

With one swift kick they were off. I couldn't believe how fast they were going right from the start. I guess a quarter mile wasn't very long of a stretch to run but damn it took them no time. Back and forth they went for a good thirty minutes and I never tired of seeing the dust fly behind them. When it was over, Canyon hooked Bud up to the turning wheel and let him walk in circles before he came over to the fence I was sitting on to kiss me.

"What did you think?"

"It's pretty impressive."

"Bud's my slowest. If you liked that, it only gets better."

"I can't wait to see."

Four horses later it still never got old. After the first two had their run I took on the responsibility of taking the one walking in the circle back to the barn to replace it with the next. It fascinated me that they had the speed and agility that they were showcasing and the fact that Canyon was creating this allowed me to respect him that much more. He was brilliant for taking wild stallions and creating a whole new line for himself.

Canyon had run the final horse for the day and I couldn't help but tell him just how proud I was of his accomplishments. "All this has been drilled into me since I learned to walk. I haven't done anything that can be called mine, yet. When one of these horses wins, the world will remember the name..."

Clap. Clap. Clap. Clap.

"Michaels!"

Both of our heads whipped around to see a man walking through the barn toward us.

"What in the hell is he doing here?" Canyon obviously was talking more to himself than me because I hadn't the faintest idea who the man was.

"What do you want?"

"What do I want? Well, that's a dumb question, boy. Seems I hear you sold a few horses a while back."

"And?"

Canyon was fuming as the man came closer.

"And half of that's mine."

"The hell it is! You have nothing to do with this ranch anymore. This is all mine."

"Sorry to disappoint you. Actually, no it's not, you piece of shit. This business was your dad's and mine, nothing about it is yours."

"You've lost your mind, old man. Why don't you go back where you came from and get the hell off my property."

"This may be your property but you sold those horses under the stable name and that is mine."

I was bouncing back and forth between the two trying to follow the conversation. At the same time, I was ready to jump in front of Canyon if necessary to keep him from killing what I had figured out to be his uncle.

"You're insane. You both destroyed the company, tore it to shreds! There was nothing left. This is ALL MINE!"

"We'll see what the lawyers say."

"Are you kidding me? Like this family hasn't gone through enough!"

"You little punk ass. You think I want to take it easy on you? I'm going to do everything in my power to make you suffer. You are the very reason this family is the way it is!"

"Me? How can you blame me? He killed my mother!"

"You little..."

His uncle was coming at him and Canyon was advancing ready to blow. Without thinking, I jumped down from the fence and was between the two of them holding them back with each arm while I screamed, "ENOUGH!"

"Darlin', I suggest you move. This is between my nephew and me."

"Ari, baby, go inside."

"Cany—"

"GO INSIDE!"

He had never yelled at me before making me tense up immediately. I didn't know what to do. If I walked away they would kill each other for sure. So I chose in that second to stay put.

"Listen right now, both of you. I'm not going anywhere. You aren't doing this today." I looked at his uncle first. "As you have stated, this is his property so you are trespassing. If I go anywhere it will be to call the police and have you arrested. You need to leave." Then it was Canyon's turn. "He's not worth this."

Both men were seething mad and I doubted they even heard me until his uncle broke the stare down contest between them and stepped back.

"You will be hearing from my lawyer!"

"As if you can find one that will represent you. Good luck!"

His uncle continued to stare him down as he walked backwards. "You just wait and see."

He turned and walked back through the barn. Canyon watched him go until he was out of sight and then kicked the bottom post of the fence snapping it in two.

"I'm screwed!"

Chapter 19

I didn't know anything about the business side of this but if he never changed the name, his uncle just might have a stake in it as he said.

"So can you switch it now? He might have some claim but only to the few you sold already, right? Anything in the future would be yours."

His hands had gone to his head out of frustration, knocking his baseball hat to the ground as he rubbed back and forth over his face and back up to his hair.

"I wish it was that simple. Everything I have built up to this point is in the name of the company. He could come after me for any future earnings from the livestock I created. SHIT!"

He kicked the broken board again. This time, it splintered and threw wood particles everywhere.

"Okay, so you fight it. We both know this isn't fair and the law has to see it that way."

"I wish you were right but I can't see it working out for me. Nothing ever does."

"Please don't give up. You tell me all the time how I need to fight. I'm here. I will help you anyway I can."

"But for how long?"

That question changed everything. "As long as you need me."

"That might be something you come to regret saying."

"Maybe, but right now it's all that I have to offer."

"Then I will take it."

The mood never went back to the place we were at that morning. There was no longer a smile that was genuine coming from either of us. We both knew his uncle had a point and the last thing Canyon wanted to do was be in business with that scum bag.

Eventually, I decided I needed to go home after hours of Canyon looking on the Internet for laws around this mess and coming up with nothing. He was so engrossed with the computer I simply kissed him goodbye and promised I would be back the next day. He muttered a simple, "Bye" in return and went back to his research.

I walked home wishing I could ask John for advice, but I knew nothing good could come from asking him anything.

The following day Canyon wasn't much better when I got there. He was sweet as usual but the light in him had burnt out. He was a shell of the man I knew two days prior. I hated his family for putting him through even more hell than he already was forced to endure.

We played with the puppies, worked with the foals and even went out for another ride trying to do anything that would allow him to clear his head. Nothing worked.

The rest of the week went pretty much the same way. I had school, Canyon trained, and then I would meet him back at his place. We worked in the barn, watched some TV, and I would go home. I didn't know what he needed but I knew being there helped. At least he wasn't alone.

Friday came and with it so did the rodeo. I got home from school with enough time to change my clothes, grab Shelby and head over to Canyon's. We pulled into the driveway but before I could even come to a complete stop, Shelby was throwing her door open, jumping from the truck and running into the waiting open arms of Canyon. The smile was back and I learned quickly Shelby was the key to it.

I got out and walked toward the two. "What am I chopped liver?"

"Hey there, darlin'. You ready to go do this?"

I walked over and kissed him before saying, "I sure am. This is going to be amazing to watch."

I didn't want to bring up how happy I was to see him smile. It could trigger him to go back which was the last thing I wanted.

"I can't wait to see the horses."

"The horses?"

He began tickling her to the point she was screaming for help before he stopped.

"Little girl, you see plenty of horses here. You better be excited to watch me."

"You're going to ride a bull. That's not fun."

"No, it's awesome!"

"No, it's not."

"Shelby!"

"Don't yell at her she's just being honest."

"Honesty can be rude and in this case it is."

"I just don't want him to get hurt."

Canyon bent down to be on her level. "I've been doing this a long time. Don't you worry, I'll be fine."

We all loaded into Canyon's truck and headed off on the hour long road trip.

Shelby wanted to play on her iPad the entire time in the back seat leaving Canyon to wonder why. I didn't want to explain in front of her that this was the standard practice with our family. The back seat didn't exist. Instead, I threw back questions periodically to her. What I got in return was only what was required to answer the question and then she was back to her game.

Canyon and I chose to fight over what music was better the entire ride. I wanted top forty where he demanded country or classic rock. Truthfully, we both enjoyed all of it, but it was fun to bicker over.

We made it to the arena right on time. The parking lot was filled with trucks and horse trailers. It was too early for the ticket holders to arrive yet. Canyon explained everything to Shelby and me as he walked us through the back area where all the riders were getting ready and then out to the arena floor. Looking up into the stands made everything different. It looked so much bigger from that view point.

"Over there you'll have the barrel racing, the steer wrestlers and the tie down roping challenge done by one person or a team of people. Those are all timed events. Then you get to see the rough rider events. That's what I'm in. There's going to be saddle bronc riding, bareback bronc riding and finally the bull riding. A lot is going to be going on but I know you are going to love this."

"So much is different from this and the PBR."

"To tell you the truth, this is what I miss the most. The PBR is the final level of bull riding. This is where it all comes from. The heart and passion starts here. You can feel it."

He was so passionate as he spoke that when I looked down at Shelby, she was mesmerized. "How did you go from being thrown by a horse to bulls if there is such a thing as bucking broncos?"

"What man wants to stay on a horse when he could have a two thousand pound bull between his legs?"

"Only the wimpy ones, I guess."

"You got that right."

He wrapped his arm over my shoulder and pulled me in for a kiss. I loved the taste of him. Whether he gave me a simple peck or we were making out, the taste never changed. I craved him.

I looked down at Shelby after we broke away expecting her to say, "Eeewww" but instead caught her beaming smile.

Eventually, Shelby and I were forced to join the waiting fans in our seats as the rodeo was getting ready to start. Canyon held my hand as he walked us to the hall door squeezing it periodically just so I would look over at him.

"I love your eyes."

"Where did that come from?"

"I don't know. I was just remembering the fire in them the first time I saw you."

"That seems like forever ago."

"I wouldn't trade a minute of it."

We reached the door to the hall and it was time to say goodbye. Shelby hugged onto his leg before letting go and said, "Don't die."

"WHAT?"

"SHELBY!"

"What? I don't want him to die."

"He's not going to die and we really need to work on that honesty thing with you, geez."

Canyon laughed then kissed me one last time before he rubbed the top of Shelby's head and started walking away. "I won't die just for you, Shelby girl!"

"Sounds good!" she yelled back before the door closed and we were on our way.

When we got to our seats, Shelby never stopped with the questions.

"What comes first? Is it the barrel racing?"

"I want to see little kids like me. Are any going to be here doing stuff?"

"When is it Canyon's turn?"

"What's a bronco? Does that mean all boy horses?"

"Do girls compete too?"

"When does the bull riding start?"

"That was cool but I'm ready to see Canyon."

"That was dumb."

"When is Canyon going to ride?"

"I DON'T KNOW!"

She wore my patience out after two hours of nonstop questions. By the third I had lost it.

"I'm hungry."

"I'm thirsty."

"I need to go the bathroom."

Finally, the bull riding started. It was the last event of the night and as much as I enjoyed watching everything else, I too was ready for Canyon. My nerves had gone into overdrive as all the cowboys lined the wall behind the metal bars bringing me back to the first time Canyon made it obvious he wanted me around. That seemed like forever ago too.

"I see him!"

I looked but couldn't find him. "Where?"

"Right there."

She was pointing but I still only saw the silhouettes of the men. Shelby began waving with a huge smile on her face as I worked like crazy to spot him and then I spotted him. Dressed in a black cowboy hat and his red plaid shirt, he looked sexier than ever waving back at Shelby.

"Do you see him now?"

"Yeah, I can see him."

He pulled his hat off with his right hand and with his left he blew me a kiss. I never felt as adored as I did when I was with him. I knew this was a big moment for him and I just prayed hard it went as good as he hoped it would.

Rider after rider were thrown. The bulls they stocked for this event were meaner than crap. Shelby covered her eyes countless times when riders would fall either underneath the bull or near their feet. By the time it was Canyon's turn, only two men had stayed on for the full eight seconds. Shelby was sitting on the edge of her seat bouncing her right leg, mimicking every move I made.

"Are you ready for this?"

"I'm scared."

I grabbed her right hand with my left and squeezed.

"He's a pro. This will be amazing, we just have to watch and see."

There was a problem with his strap or something because it was taking longer than it should. All of a sudden the bull started thrashing around in the pen. I stood up hoping to be able to see better and Shelby followed.

"What's going on?"

"I don't know."

The bull was kicking with everything he had, trapped inside the small space. I watched Canyon get yanked from him while the bull was still going berserk.

The announcer came on the loud speaker and explained that they would be trading out Canyon's bull. He had apparently turned himself around inside the holding area. The gate opened and out came one very pissed off bull without a rider kicking at anything that came near him.

After he was done throwing his temper tantrum he slowly walked through the open passage bulls used to leave, with two men in orange shirts on either side ready to close him in. It took five more minutes before Canyon was sitting on another bull. This one was named Gun Slinger.

"Is it going to happen now?"

"If nothing else goes wrong it is."

Again, Canyon pulled on the strap, but this time he followed by tapping the gate and grabbing on to it. He was ready and I was scared to death.

The door flew open and out came Gun Slinger crazier than the bull before him. Canyon moved with every turn and kick the bull threw. Just as Chett had said, he could predict what was coming and it was beautiful to watch. The buzzer went off letting us know he had made it and the crowd went wild. Shelby stood up clapping which was absolutely priceless to see the pride in her eyes as Canyon jumped off the bull.

I heard the man seated next to me gasp, drawing my attention back to Canyon, when I noticed something was wrong. He was jumping beside the bull with each move it made, while at the same time three men were on the other side grabbing at the rope. It was stuck and the longer it took, the more anxious I became.

The bull took one strong turn, throwing his back end to the right taking Canyon with him, all the while stripping the three men helping Canyon from being able to do anything. His arm looked like it could be ripped off the way he was getting swung around. Five more guys were there to replace the three that fell immediately doing everything they could to distract the bull. Thank God it worked. Another man in an orange shirt reached up with a knife and cut the rope letting Canyon free.

Gun Slinger went charging after two of the men with flags while four others in orange pulled Canyon from the dirt and out of the riding area.

He wasn't moving.

I grabbed Shelby's hand, yanked her out of her chair and practically drug her down the steps. Once we were in the hall I let go and screamed, "Follow me!"

I ran down the hall, through the door, down more stairs ending up on the dirt floor where everyone was either waiting for their turn or hanging out.

I looked back to make sure Shelby was still with me and then started pushing through people again. When I couldn't find him, I started asking. When they didn't have an answer, I started screaming his name. Clearly someone had to know where the man who just got dragged off unconscious would be located.

"Ma'am, he's with the medic. Go down the hall and make your first left."

I didn't turn to even see who was talking, I simply said, "Thank you" as I followed the path he gave me.

We reached the door when Shelby grabbed my hand and pulled me to stop.

"Is he dead, Arianna?"

"No, honey, he's not dead. He's just really hurt I bet."

"Are you sure?"

"Yes, Canyon's going to be fine."

Just then the door opened almost hitting us as a man walked out. "I'm sorry, ladies, hope I didn't get you with that door. Is there something I help you with?"

"Is Canyon in there?"

He took his hat off and then smiled.

"You bet he is and I know good and well one look at y'all's faces is just what he needs right now. Follow me."

We walked through the door and followed him back to a room with nothing but a gurney and Canyon Michaels.

"Canyon!"

Shelby tore across the space and was wrapping her arms around him instantly. I, on the other hand, was trying to get my emotions under control. Tears were falling from my face but at the same time I wanted to kill him with my bare hands. He kissed Shelby on the forehead and then looked at me.

"Come here, darlin'."

I stood in the same spot unable to move. Canyon let go of Shelby and stood from the bed, closing the space between us. Once he was in front of me his left hand lifted my chin allowing me to feel the calloused fingertips I had become all too familiar with.

"Look at me."

I had closed my eyes trying to remember why falling in love with him was a bad idea. But no matter how I looked at it, the thought of losing him kept flashing before me and it was something I no longer thought I could take.

"Hey, look at me. I'm right here and I'm not going anywhere."

I opened my eyes and looked up into his. His genuine concern for me made no sense because I was the one that was scared to death for him.

"Are you really okay?"

"Yeah, I'm good. In fact I'm great."

"How? You were stuck, Canyon! Your body was thrown around like a damn rag doll. You weren't moving!"

"This isn't my first rodeo, darlin'. I've been through plenty worse. This is all just part of the ride."

"Then I hate the ride."

"Don't say that. This is what it's about. I'm going to get hurt, it comes with the territory but you have to understand, this is where I belong."

I didn't know anymore how I could understand it and that bothered me even more. I pushed him to do this. Why couldn't I be supportive? It should have been easy but it was the hardest lie I've ever told.

"You're right. And heck, you might win tonight."

"I will, no questions about that."

"Cocky much?"

"Always when it comes to riding." His smile stretched to his eyes. He was in his element and I had to be there for him like I promised. Even if that came with my new found hatred for bull riding.

He won, just like he said. He even lined up rodeos every weekend after that for the next month out. Shelby and I stayed off to the side while we watched as he talked to all of the big dogs running the show.

"You're not really happy for him, are you?"

I looked at Shelby and wondered if I could tell her the truth or if I should protect her from worrying. "I just got scared is all. Believe me, he's on top of the world and for that I'm happy."

"You like him a lot, I can tell."

"I'm trying my best not to but sometimes the heart wants what it wants."

The ride home was spent listening to Canyon go on and on about getting back into the PBR. It was going to take some work but he was ready. All of his coming events were PBR sanctioned which meant that he would need to bring in twenty-five hundred dollars from those events for his application to qualify. It was doable if he won all of them and listening to him, he had no doubts he would do it.

We took Shelby home but Canyon wanted me to stay with him again. All that talk about him riding made me really want my own bed but I couldn't tell him that without an explanation, so instead I went with him. We made it to the couch in his family room cuddling and were watching TV before he called me out.

"What is it?"

"What is what?"

"Don't play stupid, you've been extra quiet. Something's bothering you, just say it."

"Fine, if you want the truth here it is. I don't get it. We walked in tonight and all you talked about was your love of the rodeo. The simple pleasure that came from it and then everything switched over to being about the PBR. I wanted you to be happy but now you just seem like you're on a mission to kill yourself and I don't understand. Why is this more important than anything else for you to do?"

He sat up and swung his legs around so his feet could hit the floor. Looking up at the picture of him and his mother he said, "The quarter horse business was for my mom. She started it all. She was the one with all the money when they got married. Then things changed after she had me. My dad started making decisions with his brother that she didn't like but he took her vote away from her. They started making and building a brand that soon became recognized by some of the top buyers in the industry. The horses became about the money and were no longer treated as pets the way she always wanted them to be. I know that probably doesn't seem important to you but keeping the legacy away from David means everything to me. If I can get to the PBR again I could take the whole thing. I was on my way when my dad stripped me of everything I love and caused me to quit."

"What happens if you win? How does that change anything?"

"It would change everything, Ari. The payout is a million dollar bonus."

And that made it all crystal clear. He could buy out his uncle.

"It's the only way, darlin'. I could make that and more off of Magnus but he would take fifty percent and I don't want him having a dime of it."

"I get it. Truly I do and as much as it scares me you're going to get hurt I will be here for you no matter what."

"That means everything to me. I can't lose you now."

Chapter 20

Each week that went by, Canyon got closer and closer to his goal. Shelby and I went to each rodeo praying to God that he would come out unscathed and not only did he, but he was setting new record highs for himself. Canyon seemed on top of the world but there was something he forgot that I couldn't let slip my mind. My birthday was the same day as the last rodeo he would enter before qualifying. We only had two days until I turned eighteen and a week until I graduated. Time wasn't on our side anymore.

It was Wednesday right after school let out and I had plans to meet up with Canyon over at Jason's house. Everyone else was going on and on about graduation and what they were going to do after. I only had one thing I allowed myself to focus on and that was Canyon. I needed him to be okay before I left. It was the least I could do.

Jason had the training area Canyon was using and I had started going over there and watching them work the day after his first ride. He convinced me that watching would make me more comfortable and as much as I doubted him, he was right. Getting caught up in the rope strap was extremely rare. The way Canyon rode made it almost seem easy and I knew full well there is nothing about riding a bull that is easy. It was the grace in which he did it. The way his body moved instead of the jerking you see when you watch other riders do the same thing. He had a natural gift. That's for sure.

I pulled into Jason's ready for the hug and kiss I always had waiting for me but what I got was no Canyon. I knew he was there. I parked right next to his truck. Finding it odd, I walked around back and spotted Jason right away standing next to the practice ring.

Walking toward him I asked, "Where's Canyon?"

He didn't answer but instead pointed over to the back side of the house. "He's on the phone with his lawyer. Whatever it is, it's not good."

I shook my head looking over at Canyon. "He can't catch a damn break."

"Does seem that way, doesn't it?"

I started on my way over to him when Jason yelled, "I wouldn't do that."

"Thanks for the advice."

I didn't take it. Over the last month and a half when things got tough we were what each other needed. Why would this time be any different?"

The closer I got, the more I picked up from the conversation.

"How can he do that?"

"Well do something! Stop it from going forward until I get the money."

"Delay it!"

Canyon wouldn't look at me. He kept his head down and was kicking around the dirt from under his boots.

I reached out to put my hand on his shoulder when he jerked back as if my touch could burn him. My hand recoiled but it wasn't enough to make me give up from wanting to be there when he needed me.

"All right, just call me if anything else comes up."

Canyon hung up the phone and then looked at me for the first time with rage in his eyes.

"What happened? Whatever it is, we can get through this."

"No 'WE' can't. Your precious step-dad has decided to represent David. The only asshole that would be willing to take his case is your step-dad, Ari. They are moving to freeze my assets!"

"Oh no! Oh my God! I am so sorry." I wrapped my arms around his shoulders but he was as stiff as a board. "Hey! Listen to me. They won't win."

I brought my lips to his but what I got in return was worse than the first time I tried to kiss a boy in fourth grade. I pulled back and looked in his eyes.

"You're not blaming me for this, are you?"

He leaned forward and kissed me but it was the most pathetic form of a kiss a person could give and then he pushed me away from him.

"No, Ari, it's not your fault. Nothing is anyone's fault. Shit just happens."

He walked back over to Jason, slapped him on the back and said, "Let's do this." never looking back at me. I stood there thinking, "How is my step-dad representing his uncle?" I didn't even know he had a license to practice in Montana let alone handle a lawsuit over horses. He was so far out of his league with this it could only mean one thing. He wanted to hurt me and he was using Canyon to do it.

I walked over to the metal fence where the two of them stood talking.

"Sorry to interrupt but I wanted you to know I'm gonna get going. I'll see you later back at your place, Canyon. Bye, Jason."

That got Canyon's attention. "Where are you going?"

I had started walking toward my truck when I turned to answer him. "There's a few things I need to take care of. I'll see you later."

I spun around and continued to walk to my truck until I was inside of it, turning it on. Some part of me thought he would chase me down to find out what I had up my sleeve. When he didn't, I knew he blamed me for playing a part in all this and in a way he was right. If I had never come to this stupid town, my step-dick wouldn't be here either.

I called Maddie's parents first and asked if they would mind watching Shelby for me for a few hours. Her mother answered and agreed without question. I thanked her and drove straight home. Leaving the truck on, I walked in the door and went straight to Shelby's room.

"Hey, squirt. Would you like to go over to Maddie's and play for a little while?"

"Really? I can?"

"Sure you can. My truck's running, grab whatever you want to take and let's go."

I walked back down the hall and saw John in the kitchen. He looked at me wearing an expression that could only be read one way: he was baiting me. There was a time for that and this wasn't it.

"I'm ready."

Shelby came up behind me with her backpack slung over her shoulder.

"Where are you taking her?"

"She's going over to a friend's house to play."

"What makes you think..."

I grabbed Shelby and pushed her out the door without listening to the rest of his rant. I closed it behind me and walked back to my truck waiting for him to come storming out. I thought he may have decided it wasn't worth it but was proven wrong as we backed out of the driveway and the front door flew open. I hit the gas and sped off down the street.

"What are you doing?"

"I'm taking you to Maddie's."

"What's going on?"

"Nothing you need to worry about."

"Not that again."

"Yep."

Maddie rode Shelby's bus so every time we passed her house Shelby would point it out. It wasn't too far from town and took us less than ten minutes to get there. Once we were in the driveway, Maddie was running toward the truck.

"Someone's excited you're here."

Shelby didn't say anything she just unbuckled her seat belt, jumped out of the car and ran into the house behind Maddie. I got out but Maddie's mom stopped me by holding up her hand.

"Don't worry, I got her. Go do whatever it is you want. She's safe here."

"Thank you so much."

"Anytime, hun."

I got back in and drove to the very place I had just left. Minutes later, I was pulling back in the driveway ready to kill him while my body shook like a chicken. My nerves were shot. I was scared to death but tired of him and everything that came along with having him in my life.

I threw the front door open intentionally, knowing he would come.

"What the hell do you think you are doing around here? You think you can just come and go as you please and take my daughter with you. By the way, where is she?"

"She's safe."

"What the fuck do you mean 'she's safe'? Where is my daughter?"

"Did you take the case on purpose?"

He was fuming but I caught the small smirk he let escape before he covered it up. "You bet your ass I did."

"Why? How is hurting Canyon going to make any difference to you or me? I'm leaving. You can have your precious family. He has nothing to do with any of this!"

"You took my life away from me, Arianna. You think I care who I have to take down to hurt you. You can lie all you want but this is eating you up inside, just like I want it to. I don't give two shits about that boy or his uncle."

"I didn't take anything away from you! I didn't force you to get involved. I had nothing to do with you taking that money!"

He slapped me. As hard as he could, he struck me right across my left cheekbone. My hand immediately covered it, rubbing it back and forth.

"You think I had a choice? No one would hire me. I had to take that money, you little bitch."

"You are a sorry excuse for a man. You could have protected me. You got caught up with the wrong people and used me to get out of it."

"You think you have it all figured out but you don't know shit. If that deal didn't come with the terms it did from Michael Thompson himself I would have left your ass for them to kill you. It's where you belong."

"You don't think that without me they wouldn't have killed you? I was your life preserve."

"Are you kidding me? You think you saved us? This is ALL YOUR FAULT!"

"You keep telling yourself that. I'm done being your punching bag for insults and blame. You got yourself in this mess. Now stay away from Canyon."

"Or what? He will beat me up? I'm not scared, Arianna. Not in the slightest."

"You don't have to be scared of him. It's me that's coming for you. When you least expect it, it will be me that brings you down."

I walked out, the door slamming closed behind me. My whole body was shaking so hard I thought I might possibly pass out. I managed to climb up into the cab of my truck, drove over to Canyon's and laid down on the seat breathing slowly until he got there.

Twenty minutes later I heard the crunch of the gravel crushing under his tires as his truck pulled up the driveway. I sat up and opened the door to my truck just as he got out of his.

"Hey there. How did practice go?"

As Canyon walked toward me I watched his expression change the closer he got.

"Practice was fine." He lifted his right hand to cup my jaw bone on the side of my face John had struck. "I see you didn't have a good time. Can you please explain to me why you would leave me to go there? Please, Ari, tell me because I am doing everything I can to keep myself from driving over there and killing him. Only now, if I even touch the son-of-a-bitch, I'm threatening an officer of the court. My uncle could use it against me in court, Ari! So please, tell me why."

"Calm down, baby. I'm okay and you don't need to go do anything. All I need is for you to hold me and let me know that we're going to be all right. I'm not feeling so confident about that right now."

"You and me, we're always going to be good. Even when it gets bad there's gonna be good in us. Don't doubt that."

"We are going to fix this."

"I don't see how, but I have faith."

"Your lawyer can't come up with anything?"

"My lawyer is the attorney that handles my estate. He isn't equipped to handle a case like this."

"Why not get a different one?"

"I don't have any money for a retainer."

"Then it will be up to us."

"You have far more confidence in us than I do, that's for sure."

"At least one of us does."

"Come on, let's get you inside. I want some ice on that cheek of yours. Just tell me one thing. Did you say something that made it worth the pain?"

"I sure did. Standing up to that man felt amazing."

"I'm proud of you, darlin'. Just know you aren't going back over there until all this is settled."

"You can't expect me to do that."

"I can and I am. If I can't keep him from putting his hands on you there I sure as hell can here. If he steps foot on my property, I'm laying his ass out."

I sat at the kitchen table holding ice to my face while Canyon cooked dinner for us. He was making something he called pork and bean hot dish. Only it was browned hamburger instead of pork which made no sense, seasoned salt, garlic powder, barbecue sauce and a can of pork and beans. You have no idea how gross it looked when he made my plate but then he put Parmesan cheese over the top and I flat refused to eat it.

"Just try it."

"No way."

"Come on. I know it looks gross but I swear it's good. Don't be a sissy."

I picked up my fork feeling completely on the spot with him staring at me and took a bite. Believe it or not, it was delicious. Everything he seemed to make was. After we ate and finished cleaning the kitchen, I had to leave and go get Shelby.

"You're not going by yourself."

"Canyon, you have to stop this. I'm going to be fine. You have to trust me."

He grabbed me and picked me up, resting me on the counter coming to stand between my legs. "I can't let you go."

"I'm just getting my sister and taking her home."

"I'm not just talking about tonight, Ari."

I held his jaw with my thumbs as my fingers rested behind his ears. "You have to know that what I'm doing is for you. I need you to know this."

"I don't know anything, you won't tell me."

"I can tell you that you make me feel more when I'm with you than I have ever felt before. That every day has gotten brighter because you were a part of it. That one of your smiles beats down all of the bad in my day. I may not be able to tell you everything but what I can is worth so much more."

I didn't give him the chance to fight with me. Instead, I took his lips and sucked off the taste of him. Our tongues met and everything in my body went limp. His hands went up the back of my shirt and began rubbing me up and down before they slid to my stomach.

My hands came down from his head and met with his, stopping this from going any further.

"Hey." He continued to kiss me completely ignoring the fact I was trying to stop. "Canyon." His tongue licked across my bottom lip causing my body to quiver. "Listen to me, baby. I have to go get Shelby. I can't leave her there all night."

He finally stopped. "Fine. But you will come back here after you take her home, right?"

"Yes, I will come back. I promise."

I gave him one last peck on the lips before I jumped down from the counter and started for the door.

"Don't miss me too much while I'm gone."

"Don't you worry. I won't think about you for a second."

I smiled as I walked out the door until I climbed in my truck thinking the whole time, "How did I ever get so lucky?"

Chapter 21

Shelby didn't want to leave but it was nearing seven-thirty and she still had to shower and get ready for bed.

"Maybe you can come back another time."

"Of course you can, Shelby. You're welcome at our house anytime. Maddie needs to start getting ready for bed too."

She wasn't happy about it but I finally got her to give Maddie a hug, thank her mom for having her and into the truck. When we pulled into the driveway, Shelby turned to me.

"What happened?"

"It's nothing—"

"I need to worry about? Well, you're wrong. I am worried."

"Don't be. It will all work itself out. Now come on. I need to get you inside."

I hated leaving her hanging like that but I didn't have the answers she needed. She wanted me to reassure her and that's what I was trying to do. I got out before she could ask any more questions, walked to the front door, and turned to wait for her. Once we were inside, I walked straight back to my bedroom and began to pack my bag.

"Where are you going?"

I turned to see Shelby at my door. "I'm going to stay at Canyon's tonight. I'll see you tomorrow when you get home from school."

"Are you really coming back?"

I set the bag down and walked over to her.

"I would never leave you without saying goodbye and this isn't goodbye. This is me just telling you I will see you tomorrow. Now you need to get in the shower, little one."

"Okay, but promise you will come back tomorrow."

"I promise."

Shelby got in the shower and I walked out of the door without looking back. I hated everything about that house other than that little girl.

I got in the truck and was backing out of the driveway when my gas light came on. Knowing I didn't want to stop in the morning on my way to school I decided to run by the gas station before I went back to Canyon's. The only station was in the center of town right next to the post office and the grocery store. Small town living at its finest.

I pulled up to the pump listening to Carrie Underwood's "Blown Away". I loved this song so when I got out I turned the volume all the way up so I could hear it while I was pumping. Looking around I took in just how peaceful everything looked. It amazed me how deceiving things could be from the outside. No one knew what was really going on inside the houses nearby.

The handle clicked letting me know the tank was full. I hung it up and grabbed my wallet so I could go inside and pay. All I was thinking about when I opened the door and walked in was grabbing a root beer and an ice cream sandwich. What I was met with was the last thing I ever expected.

Standing at the counter with his blond hair gelled perfectly, in his standard Affliction jeans, Doc Martin boots and the black North Face jacket I bought him for Christmas was Kale Thompson. I didn't know what to do. Part of me wanted to run and hide while the other half wanted to find out why he was there and how he found me. I didn't get the time to decide before he turned and noticed me for the first time.

"ARIANNA!"

I stood in place while he practically ran toward me and then picked me up and spun me around in the middle of the store. My hands were at my sides. I didn't hug him back. To be honest, I didn't know how to feel about any of it.

"What are you doing here?" was all I could get out.

He set me down and softly cupped my face just the way I always remembered. "Just look at you. You're more beautiful now than you ever were."

"I asked you a question."

"Wow, you're still mad at me? I get it. Is there anywhere we could go and talk?"

I looked at the girl working the counter who not only went to my school but was listening to everything we were saying.

"Yeah, there's a park down the road. Follow me."

I grabbed my wallet to pay for my gas when Kale held up his hand stopping me.

"I got this." He threw a card down on the counter and waited to sign the receipt before turning back to me.

"Lead the way."

I walked out the door and headed for my truck when Kale said, "Why don't we take my car?"

"I'd rather us both drive."

"Since when? Besides, what the hell is that thing? What happened to your car?"

"Don't come here making fun of my life, Kale. You have no idea what I have gone through!"

"Look." He came so close I could smell the cologne he always wore. How I didn't pick up on that the first time is beyond me. I must have been in shock and blocked it out. "I want to make it up to you. Please just give me a chance and hear me out."

"I said I would listen, didn't I?"

"You have to stop with the attitude. I'm trying to fix this."

"Good luck with that, Kale. I haven't heard from you since that night!"

"Are you going to listen to me or scream all night?"

"Fine. I'll go with you but don't get your hopes up."

I left my truck and got in his rental car. I wasn't the least bit surprised that it was a Cadillac; he only drove the best. Kale closed the door once I was in and walked around to get in the driver's side.

Sitting there, I continued to wonder how he found me and what he expected to happen now that he had. Kale opened his door while I sat there with my hands clasped together in my lap and got in. We drove in silence to the park I was telling him about, other than me giving him directions. Once the car was parked I grabbed for the door handle but Kale put his hand on my left inner thigh stopping me from getting out.

"I'm sorry, Arianna. For everything that I did and what happened, I'm sorry."

"I wish I could say that I forgive you but I just can't."

I pushed his hand off and got out of the car. I needed as much space as possible from him. It wasn't that I detested him. In fact, it was the complete opposite. I had loved Kale Thompson ever since the ninth grade homecoming dance he asked me to. I lived and breathed for that boy and to have him there was the hardest thing in the world for me after he left me to suffer.

I walked over and sat down on a swing and began to rock myself back and forth. Kale joined me by sitting on the seat next to me and grabbed ahold of the linked chain on either side of him.

"I came here for you. You know that, right? I'm here to take you out of this hell hole and bring you back. It's been long enough."

I drug the toe of my foot through the dirt bringing myself to a stop. "I can't go back. That's part of the deal, remember? Oh, I forgot, you wouldn't know what deal was made. You were to freakin' high at the time."

"Stop! Just stop it! You know I never would have let that happen if I wasn't. I have loved you for as long as I could love. You were my first everything, Arianna. I have been lost without you."

"Lost, huh? It sure didn't look that way on Facebook! You and everyone else seemed just fine while I was the one who lost everything. ME, Kale, not YOU!"

He stood up from his swing and came over to mine steaming mad. His arms were under mine pulling me up to him and before I knew what was happening his lips crashed into mine with a fever I had forgotten we had between us. We always fought like crazy but we made love the same way. We were intense in every respect of the word.

My hands grabbed onto his shirt while his fisted in my hair. As mad as I was, I missed him and everything that came along with our dysfunctional relationship. Reality slapped me in the face seconds later though when an image of Canyon went through my mind. I jerked away, pushing Kale off of me, panting from the adrenaline coursing through my veins. He took a step to come back at me but I put my hand up signaling for him to stop.

"I need to think, Kale. Not be convinced by what happens when we're together. That's not healthy and you know it."

"You can hate me all you want but you still love me just as much. Don't try to deny what we have, Arianna, it will always be there."

He was right. No matter how much I wanted to hate him he was my first everything too. I had never loved anyone before him. Never felt the desperation you feel when you find something you never want to let go of.

"How do you think I could go back and questions wouldn't start up? They put me here for a reason. That isn't going away."

"So we don't go back. Both of us graduate in less than a week. We can move anywhere and start all over. What college do you want to go to, I'm down for where ever you pick. It can be just you and me. Screw everyone else."

Don't think for a second that I didn't want to jump in his arms and say, "Let's go". Of course I did. If I left, not only would I get away from John but Canyon wouldn't be his target anymore. He could go on with living out his dreams and he wouldn't have me plaguing them. Shelby was going to be the hard part. Saying goodbye to her was going to crush me. The promise I made that night had my answer to Kale crystal clear.

"I can't leave with you tonight, Kale. I just can't. Shelby's here. I won't leave her without a goodbye."

"So when will you be ready?"

"I don't know. I graduate next Friday. Give me until then to decide, please."

"I have to know before then. I have to plan this perfectly. My dad is only getting more powerful."

"You've always gotten your way, Kale, but this time I need to be the one to decide and you have to let me. Your life will be fine no matter what. If I make one wrong move I—"

"I won't let that happen."

He took another step but this time I let him. He lifted my chin and I could feel his breath hit my lips right before headlights turned into the park shining right on us. I backed away from Kale and put my hand over my eyes trying to block the light so I could see who it was. Panic—pure, blood-curdling panic—went through my veins as I focused in on the one truck that held the man who changed everything for me.

"Who the fuck is that?"

Kale was standing next to me and I wished more than anything he wasn't. I didn't know what to do. Should I have left him and walked up to the truck? Yes. Did I? No. I got about halfway between the two and stopped. Torn, I just stood there like an idiot. I couldn't choose. Unfortunately, Canyon made the choice for me. I heard the truck change gears before it backed up and pulled away. Dropping to my knees, I openly sobbed, screamed at the top of my lungs and clawed my nails into the grass trying to get a grip on what I just lost.

Kale came up from behind me and sat down next to me in the grass. "What just happened?"

I didn't want to tell him anything. I wanted Canyon as far away from all of this as possible. What he and I shared was none of Kale's business.

"Take me to my truck."

"What? No. We have to figure this out together. What we do next could—"

"Take me to my God damned truck, Kale!"

I got up and stormed to his car, opened the door, got in and slammed it closed behind me. I waited as he stood in the middle of the park, not budging an inch. I wasn't either. In fact, after five minutes of sitting there, I got out and started walking.

"Where are you going? Arianna, wait, I will drive you."

I didn't stop. I was determined to get to my truck if it was the last thing I did. I heard the car start behind me but at this point I was to the top of the hill and more pissed than ever at myself. How could I let this happen? I made it halfway down the hill before Kale pulled beside me. The window rolled down and then Kale leaned his head out.

"Just get in. I'll take you to that piece of shit if that's what you really want." I wasn't sure I if wanted to be anywhere near Kale at this point. The only thing I was focused on was getting to Canyon. "Would you quit being so stubborn?"

He jerked the wheel, pulling the car across a lane of traffic and onto the shoulder of the road I was using to walk. I got in but I didn't say a word to him. We pulled back into the gas station and there was my truck, in the same place I left it. I had never been so happy to see that piece of crap in my life. I opened the door to get out when he opened his at the same time which I didn't understand.

"What are you doing?"

He looked at me like I lost my mind.

"What do you mean 'what am I doing'? What is going on with you? You're acting crazy. I just flew for five hours and drove for another three! You haven't seen me in months. What the hell is going on?"

I didn't know what to say other than, "I'm sorry. I'm not trying to hurt you right now but you have to understand. You haven't tried to contact me once, Kale! Not once! How did you even find me?"

"I went through my dad's computer. He had it in a locked file that I broke into."

"He had what?"

"The name John used to wire the money to. The banking information was there after a lot more digging. He bought the house with the money."

"So they know where I am? I thought the whole point of this was for me to disappear. Anyone can find me?"

"No. Like I said, that file was locked. I am the only one who knows the password he would use. You're safe. I promise."

"How do you know someone else won't figure it out?"

"Because no one would guess the name of the turtle he got for me when I was five. Seriously, you're good."

"Kale, I am so scared and confused right now. I love you but you need to give me space. I need to figure this out on my own."

"I have a room booked in Helena for the night. I can extend it until Friday. You have until then to let me know. I will meet you back here at the park around seven o'clock. Please don't make the wrong choice."

He got back in the car, put it in reverse, pulled back out on the road, and drove away. The fact my birthday was on Friday didn't even come from his mouth which meant neither man in my life knew just how epic this birthday was going to be.

Chapter 22

I couldn't help the tears that were falling as I drove to his house. I continued to wipe them away but more came. The last thing I wanted to do was hurt him and I had done just that.

I cut the lights as I pulled into the driveway and turned off the engine once I came to a stop. Sitting there, I tried to come up with what I should say but the words never came to me. I seemed to be having that problem a lot.

Eventually, I left the confines of my truck and walked around to the back of the house. The porch light was on but Canyon wasn't sitting there like I expected. I climbed the steps and entered the screened in area but couldn't bring myself to open the door to the kitchen.

He'd once told me I was no stranger and that knocking only proved to be for those who were, but in that moment I felt it wasn't my right to enter without it.

I raised my hand, ready to bang against the glass when the door opened. Canyon stood stock still glaring at me.

"Can I come in?"

"I don't think that's a good idea."

"Please, Canyon, I have so much to explain."

"Now you want to tell me? I have given you all the space in the world to come to me when you were ready and you choose now, seriously? Guilt doesn't help ease a situation, Ari. I think you better go."

He started to close the door when I screamed, "PLEASE! DON'T DO THIS."

"I'm not the one who did this. You are."

"As if I haven't heard that enough in my life. You don't understand. It's far more complicated than you realize."

"You're right. I don't realize anything but the fact that my girlfriend was about to kiss another guy had I not pulled up when I did. Did I get any part of that wrong?"

I shook my head back and forth thinking, how did I screw this up so bad? "If you give me fifteen minutes of your time and want me to leave I will."

"What, and go running back to whoever that was? Why don't you go now?"

"Because I love you!"

He tilted his head back and laughed. Laughed! "That's convenient. You've chosen now? You have to be kidding me."

The tears weren't coming by choice. If anything, this entire moment of my life was humiliating. So much so, that I had had enough.

"I may have kept things from you but I never intentionally hurt you the way you just hurt me."

I turned around and ran down the steps going straight to my car. After I got in, I started the engine but had no idea where to go, so I simply put my head on the steering wheel and cried. My entire body shook as I thought about just how badly I screwed thing up.

A knock on my window scared the crap out of me. I jumped, nailing the back of my head on the rear view mirror and watched it fall to the floor board.

Canyon opened my door and said five words I will never forget, "Your fifteen minutes start now," before he walked away.

I only allowed myself to be aggravated with his attitude for a second before I jumped out of the cab and ran after him. I knew my chance with him was gone but there was still room for hope that forgiveness could be given and I needed that.

I made it to the back of the house just as he sat down in his chair on the porch. Climbing those stairs I kept telling myself that I had one chance at this and I didn't want to screw this up too.

I sat down on the floor in front of him leaning against the outer wall and took a deep breath before I spilled my soul.

"The truth is, there is still so much I can't tell you but I'm going to try and do my best." I was picking at my nails doing anything to not have to look at him as I said the next part. "That guy I was with, his name is Kale Thompson. His father is Michael Thompson, the Governor of Massachusetts, and the Republicans hope for President. I've been with Kale since my freshman year, just after I turned fourteen." I glanced up, gauging his reaction and noticed his hands were in fists. Nothing about this was easy for either of us.

"My life was a lot different from what it is now. I used to go to a private school and had pretty much everything I wanted." I didn't want to cry again. If anything, I wanted to stay calm and focused so he would hear what I was trying to explain but what I told him next was harder than I ever realized. "I saw something really bad. That's the part I can't tell you about but what happened after that cost me and my family everything. It's not that I'm not ready to tell you, I physically can't. Too many bad people are attached to this. We lost our house, Canyon, John lost his job, I lost my life as I knew it and had no choice in any of it."

I wiped away the tears that fell, trying to keep some composure but I knew what I was about to say would hurt him the most. Reminding him of what he saw was not something I ever wanted to do but I needed him to understand I didn't plan any of this.

"I went in town tonight for gas. I didn't know Kale would be there. I never in million years thought I would see him here. You have to believe me..."

Canyon jumped up from his chair as started pacing the room. "Do you have any idea how scared I was? I sat in this house waiting for you to come back and then in my truck trying to convince myself not to go to your house and kill that son-of-a-bitch for not letting you leave. I told myself it wouldn't matter if I went to jail if something happened to you and I didn't do anything to stop it." He stopped pacing and knocked his hat to the ground as he ran his hands back and forth over his face and hair. "I drove to your house, only you weren't there. I spent the next twenty minutes covering every street we have in this town."

He crouched down next to me and looked me in the eye, making sure I heard this next part loud and clear. "Can you even imagine how I felt when I finally saw your truck at the gas station? Or how about when I pulled up and noticed the driver's side door was slightly open, the keys were still in the ignition, the radio was left on, your purse was lying on the seat, but you were nowhere to be found. Do you have any idea how fucking scared I was?"

He stood up and started pacing back and forth again with his hands opening and closing into fists, more angry than I have ever seen him.

"Then Chelsey told me you got in some stranger's car and said something about going to the park. I was terrified! I thought something bad was happening to you. You keep so many damn secrets from me I had no idea what was going on. Can you even imagine what it felt like for me when I saw you with him? Of course you can't. Because I would never do that to you!"

I stood up and walked over to him forcing myself to stand strong no matter what. "For what it's worth, I am sorry. I didn't do any of this to hurt you."

"But you did."

"I can't change anything that happened tonight and you may never look at what we had the same but I want you to know that what you did for me these last couple of months will be something I never forget. I will always be thankful for what you gave me back."

I turned away from him and walked down each step with purpose. I couldn't force him to forgive any hurt that I caused him but at least he knew what he meant to me. As my feet hit the dirt I looked out at the barn and thought about all the animals I had grown to love as well. I wished I had the time to say goodbye to each and every one of them but my time there was over.

"Do you love him?"

I didn't expect the question but also I didn't hesitate when I turned to answer. I was done with the lies. They destroy everything. "Yes."

He looked as though I just stabbed him in the heart. "You said you love me?"

"Yes."

"How is that possible? How can you not even see that guy for months and say that you feel the same way about him as you do me?"

"That's not what I said at all. You asked if I love him, not if I felt the same way. The two of you are so different there is no way to compare."

"Are you leaving with him? You said you didn't know where you were you going when you leave. Was that all a lie?"

"No, I still haven't made up my mind. I don't know what I'm going to do. Either way I'm hurting somebody I love."

I walked away not wanting to let him see me fall apart. I was almost to the back of the house when I felt his arms suddenly wrapped around me. I hadn't realized just how much I needed his touch until he engulfed me within it.

"Don't go."

My body went limp. I gave into the want I felt for him. The need that took me over when I was in his arms. As convinced as I was that leaving would be the best thing for him, something in that moment let me know he would rather go down fighting with me by his side than let me walk away.

He spun me in his arms and looked me in the eye. "I may look like a pathetic fool for saying this but I don't care. I'm not ready to let you go. Please, just stay with me tonight."

His lips touched my forehead first. Softly he let them trail down to the tip of my nose as the calluses on his fingers lifted my chin. I closed my eyes and felt his lips graze across mine. The taste of him brought me back home. I felt his hands across my back at the same time his tongue caressed mine. I was so completely lost in his kiss that I hadn't realized his hands had traveled down under my butt until he picked me up, never breaking his lips away from mine.

My legs wrapped around his waist at the same time my hands went to the back of his head pulling him even closer to me. He carried me up the steps, into the house, up into his room and slowly laid me down on my back across his bed.

I broke away from his lips, panting from the adrenaline coursing through my veins as I pushed him slightly up. With the bottom of my shirt in my hands, I pulled it over my head, leaving me for the first time exposed.

I heard Canyon suck in his breath as his eyes took me in. The low amount of light coming from the porch seeped into the window adding only a soft glow to the otherwise dark room. His hands slowly came down over my breasts and then hovered as if he was unsure if he could touch them. I didn't want any doubt in his mind so I brought my hands up to cover his and led them down to me. He cupped both of them and squeezed at the same time he crashed his lips back down to mine.

I felt his weight on the bed and opened my legs for him to find his place next to me. I began to rock against him, needing to release what was building up within me. He pushed himself firmer against me as he slid my bra cups to the side to touch my nipples for the first time.

"Canyon, I want you."

He didn't stop rubbing all over me but he slowed down. "I want you too, darlin', but I need to know you're not going to give me all of you and then walk away from me."

I wanted to tell him I would never do that but I wouldn't lie to him and break his heart for an orgasm or more so a selfish memory to hold on to. I stopped moving my body but instead grabbed on to his back and pulled him down on me. I needed to feel him close as I wrapped my arms around his back and began to rub my nails lightly across his skin.

"I don't want to make promises I can't keep. What I want is to share in something neither of us will ever forget. Can't that be enough?"

He pushed up to look me in the eye. "No amount of time will ever be enough with you, Ari."

He leaned forward and kissed me softly before he moved lower so he could lay his head on my stomach and at the same time he wrapped his arms around me pulling me to him. I stared at the ceiling as I ran my fingers through his hair until his breathing leveled out and I knew he was asleep. It didn't take long before I closed my eyes and gave into the night.

I awoke several hours later when I thought I heard something and realized Canyon was no longer with me.

Sitting up on the bed, I grabbed for my shirt and pulled it over my head determined to follow the sound I had quickly identified once I had woken up enough to focus. He was singing again. I made my way down the steps, through the family room and into the kitchen listening to one of the saddest songs I had ever heard.

Looking out through the glass encased within the back door I could see him play and it was beautiful. I wasn't familiar with the song so I focused instead on what he was saying. The words ripped me to shreds.

They talked about being a fool for holding on to someone when you know they are still thinking of someone else. Hoping that someday they will let go and see that the love right in front of them is more than they will ever know to understand.

I couldn't take any more of just standing in the dark hearing him pour his heart out.

I had grabbed a blanket from the back of the couch as I passed by it and wrapped it around me sheltering me from the cold. Using it now for security I clenched onto it as I opened the door to the patio. Slowly, I moved toward him, never breaking stride until I sat down in the chair beside him.

I expected him to stop immediately when he saw me but instead he looked me straight in the eye as he continued to play. The first time he was willing to bear his soul to me without any fear was the very moment I decided what I needed to do.

The last words were sung while a single tear fell down Canyon's face. He wiped it away before he took the guitar from his lap and rested it against the wall next to him without saying a word.

"What's the name of that song?"

"'Don't Close Your Eyes'. A man named Keith Whitley sang that a long time ago. It never meant much to me until now."

"I can see why."

I got up from my seat and moved to stand in front of him. I lifted my right leg, placing my knee on his left side and then followed with my left leg. I sat in his lap resting my weight on his knees and looked straight into his eyes. I could see his hope dying through his stare. I couldn't put either of us through this any longer.

"I'm not going anywhere."

"Don't tell me what I want to hear, Ari, I can't do much more of this."

"It's decided. I'm yours if you still want me."

He grabbed ahold of my back and pulled me down to kiss me with everything he had before he said, "Tell me you love me again now that I can believe you."

"You didn't believe me before?"

"Just say it again for me."

I grabbed his cheeks and looked him straight in the eye before I rubbed my nose against his giving him Eskimo kisses. "I love you, Canyon Michaels."

"Those are the sweetest words a cowboy could ever hear."

"A cowboy? What about a bull rider?"

"Those words are something totally different. I'll have to teach you all about that when we're in the bedroom."

We both laughed and it felt so good to know there was some happiness left after all that pain.

"I was thinking and did some stuff that might make you mad. Now don't tell me no or yell at me until you hear me out, okay?"

"What did you do, Ari?"

"I turn eighteen on Friday."

His face fell. I knew I had never told him the date so he couldn't blame himself.

"Don't feel bad you didn't know. Now listen. That means all of the money will be wired into my account from my dad's trust fund, insurance, and everything my grandparents left me. I have had it lined up to be deposited immediately so I could get out of here as soon as possible but it doesn't look like the funds will be available until Monday. Either way, I was also Googling some information about your issue with your uncle. I've talked to an attorney that would like to speak with you. He understands his money is coming and is willing to take this case under those terms. He's expecting your call tomorrow."

"Why would you do all of that for me knowing you might leave?"

"I thought about it every way possible. I wanted to take care of you and the mess that was created because of me to begin with. If you'd never met me, John wouldn't be here to represent your uncle. Then when Kale showed up I thought about it the other way. If I left maybe John wouldn't stay on the case because it would make no sense to try and hurt me if I was already gone. Either way I always wanted to protect you, Canyon."

"I never needed your protection, Ari. I have only needed you."

Chapter 23

The next morning I woke up to the alarm on my phone. After patting the bed beside me I quickly realized that I was alone. I missed Canyon's arms immediately so I settled for second best. I rolled over to hug his pillow when I noticed a piece of paper. I picked it up and rolled onto my back as I began to read, instantly smiling.

You have no idea how much I wanted to stay in this bed with you in my arms but duty calls whether I like it or not. Don't you dare leave this house without coming out to the barn and giving me a kiss. I love you, darlin', with everything I've got. By the way, your breakfast is downstairs on the table.

I laughed thinking about how funny it was that he read my mind long before I even had the thought. For the first time that I could remember, I wasn't worried about anything happening before I allowed myself to be happy. Instead, I felt safe knowing within days I would have my money and life would work itself out. It's okay to look at the bright side sometimes and it was all I wanted to focus on.

I went downstairs only to find a plate of my favorite eggs, along with sliced fresh fruit, resting at the center of the table. I smiled again knowing he'd been shopping and picked this up for me. After eating I decided I was going to make a detour to the barn first.

The sun was just rising over the mountain tops causing me to pause for the moment and take it all in. This wasn't the place I once thought it would be, for the first time I realized I wanted to be able to call Montana home.

"Hey there, gorgeous, whatcha doing?"

I smiled so big my molars probably showed. "Coming to see you."

I watched him walk toward me with his standard baseball hat turned backwards, a yellow t-shirt that hugged his body perfectly, jeans that fit him just right and his usual black work boots, but that megawatt smile put his sexiness over the top.

We met at the bottom of the stairs right before I jumped into his arms.

"Good morning, handsome."

"Good morning to you too, beautiful."

"So, what's your plan for the day? You're going to call the lawyer, right?"

"Listen to you checking up on me. If I didn't know any better I would think you actually cared." I knocked his hat to the ground before I kissed his perfect lips. "Hey, that's my favorite hat!"

"The next time I'm at Bass Pro I'll grab you ten more."

"You better. You keep knocking my hat off you're going to need to get a job."

"I work here, remember?"

"One that pays."

He gave my lips a quick peck before he set me down. Just then two of the puppies ran out from under the porch and started dancing around our feet, scaring the crap out of me.

"When did they get that old?" I said sarcastically. It seemed like yesterday they were barely walking straight.

"You're telling me. I can't keep them penned up anymore. They cry all day wanting to be let out."

"Are they going to be okay running around the horses and stuff?"

"They have to learn somehow I guess."

I bent down and scooped one of them up and raised it to look in its eyes. "You be careful. Those horses will kick you."

"I don't think he understood a word you just said."

I shot Canyon a dirty look before setting the puppy back down on the ground. "At least I can say I tried." I saw something move out if the corner of my eye and noticed Magnus was tied to the outer fence. "Are you going to work him this morning?" I didn't wait for his answer before I started walking over to pet him.

"No, he's actually getting picked up in an hour."

I whipped my head around thinking I clearly heard him wrong. "What do you mean picked up? To go where?"

I continued walking until I got to Magnus and as soon as my chest was close enough for him to reach, he bumped me with his head.

"I know boy, the ears. Always the ears."

I began rubbing him in his favorite spot when Canyon appeared on his other side.

"Remember I told you a while back about that jockey? He's going to take him for the next few weeks to work with him."

My arms wrapped around Magnuses' thick neck as I squeezed, giving him the biggest hug I could.

"I'm going to miss you so much, buddy. It won't be the same around here without you. Who's going to let me ride them like you do?"

"There's always, Winston. Or you could have Bud? I need to start working Lala and Percy more anyway."

"It still won't be the same."

"Damn, darlin', you're making me a little jealous. I can't have you lovin' a damn horse more than me."

"Sorry, my heart has already been stolen by this black beauty. You'll just have to be okay with second best."

Canyon ran around Magnus startling him but he paid no mind. I was over his shoulder getting spanked whether I liked it or not. We both were cracking up laughing until well after he put me down.

"So when are you going to call that attorney?"

"I promised I would, didn't I? Now stop already."

"Why aren't you as excited as I am?"

He looked back at the barn before he turned to answer me. "Honestly? I guess I just don't want to get my hopes up. I pray there is something he can do, don't get me wrong. I've just worked my ass off for the last two years. You have no idea what those horses mean to me. The idea of him just coming in and claiming it all for himself kills me, you know? He didn't do anything to deserve a dime."

I wrapped my arms around him and rested my head on his chest, feeling his heart beat a mile a minute. He was scared. I could feel it.

"This is all going to work out. I have faith."

He kissed the top of my head before saying, "I'm really glad I have you."

"You should be. I'm pretty special."
He laughed and pushed me away. "Cocky much?"
"Just keeping you on your toes."
He grabbed my hand and pulled me back to him.
"Believe me, I know what I have."

An hour later I was on my way to school. We only had four days left of classes and then the graduation ceremony was planned for the following Friday.

The parking lot when I pulled in was practically empty from all the students skipping. It was as if they had already got their diploma and felt no need to be there. By the end of the day I agreed and wondered why I even bothered showing up.

Mrs. Hemswith asked me to stay after and help get the caps and gowns sorted due to the fact the committee never bothered to come to school. I didn't have any desire to be in that building for another minute but I ended up staying out of guilt. We didn't walk out to the parking lot until almost seven o'clock that night.

Driving to Canyon's house from school I was anxious, my nerves were shot to crap, and to be honest I was scared to death. All day I couldn't focus on anything other than what the attorney said and if he was going to be able to fix this. He was Canyon's last hope and if he couldn't help him I dreaded the condition of the man I was on my way to find.

I pulled into Canyon's driveway and waited to see if he was going to come around the corner and greet me. He never did. I had no idea what to expect when I walked around the back of the house but what I found was only something I can describe to you as the best moment of my life.

Under the wood pergola that was lit up by tiny white lights stood a perfectly dressed man holding what had to be at least three dozen long stemmed red roses. He was dressed in a black suit that fit him like a glove, clean shaven with his hair gelled having no hat to speak of.

He clicked a remote in his hand and music started pouring from speakers I never knew existed. The song was something I never would have pictured him choosing. Nothing about this moment could ever lose out against the best dream a girl could have.

I walked toward him listening to Adele sing "One and Only". I know every word to this song by heart. I didn't need to pay attention to the words this time to know what it was about. He wanted to be my one, my only, forever and needed me to let him.

As I got closer, he set the flowers down on the table next to him before he held out his hand to take mine. I attempted to ask him a question but he pressed his finger to my lips before he pulled me close.

He brought his mouth to my ear and whispered softly, "May I have this dance?"

When he pulled back enough to look in my eyes he got my answer. He never let go of my hand but instead rested it against his chest as he began to rock us back and forth.

I used my other hand to run my fingers through his hair while I continued to stare into eyes that completely captured my soul. I could have stayed in that moment for the rest of my life.

The song ended with Canyon pushing me back just far enough that he could dip me. When he brought me back up we were nose to nose. Softly his lips met with mine tipping this perfect moment over the scale into epic proportion.

"This is amazing, Canyon."

"Anything for you."

We continued to dance for the next three songs before he clicked the remote turning down the volume down.

"Are you hungry? I made dinner."

He led me over to the table perfectly laid out with covered dishes.

"I'm starving." He pulled my chair out for me before I watched him unveil smoked pork chops, a baked potato and grilled asparagus. "This looks delicious."

He picked up the roses and placed them in a glass vase before sitting down across from me.

"I hope you enjoy it."

The first bite melted in my mouth. "How could I not? Anything you make is incredible."

We both got quiet but only because we were too busy eating to talk. When I couldn't fit anything more in my stomach, I covered my plate with my napkin and rested back on my chair.

"I still can't believe you did all this. Oh, and that song choice was interesting by the way. I mean, I love Adele, but I'm slightly confused."

"That was the whole point of doing this. I never want you to be confused again. I want you to be mine, Ari, for as long as I can breathe I want you to be mine."

Kale came to mind. I know he should have been the last person I thought of in that moment but it's not what you think. All I wanted was to finally be happy and that day couldn't come until I talked to Kale.

"I'm yours, Canyon, and this is by far the most romantic thing anyone has ever done for me."

"Well, I always do like to put my best foot forward. That way when it only goes downhill from here you have a memory to hold on to."

I picked up my napkin and threw it at him. "So are you going to tell me what the attorney has to say?"

"You're never going to believe it when I tell you."

"Just tell me, I'm dying over here."

"He said that if my uncle, being a proprietor, wanted to pay me for all of the time I have invested along with the cost of running the utilities, farm equipment, feed... well, you get the point. So he sent John something saying we are counter-suing for seventy thousand dollars."

"What does that mean? Your uncle pays you and he still holds control?"

"He doesn't have the money, Ari. Seventy thousand dollars is a lot of money and he doesn't have a pot to piss in. He signed the company over at five o'clock tonight, darlin'. It's all mine!"

My chair flew back as I jumped up from it and lunged at Canyon—throwing him off balance—and both of us went crashing to the ground.

"Oh my God! I'm so sorry. Are you okay?"

He started laughing. "I'm fine. Glad to see you're as happy as I am but you could have given me a little warning."

"I'm just so happy for you. This is the best news ever!"

I grabbed his face and kissed him. "You have to be on cloud nine right now. I mean, no more worrying. "I sat up and looked around. "It's all yours."

Canyon stood up and offered me his hand to pull me to my feet. "I would love to share it with you if you're staying. I don't want you anywhere near that house, Ari. John's a monster and I don't trust him, especially after this news."

"I can't leave Shelby, Canyon."

"We won't. She's coming tomorrow, right?"

"Like she would miss watching you ride."

"Then we take this one day at a time."

I helped him clean up before we ended up cuddling on the couch. "You can't be comfortable."

"Why wouldn't I be?"

"You're still in a suit. Wouldn't you feel better wearing sweats or something?"

"You don't prefer me this way?"

"I like you any way you come."

"Really? You finally admit it?"

"Admit what?"

"That first day. You were checking me out, weren't you?"

"I don't know what you are talking about."

He climbed over me to stand in the middle of the room and started with taking of his suit jacket. I crawled over to the arm of the couch making sure I was comfortable for the show that was about to take place.

"What are you doing?"

One button after another was undone until he was placing the shirt on the side chair over his jacket. Slowly he pulled his undershirt from his pants and lifted it over every ripple and bulge until it was over his head and thrown at my face. "Does this help you remember?"

He walked back toward me looking hotter than any man on the planet. I tucked my legs under me and began to bounce in excitement. I wouldn't answer him but my body language clearly screamed my approval.

"What are you thinking right now, Ari?" I bit my bottom lip while looking right into him eyes. "Tell me..."

"Okay! OKAY! I thought you looked good."

"Just good?"

"Don't beg for compliments, it's not sexy."

He pushed me down on the couch and crawled on top of me. "I don't beg."

"You were begging."

"You're the one who's going to be begging."

"For what?"

"You'll see."

He kissed my forehead and then moved off of me.

"Hey, where are you going?"

"I'm just gonna sit over here."

"Why?"

"No reason."

He was giving me a look that spoke to me clearly. How long can you last?

I grabbed for the remote control and turned on the TV. After searching the entire menu I came to realize I couldn't focus on anything other than the lack of Canyon's shirt and how freaking good he looked sitting across from me. Eventually, I turned the TV off and sat back to look right at him.

"Is there a problem, Ari?"

That's when the idea struck me. Two could play this game and after his reaction the night before, I knew my breasts were his downfall. I moved my hands slowly to my lap as to not to give away my plan.

"Nope. No problem at all."

I grabbed the bottom of my shirt and began to drag it up over my stomach but stalled mid-reveal of my bra. I watched him suck in a breath and then swallow hard as I lifted it just enough that with one slight tug my breasts were free for him to see. I didn't hesitate after that, pulling it over my head and throwing it on the end table next to me.

"Is it hot in here or just me?"

I began fanning myself as if it were one hundred degrees in that room and by the beads of sweat on Canyon's forehead he probably believed it to be true.

"You don't play fair."

"All is fair in love and war."

I held strong wondering how long it was going to take until he broke. His hands were gripped firmly on the arms of the chair he sat in but he never got up.

It was time to up the ante.

I sat forward enough that my cleavage would be all he could focus on while I reached around my back to undo the two eye hooks. Within seconds I was free from the support and let my shoulder straps fall to my elbows.

I reached back around and cupped my breasts leaving them only slightly covered by the white lace bra I had been wearing.

"That's not going to work."

Slowly, I let what remained of my coverage fall to my lap leaving me completely exposed. Canyon opened his mouth to speak but chose instead to lunge across the room at me. I giggled as he pressed me down onto the couch and immediately started kissing me. He broke from my lips and then delicately spread them across my face starting at my forehead, the tip of my nose and then went on to continue with my neck, my chest and my shoulders, finally ending up over my breasts.

He stopped to look up at me. "I'm a weak man when it comes to you."

His mouth lowered until he kissed not only one but both of my breasts before he rose up off the couch and started for the stairs. He had gotten me so worked up I was lost as to why he was leaving the room until he turned back to me and said, "I may be weak but I never lose" before he climbed the stairs and left me alone.

I jumped off the couch and ran after him up the stairs screaming, "Canyon!"

Just as I got to the top he yelled back, "Who's begging now, huh?"

Chapter 24

It was finally my birthday and all of the waiting was over. I no longer needed John or my mother for anything and I can't tell you how freeing that was for me. The only thing left to take care of was Kale.

I decided that morning that making him wait until that night was just cruel. I know it may have been insensitive but I chose to send him a text instead of meeting face-to-face. I thought at the time that it would save me from having to see the hurt I caused and for him the embarrassment of it.

All day at school I tried to think of a nice way to put it. Nothing about saying you're done with someone and want to move on is nice though, no matter how you put it.

Finally, after throwing practically an entire notebook of paper in the trash I decided on what to write.

I was getting ready to leave my last class for the day when I got my phone out to text him. It had been so long since I typed in his number that it felt almost foreign when the bubble popped up for me to use. My thumbs went to work on the tiny keyboard and before I knew it I had written this:

I want to say that first I'm sorry for hating you as long as I did. Everything that happened was the fault of all that were involved and I shouldn't have blamed you entirely for it.

I don't want you to think that I went into making this choice easily. Nothing is ever easy when you know you're going to hurt someone you love and I never want you to doubt that I loved you. I loved you for so many years it's hard to remember a time when I didn't. But life changes things and what happened will forever alter who I am. That girl would have done anything and everything for you and I wish I could say I was still her but I'm not.

So instead of dragging this out more I'm just going to say it. Don't drive all the way back out here. Get on your plane and go live the rest of your life happy. I may not be a part of it but that doesn't mean that you can't move on.

Too much damage came out of what happened that night and I think it's best if we don't be around each other to re hash it.

Good luck with whatever you chose to do and know that at one time you owned my heart it's just not available anymore for me to give it back to you.

Goodbye, Kale

My thumb hovered over the send button until the final bell of the day rang, startling me. When I looked down, it had sent. Instantly, I felt guilty. Like maybe I should have given him more respect and talked to him face-to-face instead. Regardless, what was done was done and now I just had to sit back and wait to see if he would send me a response.

We didn't have much time to fiddle fart around after school since Canyon's rodeo was two hours away.

I pulled into the driveway to pick up Shelby and just stared at the house for a while. So much bad happened in there it made it hard to imagine that I made it through it. I was glad to be leaving and after I grabbed my things I was never going back in that house again.

Eventually, I walked through the front door, ignored my mother sitting on the couch watching TV and went straight back to Shelby's room, finding her on her bed waiting.

"What took you so long?"

"So long? I just got out of school."

"You didn't come home yesterday."

"We're going to need to talk about some things on our way to the rodeo. I'll explain it all later. Right now I need you to pack an overnight bag. We probably won't be getting back until it's pretty late."

"I get to stay at Canyon's?"

"Yes, you do, now pack. I'm going to go start getting my stuff together."

I walked into my bedroom and began to look around. I didn't really have much to take that I wanted. Almost everything I owned was attached in some way to memories and none of them were something I wanted to reminisce over. That left my clothes.

I grabbed three large duffle bags and started shoving everything from my closets and my drawers into them. I needed a suitcase for my shoes but decided I really didn't need the bulk of those either so I chose five pair that I loved and left the rest.

I had made several trips out to my truck and was on my last when John pulled into the driveway. I was wondering how long I was going to be able to enjoy the peace and quiet around there before he got home and I had gotten my answer.

"What do you think you are doing?"

He slammed his car door and started to approach me as I threw the last bag in the bed of my truck before I looked him in the eye to answer.

"I'm leaving."

"Where do you think you're going?"

"That's none of your business. Oh, and by the way, sorry to hear about your case."

"I bet you are, you little bitch. You're just out to screw me, aren't you? That case was going to get me back on my feet and you had to fuck that up for me too."

"Daddy!"

Both of our heads snapped to see Shelby standing there with her hands on her hips.

"Sorry, honey, I didn't see you there."

"Say sorry to Arianna, not me."

"Excuse me?"

"You said a bad word and weren't being nice at all. You need to say sorry to Arianna."

The look on John's face was priceless. He would rather eat crap than apologize to me.

"I don't need it anyway. Shelby, are you ready?"

"I still think he should say it."

"Just get in the truck, I'm ready to get out of here."

We both opened our doors and were getting in when we heard, "Shelby, don't you dare get in that truck. Do you hear me?"

She looked at me and I could see the fear in her eyes.

"Maybe you should stay home this time and next..."

"I want to go."

"I know but Canyon and I can't take you without your parent's permission. I can't do anything about this, honey."

She looked back and forth from me to her father before she climbed back out of the truck and walked over to him. I couldn't hear what she was saying but the shock that took over John's face before he watched Shelby walk back to the truck, jump in and close the door behind her was picture perfect.

"What did you say?"

"Can we just leave?"

I turned the key and started backing up out of the driveway and out onto the road. "Are you going to tell me?"

"I told him I saw. He knows I watched what he did to you and I told him I would tell if he wouldn't let me see you anymore."

I reached across the seat, grabbed her hand and squeezed. "I'm sorry you saw what happened that night, honey."

"It's not your fault. I'm sorry he did that to you."

"Yeah, me too."

We pulled into Canyon's driveway and there he was, waiting for us. Shelby jumped out of the car as usual and ran into his arms. I, on the other hand, started grabbing bags.

"Hey, stop! I'll get those, don't worry about that stuff."

"I can carry my own bags."

"I know you're capable but that doesn't mean I can't help and it's your birthday, let me do things for you."

"Well if you really want to, who am I to keep you from it?"

Shelby walked over to me with very confused expression on her face.

"Today is your birthday?"

"Yes, it is. Remember I had said were going to talk about a few things later, this is one of them."

She hadn't waited for me to finish talking before she was hugging my waist.

"Happy birthday, Arianna."

"Thank you, sweetheart."

"How come I never knew you had a birthday?"

Canyon looked at me with sorrow in his eyes. I never wanted him to know the depths my childhood went to but he was getting bits and pieces of it whether I liked it or not.

"Well that just means we are going to have to make this one pretty special, huh?"

"Yay!"

"You don't have to do anything, Canyon. Being free is the best gift there is."

"Let me take care of this, okay?"

"Can we get ice cream? Arianna loves mint chocolate chip."

Canyon looked down at Shelby smiling, "We will definitely get some ice cream."

Twenty minutes later, we were loaded up and heading out of town. Occasionally I glanced down at my phone, checking to see if Kale had responded but each time led to my disappointment. Because there was literally nothing to look at due to the sun going down, I started to glance through the history of our texts to each other. We had a lot of funny pictures, jokes, gossip, there were ones where he would complain about his dad and then finally, the last one sent before mine that day was from the night my world was destroyed.

I don't know why I never deleted our history but then again, this was the first time I had ever gone through anything that had to do with him. When people get hurt it only can go two ways: you do nothing but go through old memories just to torture yourself or you cut off what hurt you and vow never to revisit it again. I chose the latter.

"What's got you so quiet over there?"

I shut off my screen and turned to look at him.

"Nothing important. So, are you excited for tonight? This is your last ride before you are officially back in the PBR. That's gotta be a little nerve wracking."

"Actually, I wanted to talk to you about that."

"Why? What's up?"

"I'm not sure that's what I want anymore."

"What? Why would you say that?"

"You were right when you said my love was for the rodeo. I only wanted to get back to the PBR for the money. If my uncle isn't getting any part of my company then I really think I should focus on that for a while. You know, make my last name mean something again only this time it will have respect attached to it. Besides, the PBR would take a lot of my time. They tour for months on end. I can't really do both."

I sat there and took in what he was telling me.

"So, you're saying you changed your mind? I just want to make sure that I have nothing to do with this. I want you to be happy doing what you love and I was sure bull riding was it."

"I'm not giving it up completely. I will still take on a rodeo here and there. I love the PBR but I love you more and I don't want to be away from you for months at a time."

"I don't want you to end up regretting this."

"How could I ever regret having you in my life?"

"Oh, buddy, you will for sure feel that way sometimes. That I can guarantee."

"So, what did you want to talk about?"

Shelby sat forward and poked her little head between us in the front seat.

I looked to Canyon for support. This wasn't going to be easy but I knew it was for the best. He squeezed my hand letting me know he was there if I needed him and that's all that mattered. I turned around in my seat to look at her when I said, "Well, I want to talk to you about some things you're going to have to try to understand even though you may not really like them, okay?"

She looked confused already but shook her head up and down letting me know I could continue.

"As you know, your dad and I don't get along very well. You also know that today is my birthday. When you turn eighteen that means you're an adult and you can move out. Are you understanding what I'm saying so far?"

"Kind of."

"I'm going to be staying at Canyon's from now on. I'm not going to live in the same house as you." Her eyes started to glass over and I knew I needed to be quick. "But that doesn't mean you and I won't still see each other a whole lot. Things might even get easier for you without me there to make John mad."

"I don't want you to leave."

"I know, honey, and I'm sorry, but..."

"Can I come live at Canyon's too?"

I shook my head in disbelief and looked at Canyon wide-eyed. He didn't say a word but simply squeezed my hand again.

"You can have sleepovers but I think for now we need to just take it slow."

The last thing I needed was step-dick getting pissed and deciding to move and take her away from me.

"But I don't want to be there without you."

"For now it's all we can do. I love you, Shelby, with all my heart. I will never leave you."

"Do you promise?"

"I swear."

"Don't forget."

"Never."

We got to the arena a couple minutes early and decided to hit the vendors for some non-healthy snacks before the rodeo started. I picked a huge soft pretzel with cheese while Shelby and Canyon went straight for the funnel cake.

"How can you both love those things so much? One or two bites and I'm done. I bet either of you could eat the whole thing by yourself."

Sticky fingers and all they both looked at each other and said, "Yep." Shelby started giggling making Canyon laugh out loud.

We didn't have long after that before it was time to say goodbye to Canyon. Shelby gave him a hug and wished him luck. I, on the other hand, wrapped my arms around his shoulders and gave him the best kiss I could give.

"Have fun out there, stud."

"Oh I will. Just having you here means everything to me."

He gave me one last kiss before he started walking away. Shelby and I turned to go find our seats when I heard Canyon say, "Don't think I didn't know you could be leaving with him right now."

I whipped around to see him wearing that trademark smile while my jaw was practically touching the ground.

"How did you..."

"I love you, Ari."

Then he turned and walked away.

I stood there in awe. How could he have known?

"You were going to leave tonight? Where were you going to go?"

"There's just a lot that you won't understand."

"Yeah, yeah, yeah. When I'm older. Gosh, when am I going to be older already?"

I laughed and then grabbed her hand and started swinging it back and forth as we walked. "Hopefully not for a long time."

Shelby did a lot better this time around. You could say she was becoming seasoned to the rodeo experience. She kept her questions to a minimum of one or two per event and only went to the bathroom twice before the bull riding started, allowing me to sit back and try to enjoy the show.

I kept wondering if Kale was so pissed at me that he didn't have a response or worse if he for some reason hadn't checked his phone and was waiting for me at the park confused and angry. I even contemplated calling him at one point but talked myself out of it. There really wasn't much of a chance he hadn't seen the message and the last thing I wanted was to pour salt in the wound.

Most of the riders had done a decent job that night leaving it down to the score to decipher the winner. Two men had scored extremely high making me grateful Canyon was no longer banking on this ride to be in with the PBR.

When the announcer did call his name, Shelby and I were out of our seats and screaming for him causing all the spectators to stare but I didn't care in the slightest. He looked over to us giving us that smile you know I love so much before he climbed on his bull and strapped his hand in.

There was a time I was petrified watching him but that passed long ago. My adrenaline was pumping hard through my veins waiting for that gate and when it did it was amazing.

Canyon got one of the larger bulls who in no way shape or form wanted him on his back. That bull did everything in his power to shake him but Canyon twisted and turned right along with him. It really was beautiful to see. He had a gift that most men dream of having.

When the buzzer sounded, he didn't jump off like we all expected. Instead he continued to ride making the entire arena stand on their feet. I didn't know what he was thinking unless he wanted to prove he belonged in the PBR regardless of if he went through with it.

When he finally jumped off, the crowd went wild when Canyon threw his hat up in the air. Both hands were raised as he waved to all the onlookers while the men in orange took care of getting the bull out of the circle.

I was on my feet clapping along with the rest of the fans more proud than I had ever been. He definitely went out of this one with a bang.

An hour later, we watched as he was declared the victor. I grabbed my phone and made sure to take as many pictures as I could hoping one of them would be worthy to frame on his wall of accomplishments. He never stopped smiling the entire time letting me know this was everything he ever wanted and I couldn't have been happier for it.

After it was all said and done, we met up outside the area the participants were gathered. Men and women made sure to pat his back as they made their way to their cars and told him things like, "That was amazing," or, "Hell of a ride, man".

Me? I simply gave him a kiss and said, "I love you, Canyon Michaels."

"Those are the best words I could ever hear."

Shelby didn't really understand the magnitude of what had happened so instead of boasting about how great he was, she went with, "Can we go get ice cream now?"

I laughed while Canyon swung her around before she ended up in his arms.

"Have I ever told you that you're my favorite little girl in the whole world?"

"No, but you can."

We both cracked up at the blunt honesty she possessed.

After we stopped for ice cream, because you know we really had no choice, we headed for home. Shelby fell asleep ten minutes after we got back on the road leaving Canyon and I to talk openly without worry.

"Are you going to tell me why you think I would have left tonight?"

"It's your birthday. You always said that's when you were going to go. Why wouldn't I think with him showing up it wasn't to collect you?"

"I wouldn't have, you know. I was planning on graduating first. I would never have left you and Shelby without a proper goodbye."

"I can't see anything being proper about having to say goodbye to you."

"Well now you won't have to for a while."

"A while?"

"I still have some things I need to deal with and me staying with you could bring it all crashing down around you. You have to trust me, Canyon, I love you too much for you to get hurt any more than what I've already caused."

"Why do you treat me like I'm weak? Nothing can be worse than watching my mother die by my father's hand, Ari. Whatever you think I can't handle I assure you I can."

"I never meant to make you feel weak. If anything your strength is what propelled mine. This isn't about what you can handle and as far as testing those boundaries, that's something I never want to happen. Can't you see that with loving you comes the need to not bring harm your way?"

"You don't think that same feeling could belong to me? That I don't own it too? I want to protect you from anything and everything, so when I say you treat me as weak I mean it. Why can't you open up to me and let me be the one who keeps you safe?"

I had never had anyone in my life tell me that and I wanted more than anything to have someone be by my side instead of feeling all alone. I wasn't a fool though. It would do nothing but bring the danger to him and I refused to be a part in that.

We were pulling into the driveway and I knew that once we were inside I could reason more with him and get him to understand.

"Can we just talk about this once we get in the house and put Shelby to bed?"

"Yeah, I'm not ready to... What the fuck is he doing here?"

I looked up and with the headlights shining right on him there was no question of who was staring back at us

Chapter 25

I jumped out of his truck as fast as I could and ran straight to Kale.
"What are you doing here?"

"Are you kidding me? You think you can leave me an explanation like that on a fucking text and I would be okay with it?"

"How did you find out where I would be?"

"You drove straight here the other night. Did you think I wouldn't want to know who you were running to instead of staying with me?"

"That's not..."

"You need to leave now!"

Canyon was standing behind me and the authority in his tone had even me flinching. I turned around to look at him with an expression that begged him to give me the space I needed to handle this but he didn't waiver for a second.

"Did you not hear me clearly?"

"You can go fuck yourself. Arianna owes me an explanation and I'm not going anywhere until I get it."

Canyon went to lunge for Kale but I grabbed him and tried my best to hold him back.

"What else do you want from me? I told you I wasn't going with you, what more do you want?"

"Let me guess, you told him everything didn't you? You opened your damn mouth..."

Canyon was getting harder to hold back. I knew he could easily break free if he wanted to, making me grateful that he had enough respect to let me handle this the best I could.

"I haven't told him ANYTHING! He has nothing to do with this!"

"He has everything to do with this. You want to stay here in the middle of fucking nowhere go right ahead. You have no idea how much you just screwed up!"

Kale started walking away at the same time Canyon grabbed my hand. I pulled out of his grasp and ran after Kale screaming.

"I didn't do anything, Kale! You did and you let me take the fall for you. Don't come here and threaten me just because things aren't going the way you want. Do you think me losing everything was easy? You haven't lost shit!"

He turned around and when he did he walked straight at me until I could feel his breath hit my face. "You think I didn't lose anything? I lost you!"

"You lost me the second you chose to cut me off and let me take the fall."

"You didn't take any fall. They made you disappear, big deal! You brought the drugs that night don't forget. You could have gone down with me!"

I started hitting him. Like full-fledged slapping him in the face, beating my hands on his chest kind of hitting him. He tried grabbing my hands but I wasn't giving up. The rage I felt allowed me to finally get it all out. All the pain and hurt I felt from him abandoning me when I needed him the most.

"I HATE YOU! DO YOU HEAR ME? I HATE YOU! JUST LEAVE! LEAVE!" Canyon pried me off of him but it didn't stop me from kicking and screaming. "I NEVER WANT TO SEE YOU AGAIN! I HATE YOU..."

"Oh you don't have to worry about that, bitch. I have no desire to have your skanky ass any..."Canyon set me down and before Kale could finish, Canyon's fist met with his face. Kale dropped to his knees yelling, "You son-of-a-bitch! I will fucking sue you!"

I walked over to Kale and crouched down to his level so Canyon couldn't hear.

"I don't even recognize you anymore. You're nothing like the guy I fell in love with and if you think for a second you are coming after him I will gladly take the charges, but I'm taking you down with me."

I got up and walked back over to Canyon completely ignoring the fact Kale was still there and looked down at his swollen hand.

"Are you okay?"

"No. I want that piece of shit off my property and as far away from you as possible."

"He's leaving and I don't think he will ever be back."

I heard a car door close behind me and turned to look when the headlights came on. As Kale pulled away, my anger faded and sadness took over. It wasn't a lie, what I had said to him. He really was nothing like who I gave all my firsts to and that hurt more than I can explain. What he was now was a mini version of his father, the very thing he hated all those years and it broke my heart.

Canyon wrapped me in his arms then whispered in my ear, "Are you all right?"

"No."

"I kind of expected that. Come here, darlin'."

There is nothing good about crying on one man's shoulder for the loss of another but I was just so tired of it all and the tears I attempted to hold back came anyway.

"I'm sorry, Ari. I know none of that was easy for you."

"How can you be so understanding about something like this?"

"Because as much as I hate that dude I'd be the same way if I lost you."

The idea of us going through this crushed me. I couldn't imagine him saying horrible things and hating me the way Kale did.

"I have so much to explain to you about what he said. I made a lot of mistakes, Canyon, but I didn't deserve this. He did—"

"Why don't you go in and pour yourself a hot bath and soak while I get Shelby up to bed?"

"Oh my God! Shelby! I forgot all about her! Did she wake up? If she saw..."

"She's still sound asleep. I can see her from here."

I had almost suffered a heart attack. The last thing I ever wanted Shelby to hear was my involvement with drugs and what was caused because of it.

"Are you sure? I can get her."

"I'm going to tell you one last time, go get in the tub. I'll be there in just a minute. You do have a lot of explaining to do and just so you know, I'm done with the secrets. They're coming out tonight whether you're comfortable with that or not. I love you, girl, whatever happened won't change that."

He patted my butt, grabbed my cheeks and kissed me before he walked away to collect Shelby. I hated the idea of him judging me but the truth is, Kale never would allow himself to believe me which meant he already thought Canyon knew. So what difference would it make anymore is all I thought about as I walked into the house and up the stairs to the bathroom.

I must have soaked in that tub for a good thirty minutes before Canyon knocked, asking through the door if I was doing all right. In truth, I was stalling. I hated the idea of admitting everything that I've done and what it caused, but it was time for him to know the truth and then I would just have to live with the consequences if he chose to walk away from me. At least my bags were already packed.

"Yeah, I'm okay. I'm getting out now."

I reached for the towel that hung from the wall next to me and wrapped myself in it. It was now or never.

When I opened the door I found Canyon standing across the hall, holding out a pair of my pajamas.

"I thought you might need these."

"Thank you. Would you mind making me some hot chocolate? It's going to be a long night and I need something to calm my nerves."

"Sure, go get dressed and I'll just meet you downstairs."

Ten minutes later I was sitting on the couch, facing Canyon, about to spill my guts, literally. The need to vomit was not far off. Canyon held my hand as I started to explain the worst night of my life in detail.

"You have to understand that the girl I am now is nothing like who I was. You wouldn't have liked me much back then."

As I went into explaining it my mind flashed back to that night.

It was a typical Friday night. The same group of people from school partied together every weekend without fail. It wasn't a question of who would be there but more where would we be. The party moved to a different location nightly and on this particular one Kale decided to have it at his dad's mansion. We all knew he was crazy for trying to pull a party off there but Kale's dad had pissed him off and he was going to do anything he could to give the same feeling back tenfold.

My dress for the night was more wrinkled than the kind you can get away with so I was running late after I had to steam it. My two best friends, Margie and Emma, were texting me non-stop about how kick ass the party was and wondering why I wasn't there yet.

I had just walked out the door and got in my car when my phone chimed again. I assumed it was either of them, but I was wrong. This time it was from Kale. He and I had talked after school and he knew I would be late so I wasn't sure what he needed until I read the text.

Hey, doll, do me a favor and swing by Derrick's house for me and pick up the package. I've already worked out the payment but I need you to go to grab it. Go to the back door and knock three times. Don't ask questions. Just bring it straight here and DON'T GET PULLED OVER.

I love you and will see you soon.

Here's the address in case you don't remember

11454 Highlington Parkway South.

I hated that he put me in that position and instantly thought about skipping it and just going straight to the party, pretending like I never got the text. But as I drove closer to the Senator's I told myself it wouldn't be a big deal; it was just cocaine. Kale had been picking it up from this guy Derrick and another guy named Brian for over two years. His dad had several cops underneath him that stole the drugs from the evidence locker and resold them on the streets. Kale was always the supplier when it came to the parties and people had come to expect it. Derrick was just one of the two Kale had worked out a deal with so I told myself it wouldn't be a big deal.

I pulled into Derrick's driveway, walked around to the back of the house and knocked three times like I was instructed. The man that answered was nothing like what I expected him to look like. I had always stayed in the car when Kale made a run so to say I was surprised would be an understatement. As a police officer you would think he would have been younger and fit but this man was about eighty pounds overweight with very little hair to speak of. He had jeans on that barely fit under his gut and a black t-shirt that didn't make it down to meet his pants.

He didn't say anything to me but instead pointed a gun in my face.

"What do you want?"

I almost pissed my pants standing there. I had never had a gun pointed at me before and all I thought about was running but I feared he would just shoot me in the back.

"I was asked to pick up a package for Kale Thompson."

He grabbed a bag from the counter beside him and shoved it at me, never taking the aim of the gun away from my face.

"If you even think about taking that for yourself I will hunt you down and kill you. Don't fuck with me."

I grabbed a hold of the bag and took it from him without breaking eye contact. "I won't."

He pulled the gun back and then slammed the door in my face.

I hurried back to my car and threw the bag under my seat, crying like a baby, but also ready to kill Kale for putting me in that situation to begin with. By the time I got to the Senator's my foot had stopped shaking over the gas pedal. I had made it somehow. I grabbed the bag and walked straight into the house finding Kale waiting for me on the other side of the door.

"Hey, doll, thanks for grabbing this for me. He didn't give you any problems, did he?"

He leaned down and gave me a kiss but I pushed him away, still angry.

"No, not unless you call shoving a gun in my face a problem, Kale! Why would you ask me to do that?"

He wrapped his arm around my shoulder and led me into the open room filled with all our friends while he said in my ear, "Don't let that freak you out. He just wanted to make sure you were good and not someone trying to get a free score."

"Well, I'm never doing it again. Do you understand?"

"Sure, whatever you say. Now come have some fun. The party is just getting started."

He walked with me into the kitchen and was grabbing me a beer when I saw Emma for the first time that night.

"What's up, girl? What took you so long?"

I looked over to Kale only to catch an expression that clearly said, don't dare say a word.

"My dress needed to be steamed."

"Don't you just hate when that happens? Oh my gosh, did you see Curly's new Prada bag? It's to die for."

"No! Did her mom hook her up again?"

"Come on, you have to see it. It's in next season's collection!"

She pulled me away but it didn't require much work on her part. Back then all I cared about was the newest fashion trend.

I didn't see Kale over the next two hours while I played a few drinking games and talked to all my friends which started to piss me off. Sure, we were never attached at each other's hips, but we always spent some time together and he had completely ignored me since I walked into the house.

Looking around I noticed a few people were acting as if they were about to pass out instead of bouncing off the walls like they normally did after getting high. Nothing about their behavior seemed normal. Not when these few seemed to be the first to go after the cocaine every time it was offered.

I didn't bring attention to what I questioned but instead went looking for Kale. I walked from room to room socializing, trying to not call attention to that fact that I was boiling mad.

I looked everywhere and when I continued to come up empty I started going through the upstairs bedrooms.

Fear took over as I let my imagination run wild. With every door I came to I began to picture finding Kale cheating on me with another girl. When I got to his dad's room and opened the door what was in front of me surpassed my worst nightmare.

Kale was standing over a girl named Dorian Baker. She was a sophomore and played on the soccer team at our school only now she was lying on the bed twitching with a belt around her arm and a syringe still lodged in it.

"What the hell, Kale?"

"She just started acting funny. I don't know what's going on, Arianna, and I am freaking out."

His words came slow and almost slurred, which only meant one thing, he was just as high on whatever everyone was taking.

All of a sudden. Dorian started making this gurgling sound. It was something I've never heard before and never want to hear it again. The look Kale gave me was filled with pure panic before he said, "Call my dad."

"What the hell is going on?"

I walked over to her and grabbed her hand but immediately let it drop back down on the bed and started screaming at him.

"Kale, she's cold! What did you give her?"

When he didn't answer me I asked again. After he chose to stay quiet a second time I slapped him straight across the face.

"WHAT DID YOU GIVE HER, KALE!"

"JUST CALL MY DAD!"

I grabbed my phone out of my clutch and with my fingers hovering over the key pad I asked, "What's his number?"

"555-453-2766!"

I dialed as he rambled the numbers off and as it started to ring I looked down at Dorian again. Her eyes were open but her lips were turning blue.

"Help her! Get that needle out of her arm, Kale! What is wrong with you?"

The phone went to voice-mail.

"Should I leave a message? Kale, should I leave a message? Answer me! What should I do?"

I hung up and was already dialing 9-1-1 when it started to ring with Kale's dad's number.

"Hello? Arianna, what's going on?"

"Mr. Thompson, Dorian... Kale... she's not right, she's turning blue..."

"Where are you?"

"At your house. I'm calling 9-1-1. I'm scared!"

"I will call 9-1-1, honey, don't you worry about it. Where is Kale?"

"He's sitting on the bed with Dorian. He's not acting right either, sir. We need help!"

"I'm on my way. Don't worry. Just close the door to the room and wait for me."

"But shouldn't we..."

"No! I will take care of this. Just stay put."

He hung up on me.

I made sure the door was locked and then looked at Kale again. He was practically asleep.

My body sank to the floor but then I started to think. Whatever Kale had given Dorian, she was clearly overdosing. I looked at my phone again deciding to search Google for how to treat an overdose. The results varied on what the victim has taken and in this case I had no idea.

I looked up everything a person could shoot up but all of the symptoms were similar. I finally found something that said if the skin turned blueish purple and they make choking sounds it could be heroin. Heroin!

I read that you should check their mouth to make sure that the air way is open and that they didn't swallow their tongue. I climbed off the floor and was standing next to the bed, scared to touch her, but I knew it could mean the difference between saving her life or letting her die.

"Dorian, can you hear me? I'm going..."

A knock came from the door and someone was turning the handle. I didn't know what to do. The knock came again but this time with it I heard Kale's dad call my name. I rushed over, unlocked the door and swung it open screaming, "Help them!"

Four men came in the room after Kale's dad.

"What did they take, Arianna?"

"I'm not sure. Kale had me pick something up from Derrick. I think it might be heroin!"

"Lucas, Matt, get the girl out of here. Jeremy take care of Arianna."

I was glad Kale's dad was going to get Dorian help, but what about Kale?

"Is Kale okay?"

His father walked over to his side of the bed and slapped him hard in the side of the head. Kale's hands went up in the air before he said slowly, "Why did you hit me?"

"You sorry piece of shit. How dare you invite all these people into my home and steal from me!"

All of the sudden my arm was being pulled, dragging me out the door and into a different bedroom before the man closed the door behind him.

"Sit."

I sat down on the bed not understanding what was going on at all.

"What's going to happen? Can I go to the hospital with her? Is Kale going to be all right?"

I tried to stand up when he walked over and pushed me back down.

"You brought those drugs here?"

I didn't understand. What did that have to do with anything? "I didn't know what was in the bag. I thought it was cocaine."

"So you still thought it was okay to bring cocaine?"

"Well, no, but..."

"You did this, you know. If she dies it's your fault."

"No it's not! I didn't even know anything about this. I just came upstairs to find Kale and he was shooting her up!"

"She administered her own dose. Kale didn't do anything but find her just like you did. Don't try to blame this on him. All of this falls on you."

"No it doesn't! Now let me out of here so I can see Dorian and Kale."

I tried to push past him but this time he threw me on the bed. I began to scream at the top of my lungs as he held me down and tried to cover my mouth. When his hand turned just slightly it was enough for me to bite it and I did as hard as I could.

"You little bitch," came before he back handed me straight across the face.

The door flew open, slamming against the wall and in walked Michael Thompson.

"Get off of her."

"That little bitch bit me!"

"I don't care. Her screaming can be heard down the hall."

The man climbed off me and went to stand next to Kale's dad.

"Arianna, are you aware of what you've done here tonight? Do you know how much trouble you could be in?"

"But, sir, I had no idea what they took. I just found them like that. Is Kale okay? Can I see him?"

"It's best that you don't. Here's the deal, honey, you're going to go to jail for a very long time. I don't think Dorian is going to make it and you supplied her the means to overdose."

"No I didn't. I just picked up a package from Derrick because Kale wanted me to and then..."

"That's enough! You won't say another word, do you hear me! What you think happened is wrong. You did this and you are going to jail possibly for murder unless you listen to me very carefully."

I didn't understand why he kept saying things like that and it scared me beyond belief.

"You're going to move tomorrow. You're going to go far away from here and you will never speak of this night again. I will take care of the charges you would be facing but you need to sign something promising me to keep this quiet. Do you understand?"

"What? No! I don't want to leave. Where would I go? I have no money, I'm not even eighteen..."

"It's already taken care of. John no longer has a job and won't get one either...

I began to cry when he patted my leg.

"Don't feel bad, he was so deep in debt from his gambling they were about to put a price on his head anyway. What idiot gets two hundred grand in the hole anyway? You're actually saving the son-of-a-bitch."

"Please don't make me leave. I won't say a word, I promise. Just let me stay with Kale."

"You don't get that choice. You're going to get as far away from me and my son as possible or you're going to jail for the murder of Dorian Baker."

"I won't do it! I'll tell the police what happened and they will..."

He put his finger in my face scaring me even more when he said, "You listen to me, little girl, I will make your life end before you get a chance to live it or you will sign these papers. The only reason I'm even giving you a choice is because for some reason my son asked me to. Otherwise you would already be taken care of."

"Let me see Kale! I don't believe you! He wouldn't have told you to do this. KALE! KALE!"

Two seconds later, Kale walked in the room with one of his dad's men holding his arm.

"Did you do this? Please tell me you didn't. You know what you did, Kale! Don't let them do this to me! Please, Kale!"

He looked down at the ground and said nothing. "You have a choice, Arianna, and you need to make it."

"This isn't right! You're making me do something and acting like I'm getting a choice when you know damn well I'm not. Why?"

John walked in the room followed by two more men. "John. As you can see we have a situation..."

I was up and off the bed running for him screaming, "John, help me! They're making us leave! Tell them they can't do that. Tell them..."

Just as I grabbed on to his arm he knocked me to the floor when Kale's dad started to speak.

"You no longer have a job, John. I've ensured you won't get another one either. You're going to take the money I am offering your family to relocate and pay off your debt or you can deal with the hole you're in with the Masser family. Ha! You didn't think I knew about that? Well, you're an idiot, because I know everything. So what's it going to be?"

"John, don't listen to them! We don't have to do this..."

I crawled up his leg begging and he simply kicked me off as if I was nothing.

"How much money are we talking?"

I looked over at Kale and begged him with my eyes to do something but he went back to staring at the ground and I knew I was done. The second John asked that question was the day my life stopped.

The next morning movers were in our home packing everything up by five a.m. We were in the car on our way here by five that night.

I wasn't allowed to say goodbye to anyone. One day I had everything and within twenty-four hours it was destroyed.

Canyon never once interrupted me to ask a question or even made a noise. Instead, he held my hand and let me tell my story until it was over.

"So they coerced you into signing a confession to hold over your head?"

"That's exactly what they did and I signed it."

"What ever happened to Dorian?"

"That's the worst part, I don't know. I tried to look up obituaries but I never saw one for her. Maybe they covered that up too."

"I want to kill each and every son-of-a-bitch attached to that night."

"You can't say anything, Canyon. If any of this comes out, do you know what they would do? Michael Thompson is possibly going to be the President of the United States. He would have no problem killing you or me if we thought about standing in his way of that."

"What are you supposed to do? Stay hidden forever? If that's the case, why was Kale here?"

"He wanted us to run away, to go to college and if we were together maybe his dad would let it all go."

"How stupid is he? That would only piss his dad off more. How could you even consider going?"

"If it meant keeping you away from the threat and possibly having John drop the case it was worth it."

"I don't agree at all with that. Tell me the truth. What changed your mind?"

"I kind of fell in love." He smiled but this wasn't really one of those feel good moments where a smile or a kiss made everything okay. "I need you to tell me what you think of me now."

"What do you mean what I think of you?"

"You have to have an opinion of what I did. I brought those drugs there. I killed Dorian."

I wiped the tears falling from my eyes as I waited for him to tell me. He let go of my hand making me think, "Here it comes," but instead he wrapped me in his arms. I broke down and bawled like a baby as he pet my hair with one hand and rubbed my back with the other.

"You made a mistake that you will have to live with for the rest of your life, Ari, but that doesn't define who you are. The fact you have kept this secret for as long as you have, holding all of this in, is unbearable to believe. You're not alone anymore, darlin'." He kissed the top of my head and let me cry more before he continued. "I'm here and I'm not going anywhere. This doesn't make me love you less. Don't worry, baby, you're gonna get through this. We are gonna get through this together."

I can't tell you how much I needed to hear those words. It was the biggest weight off my back and for the first time in months, I believed I was going to be okay.

I looked up into his eyes and said, "Thank you, Canyon. I never knew how much I needed you until right now."

"Really? Because I figured that out a long time ago."

"You know what I mean."

"Yes, I do, and as screwed up as this night has been, what I think we both need is some sleep. We can think more about what to do tomorrow."

"There isn't anything left to do."

"Tomorrow, Ari, I'm exhausted. It's three o'clock and I need to get up in a little over an hour."

"Oh my God, I completely forgot. I will do the chores and you can just sleep in this time."

"Yeah right. Just come to bed with me."

He pulled my arm until I followed him up to his room.

"Where is Shelby sleeping?"

He looked down the hall at his parent's room.

"I put her in there."

"Canyon, you didn't have to do that."

"Just please come to bed with me."

I followed without a word until I was wrapped in his arms listening to him sleep. Only then did I say, "I hope I can someday deserve the love you give me."

Chapter 26

The following morning I did wake up before Canyon, only it was more like seven-thirty, versus the five it needed to be. He looked so adorable that I wanted to snuggle up and kiss him but I had another plan that required him to stay asleep.

Sneaking downstairs, I found Shelby was already up and watching TV quietly.

"Are you hungry, honey?"

"I already ate a bowl of cereal. Is that okay?"

"Yeah, I'm sure Canyon won't mind. Did you happen to see my bags anywhere?"

"He put them on the porch out back."

"Thanks. Did you want to help me out in the barn? I need to start taking care of the animals."

"Can I really?"

"Of course but I wouldn't be so excited yet. It's hard work."

"I can do it."

"I know you can. Now turn off the TV so we don't wake Canyon up and let's go get started."

An hour later I had cleaned all the crap out of the stalls while Shelby cleared the sawdust. It felt like years had gone by since the first day I worked there. Somehow I completely fell head over heels in love with not only the man who owned all of it but every animal that came along with him.

In just those couple months, the foals had grown so much they could be considered small horses. The puppies were no longer innocent babies but holy terrors, spooking the horses non-stop. The kittens were getting more and more curious of the world around them too and began venturing off away from the barn, out into the corral and even up to the house. Who knew a city girl like me could find true happiness out in the country?

I had just finished putting water into every trough and was heading back into the barn when I heard Canyon's voice for the first time. I quickened my step until I rounded the corner and saw him crouched down petting one of the pups with Shelby.

"Good morning, handsome."

He stood and flipped his hat backwards.

"Good morning to you too, darlin'. What have you done?"

"Everything you taught me to and more. I even shoveled out the poop." I was so proud of myself I couldn't help but brag.

"You did? Seriously?"

He started looking in each stall.

"I did the pee part! It was gross."

We both laughed. I remembered feeling the same way on day one.

"I can't believe you both did all this for me."

I walked to him saying, "I have to earn my keep if I'm going to be staying here now, don't I?"

He waited until I was close enough that he could grab me and pull me in before he said, "You don't have to lift a finger here to be welcome, but I sure do appreciate it."

"Anything for you."

He kissed me and patted my butt before pulling back.

"Well if that's all done what do you girls say about going for a ride?"

Shelby jumped up from the floor and ran straight at Canyon.

"Really? Seriously? I can go on a ride with you guys?"

"If your sister here says it's okay, then absolutely."

Shelby looked up at me with more hope in her eyes than I can remember.

"Heck yeah! Let's get them ready. Shelby you're gonna learn what it takes to be a true cowgirl."

"I don't want to be a cowgirl."

We had started to walk towards the tack room when both Canyon and I stopped dead in our tracks.

"What do you mean you don't want to be a cowgirl?"

"I just want to be a princess with a unicorn, remember?"

Canyon laughed and I just shook my head before I said, "Oh, that's right, a unicorn. Well, even unicorns need to be taken care of and this is part of it. Grab some of this stuff and take it out back."

She gladly took the blankets I handed her and walked away while Canyon and I grabbed the saddles.

"She's one of my favorite things."

I stopped and looked at him thinking the same thing about him for loving her like he did.

"What?"

"You're just too good to be true."

"Oh don't start that."

"Start what?"

"Doubting me again. I am what I am, girl, believe me, I'm not good enough to have you but instead of wondering why, I just thank God for it. Get what I'm saying?"

"Yeah. Actually, I do."

"What else do we need?"

Shelby was already back and ready for more.

"Here." I handed her the bridles.

"Now be careful when you walk that you don't trip over the reins."

She put her hands on her hips and with sass I have never seen her sport, she said, "Canyon! I'm not an idiot" and then walked away holding them above her head.

He looked at me and we both laughed.

"See what I mean?"

Twenty-five minutes later we had Winston and Percy saddled up and ready to go. Canyon insisted Shelby ride with him even though I felt Winston would be better at having two people on him at the same time.

"You think the horse matters? You've never had someone ride with you and I would prefer that someone to not be Shelby the first time that happens."

I almost told him to make sure she was safe but then I remembered who I would be talking to.

"Good point. Are you ready?"

He turned around and grabbed Shelby, lifting her up onto Percy before he climbed up behind her.

"Yep, what are you waiting for?"

"Nice one."

I swung my leg over Winston and was ready to go. "After you."

He kicked Percy but then looked back at me. "Keep up, okay?"

"Don't you go too fast with her on there."

"Oh stop nagging and let's have some fun."

He took off, leaving me to catch up. I laughed as I was forced to push Winston further than I ever would have, considering he wasn't Magnus. Once I caught up, the two horses ran side-by-side through the open range.

Every once in a while I would glance over at Shelby and watch her face as she took in the countryside for the first time like this and I remembered feeling the same way, she was in awe. It was nature at its best.

Eventually, we slowed at the creek Canyon had talked about learning to swim in as a kid. It wasn't really a creek but more of a slow moving river with as big as it was.

"You want to go?"

My head snapped in his direction. "Go what? Swimming?"

"Yeah, why not?"

"I don't know, maybe because we don't have suits on?"

"Who cares? It will be fun."

Shelby looked at me with a smile so big I could practically see all her teeth. "Please, Arianna?"

"Are you both crazy?"

Canyon got down and grabbed Shelby, pulling her from the horse. "Just live a little, Ari. Come on, it will be fun."

I stayed on Winston not paying them any mind. "What do you plan to do with the horses?"

"They'll just graze around. Don't worry, they won't run off. Come on!"

I hesitated but when Canyon led Shelby down to the water leaving me, I decided to hell with it. I climbed off Winston and he instantly went over to eat the grass with Percy, leaving me with no excuse. I walked toward the tree line and could hear the two of them laughing. Once I was over the bend and could see down the embankment every part of my hesitation went out the door. Canyon and Shelby were already in the water swimming around having a blast.

"You guys didn't want to wait for me?"

"You took too long. Come on, get in. The water feels great."

Shelby ignored the fact I was even there and continued to enjoy swimming.

I looked over next to me and saw a rope swing was secured to a post giving me an idea. I have never been one to slowly walk into water. Well, not unless it was warmer in it than the temperature out of it. It was either I jump in or it's not going to happen.

I untied the swing and walked backwards until I had the rope secure and then screamed as I ran as fast as I could before my feet left the ground. Swinging out over that water was one the most fun things I had ever done. When I got to the middle of the creek I let go, falling close to fifteen feet before my body plunged under the surface. The water instantly put my body into shock from the bitter temperature of it. By the time I made it back to the top and could catch my breath, I was screaming again. Only this time I was forced to monitor all the use of profanities that were coming to mind.

"What the hell! It's freezing! You lied to me!"

Shelby swam toward me. "I didn't say anything, so you can't say I lied."

Canyon was laughing from the moment I let go of the rope.

"It's not funny!"

"Yes it is. Don't be a baby, you'll get used to it."

"You could have been honest and warned me."

He swam over to me and I watched in slow motion as he raised his hands up in the air before they dropped on my shoulders and dunked me under the water.

I came back up ready for war when Canyon said, "You wouldn't have gotten in!" as he swam away from me.

I fought against the water to race after him until I could grab onto his back and then wrapped my arms around his neck. I tried with all my might to push him under but he was entirely too strong for me to win. We were all laughing at my failed efforts until I half-heartedly gave up and enjoyed the fact that we were all having fun.

"Shelby, you should go swing. It's fun."

"You'll let me?"

"Absolutely! Canyon and I'll stay down here and watch you."

She swam over to the bank and started climbing up while Canyon pulled me around to face him. "I love you, darlin'. I know I've said this a million times already but I really am glad you're here."

I didn't know where that came from but obviously our conversation the night before wasn't far from his mind. "I love you too and I never want to leave." And I meant it.

"Say that again."

"Which part?"

"The whole thing. I don't think I'll ever get used to hearing you say it."

"You will one day when I'm old and fat. You'll be wishing you never wanted this after all."

He looked me in the eye and I knew what he was about to say would melt my heart. "Damn, you're right. I may want to rethink this after all." I was wrong. I tried to push off of him and swim away but he just laughed and pulled me in tighter. "I'm just teasing you, girl."

"You think you are but you just wait and see how miserable I make you in a few years."

"I'm looking forward to it."

I smiled and gave him a kiss right when we heard, "Hey, guys, watch!"

Just as we looked up, Shelby was running straight off the ledge. I didn't realize how crazy high you got on that rope until I watched her swing out. When she let go she screamed at the top of her lungs as she plunged in to the water.

I nervously let go of Canyon and swam over to her when she came up for air.

She grabbed onto me and just as I opened my mouth to ask if she was okay she blurted out, "That was awesome!"

"Really? You had me freaked out when you screamed like that. I thought you were scared."

"No way, that was awesome! Canyon, it's your turn."

We both looked back to give him trouble but he was already on his way up the bank.

"I'm on it, girls. Are you going to catch me?"

Shelby and I looked at each other wide-eyed.

"Not me."

"Not me either."

"Well then you better swim fast 'cause here I come!"

Canyon shot out over the water, forgetting the rope, and pulled his knees up right before he made the biggest cannon ball splash in history right next to us. Shelby and I both screamed at the top of our lungs as waves crashed over us. Canyon came up and we all laughed and played over the next few hours, letting go of all the bad and just enjoyed the moment we were in.

Eventually, it was time to get back to work and I had to take Shelby home. I hated seeing her cry but I couldn't keep her with me even though it was all I ever wanted.

"Hey, do me a favor, huh? Can you make sure that you come back tomorrow? I don't think I can handle all the puppies running around while I'm working on your horse. I really could use the help."

Shelby wiped her snotty nose and looked up at Canyon with her red swollen eyes.

"My horse?"

"Yeah. I seem to remember Ari telling me something about you wanting your own and I have the perfect filly for you if you want her."

My face almost matched Shelby's with the disbelief we were both dealing with. "Really, Canyon, you will let me have one?"

"You bet, hun. I'd do anything to make you smile. But you have to do your part too. She's going to need lots of love and care that I can't give her so I'm going to need you to be here every day. Will that be something you can handle?"

"Yes, yes, yes!"

She ran into his open arms as he picked her up from the ground and swung her in a circle. I stood back smiling at the two people I loved most in the world and thought, this is what life's all about.

"I hate to break this up but, Shelby, I really need to be getting you back."

Canyon hugged her one last time before he set her down and she ran to my truck and climbed in.

I walked over to the greatest man in the world, took both of my hands and rested them on his cheeks while I stared into his eyes.

"You are something amazing, Canyon Michaels." I didn't give him a chance to respond before I softly pressed my lips against his.

When I pulled back he grabbed me and yanked me forward so he could kiss me again. "You, Ari, are what makes me what I am. Now hurry up and take her back so we can get to work."

"Yes, sir."

"Don't start that with me."

I walked back to my truck with a smile on my face and got in.

"Can you believe he's giving me my own horse?"

I turned the key and started to back up when I said, "You deserve it, Shelby. You're a good girl and he loves you so much."

"I love him too."

The smile she wore all the way back to the house melted my heart.

We got out and I grabbed her bag to carry it in for her. I hated the idea of entering that house knowing I didn't have to anymore but Shelby ran in straight to Mom and John screaming, "I have my own horse! My own horse!"

Neither of them said a word. They were waiting for me to walk into the room.

"What do you mean you have your own horse?"

"Canyon gave her to me. She's mine! And I get to take care of her every day."

"That's great, honey. Why don't you go jump in the shower. You stink."

"No I don't. We were in the creek swimming all day. I can't smell."

"Well you do and I said get in the shower now!"

Shelby huffed but still walked down the hallway and disappeared in to the bathroom.

My work was done. I had gotten her back home safe and felt no reason to stick around. I walked out the door, closing it behind me when it flew back open with a raging lunatic coming right at me

"You can tell your precious Canyon he can keep his fucking horse! I don't want his pity and he had no right getting my daughter's hopes up."

I spun around and walked until my finger was almost touching his nose.

"Your daughter was bawling her eyes out because she didn't want to have to come back here and live with you! You! So don't you dare blame anyone but yourself for the fact she hates you. You did that all on your own."

I turned and walked to my truck wishing I never had to see him again.

All of a sudden my head was yanked backwards. He had my hair and was pulling me away from my truck while I screamed at the top of my lungs.

"I am so tired of you!"

He shoved me down to the ground and was pushing my face into the gravel with his knee. I tried fighting back but there was nothing I could do.

"Go tell Canyon I said to stay the fuck away from my daughter or he will lose everything he owns. Don't fuck with me!"

He pushed down one last time with his knee before he let go of my hair and stood up to walk away.

I sat up and screamed, "I hate you!"

With both of my fists filled with rocks, I threw them as hard as I could at his back but he never bothered to turn around. Instead, he continued to walk into the house as if I wasn't even there and slammed the door behind him.

I wiped my face to try to get the small bits of gravel imbedded in my cheek off. It hurt like hell but I got up and sat inside my truck using my rear view mirror to get out the rest. Nothing short of killing him would ever be justice enough for that man.

I drove back to Canyon's dreading the reaction he was going to give me when he forced me to explain what happened. Once I pulled up and realized he wasn't waiting for me I took the advantage and went into the house to shower and get cleaned up. From the upstairs bedroom window I could see him running Percy and knew I would be okay.

After I got out of the shower I decided that the old me didn't need to be completely buried. I may have hated a lot about who I was but it didn't mean that wanting to feel pretty had to go with it.

Taking the time to curl my hair and apply my makeup actually felt good. It's crazy how an everyday ritual that feels almost like a chore can turn into something uplifting. I liked who I saw back through my reflection.

Choosing the clothes was a lot harder. The old me would have gone straight for a dress and heels but I wasn't her anymore. I needed to find comfort in who I was becoming. So instead of the dress I found a denim skirt and a blue plaid button up shirt. The yellow tank top I paired with it just peeked out from the few buttons I left open. My cowgirl boots were the last accessory I put on before I was ready for Canyon to see me.

I walked out onto the porch feeling way more insecure than I had upstairs. What if he didn't care for me with all the makeup and hair? He never once made me feel less than beautiful when I was completely natural. So many thoughts were going through my mind when I opened the door and put myself on display. Canyon happened to be walking back from the training run with Skyla, one of the mares. His body glistened from the sun bouncing off of the sweat pouring from him. With his hat backwards and only his jeans and boots on, he made for possibly the sexiest man alive in my eyes. But none of that compared to the look in his eye when he looked up at me for the first time. I wasn't sure how he would take my new look but nothing beats a man stopping dead in his tracks. Even Skyla was jerked to a halt when her lead rope wasn't moving along side of her anymore.

My smile was as big as it could get looking at him, watching him stumble for words.

"Are you going to say something?"

I took one step at a time, trying my best to not look like I was putting too much thought into it until I was on flat ground and approaching him.

"I ah, um... Ari, you are stunning."

I hadn't thought my smile could stretch further but it did.

"Let me take you out tonight."

"Wait, what?"

That was not what I expected to hear.

"May I have the honor of taking you out to dinner? I know any normal man would want to tuck you away and keep you all for themselves but, darlin', I would rather show the world what's mine. You are beauty at its finest and..."

"Stop! You're killing me. Yes, I'll go to dinner with you."

"Why did you cut me off?"

"Because. No one wants to hear all that. It makes me uncomfortable."

He let Skyla go and hopped over the fence that stood between us.

"You will get one thing straight right now and with this, I won't budge. You deserve to hear these things and I'm going to tell you whenever I feel like it. It doesn't make you conceded or vain, it makes you loved and there is nothing wrong about that."

I closed the space between us and moved to kiss him when he grabbed my arms to stop me.

"I'm all dirty, darlin', you don't want to do that."

"Don't tell me what I want to do. If I want to kiss the man I love I'm gonna damn well do it."

He smiled at me before my lips touched his. The taste of that man. God help anyone who had ever had him prior to me and had to let him go. With each swipe of his tongue or pull on my bottom lip I was done for. Just as we were both getting into it, he pulled back, short of breath.

"Let me shower real quick. I don't want to mess you up. You look all fancy. Just give me twenty minutes please."

I couldn't drop my smile if I tried. "Take all the time you need. I'll go put Skyla on the wheel and take Percy back in for the night."

"Sounds great to me, thanks."

He started walking to the house while I squeezed myself through the fence.

"Hey, Ari!"

I came up on the other side to find him standing on the steps.

"Think about what your favorite song is."

"My favorite song? For what?"

"Just do it for me okay? I don't need to know right now. Just think about it."

He walked into the house as I laughed to myself.

I knew the answer to his question. I'd had listened to it every chance I got since the first time I heard it. Why he wanted to know was going to be interesting to find out.

Chapter 27

When Canyon came around the corner into the barn I could smell him before I saw him. The cologne he was wearing was something I could drown myself in and die happy but what I got to look at topped even that.

He had shaven, cleaning up the scruff on his face I had come to expect daily. The jeans were crisp with a royal blue button down that pulled the tan coloring from his skin out and made him almost look golden. His hair was gelled up in a messy way that took his sex appeal to heights I didn't know were possible as he walked toward me. I stopped petting Triton and said, "Hey there, good lookin'."

"Hi to you too, sexy."

When he wrapped his arms around me and kissed me tenderly on the forehead I thought to myself, this is a memory I will hold onto forever.

"You about ready for dinner?"

I was starving so the answer wasn't hard to come by. "Absolutely. Where would you like to go?"

"I'm taking you to the best restaurant in a forty-five mile radius. You like seafood, right?"

"I haven't had any since we moved here."

"I figured that. I just wasn't sure you liked it."

"Can I tell you how excited I am?"

"Why don't you wait until we're in the truck? This is going to be a long drive."

He wasn't kidding. The restaurant was almost an hour away but holy crap was it worth it. When we walked in, the mood was as romantic as something you would find from a five-star restaurant in the heart of Baltimore. I didn't think it could exist way out in the middle of nowhere Montana but Canyon had managed to pick the perfect place for us.

I felt slightly under dressed by the setting but looking around had me more at ease. People there didn't make you feel like you needed to adorn a seven-hundred-dollar outfit to enjoy good food and for that alone I respected them.

We were led to a table in a far back corner, giving us privacy from the main dining area in the center. A low lit pendant hung from the ceiling centered above our table. It was the only light we had to see with other than the soft glowing candle resting as a centerpiece. Canyon pulled out my chair before he took his seat across from me.

After giving the waitress our drink order we started looking over our menus. My mouth watered at the mere thought of lobster. It is my favorite food on the planet and seeing it listed on the menu had me smiling from ear to ear.

"You see something you like?"

I looked up at him and asked, "What sounds good to you?"

"I'm going with the lobster."

"That's what I was thinking too!"

You wouldn't believe what they brought out for us. The lobsters were the size of small dogs and oh my God did it taste amazing. We stuffed ourselves to the brink of being miserable before we both sat back and laughed.

"That was freakin' delicious."

"Did you think of that song yet?"

"Where did that come from?"

"I'm still waiting for the song if you came up with it."

"I did."

"Are you going to make me torture you to hear it?"

"'Let It Be Me.'"

"What?"

"The song you sang me the other night on the porch. By Keith Whitley?"

"You mean 'Don't Close Your Eyes'? How can that be your favorite song? I sang that at one of the saddest points in my life thinking you were leaving."

"It was the words that made my decision to stay."

"But how is that your favorite?"

"Because it was the best decision I have ever made."

"You ruined my surprise by this, I hope you realize that."

My jaw dropped. Even though he wore a smile I never thought my love for that moment could ruin anything. "How?"

"Never mind. Would you like to share a dessert with me?"

"Uh no. I couldn't eat anything else if I tried. Besides, what did I say wrong? Would you like my runner up?"

"Yes, please."

"Well I know you live in the sticks but have you ever heard of Ed Sheeran?"

"'Thinking Out Loud', maybe?"

"That's the one. How did you know?"

"Because every woman on the planet loves that song. And it's perfect."

"Perfect for what?"

"Us."

That was like the gospel spoken. He was more right than he knew. I always hoped someday I would find someone who could love me like that and I had it from the man I least expected letting myself fall for. I think my smile was his answer because the next thing I knew he was standing up and pulling my chair back.

"Are we leaving?"

"Yes, darlin', I have other plans for tonight."

"Really? With who?"

"Only the most gorgeous woman on the planet."

"Are you trying to make me jealous?"

"Not one bit being it's always going to be you."

We both wore matching grins as we walked hand in hand into the house after the long ride back. I think we were both anxious as to what the rest of the night had in store. I had never felt so full of everything. I know that doesn't really make sense to you but when you go from feeling completely empty to having something that truly completes you, it can do amazing things and I wanted to pay him back the only way I knew would solidify what we had when we were together.

He thought he had a surprise for me but what I had for him was something just as special.

Canyon turned on the TV while we laid on the couch cuddling but my mind was racing with the thoughts of how I was going to pull this off. Eventually I rolled over on my side facing him and said, "I'm going to go change into something more comfortable."

He was so engrossed with what he was watching that he barely murmured an, "Okay "while I slipped out of his grasp.

Climbing the stairs I kept thinking about how awkward this all was. I wasn't a virgin and I seriously doubted he was either but something about what was going to happen had me more nervous than the first time I ever had sex.

I took off my clothes and grabbed the sexiest underwear I owned. What I couldn't decide on was if I should cover it all up or prance down the stairs and see his reaction. Most girls would prefer the man to take this decision from them and let them make the first move. Well, I'm not like most girls and the need to make this moment perfect for him was all I could focus on.

I decided that the barely naked approach was the way to go.

I reapplied my makeup and shook my curls out a little bit, trying to make myself more confident than he'd ever seen me. I got to the top step though and then ran back into the bedroom for my boots. If anything was going to make a cowboy blush it was his girl in nothing but her boots.

Back at the steps I started to doubt myself and the whole idea. What if I tripped and fell? I mean, how stupid would I look? I told myself it would be okay and I just had to go for it. Each step was better than the one before. My confidence grew higher and by the last one I felt on top of the world. Only Canyon never looked away from the TV. I stood there holding onto the banister for what felt like forever until finally I cleared my throat.

He was watching the PBR and I couldn't expect him to know what I was up to but a simple glance in my direction would have at least been something. The longer I stood there the more aggravated I got. I cleared my throat again and watched him once again completely ignore me while he picked up his beer and took a drink.

I decided the subtle approach wasn't working so instead, I walked in front of the television. Watching Canyon's eyes swell bigger than saucers was worth its weight in gold. Getting beer spit all over me was not.

I was speechless if you can only imagine, shaking my arms attempting to rid myself of the drops of beer now covering me.

"Holy shit!"

"You could say that. This is so not how I pictured this moment going."

Canyon was up off the couch and dashing to the kitchen, for what I was unsure of, until he brought back a roll of paper towels and began patting my body down.

"I can do that." He ignored me and continued to try to dry me. "Canyon, I got it!"

He was down on his knees when I ripped the towels out of his hand.

"Hey! Don't get mad at me because you decided to come down here naked. What the heck did you expect me to do?"

"I'm not mad, I'm just embarrassed."

I was wiping off my stomach when Canyon grabbed my hand and stopped me.

"What are you doing?"

"Why would I let it go to waste?"

He brought his face to my stomach and then drug his tongue from my navel all the way up to the underside of my breast and holy crap did it feel good. I felt his hands grab onto my hips and pull me forward as his tongue went back to cleaning off my body. He rose up on his knees while his hands climbed up my back until he grabbed onto my bra strap and I felt the tension release. One strap at a time fell from my shoulders as I stood there covered in goosebumps.

This was not how I planned this at all but I couldn't think much because the next thing I knew, Canyon had both of my breasts in his hands.

"Tell me you came down here for me so I could do this to you."

His tongue flicked the tip of my breast and made me want to scream.

"Yes."

He kissed the other one dragging his tongue between the two.

"Ari?"

"Yes?"

"Can I take you to bed?"

"Please."

He rose up to meet me at eye level with a look in his eye I had never seen. It was primal. I thought he would take my hand and lead me up the stairs but instead he scooped me up in his arms and carried me the entire way.

We never let each other go with our eyes as he laid me down softy on his bed and then stood at the end of it.

"You are the most beautiful thing I have ever seen in my life."

"Come here."

He crawled onto the bed, hovering over me until he brought his sweet lips down to mine. I loved the taste of him. The slow pulls he took to my bottom lip. I loved everything about this man and the idea of what he would do entranced me.

"This time I'm not going stop this from happening. I'm going to make the sweetest love to you that both of us will ever know."

He backed off the bed, taking my panties and boots off in the process before I watched as he slowly stripped off his clothes. The body that first caught my attention long ago out in the fields was now standing before me completely bare.

"Tell me you want me, Ari."

His weight sunk into the bed as he climbed back up me.

"It's all I will ever want."

When he lined himself up in between my legs I thought I might pass out by the trauma my body was about to ensue from the size of him alone. It had been months, but it felt as though I had never experienced anything being inside me as he began to stretch me from the inside out.

His arms gripped onto me as he buried his head in my shoulder. Another slow push came. This time I thought I was going to split open. Canyon lifted up as my hands fell to his waist and each time he would move forward I would use resistance against him.

"You have to calm down, darlin'. I promise I will never hurt you, just trust me to make you feel good."

He pushed again and this time I screamed bloody murder as his end became one with my beginning. We both didn't move for a second letting nature work its magic while my body adjusted to comfort with his size.

Canyon looked down into my watering eyes and then kissed the tip of my nose.

"I love you so much, Ari."

"I love you too. So much it actually hurts at the moment."

He started to shake and I knew it was from the laughter he was holding in. I didn't even try to restrain myself. I needed the distraction and laughing did just what I needed it to.

"I can't believe we're laughing right now. I haven't been with a girl in so long and the first time I'm back in the game, I make you laugh."

I rose up on my elbows and grabbed his cheeks.

"If we can't laugh, what is there left?"

He pulled slightly out of me and then plunged back bringing with it the most incredible sensation.

"I will show you what's left."

I fell back down to the bed and closed my eyes while I fell into a euphoric coma as he rocked in and out of me.

"Don't close your eyes. Open them up and stay with me."

My eyes opened and set their focus on the most beautiful man bringing levels of pleasure to me I had never reached. The pain disappeared leaving in its wake the most sensual experience of my life. I let my hands wander across his body, feeling every dip and curve along with the tightness of each muscle as he used them. With one legged wrapped around his back and the other left straight I had access to the point we came together. Slowly, I rocked with him as my right hand came down and began to rub myself.

"Holy shit! Don't do that. You're going to make me…"

"I'll stop. I just wanted to make you…"

"You being under me right now makes everything the best it can be. Now let me take care of you."

No more words were needed as the pace we had been maintaining went all to hell when Canyon grabbed ahold of my leg, lifted it over his shoulder and began his assault on me. My climax was building out of control and I knew Canyon was holding back to let me finish.

"OH MY GOD! Get there, baby, because I'm going to lose it."

Seconds later I was in climax bliss squeezing on to him in a rhythm only a female body possesses.

"Ooohhhhhhuuuuuuhhhhh!"

He pulled out, falling on top me, taking my mouth like he had just taken my body as he finished.

"That was the most amazing thing I've ever felt. Thank you."

He looked like he was going to say something equally as sweet but he got distracted.

"Damn, let me get a towel."

The second he lifted up I agreed, feeling the remains of what he left behind.

"I probably could have told you I'm on the shot."

He looked at me like I had just spoken Spanish.

"The shot is a form of birth control."

I watched the light bulb go on and began to laugh.

"Don't laugh at me. I should have worn a condom but I forgot all about it when I saw you downstairs. Which is why I couldn't hold out for crap."

"You don't need one is what I'm trying to say. Wait, that was fast for you?"

He grew hard again and my eyes practically popped out of my head. "No way!"

"What do you mean no way? You just told me I can ride bareback, darlin'. Those are words every man lives to hear."

He lowered himself back down on to me and for the next few hours we discovered what true love making was until our bodies decided we had no choice but to stop. As I lay there wrapped in Canyon's arms all I could think about was how nothing in the world could compare to being this happy.

"Hey, are you asleep?"

I lifted my head from his chest. "No, but I should be. I have no energy left."

"Let me up for a minute. I want to go grab something."

I rolled over allowing him to slide out from under me. While he got up and left the room I nuzzled back into a cozy spot and drifted off before I knew it.

I woke to the sound of guitar strings. Nothing could have taken me more by surprise then Canyon sitting down on the bed playing "Don't Close Your Eyes" to me. I sat up and scooted myself back until I could rest my body against the headboard, clutching a pillow in my lap as I watched him sing the most amazing lyrics come from the man that I loved. I know this song isn't romantic. If anything it's a tear jerker but as I've said before, joy can arise from heartache and sometimes it can be the most powerful kind.

When he played the last chord, I crawled across the bed to kiss him sweetly.

"What happened to 'Thinking Out Loud'?"

"I asked for your favorite for a reason."

"I will forever be grateful for that song, Canyon. Thank you for that."

"Oh I know how you can thank me."

"Seriously?"

"Absolutely!"

Only this time when he grabbed ahold of me he simply pulled me to him, wrapped his arms around me and said, "Goodnight, baby girl."

Hours later I woke up to a sound I had never heard before. I was so exhausted that I tried to play it off as a dream and go back to sleep but when I heard it again, there was no mistaking real from fantasy and if anything this was an all-out nightmare.

I sat up quickly and saw light coming from what should have been a coal black night. I shoved Canyon and screamed, "Wake up" as I jumped out of bed and ran to the window.

"OH MY GOD! OH MY GOD! CANYON!"

Not another word was needed before he was out of bed and running to see what had me so upset while I was grabbing for my clothes.

A scream came from outside that broke both of us.

"NOOOO!"

It was almost impossible to breathe as I watched the man I love crumble into a thousand pieces as he threw on a pair of pants and ran out of the room. I wasn't far behind him with only his shirt and a pair of panties.

When I got to the back door it was swinging shut from Canyon running through it straight for the barn that was completely engulfed in flames. The animals were trapped and screaming for their lives and there was nothing we could do. I ran after Canyon, trying to pull him back but he threw me off, making every attempt he could to get inside. The blaze was too high and completely out of control.

I ran back in to the house and grabbed the phone. My hands were shaking so badly that even dialing 9-1-1 was difficult. I told the operator the address followed by, "Get out here! There's a fire and we need help!" before I hung up and ran back out to a night sky now blocked out from the smoke billowing from the inferno.

"Canyon!"

I could no longer see him.

"CANYON!"

I ran around the barn trying to find him, screaming his name over and over again but I never got a response. I fell to the ground and covered my ears, rocking back and forth trying to block out the sound of the death happening before me.

"CANYON!"

He was inside. I knew in my gut I had lost him too and nothing can allow me to describe the pain ripping me apart.

Chapter 28

I could hear the sirens in the distance coming our way but it didn't matter. The sounds coming from the barn were drowning them out.

Everything I loved was gone.

Firetrucks pulled into the driveway and men started running around the building that was now collapsing within itself using hoses to spray it down but nothing was helping. I sat back and wondered, how can God be so cruel?

"Ma'am, excuse me, ma'am, I need you to come with me."

I didn't move. There was no reason. If anything I only wished I had been brave enough to run into the fire too. At least my misery would be over.

I heard the firemen coming in and out of the barn but I didn't really listen. I didn't care about anything anymore.

"Ma'am, I'm going to have to move you."

He scooped me up, taking away my choice and brought me around to the front of the barn where the ambulance was waiting to take away the one man who stole my heart, vowing to never leave me but did anyway.

When I was set down on the steps, I noticed everyone running to the back. I didn't care to live, more or less move. The horses, Canyon, I had lost everything.

"Get the stretcher over here now!"

I looked up and saw them laying Canyon's body on the ground off in the distance. My entire body began to shake as two men lifted the stretcher and started to carry him toward me.

I whispered to myself, "Please don't. Please. I can't see this, I just can't" before I got up to run into the house but a woman grabbed my arm.

"We're taking him now. Would you like to ride with us?"

I couldn't believe she would ask me to do something like that. I shook my head back and forth when words wouldn't form, feeling even worse for being so selfish. Canyon would never have let me go no matter how awful it was.

"Honey, he just might need your strength."

"What kind of sick person are you?"

"Look it's up to you but either way we're leaving. Do you want to come or not?"

Something about her agitation made me think. "Are you telling me he's alive?"

"Yes, dear, that's exactly what I'm saying and he's going to need you."

I was up and running as fast as I could for the ambulance they had loaded him in. As soon as I reached the back, I climbed in and crawled straight to his side.

He had a few burns that weren't nearly as bad as I expected them to be but he wasn't responding when I touched him. I looked at the paramedic on the other side of Canyon and asked, "Why isn't he..."

I was shaking so badly, afraid to finish my sentence.

"We sedated him. He suffered from severe smoke inhalation and needs oxygen."

I wiped the tears from my face and tried to steady my hands while I asked, "How did he even survive being in there?"

"They found him in the tack room along with a young foal. He had them both covered with a fireproof blanket."

"So he saved a horse too?"

"She's a fighter, I tell ya."

I looked down at my hero and grabbed ahold of his hand.

"Thank God for that blanket."

"You can say that again."

When we got to the hospital they took him from me again. I didn't want to let him go but the ICU wouldn't allow me in. Instead I was taken to a room full of scrubs. I hadn't once thought about the fact that I was still only in Canyon's shirt and my panties. Who would think about what they were wearing in a situation like I was in?

I changed and then made my way to the waiting room when I realized that I had no one to call. No one to lean on. All we had were each other and I wondered if he thought about that before he ran into the barn. That thought triggered memories I wasn't ready to reminisce. We lost everything but ourselves. It wasn't as if the animals were mine but I loved them equally and their pain in death crushed me to a core I hadn't known existed prior to that day.

I tried drinking some coffee, hoping to hear something from the staff but in the end sleep won out.

Hours later I was being shaken awake by a nurse with bright red hair. The second I opened my eyes and saw her all I thought about was...

"Oh my God, Shelby!"

"I'm sorry, dear, who?"

It all came crashing down on me. The animals, almost losing Canyon...

"Excuse me."

I ran straight to the bathroom located across the hall. Throwing a stall door open, I hit my knees on the cold tile floor and violently began to vomit. When I had expelled all there was I sat back on my heels and screamed at the top of my lungs. The nurse from the lobby scared me when cold hands graze my neck before pulling my hair from my face.

"I heard what happened and I'm so sorry. But what you need to hold onto right now is your strength. God gives us more than we require and it's times like these that you have to tap into your reserve."

"How is he?"

I wiped my mouth with the back of my hand and then turned to look at her.

"He's got some pretty bad burns but none are past third degree. I just wish that poor boy would have worn a shirt."

I stood up and said, "Excuse me" while I passed her on my way to the sink to rinse my mouth out. I noticed she didn't tell me he was going to be okay. At least she didn't lie to me.

"Can I see him now?"

"I'm sorry. We're still keeping him comfortable while we treat the burns."

"How would being there make him less comfortable?"

"The doctor intubated him just in case his air way swells. Right now we just want him to sleep."

I didn't care if he was asleep or not. I just wanted to be with him. See him with my own two eyes.

"I thought I lost him. When I couldn't find him I thought..."

Her hand rested on my shoulder. "He's going to be just fine. Time is what he needs. He's always been a tough one, even as a child."

I wasn't expecting that one.

"You know him?"

"I'm sorry, I haven't introduced myself yet, have I? My name is Hillary Michaels and it's nice to meet you."

"MICHAELS?"

"Yes, unfortunately I bear the name but please don't lump me in the bunch. I married Canyon's cousin and before you ask, no we are no longer affiliated with his father's side anymore."

"You said anymore. Like once upon a time you were?"

"Honey, when that boy's mama was here we were as tight as two friends could be. Sharon was the most amazing women you could ever know."

"I really just need to see him. Please, even if I don't get to go into the room, can I just see him?"

She looked perplexed but answered me with exactly what I needed to hear. "I could get in trouble for this. Whatever, you only live once right? Follow me."

I was two steps behind her the entire way until we reached his door where I found a small window but that was as far as I could go. I was grateful to even get this.

I peeked through and when my eyes landed on him, my heart began beating so hard I'm surprised others couldn't hear it. At the same time that I felt relief, rage also took its place. For so many reasons I was angry. Why did it happen in the first place? Why did all of those beloved animals have to suffer and last but most importantly, why did Canyon risk his own life?

"We have to go now. I can't chance anyone seeing you here any longer."

I stayed in place for one more second, just to touch the glass and wished it was him before I turned back to Hilary and said, "Thank you for bringing me here."

"You're welcome."

Once we were back out into the waiting room I was met by police. The last thing I wanted was to relive what happened but I had no choice when I heard, "We need to ask you some questions."

Twenty minutes later I had told every detail I knew to the officers. "Thank you, ma'am, we'll be in touch."

They walked away without so much as an "I'm sorry". I can't tell you how much I wanted to chase them down and ask if they would like to be questioned just after a loss like the one I was feeling. Of course I knew they were just doing their job but my patience was absent and my kindness was spent.

Hilary checked on me several times suggesting I go home and get some rest but two things were stopping me. The first and most obvious was I had no way to get there. Second, I didn't want to see the remnants of what was once my favorite place in the world.

"He's going to be sleeping the majority of the day, sweetheart. You deserve to do the same."

"I can't go home."

"Sure you can and I'm going to make sure you're not alone in doing it. I get off in a half hour. Just hold tight and I will be back soon."

She patted my leg before she walked back through the double doors leaving me once again. I knew without her I wouldn't have been told anything. Hospitals are tricky about who they give information to and with me not being family I would know nothing.

Thirty minutes later Hilary walked out with her keys in hand and her purse slung over her shoulder ready to go.

"You look like you're about to fall asleep sitting up. Come on, let me get you home."

"I appreciate this but you have no idea how much I don't want to go back to that house."

"Oh, I was thinking I was taking you back to your parents. Do you not have any either, dear?"

That was a question that took some thought to answer. I never really had parents the way that most kids do and so that's how I answered.

"No, I don't. I have been staying with Canyon."

"Oh, well that is more complicated isn't it? Just the same, you need rest so follow me."

I walked behind her through the parking garage until we reached her car.

"I feel bad asking you to do this."

She turned to me with a stern reprimanding look.

"You didn't ask, I offered. Now get in the car, sweet child."

She hit the button to unlock the doors and got in while my hand hovered over the handle as she turned the car on. The window began to roll down when she leaned across the seat and said kindly, "It's going to be hard but remember, you're not alone."

Hilary didn't talk much or ask me questions like I expected her to. She simply let me have the quiet I very much needed to get my thoughts in order. After twenty minutes they were just as jumbled as before. I missed him already and the idea of walking into that house knowing he wouldn't be with me, sleeping in his bed without him beside me… it was haunting.

Hilary was kind enough to try and drown them out with music. I had never heard "Night Changes" by One Direction before but damn did they have it right, so much can change in one night.

I wiped the tears from my cheeks as they fell wondering how I could conjure up some of that strength everyone apparently thought I had, but was coming up empty.

"You know you can think about all of the things that you lost or you can think of what you still have."

"I can't get it out of my head. The sounds of all of those poor animals suffering. The idea of losing him…"

"I remember after Sharon passed when Canyon's father had David sell all of her horses. That in itself would have killed her. I don't know how that young man managed to rebuild after that but he can do it again."

The horse! He saved one, a girl!

"Oh my God, Magnus!"

Hilary looked at me like I was insane.

"Magnus is Canyon's prize stallion. He's with the jockey. I bet that's why he saved a female."

"He managed to save one?"

"Yeah, the dumb goof. That's why he must have gone in."

"See? If he wasn't willing to give up you shouldn't either."

That was something I could debate but she wouldn't understand.

By the time we pulled into the driveway daylight had broken. There was no longer a barn standing strong in front of us, instead there were two cars I didn't recognize.

"Who could that be?"

243

"I have a feeling we're about to find out."

We both got out of the car and walked toward what was left. I was shaking uncontrollably and Hilary must have noticed because the next thing I knew she took my hand and squeezed.

Two different men were walking around the scene looking for something.

"Can we help you?" Hilary asked.

They both looked up and then the man closest walked toward us.

"This is a crime scene. You can't be here."

"I live here."

"Then excuse me, ma'am, but we need you to stay out of this area until we complete our investigation."

"Who are you?"

"My name is Duncan and I am the laboratory analyst." He handed me a business card. "That over there is the lead fire scene investigator, Shane Collins. He might need to ask you some questions hold on one second."

"Hey, Shane! This is..." He looked back at me. "I didn't catch your name."

"Arianna."

"This is Arianna. She lives here."

The man named Shane began to walk towards me while Duncan went back to work. I glanced at Hilary and realized just how grateful I was that she was there and I didn't have to do this alone. When the man named Shane reached the two of us there were no nice pleasantries exchanged. He simply made his approach and then started firing questions.

"Do you have anyone in mind as far as who might have started the fire?"

I knew it couldn't have happened by accident but for someone to do this, it was unbelievable.

"Are you saying someone did?" Hilary took the question right out of my mouth.

"I can't officially pronounce it as arson until our investigation is complete but it sure looks that way to me."

The first person that came to mind was John and what he'd said the last time I had seen him but I wasn't sure if I should throw unfounded blame.

"I'm aware that there was a feud over ownership of the stables with a—" he looked down at his report "—David Michaels. Is this someone you would consider a threat?"

That name hit me like a ton of bricks to the face. He may have hated Canyon for taking the business but he wouldn't have killed innocent horses to sever the ties completely, at least I thought.

"Yes, absolutely I believe he could have done this."

I was stunned silent. I knew Hilary was there to support me but I had no idea she would blame someone outright.

"And who are you, ma'am?"

"My name is Hillary Michaels and David is pure evil, just like his brother. I don't doubt for a second that he would go to any lengths possible to punish Canyon."

"Well, we have your statements, now you need to let us do our job."

I heard him speak but I couldn't wrap my head around the fact he said arson. If someone did this they deserved to pay.

"John McCormick," I blurted out without premeditation.

"Excuse me?"

Hilary looked just as shocked to hear me speak for the first time since I told them my name.

"He lives in the next house down the road."

"And what leads you to believe this man would be involved?"

"He's married to my mother and the last time I was there he said something like he will make sure Canyon loses everything he owns."

Hilary gasped while Shane the fire investigator started writing things down.

"Thank you, ladies. Now please, we need to get back to work."

"Who will clean this up after you're done?"

"That's up to you to hire a crew. My job is to nail the son-of-a-bitch responsible."

That was the last thing I wanted to hear. Canyon didn't need to deal with any more than he already had.

"Do you know of anyone I can call?"

He started digging through a pocket of his jacket when he pulled out a stack of business cards. After sorting through them he pulled one out and handed it to me. "Ask for Jeff." And then he walked away.

Hilary turned to me and said, "Do you really think your step-dad could do this?"

"I think it's possible that he could do anything to hurt me or the people I love."

"So that's why you said you have no parents?"

"I'm sorry if I misled you. I just don't really consider either of them anything close to what a parent should be."

With sympathy in her expression she wrapped her arm around my shoulder and said, "Let's get you inside."

Ten minutes later Hilary had drawn me a bath and was saying goodbye.

"Thank you for all your help."

"It was no problem at all, dear. Now you get washed up and then get some rest."

She let herself out while I stripped out of the scrubs I had been wearing, climbed into the tub and openly sobbed.

If John did this, I was the one responsible. I pushed him too far the last time I was there and I knew it. But what if it was David? In the end it didn't matter. Canyon lost almost everything he had worked so hard for.

I woke up in ice cold water and realized I had fallen asleep what had to have been a long time ago. Getting out, I told myself that it was a good enough nap being all I wanted to do was get back to Canyon anyway, so I rushed to get dressed, grabbed my phone, and headed out the back door.

The men were gone leaving no distraction from the pile of wood and ash but there was one thing out of all of the saddest that brought a smile to my face. Nyah. I walked out to the corral where they had left her and felt the weight of my sadness return. She no longer had a mother to care for her and after everything she'd been through she was left alone. I tried to pet her but she was still to skittish which I understood completely. I needed to get the mess cleaned up and to find her a place to stay while it was being done. I went back in the house and grabbed the business card Shane had given me and dialed the number. I knew because it was a Sunday it was a long shot and I was right. It went straight to voicemail. I left him a message with all the details and asked that he get back to me as soon as possible before I walked back out the door and to my truck.

I drove straight to Canyon's friend Jason's house. When I got there I found him out back after I rang the doorbell several times.

"Hey, Ari, what brings you here? Canyon's not—"

"No, I know. It's just, well, there was a fire last night and ah…"

"Holy shit! Is he okay?"

"I think he's going to be but he lost the barn."

"Oh dear God almighty!"

"Yeah, well he managed to save one foal. She's in the corral but I have nothing to feed her. I'm on my way to the hospital to see him now and have nowhere to take her. To be honest I don't even know anyone here. So I was wondering if you wouldn't mind..."

"Don't even ask. Consider it taken care of. I'll go get her now."

"Thank you so much. You have no idea how much I appreciate this."

"It's no problem at all. Please tell Canyon I'm willing to help any way I can."

"I sure will. Thanks again. I don't mean to cut this short but I really need to get back to the hospital."

"No problem, go. I'll take care of..."

"Nyah."

"Nyah. She's going to be one spoiled girl."

Driving to the hospital, I turned the radio off and rode in silence. I didn't need any distractions what I needed were answers I just didn't know where to find them. When I got to the ICU floor I checked in with the nurse on duty.

"Hello, my name is Arianna and my boyfriend Canyon Michaels was admitted here late last night."

"Yes."

Yes? That's all she was going to give me.

"I understand your policy regarding family but he has none. I'm ALL he has so if you wouldn't mind telling me a little more than yes, I would appreciate it."

"If you understand our policy then you know I can't release any information regarding the patient."

"Did you hear me? He has no family. His mother was killed and his father is in prison so what does your policy say regarding that?"

I had no patience left. If I had to tackle her to the floor I was going to get answers.

"I think you can leave now or I will have you escorted out by the police."

"Are you kidding me? Do you know what I've been through! I'm not going anywhere and if you feel the need to call the police then call them!"

"Can I be of any help here?"

I turned around to see a man standing behind me wearing a doctor's coat but I kept my eye on the nurse with the phone receiver in her hand, ready to dial.

"You can try all you want but like I told whatever her name is, I'm not leaving until I see if Canyon's okay."

"You wouldn't be Ari, by any chance?"

No one other than Canyon called me that. No one. It gave me chills just hearing it come from the man's mouth.

"Yes, that's me."

"Well it seems we have two individuals willing to fight tooth and nail to see each other. My patient hasn't stopped screaming your name since we pulled the tube out."

"He's awake?"

"Undoubtedly and won't shut up like he's been instructed to do since."

"Can I see him?"

"Give me a few minutes but yes. I will bring you back myself."

I wiped the tears that began to fall, walked over to sit in one of the waiting room chairs, and started what felt like the longest few minutes of my life.

Chapter 29

The doctor came to get me like he promised and led me back to Canyon's room. As soon as the door opened, chills ran across my body as I ran to his bedside. Nothing prepared me for the overwhelming emotions we both would feel as I wiped the tears falling from his eyes.

"I was so scared, Ari." His voice was hoarse but I could clearly understand what he was saying and to be able to say hearing him came with a joy I can't express to you properly.

"Don't cry. Please, you're here and going to be okay. That's all that matters."

"I'm sorry I went in. I just thought maybe I could save some of them."

"You did."

"She made it?"

"Yeah. I talked to Jason and he's going to get her and keep her for a while for you."

"I couldn't let Shelby lose..."

"Shelby? What are you talking about? I thought you saved her for Magnus to breed with."

"I didn't even think about that. I just kept thinking, I promised Shelby a horse and I didn't want to..."

I snapped. "Are you kidding me? You risked your life because you didn't want to hurt Shelby? I almost lost you. I could have lost you!"

"Please don't be mad at me. I'm sorry. I screwed up."

I wanted to slap myself for being so insensitive. How could I yell at him for doing what he thought was right even if it was just plain stupid?

"No, I'm sorry. I was convinced I was never going to see you again and then when they pulled you from the fire and you weren't moving, it was the worst moment of my life."

"Knowing I couldn't get out to you was the worst moment of mine."

I was wiping my own tears along with his before I bent down to kiss his forehead.

"It's going to be okay now that you're safe."

We both stared at each other saying way more than the words coming from our mouths. We were all each other had. Eventually, I needed to ask the questions I wasn't sure I wanted to know the answers to.

"How bad did they say the burns are?"

He had parts of his arms and chest covered in bandages.

"They told me they are mainly second degree with some spots being third. The back of my arms are the worst."

Relief flooded me. "Are you in a lot of pain?"

"Not really. It kind of stings but otherwise I'm ready to get out of here. I spent too much time here as a kid when my mom would get a beating...."

"Well, thank goodness you finally calmed down."

A nurse who looked no older than Canyon walked into the room interrupting him and headed straight for the machines beside his bed. "You must be the infamous Ari?"

My face turned bright red when Canyon answered, "The one and only girl for me."

"Is he always this sweet or is it the pain meds talking through him?"

"It might be a little bit of both."

She looked down at Canyon. "Well, all I can say is God is for sure on your side. You could be discharged by tomorrow if you keep responding like you've been."

"What do you mean responding?"

I wasn't sure what he needed to do but the sooner he could get out the better.

"Well he's got a med button that he's barely pushed, he came off of his tube talking away and..."

"I'm a man. We don't lay around all day and whine about something hurting. I'm going to be fine, so the sooner you can get me out of here the better."

I looked up to see the nurse smiling. "See what I mean?"

I laughed at the same time I grabbed his hand and looked in his eyes. "No one is doubting you're a man. But you need to stay in here until you're better."

The nurse typed a few things into the computer and then turned back to us.

"I'm done here for now. If you need anything, just hit the button, okay?"

"Will do. Thank you."

"You're welcome. It's nice to meet you, Ari."

"Nice to meet you too."

When we were alone again I sat down on his bedside and just stared at him.

"What are you looking at me like that for?"

"I love you, Canyon."

"I love you too now tell me what's got you wearing that I'm keeping secrets again look."

"It's not anything you won't find out but right now I don't want you to worry about anything other than getting better."

"I thought we were done with keeping secrets. Stop protecting me."

I didn't know how to bring it up without upsetting him and it weighed heavy on me. I just decided it was best to be honest.

"They asked me today who could have done it."

He lost all the color in his face. "What did you say?"

"Do you know a Hilary Michaels?"

His body went stiff. "How does Hilary have anything to do with this? She would never in a million..."

"She drove me home after I rode here in the ambulance with you. Don't worry, she's on our side. They don't think she had anything to do with this."

"Then why did you bring her up now?"

"She told the arson investigation guy that David could have done it and..."

"That son-of-a-bitch!"

He tried to sit up quickly but then winced from the pain.

"Canyon, calm down. I don't know that it was him. John said something the last time I saw him and..."

His body flew back against the bed before he said, "Are you kidding me? Why? Why would anyone hate me so much? I didn't do anything wrong!"

He began to shake as tears poured from his eyes. I climbed into the bed with him, careful not to lay on his arm but I needed to be as close to him as possible. There isn't anything worse in the world than watching the strongest man you know crumble.

My own tears soaked the sheet under my face as I buried it into the crook of his neck. We cried until our bodies no longer had tears to shed. After that we just laid there in silence. What could be said to make any of this better? Instead what found us was sleep.

I was awoken by the sound of someone clearing their throat. When I lifted my head I saw a man standing at the end of the bed. Nervously, I worked until I gained focus, coming to realize it was the doctor from the lobby.

"Sorry to disturb you but I need to assess my patient."

I sat up and slowly scooted off the bed while Canyon continued to sleep.

"Thank you for letting me see him."

"There was no other way to get him to calm down. He's finally doing what he needs. Sleep is the best thing right now for his body to heal."

"He's very lucky, isn't he?"

"All I can say after reading the report is it's a miracle. He should have died, there's no question about that."

I already knew that, but hearing it out loud still felt like a knife was being shoved into my chest.

"He keeps telling me he's okay but it's too hard to believe. I know those burns have to be bad."

"He's telling you the truth. He will have minimal if no scarring at all. When I claim a miracle, this is what I mean by one."

I wiped my tears before saying, "How long before he can come home? He hates hospitals."

"I want to keep the dressings clean so I would say at the earliest, tomorrow evening."

The nurse was right. That meant I had to get ahold of the Jeff guy soon. I wanted all of the debris cleared before he came home. It was hard enough for me to see. I couldn't imagine Canyon having to relive it also. I know he said I protected him and that he could handle it but I would always want to protect him. He was my everything.

"That would be amazing, thank you so much."

"I think what's best is you give us the help we need to treat him."

"How?"

"Give him time. Don't push too hard to get him back to health. He needs to rest."

"Yes, sir."

"Can you give me a minute so I can treat his wounds?"

"Sure. I'll just be out in the hall."

I closed the door behind me as I walked back towards the waiting room. I had so much to be thankful for but I couldn't stop thinking about who would do this. I glanced down at my phone and decided to call Jeff again. This time he answered. I went over who I was and what we needed. The one thing going in our favor was he had already heard from the arson team which meant the investigation was complete. It was no longer a crime scene and he could clear it out.

The plan was to start the following morning and take the better part of two days to complete. It wasn't what I wanted to hear but it was what it was. If it meant Canyon could start over than that was what we needed to focus on.

The doctor came out to meet me, tapping my shoulder to bring me out of my thoughts.

"I gave him a sedative to keep him asleep for the next few hours. If there are things you need to take care of you have time to do it before he's awake again."

I knew one thing I was going to do and that was have a visit with John. I would know immediately if he had done it. He was never good at holding back the smirk he wore when he was able to hurt me.

"Thank you. So what do you think? Three hours?"

"More like five."

"Okay. I will be back."

"I'm counting on it. I don't need the same experience as we had earlier if you know what I mean."

"I do and I promise that was all worry talking. Now that he knows I'm safe he will be fine."

"Let's just not test the theory."

He smiled and then walked back down the hall.

When I got in my truck I wasn't sure if I should go by the police station and see what they'd found out or just head straight to John's. My anger won out as I got closer to town. I had to know the truth. If it was John I was ready to see him go to jail once and for all.

When I pulled into the driveway something felt off. I can't explain it but I knew to prepare myself for anything as I approached the house. I knocked a few times and when no one answered, I let myself in. Standing on the other side of the door was a raging mad John.

Not a word was spoken before I was being spun around and slammed against the wall behind me. His right hand came up and locked itself in the front of my hair before he pulled forward and then thrust my head back into the drywall behind me over and over again.

I tried with all my strength to push him off of me and when it didn't work, my hands found his face. I dug my nails as hard as I could into his skin and wouldn't stop until his screams matched my own and the hold on me let up.

It was hard to see but I could make out for the most part John grabbing his face while he continued to scream. I looked down at the blood on the tips of my fingers and realized what I had done, for the first time feeling no remorse.

"Did you do it, you son-of-a-bitch? Tell Me! Did you do it?"

He was bent over but instead of standing up, he began running straight at me, tackling me to the ground. I kicked and threw my arms around, anything I could do to keep him from climbing on top of me, but it didn't work.

My arms were pinned under his legs as he backhanded me directly across the face.

"You gave them my name? My fucking name!"

SMACK!

"Are you crazy?"

SMACK!

"You stupid little bitch."

SMACK!

"You got everything you deserved."

SMACK!

It was getting harder and harder to hear him over the ringing in my ears and my sight went blurry before everything went white. One thing was for certain though. I knew he didn't do it before I completely blacked out.

The next thing I knew someone was lifting my head to put something under my neck. Voices were talking all around me while I was lifted off the ground and carried out of the house. Lights were coming from every emergency vehicle possible parked in the driveway. I tilted to the side and saw John's head being pushed down before he was shoved into the back of a police car. It all seemed like a weird dream until I thought about who could have called them to come find me and my mind flashed to Shelby bringing me back to reality.

"SHELBY!"

"Calm down, ma'am."

"SHELBY!"

"Ma'am, you need to calm down. There is no one here by that name."

"My little sister. Bright red hair?"

"No kids around here for what I can see."

"Who called this in? She has to be hiding somewhere. Find her, she's scared!"

"Duncan! Hey, can you come over here for a second?"

The emergency responders stopped moving me when a man with silver white hair and black rimmed glasses came to stand over me. The very same man that had been at the hospital questioning me.

"What's the problem?"

"She thinks her sister might be here and hiding somewhere."

"No, your mom took her earlier when I came by."

"So who called?"

"Called?"

"To report this."

"No one. I had just left and passed you on the road. Something made me turn back and thank God I did. He was going to kill you."

"Thank you for coming back."

"What made you want to come here anyway?"

"I had to know if he set the fire...."

"And?"

"He didn't."

I fought and lost the battle. They demanded I be taken to the hospital to check for skull fractures. The last thing I wanted was to show up in an ambulance but again I lost. The only thing that came from any of this worth a crap was John was now in jail. I would do anything to keep him there forever.

On the way there the paramedic was constantly checking my vitals and putting a light in my eye. I was just about to tell him I was fine and to stop it, it was annoying, when a sharp pain hit my chest and I heard, "She's crashing!" before everything went white again.

Chapter 30

I woke up this time in the hospital. Several nurses were shuffling around when I realized something was in my nose. My hand came up to my face where I found tubes.

"Those are nasal probes. Please don't try to pull them out."

I let my hand drop back down to my side but there was still pain coming from my chest.

"What happened?" My words didn't come out as clear as they should have and the volume I normally maintained was minimal at best.

The same nurse leaned down over me to hear and then rested her hand on mine. "Your left lung collapsed. We had to drain the fluid and need to make sure that it is re-expanding. You might have a tear. The doctor is ordering an x-ray now."

I had no idea what she was saying but it hurt to breathe. How could my lung be torn?

"Just rest. It will be better for you."

She pushed a button and then the pain started to disappear as my eyes got heavy once again. All I could think about was Canyon as I fell back into sleep.

The next time I opened my eyes I could see a man waiting by my bedside.

"Welcome to the world of the living, Arianna."

"Thank you."

"Seems you're going to be just fine after all. After we checked, your lung began holding air again. Not to say you still don't need to take it easy, but you're out of the woods."

"Canyon."

"Excuse me?"

"Canyon Michaels is upstairs. Can I see him?"

"You are upstairs. We admitted you this morning."

"This morning? I came in here this afternoon."

"No, that was yesterday. You have been sleeping on and off for the last twenty-four hours."

"Oh my God! Canyon!" I still couldn't scream but I wanted to.

"You need to settle down. You have a fractured rib. That blunt force affected your lung also. We need you to stay in bed and rest."

"I've been sleeping for a day, isn't that enough? I need to see Canyon."

"Let me go see if he's still admitted. What was the last name again?"

"Michaels."

"Okay, I will go check and be right back."

I sat in bed and waited for what felt like forever before the doctor came back in.

"We located him and I spoke with his doctor. He was released last night and apparently found out you were here. Would you like me to find him?"

"Yes, please, yes."

"All right but if this means you aren't going to settle down, I will make him leave. Am I understood?"

"Yes. I just need to see him."

Ten minutes later I saw Canyon cross the threshold of the doorway led in by a nurse. As soon as my eyes came into contact with his though all hell broke loose.

"WHAT THE HELL HAPPENED TO YOU?"

Canyon was running to my side screaming the whole time while his hands softly caressed my swollen face.

"WHO DID THIS?"

"I'M GOING TO KILL THE SON-OF-A-BITCH!"

"Canyon, settle down. He's in jail now."

"WHO?"

"John."

"ARE YOU KIDDING ME? DID YOU GO THERE?"

"Canyon, let me explain."

"That's enough! If you can't get yourself under control I will remove you immediately."

Canyons demeanor changed in an instant followed by tears falling from his eyes. "I'm so sorry, darlin'. I'm so sorry."

"This isn't your fault. Stop it. I knew going there that he would be mad."

"Why would you go to begin with?"

"I needed to know if he did it."

"There are police for that, Ari! You didn't need to be anywhere near that psychopath."

"He can't hurt me anymore, Canyon. It's over."

"Oh no it's not. When I get..."

"Sir, I need her to remain calm!" The nurse was rude but she made her point clear before she looked at me. "Don't overexert yourself or I will make him leave. Am I understood?"

We both agreed before the nurse left the room giving us the time we needed.

"When you weren't here when I woke up..."

"I planned to be back by then. I'm sorry I worried you..."

"You're sorry? Don't ever say that again to me. You have nothing to apologize for. That asshole had no right touching you. What are they charging him with? What did he do? How did they get him?"

I spent the better part of five minutes going through all that I knew.

"I flipped after an hour and forced them to let me go. I took a cab home but when I didn't find you there, I drove everywhere until I came back here to see if you showed up. When I found out you were admitted the stupid bitch wouldn't tell me anything else. I've been waiting since and let me tell you, there is nothing worse. I'm going to kill that son-of-a-bitch. What was the officer's name that came back for you?"

"Duncan something. I didn't get his last name."

"I'll go by the station and make sure they press every charge they can against him. I never want him to see the light of day."

"I don't think they can hold him for long. Aggravated assault isn't a large enough charge to keep him. He'll just get a court date to appear."

"Not if I have any say in the matter. Oh, baby, I hate this! What more can happen to us? Seriously, what else? I thought I was scared before but when you didn't come back and I had no way of finding you..."

"I'm here now."

"But look at you!"

"Do I look ugly?"

I felt a tear fall from my face and knew I couldn't hide my sadness any longer. He was right. We had gone through more in the matter of a couple days than most people have to deal with in a lifetime.

"You will always be the most beautiful woman in the world to me."

"That's not funny. What did he do to me? I haven't seen a mirror."

"You don't need to. All you need to know is I'm not joking when I say you're beautiful, breathtaking, jaw dropping, gorgeous. Now you need to stop talking. The doc said, so no more arguing."

"You did that on purpose."

"Shhh!"

Canyon came over to lay in my bed with me. He brushed the hair off my forehead to kiss it before he snuggled into my side.

"I love you, Ari."

"I love you too but I'm tired of saying this under these circumstances. Everything was finally going good for us. Why does anything I touch go to hell?"

"This wasn't your fault, Ari. None of this was your fault."

"Why do I feel like it all is then?"

"I don't know baby but I'm here to make it all better for you. Nothing will come between us. Nothing."

Canyon left to go to the police station that night when the nurse came in and said visiting hours were over. He promised to be back in the morning first thing before he kissed my forehead and said goodbye. I couldn't help but feel bad. Jeff must have started cleaning the property and now it was on Canyon to deal with it instead of me. My last two days of school would be missed and if they kept me any longer I would miss graduation too. Shelby had to be worried out of her mind without hearing from me and her dad being gone.

So much worrying had me wishing for sleep so when it came I was grateful.

The next morning I woke up with Canyon staring at me.

"Good morning, darlin'."

"Good morning. What time is it?"

"Five-thirty."

"It's still so early."

"My body doesn't let me sleep in and I didn't have anything to do so I came here instead."

It broke my heart and he could tell.

"It's okay, Ari. I'm okay. I hate that they suffered but with you I can get through anything."

"I just hate all of this. What's next? Someone hurts you or me?"

"They will find out who set the fire and we'll make sure they suffer like they all did. No one is going to hurt you again. I'm never letting you out of my sight."

"That's not realistic."

"It is to me. It's the only way it will be from now on."

"So, I'm your captive?"

"No, you're my love slave."

I laughed. For the first time in what felt like forever I laughed. Canyon smiled so big all of his teeth were showing and that in itself was priceless to me.

"I talked to your doctor earlier too. He said you might be able to come home today."

"Really?"

"Yeah, he said the tests have all come back positive. You're breathing on your own like nothing ever happened and there is no reason you can't be healing at home."

"Does that mean I get to take these things out of my nose?"

He laughed and then said, "Probably but I will miss how sexy you look in them."

"Yeah right. I saw myself last night when they woke me up for the millionth time to re-test me. I look awful."

"What you saw is what he did to you and speaking of him, I went by the police station last night and you will never believe who they had there."

"Who?

"David."

"No way!"

"Yep, they were questioning him. I had no problem telling them that John was David's representation through our legal matter also. They could have both collaborated to pull this off."

"But I told you, I don't think John did it. He would have rubbed my face in it."

"It doesn't hurt for them to figure that out themselves. As long as they are holding him I'm happy."

"What did you do when you saw David?"

"We don't need to get into that."

"What did you do?"

"Let's just say his face probably hurts and will for quite some time."

"In the station? Are you crazy?"

"No, I'm pissed!"

I couldn't argue with that fact. Once the pain settles anger takes its place.

"I understand. I just don't want anything more to happen."

He kissed me softly and then looked me in the eye. "He's going to suffer for what he did."

"I really hope so. Totally off the subject but have you checked on Shelby? She has to be freaking out and the only thing she has is our mother."

"I'm sure she's in school right now. I can run by there this afternoon and take her out for ice cream or something."

"Will you please bring her here? I need to see her."

"Of course I will."

"Thank you. How are you feeling? You've been so focused on me you haven't said a word about your burns."

"Darlin', any bull rider would laugh if I complained about a few burns. It's nothing."

"You were burned from a fire, Canyon! No one would laugh if you admitted it hurts."

"Cowboy up."

"What?"

"It's a phrase that means toughen up and get back to getting."

"You are crazy, Canyon Michaels."

"Crazy in love with you."

"That will never get old."

"I hope not because I plan to say it forever."

They took the nose plugs away and x-rayed me one more time before I was told I was clear to leave. Canyon was as shocked as I was that I could be discharged before he left to go get Shelby. I, on the other hand, was ecstatic to leave that hospital behind us. Never in a million years would I have thought we would both be there within the same day. I began to understand his hatred for them.

The ride home was a somber one. I hadn't been there in days and when we pulled up to see the barn cleared, it hurt. It was as if it finally sank in that everything was gone.

"Come on, you need to get out and let me get you inside. You're not one hundred percent yet by any means and you need to take it easy like the doctor said."

I opened the door and climbed out, closing it behind me. Walking toward the back of the house, I felt a tear hit my cheek and then another. It was all gone. The corral still stood and the walking ring but that was it.

All of a sudden, two puppies came around the corner and were running right at us until they reached our feet and were jumping around.

"Oh my God they made it!"

I bent down and winced from the pain but nothing was going to keep me away from those babies.

"Yeah, I found these two yesterday. I guess it paid off after all having them run around where ever they wanted."

"So it's just them? Their mom and dad didn't..."

"Oh no, I saw them too. I wouldn't doubt if a few more start popping up here and there. They never really hung out in the barn unless we were in there."

"Thank God for that."

I was petting their heads and rubbing their little wiggling bodies as much as they would let me.

"Come on, Ari, you need to go relax."

"Knowing they made it is way better than sitting on some stupid couch."

"Hey! Don't fight me on this. The pups will be here when you're better. Now move."

I hated letting them go but he was right. It hurt to lean over and I needed to rest.

"Fine, grumpy. Let's go."

After Canyon got me situated on the couch, he left to go get Shelby. Sitting alone in that house made me think about how much has happened there. Remembering the first time I saw it or how I assumed some happy family lived within its walls. So much can't be seen from the outside looking in like we think.

I wasn't sure if Canyon would even want to stay after the fire. Would it be easy to rebuild the barn or would it be simpler to move on and let all of the bad memories stay within these walls? But then I remembered all of the joy we shared here. It was also a place of happiness and love after all. We made it that way.

I heard Shelby's voice which broke my thought. The sweet sound sent chills all over my body but when I heard the gasp it broke my heart.

"What happened? Where are they?"

I wished I could be out there to help him but instead I sat and listened.

"Well, princess, there was a really bad fire. God has them now and they are all happier than ever."

Her sobs were obvious as she gasped for breath between each one. When I heard the first I was up and off the couch trying to get to her as fast as I could. I swung open the screened door and found her in Canyon's arms.

"Hey, little lady."

Her head popped up but when she saw me she began to cry even harder. Stupid me forgot I would look like a monster to her.

"Hey," I walked down the steps, "Don't cry. Canyon has a surprise for you."

She didn't break from her tears and wouldn't look at me.

"Why don't you take her over to Jason's and show her? It would probably be better to do that anyway than having her here with me."

The look in Canyon's eyes matched mine. It was sad and unfair but she was a child and things of this nature are scary.

"You know what? No. I won't do that."

He set Shelby down and held on to her shoulders so she was looking him square in the eye.

"Your sister loves you very much. She was extremely excited to see you which is why I brought you here. Now I know it's a sad day. I know you loved the animals just as much as we did but your sister has had it worse than all of us. A very bad thing happened to her and I refuse to let this make her feel bad. She may look different but she is still the girl that will always love you like there's no tomorrow and right now it's today. Go give Ari a hug and tell her you love her. She needs that more than you or I need anything."

Shelby's head turned in my direction before she began to slowly walk to me. The closer she got, the quicker her pace until she was in an all-out run into my arms.

"I'm sorry, Arianna. I love you so much."

"Oh, Shelby, I love you too."

She pulled back and looked up at me.

"Daddy did that to you didn't he? That's why he's not home."

I didn't know what to say. She was so young and didn't need to be polluted by things like this.

"I hate him! I never want to see him again and I hope he never comes home!"

"I know it hurts but he's...."

"Don't make me love him anymore, Arianna, please. I don't want to. He's mean and a bully. Mom doesn't even talk to me. I don't want to be there anymore."

I never realized I was pushing her to accept him. The whole time I was hoping she could have a different childhood then I had. Maybe that just wasn't possible."

"I will think of something. Don't worry anymore. It will all work out."

"Who wants to go to Jason's now?"

"You'll let me go?"

He smiled his megawatt smile at me and then said, "I think you deserve to see it too."

Chapter 31

I was thankful Jason wasn't home. I definitely didn't want to see anyone with my face still swollen and bruised.

Shelby's, on the other hand, when she saw Nyah and learned how Canyon saved her, was something I will never forget and it was the best thing to let my thoughts go. Looking over at Canyon and seeing the pride in his eyes when he led Shelby into the corral and over to her was just as beautiful.

We stayed the better part of an hour before it was getting dark and we needed to get Shelby home.

"So she's really all mine?" was asked as she closed her door and got buckled in.

"Of course, I gave her to you, didn't I? So when I get the barn rebuilt you're going to have a lot of work to do."

"Oh I'll do it. She's mine so I will do it all. Even her poop."

We both laughed as Canyon grabbed my hand and squeezed as we backed out of Jason's driveway and headed out onto the road.

"You hanging in there, darlin?"

"Yeah, I just need to take some more medicine soon."

"Damn it! We should have brought it with us." He looked down at the clock on the dash. "You should have taken it ten minutes ago."

"I'll be okay, we'll be home soon."

"Can I just say hearing you call it home is the sexiest words you could use."

"Really? I'll have to remember that."

"Well, not really. I still need to teach you those."

Minutes later we were pulling into the driveway. My body began to shake as all the memories came rushing back to me.

"Please don't make me stay!" came unexpectedly from the back seat as Shelby began to scream and cry when Canyon parked the truck. I wanted to hold on to her and tell her that she didn't have to. That she could stay with us forever and never have to go back, but reality would never allow that. I wasn't her parent, I wasn't her guardian, all I was was a sister who knew that she never belonged in that house again with an absent mother who would do nothing to stand in the way of a crazy father that at any time could snap on her just like he did me.

"It's going to be okay, Shelby. He's not here and you know she would never hurt you."

"She doesn't even talk to me unless she has to."

I got out and jumped into the back seat, taking her in my arms. "Someday it won't be like this but for now we have to stay strong you and me. Can you do that? Can you please be the big girl I know you are? All you have to do is walk in there, get in the shower, go to bed and go to sleep. Tomorrow is a new day and we never know what it will bring."

She sniffled a few times but then dried it up. "Will you come get me again?"

"You bet."

She wrapped her arms around me one last time before she climbed out of the truck and headed straight for the front door.

"Call me, Shelby, if you need absolutely anything!"

She turned and smiled before the door closed behind her.

"Damn that was rough."

"The hardest part is letting her go but we have to."

Canyon chose to drop the subject and instead asked, "You want to climb back in front?"

"No. It hurts to bad to move again if I don't have to. Please just take us home."

"We'll be there in two seconds, baby."

When we got back to the house, Canyon led me inside and sat me down on the couch before he went to the kitchen for my pills and a drink. When he came back in the room holding out his hand for me to take the meds from him he said something I wasn't expecting.

"I'm going to call a lawyer in the morning. There has to be something we can do about getting her permanently moved here."

"There isn't. John isn't a threat to her. They would laugh us out of court."

"Then I need to get started on the barn as soon as possible. I'll talk to the insurance company and see when they can cut me a check. The sooner I get Nyah back here the better. He can't keep her from visiting."

"Speaking of the barn, are you planning to catch any more?"

"I'm hoping Magnus takes this race. If he does, the payout will be huge and his stud fees alone would allow me to buy more."

"I love that you don't let anything stand in your way."

"I have to make a life for us somehow and this is all I know."

"You could always get back in the PBR..."

"And leave you? Never."

"I love you so much, Canyon, and we don't need to worry about money. If you want to ride I will support you. We can find a way to make it work."

He sat down next to me and brushed my hair away from my face.

"I'm right where I belong."

Several hours later we were heading up to bed, exhausted from the last few days. I knew I had slept a lot at the hospital but with them waking me up constantly for testing I was looking forward to a solid night of being in Canyon's arms again.

After we brushed our teeth, Canyon climbed in bed and held his arms open for me. As I found my comfort spot I whispered, "You know me too well. This is exactly what I need right now."

"I was looking out for myself on this one, darlin', but I'm glad I could please you in the process."

We both laughed but the longer we lay there the more I tried to block out the memories of last time we were in that bed together. It was the best and worst moment of my life.

"You thinking about it too?"

He startled me. I wasn't sure if he'd fallen asleep yet.

"Thinking about what?"

"I felt you get stiff, Ari."

"It's really hard not to."

"You're telling me. I'm a guy."

"Canyon! You know what I meant."

He tickled me lightly enough that I wouldn't jerk out of his arms before he said, "Someday it's gonna get easier."

"I hope you're right."

"I know I am. Now try to get some rest."

He pulled me in a little tighter and kissed my head before I nuzzled into his neck.

"I love you."

"I love you too."

I woke up in more pain than I had felt since the day it all happened. Rolling over, I looked at the clock and it was almost four-thirty in the morning. I was five hours overdue. Not wanting to wake up Canyon I slid from under his arm and tip-toed out of the room. My medicine was still in the kitchen forcing me to go downstairs to get it.

Once I was on the main level I saw the blinking light from my phone illuminating the kitchen on and off.

Panic set in when I remembered telling Shelby she could call me. What if John came home and Shelby mouthed off? How long ago did the call come in?

When I got the phone in my hand and activated the screen every emotion changed.

I didn't find Shelby's number, instead I saw Kale's. I had no idea what he would want unless he was in trouble somehow too. Did his Dad find out he came to visit me?

So many thoughts ran through my head as I hit the key to voicemail.

YOU HAVE ONE UNHEARD MESSAGE. TO LISTEN TO YOUR MESSAGE PRESS 1.

I followed directions and when I heard his voice I was instantly confused. He didn't sound scared or sad. If anything he sounded high as a kite and pure evil as he rambled on about how good we could have been together and how bad I messed up by choosing Canyon. Then everything changed.

"I'm sorry if my birthday present got there a little late but sometimes things don't go the way you want them to. It sure does burn when that happens doesn't it, Arianna? Oh well, I'll be sure to make it up for your graduation."

I heard my phone bounce off the floor as my body began to shake uncontrollably. I grabbed onto one of the chairs and sat down trying to convince myself that this was a nightmare that I needed to wake up from. Pinching myself did nothing other than cause me pain.

I knew Kale wouldn't have come to Montana again to do it himself which only meant he hired someone or he told his dad that I talked. Either way, Canyon, Shelby, everyone I loved was a walking target.

I got up from the chair and crept up the stairs to the doorway where I watched Canyon sleep. I couldn't do this anymore. We would never find peace until every last one of them were behind bars. There was no way I could sit back and wait for what Kale had planned after graduation, or what was to come after that. As much as it was going to kill me to leave, I had no choice anymore. That message took it away from me.

I turned around and walked down the stairs. When I got back to the kitchen I searched through every drawer until I found what I was looking for. Grabbing a pen and some paper, I sat down at the table mustering up all the strength I had and then I began to write.

My dearest love,
I know you will never forgive me for not waking you up to at least say goodbye but I am no fool and I know you wouldn't have let me go. I'm not trying to just protect you this time Canyon.
What I need to do will keep you and Shelby alive and that changes everything about me not treating you as a man. This is your lives at stake and I won't chance that, worrying about such things as your pride.
You are the strongest man I know and I am drawing from that strength to do what needs to be done. I would never have possessed it had I not met you. You will forever be my everything.
I don't know what's going to happen so it wouldn't be right to ask you to wait for me. I just want you to be happy. Do what makes you smile and know that I will never forget you.
I love you, Canyon Michaels.

I got up from my seat scared to death. What if he listened to the lies I had written? The last thing I ever wanted was for him to move on. This wasn't something I had prepared myself for.

It wasn't fair.

I grabbed the piece of paper one last time and scribbled, **P.S. When this is all over, promise you will still let it be me.**

I realized how selfish that was and went to throw the paper away and start over but instead I grabbed my phone from the floor and ran as fast as I could to my truck, crying the whole way. I deserved to be a little selfish. I was the one having to do the right thing and in that moment nothing felt right about any of it.

I backed my truck out of the driveway and stopped when I hit the road, taking one long last look at that house and prayed one day I would get to see it again before I put it in drive and left it all behind.

I waited until I was out of town before I pulled over on the side of the road. I had no idea where I was going. After a few searches through Google I came up with my answer, Helena, Montana. Driving there was the longest ride of my life as I got further and further away from everything that I wanted to drive back to. By the time I parked and reached the main door of the building, my hands were shaking and I couldn't hold back my tears. Everything I had loved about my life was about to disappear once I walked through the door and I wasn't ready to say goodbye.

"Excuse me, ma'am, are you trying to go in?"

I didn't expect the interruption and when I turned, I found a tall man with blond hair, dressed in a business suit with his briefcase in hand.

When he saw my face his entire demeanor changed. "Please let me show you inside."

I had forgotten how I must look to him.

"That would be very kind of you."

He opened the door and held it for me to pass through. Once I was inside I realized that showing up in the middle of the night wasn't the best idea. I didn't pay attention to their hours to see when they opened.

"Is no one here?"

All of the lights were off making my question a stupid one.

"We don't open until eight-fifteen."

He walked over to a wall on the opposite end of the room and flipped a switch, turning the dark space into a well-lit one.

"How can I help you?"

"I'm sorry. I'll just come back later when you guys open."

I started walking for the door when he grabbed for my arm to stop me.

"You didn't come here to leave so please, let me see if I can be of any help to you. My name is Agent Bertel by the way."

I looked at the door one more time before I realized it was now or never.

"I'm not sure if this is where I need to be but I have some information that I think you guys would like to know about."

"Well, in that case, why don't you follow me? My desk is right back this way."

I walked behind him until he pulled the chair out that sat on the opposite side of his desk.

"Why are you here so early?"

"It looks like I needed to be."

"That's not an answer."

"Would you believe me if I told you I woke up thinking I forgot to send a file and couldn't go back to sleep until I made sure?"

"That would make more sense."

He walked around and sat down before he grabbed his laptop out of his briefcase and set it on the desk.

"Give me two seconds to check that file."

I had nowhere else to be. Time wasn't an issue.

"No kidding. Well it looks like I came here just for you then."

He closed the screen and then focused on me.

"Why don't you tell me what happened?"

"I'm scared."

I was more like petrified but my life was worth losing if it meant I could protect them.

"I clearly can see you shaking. What is your name? Maybe that's a better place to start."

"Arianna Dubray."

"Okay, Miss Dubray, who hurt you?"

"That is the least of my concerns. What I need to know is that you can protect me once I tell you."

"I will do everything I can to make that happen."

I grabbed ahold of my knees trying to get them to stop shaking but there was no use.

"Can I get you something to drink maybe? Something to calm your nerves?"

"I think I better just start now while I have the nerve."

"I'm ready when you are."

"Michael Thompson is...."

I couldn't do it. I was committing suicide. I closed my eyes and then found myself standing up to leave.

"As in Governor Michael Thompson?"

My eyes opened and before a thought went through my mind my mouth started moving.

"Yes. Governor Thompson. He's evil. He will kill me if he knows I'm here. He will kill my little sister just to hurt me. I need you to protect her at all costs."

"Listen, Arianna, you didn't find this FBI office by accident. Now you need to have a seat and start at the beginning."

His tone was solid. He wasn't going to let me leave and I knew it after I spoke Michael's name. I sat back down and took a deep breath in before I let it all go.

"Michael Thompson has a son named Kale who was my boyfriend for almost four years. Kale hated his father and always talked to me when he was upset. I know way more than I should about that man. He has been working with the police force in Baltimore since before I ever knew him and has multiple cops stealing drugs from the evidence room, reselling them on the streets. Kale eventually started using this to his advantage. He knew his father would never turn him in so he supplied all of the drugs to our school parties..."

"I don't mean to interrupt you but do you have any facts to back these claims up?"

He didn't believe me and I couldn't blame him. All of this seems ludacris if you weren't there living it. That's when I reached down into my purse and pulled out my phone.

"I have it all in here."

I opened my text and scrolled to the furthest location it would allow in my and Kale's history.

"These are from when they would fight over how much Kale would take and how much money Michael would lose because of it."

His face was stoic as he read through the few I had shown him so far.

"If you go further you will see pictures of the piles of cocaine Kale would get. I'm sure you can imagine how that always turned out between the two of them."

"Is this everything?"

"Not even close."

I let my finger swipe until we came to that night when he asked me to pick, it up for him.

"This is the address of one of the cops he used as his supplier, only that night it was heroine."

"And you know this because you were the one who got it this time?"

"Yes."

"Would you mind if I recorded this conversation?"

"Between us?"

"Yes."

"Who will hear it?"

"It will be evidence."

"Will Michael know? He has people in every facet of the law on his side. He can't know this was me. He will kill me."

"I promised I will protect you and I will. As I said before, you came to the FBI for a reason. We are the best at what we do. Now, is this all the evidence you have?"

"No. There's more."

"Then let me turn this on."

He hit a few keys on his computer and then turned it to show me he was using his web cam before he moved it back to face him.

"Okay, keep going."

"That night I didn't know it was heroine when I brought it. I was so upset when I got to the Governor's house after that cop put a gun to my head and threatened to kill me that I kind of ignored Kale for the better part of an hour or so before I noticed he was missing. When I found him in Michael's room he had another student from our school, Dorian Baker, in there with him. She was overdosing on the bed with the needle still in her arm. Kale was high and freaking out. He told me to call his father Michael for help. I did, but Michael instructed me to not call 9-1-1 and to lock the door instead, saying he would handle it. Ten minutes later, Michael came with four other men and took Dorian away. Then they told me I would go to prison for murder because I brought the drugs that killed her. Michael called my stepfather John and had him come to the house. When he got there they started talking about John owing money to one of the largest organized families in Baltimore. Michael offered to pay off John's debt and to wire money into an account for him to relocate our family and disappear or he would hand John over to the family and turn me in. We moved the next day."

"Okay, I'm going to stop you there. What happened to Dorian Baker?"

"I don't know. Like I said, we moved the next morning."

"So you think Michael Thompson wired money to an organized family, which one?"

"The Masser's."

His eyes lit up like a Christmas tree.

"Please continue, or is that the end?"

"No, there's more. John took the money and we moved here to Montana where no one was supposed to be able to find us. It worked for a while but a few weeks ago Kale showed up trying to get me to leave with him. I knew we weren't supposed to have any contact but he told me how he found me. Kale broke into Michael's computer where he has files with all of the money transfers in it. The password is Kale's first pet's name, Misty."

"You kept all of this information between you and your phone? I'm impressed. Keep going please. "

"My stepfather, John, is currently in jail for doing this to me." I pointed to my face. "I have a recording of a conversation between him and I where he confirms everything I said and even threatens Canyon."

I grabbed my phone again, went into the microphone app I used that day and pressed play. You could hear him screaming about if he hadn't taken the deal from Michael I would have been dead.

"Wow. You really have your shit together, little girl. Pardon my language."

"I never knew if they would kill me or not and I wanted you to catch them."

"That was very smart thinking." He put his hands down flat on his desk. "Well if that's all the information we need to move forward and..."

He could tell I was about to throw up. This was the hardest thing I have ever done in my life.

"Are you okay? Do you need to take a break?"

"No..."

One deep breath in and then out.

"There was a fire. My boyfriend Canyon had a quarter horse business and... I'm sorry this is still so hard... As you can imagine when there's a fire, the whole barn was turned to ash and everything within it. I almost lost Canyon inside as well. We didn't know who did it until a few hours ago when I got a message from Kale."

I took my phone from the desk one last time and played the message on speaker. After it played through I set it back down.

"I don't think Kale could have done this alone. He sounds high and probably has been for a while now. Anyway, I need you to keep them safe. He said more is coming and I believe him. Please help me. I know I have to go to jail for what I did and I am willing, just don't let them hurt my sister or Canyon. I will do whatever you need me to."

I wiped the tears falling from my eyes but tried to stay as strong as I could. This was the right thing to do and I should have done it a long time ago. I might have been able to keep a lot of this from happening to begin with.

He typed a few things into his computer and then closed the screen before he looked at me again.

"You're not going to jail. You didn't do anything but make a colossal sized bad choice by mixing yourself up with these people to begin with."

A sound came out of me that I had never heard as I cried. I was so exhausted and relieved. I had no idea what I expected him to say but that wasn't it. I never thought there was an option other than jail for me.

He stood up and walked around the desk placing his hand under my arm, lifting me up until I was wrapped in his arms.

"You're going to be okay now."

"What happens next?"

He let go of me and rubbed his hands over his face a couple of times before he said, "First things first, you're safe and you're going to stay that way. Second, where is your mother?"

"She's not a mother but she is with my sister."

"You need to write down that address so we can go get them before we do anything else."

"What about Canyon?"

"The arrests will start taking place I would assume later on today. Our DC office already has all of the information. Once they confirm your story this will be broken wide open. Canyon isn't a liability here. They want you. That's why once we have collected your family you will all be protected and possibly going into the witness protection program."

"Witness protection? Like fake identity kind of program?"

"That's my suggestion but I don't get to make the decisions like that. Write down that address. I'm going to send a car for them now."

Chapter 32

Shelby walked through the door of the office several hours later. The second she saw me she screamed, "Arianna!" At the same time I was running straight to her and wrapping her up in my arms. Looking over her shoulder I waited for my mother, but never saw her come in.

"Shelby, where is mom?"

"She didn't want to come. They told her she was in danger but she stayed and told me to leave. What's going to happen to her, Arianna? Why did they bring me here? Where's Canyon?"

I was stunned our mother would just let her go like that. She always was absently there but for her to give Shelby up broke my heart. I don't think Shelby understood the magnitude of the situation.

I let go of her and stood up grabbing her hand and leading her back to the room I had been placed in once the office opened. When Bertel sent the information in, US Marshalls began showing up within the hour.

"Arianna, what's happening?"

Once I got her seated I tried to explain things the best I could.

"When we lived in Maryland there were a lot of bad people. They wanted to hurt me and that's why we had to move. Unfortunately your dad is kind of with those people. I never wanted you to know any of this but it looks like they found me again. My biggest concern is you. I never want anything to happen to you so I've asked them to bring you with me."

"What about Canyon?"

"They don't want to hurt him, honey, and I don't want to bring him into any more danger. I love him too much for that so I have to let him go."

I didn't know I was crying until Shelby wrapped her arms around me and said, "Don't cry, he will understand because he loves you too and when this is over we can see him again."

I never thought Shelby could grow up so fast. The fact that she was comforting me instead the other way around was something that just made me love her that much more. I didn't think it could ever be possible but it happened.

"I hope you're right. There's a very good chance he read the letter I left for him this morning and hates me."

"Yeah, that too. Let's hope for the other. I don't want him to hate me too and I want to see Nyah."

I smiled at her lack of restraint.

We ended up staying in that room until twelve o'clock before Bertel came in.

He sat on the edge of the desk and folded his arms across his chest.

"Here's how this is going to work. Two US Marshalls are going to be taking you on a flight. I don't know where but that's for your safety. Chances are they will have you stay in a hotel for the first few days. Then your new names and background will be chosen. You don't get to pick anything since what comes to mind first is something you might have shared at one point and not remember it. We need to talk about how your life will change with all of this. Now, Arianna, you asked for protection and we all agree you will need it. Shelby, do you have any questions you would like to ask?"

"So we won't be us ever again?"

"Unfortunately there will never be a day when you will go back to what you were. Not unless we can secure your safety."

"Why do the bad guys want to hurt us?"

Bertel looked at me before he turned back to my sister.

"Sometimes people can just be bad. They won't find you, I can promise you that."

Two hours later we were boarding a plane. Three hours later we touched down in Huntsville, Alabama. The Marshalls wouldn't talk to us much so we relied on each other. I knew we were as safe as we ever could be but it didn't feel right without Canyon by my side.

Just as Bertel had said, we were placed in a hotel but it was eight days later when the news broke the story that everything changed.

Shelby and I were sitting on the bed watching TV. I couldn't have cared less what was on and in fact I hadn't really cared for anything. The more days that passed the more I missed his smile, his huge arms wrapping themselves around me. I needed him like I needed air to breathe and it wasn't getting any easier as time went on.

One of the Marshalls by the name of Duke came into the room and didn't say a word before he turned the TV off.

"It's time to move. All the arrests were made today and the media is going berserk."

"Where are we going?"

He grabbed the few bags of clothes they had provided for us but were to remain packed at all times.

"It looks like you got your wish after all. Now let's move."

Both of us got up and followed him out the door and into the waiting black SUV parked outside.

We were on the interstate before he said another word.

"The bureau has provided you a small farm right outside of Rainsville. There is a community college there for you to attend and Savanah you will have an elementary school right down the road."

I hated hearing her called Savanah. This new name thing was the worst part. She would always be Shelby to me. When any of them would call me Tori I didn't even look up. How do you go by a different name after eighteen years of being something else? I was grateful for their help but was getting crabbier with each passing day.

"When you say small farm what does that mean?"

"Savanah said she lost a horse so we have done our best to replace what life you had."

Shelby's face lit up.

"We will have horses?"

"Only two."

Shelby grabbed my hand and squeezed it.

"Did you hear that? We get to have horses!"

I wasn't as happy.

"How are we supposed to pay for all of this? All of my money was tied to my old name."

"We've taken care of the cost."

"There's maintenance. Horses need a lot. Do you plan to continue to pay for it all? What do we do for food or clothes?"

"Your money is still yours. We will also be helping."

"How is my money mine? Can't they trace it?"

"Not when we handle things. You have nothing to worry about."

That was a lot easier for him to say.

It was late afternoon when we pulled up to the farm house out in the middle of nowhere.

"So who owns this?"

"You do. All one hundred and forty acres of it."

It was all overwhelming. Small farm my butt. How was I supposed to take care of this and Shelby? I needed Canyon. I hated doing any of this without him. I knew leaving him behind with the best thing for him but it was the worst thing I ever could have done for myself.

We were led inside and to my surprise, it had all been updated. Everything was brand new and gorgeous from the maple cabinets and trim to the almost black hardwood flooring throughout. It was also fully furnished. Not one detail was missed.

"Do you think you girls will be okay here?"

"Shelby immediately responded with an astounding, "YES! This is perfect for us, Arianna, um, I mean, Tori."

"You can't do that again! Do you not understand the depths this situation takes? It's your—"

"Don't snap at her! She's a little girl who didn't ask for any of this. It was an accident. It won't happen again."

"I hope not or we move you."

He walked out of the room delivering our bags to each of our bedrooms was my guess. I looked down at Shelby and saw tears in her eyes.

"I'm sorry, Tori. I didn't do it on purpose."

"I know you didn't, sweetheart. This is harder than we both ever thought it could be but we'll make it through it. Do you want to go see the horses?"

"Yeah!"

We walked out the back door and about half an acre back sat a large barn. The closer we got the more impressed I became. Once we were inside I counted ten stalls per side. There would be plenty of room for more if I decided we could handle it. I never would have dreamed of owning my own before Canyon but something about being surrounded by horses made me feel closer to him somehow.

"Oh my gosh, Tori, come look!"

In one of the stalls held a small black and white painted foal.

"She's so pretty!"

The stall next to her held a black stallion that took my breath away. He looked exactly like Magnus. Shelby must have thought the same thing.

"Oh my gosh doesn't that look like MAGNUS?"

"He sure does look like him doesn't he?"

"Is that what you want to call him?"

"No. Magnus will always be Magnus. I won't do that to him."

"He's still alive? I thought Canyon lost all of them but Nyah?"

I couldn't believe she didn't know.

"We didn't tell you? Canyon sent him away to stay at the jockeys before the race..."

"What race?"

"Delta Downs. It will be...Holy crap! Next week!"

"Will it be on TV?"

"We can go check!"

Shelby ran back in the house screaming Duke's name. "If I could maybe see Canyon for a second it would make it all better", I thought as I walked back in after Shelby.

She and Duke were sitting down at the table already with his laptop open.

"It looks like we can get that if you girls want to watch."

"Oh thank you, thank you, thank you!"

She was excited and I was too but I needed to know how long it was going to take before we knew if we were ever going to see Canyon again.

"Why did we need to move so fast? Getting arrested doesn't mean they won't get out does it?"

Duke looked up at me.

"They will all have the best attorneys a person can get. Our case is rock solid though, they won't be able to penetrate it."

"So bail is a possibility? They could be released today?"

"That's not likely. Their risk of fleeing is too high."

"When do the trials start?"

"When the dates are set I will let you know."

"That's it? We just sit and wait?"

"No. You move on with living your life as best you can."

The following week, Magnus won! Shelby and I were jumping up and down on the couch in the family room like fools as he crossed the finish line. It actually worked. I was so happy for Canyon. He truly deserved this. Something positive instead of all the crap life had dealt him.

Duke watched us while wearing a smirk on his face as we screamed and ran around the room. It was the first time I ever saw his US Marshall expression falter. Having a live-in statue of a man isn't fun let me tell you.

"You smiled! I caught you."

"No I didn't."

"Keep denying it but I know the truth. You have a happy side buried in there just itching to get out."

"You're delusional, Savannah."

We waited patiently for them to show Magnus's owner but Canyon never made it on the screen. I sat back disappointed but Shelby curled up next to me rubbing back and forth on my arm to comfort me. We never talked about him much but that was purely to ease the pain. Every night when I tucked Shelby in for bed we would share a look that we both understood. We wanted our old life back but really all that meant was Canyon.

Shelby had the summer off from school and I didn't enroll in any classes so we could spend as much time together as possible. We did manage to talk Duke into letting us get all the tack necessary for us to be able to ride the horses though. We named the stallion Cain and he was just as gentle as Magnus. The foal was named Stella. With us wanting to ride, Duke was forced to learn how to as well and we got another horse for him named Tucker. He would never have let us otherwise.

Over one hundred acres made for a lot of room to explore and the land was beautiful. We had nothing else to do so we took advantage of it as often as possible. I actually became good at it, if you can believe that.

By September I had even taught Shelby how to do everything on her own and nothing made her happier. Stella was almost full size and with her sixty-five pound self she could ride her. I had never broken in a horse but after watching Canyon I learned as I went along and she turned out sweet as could be.

Life was finally beginning to feel somewhat normal. We took care of the house and the animals but otherwise we just tried to have fun. I had given up on anything being different and decided to live as Duke had said months before.

The trials began and it was televised on CNN. John's case never made it to court. He took a plea deal and has to serve ten years. Ten wasn't long enough if you ask me but anything to keep him away from us was better than nothing.

Four officers pled out and were serving five years for smuggling drugs from the state.

I asked periodically about our mother but found that she never tried to find out anything about us. It was as if we never existed to her. I wasn't shocked but it broke my heart for Shelby. At least she had me and whatever happened nothing was going to change that.

Kale and Michael refused to plea. They wanted to clear their name but Duke assured me it wouldn't happen.

One night when Shelby and I were laying around watching TV, she was, as usual, flipping through the channels when I screamed "Stop!" I saw ESPN was airing the PBR. Watching it all again reminded me so much of the days when Canyon and I would lay around and cuddle. It brought back so many memories I wanted to hold onto forever. I saw all of Canyon's friends and remembered his voice as he would walk me through their rides. It was as if he and I were watching it all over again until Shelby screamed, "Oh my God!" as my finger nails dug into the couch cushion. Canyon was in the chute! Canyon was in the chute! My Canyon was right there on TV!

He looked more handsome than I ever remembered when they zoomed in on his face. He wore the same cowboy hat and I recognized his shirt as one I had told him I loved. My heart actually hurt seeing him. I had no idea I would feel so much pain when it was all I believed would make me happy at one point. I missed the feeling of his facial hair scratching my cheek so much that I actually brought my hand up and rubbed it wishing I could still feel the light burn it always left afterwards.

The gate opened and out he came on the back of a monster of a bull. It had been so long but nothing seemed to change. He still was able to calculate every twist and turn as if each move was choreographed. He was meant to do this and it was so beautiful to watch. I could see the glory all over his face as the buzzer went off and he jumped off clean, throwing his hat in the air. I smiled. For the first time I was happy about some part of the decision I made. He was where he always should have been and he never would have done it if it meant leaving me.

He had moved on and as much as that hurt I was glad for him.

"He did so good!" shouted Shelby.

"Yes he did."

Religiously I watched each and every event they had from that point on. It was the only way I could see him but I was grateful I at least had that.

Canyon went on to be ranked number one, beating out all of the other riders. Each time he would have a clean ride I got to see all of those teeth as his smiled beamed brighter than the stars at night.

Each time I would fall asleep at the day's end I would dream of how things could have been different, but each morning I woke up living the same life without him.

Chapter 33

The day I was dreading came whether I wanted it to or not. It was the final day of the trial and I was being forced to testify. The team of lawyers Michael hired had done a good enough job that the US Attorney needed me to seal the case making me the key witness as I was told. For three weeks prior they warned me, "It might happen" and then, "It's going to happen" but nothing prepared me for the two in the morning shake and wake I got that it was time.

We flew into Washington, DC's Dulles airport at seven-thirty in the morning. Shelby was kept back at the house under the security of three Marshalls. I never got to say goodbye to her so I could only imagine when she woke up and was told where I went she let them have it which made me smile. She was more of a spitfire than ever after being basically trapped.

I had eight Marshalls escorting me from the second we left my house. I know that seems crazy but once the Masser family was outed, Shelby and I went deeper into hiding.

The large group of us didn't fly on a plane with everyone else. It was private, ensuring that no one could be on the flight to hurt me. We actually drove straight onto the tarmac when we boarded and had a van on the ground waiting for us to land. No one spoke on the flight other than when I was asked if I was hungry or thirsty but I refused everything with fear that whatever went down was going to come right back up. I had never been so terrified. It wasn't as if I had that fear initially but the level of security they were using to protect me let me know something was coming after me, they just weren't telling me who or what.

Once we walked off the plane and down the stairs, one of the Marshalls pulled my arm until I was right next to him, having me duck until we were all secure inside the van and the door was closed. My entire body was shaking. I tried to control my nerves but nothing was helping and all I got in return as we rode away from the airport was, "You're with the best of the best. We haven't failed yet and you won't be our first."

"Am I going to get prepped first? What are they going to ask me?"

One of the men from the front turned in his seat to face me.

"The attorney will meet with you when we get to the courthouse."

"Are we going straight there?"

"Yes. Trial starts at nine so we don't have a lot of time."

I had nothing left to ask so the remainder of the car ride was in silence.

When we pulled up to the back of the building, the two men in the front got out and secured the area before the door was opened and I was being pushed out and rushed inside. There was no one in the hallway I was ushered through until we reached a room at the end of it with a man waiting inside.

The door was closed after I entered leaving him and me alone. His body rested back in his chair behind a mahogany wood desk until he stood to welcome me.

"Hello, Arianna. My name is Andrew Clark. It's nice to finally meet you. Before we start I would like to thank you on behalf of the United States Federal government for your participation in providing the evidence needed to bring the justice required here. Unfortunately, as you know, we still need your help."

As he talked I stood perfectly still next to the door. Nothing about turning the information in was going to do any good if they didn't convict him. That weight was falling on me.

"What do you need me to do?"

"I'm going to go over a series of questions and help you answer them with only the facts. We don't need opinions, they will tear you to shreds if you even give one. I will not lead you for answers so you need to be prepared."

I was officially about to throw up.

286

"The blessing here are those texts you saved. They can't be accused as hearsay. We have confirmed that these are in fact authentic therefore there is no room to discredit them from my opponents. The money transfers in which you provided the password for the files will secure his fate. Now are you ready to get started?"

I looked closely at the man as he spoke. He had to be in his mid-forties. His suit was tailored to fit someone much larger and his brown hair needed work. He combed over what was left on top and I thought to myself, this is who I have to leave my future in the hands of?

"Will he be in the courtroom?"

"Yes."

"Do you really think we can win this?"

"I have no doubt."

"Then I guess let's get started."

Three hours later, after I changed my clothes and did my hair, I was being led to the stand. Looking pretty was the last thing I cared about but I was told that it was a must for people to see me as a credible witness.

The courtroom was packed tight with people and reporters but the only person I could focus on was the man that scared me to death sitting at the table to the right of the room.

I took my seat and swore over the Bible to state the truth while everything in me wanted to just get up and run as fast as possible as far away as I could be from all of this but if it meant we were finally going to be safe I had no choice.

The questions came just as we practiced. Each one had me identifying who sent the each text, where the pictures where taken, the address of the officer I picked up the drugs from and lastly the night Dorian died.

When I was cross-examined, the attorney tried to ask if I was jealous that Kale had been dating my best friend behind my back which I didn't know had happened. He tried to upset me but nothing about Kale would make me feel anything but rage. Finally, he tried to make me the person who shot Dorian up and Michael the hero.

"You can spin this any way you want but the fact is, he came in and covered it all up. He never called 9-1-1 like he told me he would."

I sat forward in my chair. "You can try to make it look like I was at fault and partly I am. I never should have trusted Michael. I never should have listened to his son and called him in the first place. But the fact is he is the one who chose to cover all of this up and pay everyone off to do so."

"Do you know for a fact that he didn't have Dorian taken to a hospital? That maybe he did everything he could to help her?"

"You tell me. All I know is he didn't go with the men he instructed to get rid of her. He chose to stay and threaten me just like you are doing."

"I'm not threatening you. If this makes you feel that way maybe you don't know what a true threat even is and you have been misjudging my client."

"You're right. I'm sorry. You didn't threaten, you made accusations that are unfounded. None of mine are. As far as your client goes I've never been threatened worse in my life and that goes with me saying this unwavering."

"I'm not so sure about that. Why did it take you so long to come forward if my client is such a vile man?"

"Fear. He convinced me I would be killed if I talked."

"And yet you're here talking. Hmmm, sounds more like a personal vendetta against him to me."

"I held up my end. I lost all life as I knew it and was uprooted to move to the middle of nowhere. I didn't say a word and I did everything I was supposed to do yet they still came after me. They were threatening people I love. That is the reason I'm here today. That is the reason I'm putting my life on the line right now to speak up. And you nor anyone else will ever tell me that I'm doing this as any kind of vendetta. Is this personal? You're damn right this is personal. The man you're defending is a monster!"

He threw his hands in the air and finished with, "I have no more questions."

I was being led from the stand when the US Attorney stood and announced he was calling Dorian Baker to the stand. My feet stopped moving and my head snapped in his direction. There was no way I was hearing what he just said correctly. The rear doors opened and sure enough Dorian was standing right there looking at me. She was beautiful. It was like seeing a ghost. How did no one tell me this? How could they lead me to believe she died? I glanced over to Michael who looked just as shocked as I felt.

Someone tugged on my arm and jerked it out of the bailiff's grasp.

"Don't touch me."

"Miss Dubray, you must come with me."

"How is this possible?"

"You need to move."

"How is she here? Can I please stay? I want to hear what happened."

"I will escort you to a room with live feed but that's the best I can do."

I never took my eye off of her until the door closed ending my ability. I was put in a room with nothing but a table and chairs along with a television but that was all I needed.

They had already sworn her in and made her state her name for the record but I hadn't missed anything else.

"Dorian, can you tell me what you can remember from the night in question?"

She looked scared to death. I could relate. I was just in that position.

"I was at a party at Governor Thompson's house. His son, Kale, always had the best parties and this time I was invited. I was so excited to be with the cool kids that when he asked me if I wanted to get high I agreed. I had never put anything in my vein before but Kale told me it was the best high I would ever feel. I didn't know how to do any of it so he told me he would do it the first time to show me.

"Nothing felt right about it and a few minutes later I felt really sick. I remember Arianna coming in the room. All my thoughts were blurring in and out so all I can say is she was trying to help me. She screamed a lot at Kale and the next thing I remember is being carried out of the house by two men and put into the backseat of a car after Governor Thompson told them to take care of me.

"I am embarrassed to even admit I was stupid enough to try the drug. It was the scariest place I have ever been in my life. I thought I was going to die. The car stopped and I was carried again. This time to another car. I heard one ask the other, 'Should we give her more to finish it?' Then I heard, 'No. She'll be gone in less than ten minutes. Michael said to just leave her. It will look like suicide.' I was thrown in the driver's seat, they did something to my left arm and then I heard the car pull away. I did start to fall asleep and told myself if I was going to die at least it wouldn't hurt before I closed my eyes and welcomed God to take me.

"When I woke up, it was daylight. I opened my eyes and looked down. There was a needle hanging out of my arm. I jerked it out and threw it on the floor board freaking out. The more I looked around I realized I was in my own car! They must have brought it out there to set it all up. I was scared and didn't know what to do so I drove straight home.

"My parents were out the front door and running to my car when I pulled into the driveway. They were so worried when I didn't come home and no one knew where I was. Once I told them what happened they wanted to go straight to the police but the more we talked about it, it made more sense to disappear and let Governor Thompson think I did die than to try to prove I didn't do it on my own. My parents sent me to live with my grandparents in California that day. I have been there ever since until the police came to their house and told us about this."

"So you remember Michael Thompson being there?"

"Yes. There is a lot about that night I don't remember clearly but he—" she pointed right at him "—was there. And he wanted them to leave me for dead."

"Can you explain to us how your parents came to the decision to hide you?"

"Governor Thompson is an important figure in Baltimore but more so a scary one. He wanted me dead and if I wasn't, he would ensure I would be."

"So did your parents have a funeral? Try to help us understand."

"No they didn't have a funeral. Instead they treated it as if I was a missing person."

"Did they file a police report?"

"No but they told people they did. They didn't want to break the law but they would have if it meant protecting me."

"I have no further questions."

Cross-examination came and boy did he go after her.

"You went into the situation willingly, correct? No one forced you to take the drugs?"

"Yes."

"How are we supposed to believe that you didn't lie to your parents about getting high on your own and made up a story to keep yourself out of trouble? My client says you were taken to Johns Hopkins hospital and dropped off there."

"Well then your client is the one lying."

"So you are telling us that you were high as a kite but you remember every detail about where my client instructed them to take you?"

"Yes."

He looked stunned. It was clear he thought she would argue with him so by just giving a "yes" he had nothing to come back with. I thought I was brought there to seal the deal but it was clear as day that she was everything we needed to win. I was so proud of her strength.

"Don't you think maybe the two men decided on their own to take you elsewhere? That my client had nothing to do with that?"

"Not after I heard what they said. The answer is no. There is no maybe. Your client wanted me dead to cover up for his son."

And that was it. There were no more questions. The defense rested and the trial was over. Now we had to wait for the grand jury to decide what happened next.

Chapter 34

I walked out of the room, past the guards and almost made it to the doorway I knew Dorian would be coming out of before I was grabbed.

"Let me go."

"You need to tell us what you want not be a foolish child and run from us. Nothing good can come from it."

I spun to face the curly blond haired man who held me back. "Fine. Let me speak to Dorian please."

I knew it was for my own good but this protection was getting very old. I missed life where you could do something as simple as go to the bathroom without reporting it.

"You will go back to the room you were put and I'll see what I can do. Until then, don't move."

I continued to look him in the eye trying to decide if he was telling the truth or not. This was my one chance to spend time with her and I wasn't going to let it go by without a fight.

"I'll get her! Now go."

I walked back in the room and waited nervously. Five minutes later the door opened and in walked Dorian. I scaled the room in seconds until I could wrap my arms around her.

"I'm so sorry you had to go through all of this."

"Don't be. At least not you. You didn't do anything but try to help me.'

"I could have done more."

I pulled back to look at her. "I thought you died that night."

"So did I, until I woke up."

"I'm so glad you're okay."

She wrapped her arms around me again and pulled me close while she began to cry on my shoulder. My own tears began to fall as I realized only she and I could truly share the pain that the one night had caused. Eventually, she broke our embrace and wiped away her tears.

"I have to get going but it was so nice to see you."

"Thank you for coming here and doing this. You just sealed his fate. I'm proud of how strong you were out there."

She smiled and walked to the door before she turned back one last time.

"Hopefully now we can go back to living normal lives again."

I stood there thinking, "I hope you're right" as the door closed behind her.

Several minutes later an older guard with grey hair that stood about six foot two or three walked in.

"Are you ready?"

"Where do I go now?"

"Home."

"What about the verdict? I want to be here for that."

"We have no way of knowing how long that will take for them to deliberate and we need to keep you safe."

"I've already testified. You kept me safe like I asked but isn't the real fear going to be coming if he's acquitted? Right now there would be no reason to come after me. Please, let me stay for a while and see what happens."

"I'm not authorized to make that decision."

"Then can you please ask someone who is?"

"Hold on, I will be right back."

I knew they would say no, but in my gut I felt like it wasn't going to be long before they decided. They had all of the evidence they needed to convict him. I waited an hour before the blond headed guy walked in.

"So?"

"They've agreed to let you stay. I can't believe it and truthfully I feel it's a mistake but I have no say in this. So, are you ready?"

I couldn't believe they agreed to it.

"Absolutely. I've been stuck in here for hours."

"Well where you're going won't be much better."

He held the door for me as I walked through asking, "Where to next?"

"Oh you'll find out."

Two hours later we were in a motel room. Not a hotel room but motel. You know what I'm talking about, right? It smelled like mold and cat pee but I refused to complain. I was still in DC after all. The only thing I asked was that they let me talk to Shelby, just so she knew I was okay.

They didn't see any problem with it which shocked me. They always had a problem with everything I wanted to do.

I was handed the phone and a smile spread across my face immediately when I heard her sweet voice.

"Hello?"

"Oh my gosh, Savanah!"

"Tori! I am so glad it's you! Are you okay? What happened?"

"I had to testify today and yes, I'm okay. How are you?"

"I'd be better if Duke would let me do something by myself. He follows me everywhere!"

"It's only because he worries about you."

"I still hate it. When are you coming home?"

"Soon. I just want to be here when they announce the verdict. For some reason it's just very important to me that I get to see him go to jail. I know this is hard for you to understand and I'm sorry that I'm not there for you but I promise I will be soon. Please don't give Duke too much trouble. I want him to protect you the best way he can and that means you have to cooperate with them. Be the big girl I know you can be okay, honey? I've got to get going but I just wanted to tell you how much I love you."

"I love you too. Be careful."

"I will. Don't you worry your pretty little head about me."

"Goodbye, Tori."

"Bye, baby girl."

I handed the phone back to the officer and then turned to look out the window. There were guards in the parking lot outside of my room and a chill washed over my body. For some reason I was convinced the threat was gone but obviously they felt different.

I walked back toward the bed and sat down. It was seven more hours before I heard the words I had been longing for.

They had come to a decision and were announcing it at nine a.m. In less than twelve hours my life would forever be changed.

The morning came for most of the officers like it should. For me, I hadn't slept a wink. It was insane sharing a bathroom with all of them but eventually I was able to shower and clothes were brought in for me to wear. I wasn't the type to adorn myself in designer clothing any longer but they brought me labels I hadn't seen in over a year. I held the dress and shoes out and said, "I can just wear jeans and a regular shirt. I don't need you to spend this much on me."

"You will probably be interviewed after the verdict is announced. Wouldn't you like to present yourself the best way possible? People will judge you no matter what. We are just trying to lessen the blow."

It didn't take me long to say, "Thank you" and head to the bathroom to change.

By eight fifteen we were piling back inside the van and heading to the courthouse. My skin crawled from the idea of seeing Kale but I wouldn't back down if he was there. That son-of-a-bitch was going away too and if they needed my help I was ready. There was no longer a fear of what was going to happen but a fighter inside me wanting my life back come hell or high water.

When we pulled up to the back of the building there were reporters staked out already.

"SHIT! This is what I was afraid of!"

All the men began talking at the same time while I looked out the window thinking, what has happened to my life? This is what it's come to?

"On the count of three we move!"

"One, two, three!"

The door opened and I was in full cover mode as they ushered me past the cameras and into the building. Once we were secure inside, they took me straight to the court room.

People were packed in on both sides leaving only the space that was apparently being held for me. I walked over to the far side of the room and took my seat with officers on either side of me. The room which had gone quiet when I walked in became one where you could easily tell I was being gossiped about. I didn't care. I was there for one thing and one thing only.

At nine o'clock on the dot, the judge walked into the room. Michael and his team of lawyers were seated at the defense table and Andrew Clark sat at his. Everyone got quiet when the judge asked the female juror who was the only one standing if they had reached a unanimous decision.

"We have, Your Honor."

"On the charge of..."

The judge listed each charge separately and each time the juror came back with, "We find the defendant, Michael Thompson, guilty."

I had never felt so relieved in my life. It was as if each time she said it a piece of me was returned. In the end he had been found guilty of eleven charges total and was to serve thirty years. I couldn't stand. I was shaking all over. It was done. He was never going to be able to hurt me again.

"Are you okay?"

I turned to my right and saw one of the officers looking at me concerned as he held his hand up to his ear bud listening to something other than me.

"This is the best day of my life." I said it softly. You would think I would have screamed it from the rooftops but I was still in shock.

"Well I have other news for you. You're never going to believe this but his son just pled out on all charges. He's going to serve five years with no minimum. Once he heard about his dad he had his lawyer call it in. We just got word."

Tears were pouring down my face faster than I could wipe them away. While the room was emptying out I stayed there shaking.

"Does this mean..."

"You're free? Yes it does. You get to be you again. How does it feel?"

I looked up at him and saw he was wearing a smile.

"It's unbelievable. I need to get to Shelby!"

The second she entered my mind I couldn't focus on anything else.

"Don't tell her. I want to be the one, please."

"I will put in a call to make sure of it."

"Excuse me. I don't mean to interrupt but..."

The sound of that voice.

The mere sound.

It was something I wasn't sure I would ever be able to hear again.

When I looked over my shoulder I felt like I had to be dreaming.

This couldn't be real, and yet standing there was the man who filled my dreams with a life I never thought I could have again.

I stood from my seat and turned to face him wanting more than anything to throw my arms around him and never let go but I was reserved. What if he moved on and just needed closure? What if he didn't want me?

"Can I have a minute alone with Ari, please?"

Just hearing him say my name meant everything as I stood stock still like a deer in headlights.

"Sure thing. She's free to do what she likes."

The officer winked at me and then walked away leaving us alone in the room.

Canyon walked around the row of seats and took the one next to me. I followed his lead and sat back down. We both just stared at each other as if this moment was still part of a dream and at any moment we were going to wake up and it would be over.

Eventually, I had to say something. My biggest fear of all things was that he would never forgive me for the way I left.

"Do you hate me?"

He didn't answer right away so I knew I wouldn't like what he was about to say. "I did."

It was like a slap to the face that I deserved.

"You have every right to."

"I understand now. It was hard but it couldn't have been easy to leave. I know I couldn't have done it."

He wouldn't have. He would have never parted with me and for that I will forever regret leaving him behind.

"I'm sorry, Canyon. I wish I could take it all back but at the time I felt like it was the best choice for you."

"You didn't have the right to decide anything for me. I would have understood. We could have at least had a goodbye."

I wanted so badly to fall in his arms but I couldn't. This was the goodbye he needed. I knew it and it killed me.

"I had to see you again. I need to know that you moved on so I can."

"Move on? I have never moved on."

I turned in my seat to face him and grabbed ahold of his hands.

"I have watched every event you were in. I watched Magnus win. I have done everything I could to be as close to you as possible when I couldn't."

"Would you have come back if I wasn't here right now?"

I had no hesitation answering him. "I would have found you regardless of where you were."

"That's all I needed to know."

He stood up and I thought he was going to walk away. A blood curdling scream was about to escape when he picked me up out of my chair so fast I didn't see it coming before his lips came crashing down on mine.

The feel of his lips, his facial hair, his everything: it was all I ever wanted. I was lost in him and never wanted to find my way away from him again. Every swipe of his tongue had me dying for more. I never wanted this moment to end. Eventually we realized we were still in public and laughed at the complete loss of control we both fell into.

Canyon put me down and grabbed my cheeks as he looked into my eyes.

I could see the love was still there and I was ready to prove that I deserved it. He just needed to let it be me.

As if he read my thoughts he said, "Darlin', it will always be you" right before he kissed me again.

The two of us flew back to see Shelby together. I told him about our mother leaving us and how Shelby by law is mine. He couldn't believe she would be so cold but I assured him she always had been and nothing about that would ever change. He told me all about his riding and how Magnus was doing. He even rebuilt the barn and purchased ten new horses. I told him about the three we had at the farm and how Shelby was riding all by herself.

"Are you kidding me? I wanted to teach her."

"Oh, it gets better. I broke in her horse all by myself."

"No way! Look at you, cowgirl."

"I know, right?"

"So what do you want to do now? Are you planning on staying down here?"

He said it so casually. As if we were just old friends catching up and it worried me.

"I never thought I would be free to decide. I don't want to be away from you if that makes sense."

"It's the only answer I was waiting to hear."

My smile spread from ear to ear then he grabbed my hand and kissed it.

"I still love you, girl. Even after all this time apart. Just seeing you today made everything clear. You're all I will ever want or need."

"I love you more than I will ever be able to prove."

"Well I'll let you die trying then, how does that sound?"

"I think that's the best plan ever."

When we pulled up into the driveway Canyon's jaw dropped.

"This is yours?"

"I think so. They bought it so I'm not sure if I have to give it back or not."

"This is amazing."

He was looking all around and it actually made me laugh but when I looked at the same things all I saw was my time without him.

"It was hard to enjoy without you. Everything here reminded me of back home."

"So you consider Montana home?"

"I guess I do."

He looked at me with a light in his eyes I wasn't sure twelve hours before that I would ever get to see with my own again. I watched his mouth open as if he was going to say something, but instead it spread into that megawatt grin I had seen so often in my dreams lately.

"What's that smle for?"

He grabbed my cheeks and kissed me before he pulled back, gazing into my eyes and said, "Then let's go get Shelby and make it that way."

"Really? Are you sure?"

"Nothing could ever make me happier."

Epilogue

Some people like to use their imagination, some people like to know the ending before the beginning ever starts, but I'm here to tell you my story is far from over.

Let It Be Us Coming Soon

LET *it be* ME

Acknowledgements

I want to thank so many for Let it be Me.

The first has to go to Mac Robinson for being the most amazing muse I could ever ask for. Without you there never would have been a Let it be Me to begin with. You working along side of me through out this means more to me than you will ever know. You are a true inspiration and I am so proud to call you a friend. Your talent shines only slightly on this cover as you are much brighter than any cover could ever show. Thank you again for being everything that this book began with.

Kara Bailey, thank you for your awesomeness that can never be matched. You will always and forever be my sounding board. You give me confidence in ideas I'm scared to follow through with. You do anything and everything to make sure I continue to challenge myself. Through this wild ride I have had you by side and I will never let you go. Thank you because without you it would be one lonely carousel instead of this wild Rollercoaster adventure.

Wendi Temporado, thank you for all the work you do to ensure my work is perfection. I am not perfect by any means but no one ever know otherwise because you are simply the best at what you do.

BARBARA SPEAK

Rebecca Pau, you make every cover stand out from the rest. You not only let your creativity shine in your work but you make sure it's everything I could have dreamed of and more.

Heather Moss, the trailer for this book is EPIC and I can only say thank you which will never seem to be enough. This book would never gotten into as many hands as it has if it weren't for Like a BOSS book promotions. I owe you more than you will ever know.

My BETA readers, Jennifer Mitchell, Heather Moss, Rhonda Craft Arl, Nicole West and Amanda Barbee. You guys came back to me with nothing but the most amazing feedback. Writing a story is one thing but without someone combing through it with a fine tooth comb it can never be at its best. All of you make me so proud to know you are on my side. Thank you from the bottom of my heart.

Speak's Soldiers, each and every one of you do what you can to push my name out there and promote the hell out of my work and for that and many more reasons I love you to pieces. I need to shout out Tara Broadwater for her exceptional ability to hit every group there is. Vicci Kaighan for your mass post abilities and Tammy Hamilton for your research and insight as to what it will take to get me to the next level.

My family, oh how I thank you. For all the times my head is behind my laptop screen and I hold up my finger begging for one more minute to finish a sentence. For excusing my phone being in my hands at all times otherwise. For letting me vent frustration you never caused but still loving me anyway because you know that I am doing all of this to try to secure your future. Thank you most for loving me and making my life everything that it is because I get to have you in it.

Lastly, to my amazing readers. Some of you have stuck by me since the very beginning. Your passion and love for my work fuels my creativity like you will never begin to understand. I can't do this without you. A book can be great but without readers talking about it, it never gets noticed. Every message I receive with someone telling me how one of my books effected them, it's absolutely euphoric. Thank you! From the bottom of my heart, thank you.

LET *it be* ME

Cover models Mac Robinson and Alexandra Jones
Photography by Kaylyn McClendon.

Made in the USA
Columbia, SC
12 August 2017